RULE OF CAPTURE

AN HISTORICAL MYSTERY

ONA RUSSELL

SUNSTONE
PRESS

SANTA FE

Sunstone books may be purchased for educational, business, or sales promotional use.
For information please write: Special Markets Department, Sunstone Press,
P.O. Box 2321, Santa Fe, New Mexico 87504-2321.

Cover design › Lauren Kahn
Book design › Vicki Ahl
Body typeface › Adobe Caslon
Printed on acid-free paper
∞
eBook 978-1-61139-354-5

Library of Congress Cataloging-in-Publication Data

Russell, Ona, 1952-
  Rule of capture : an historical mystery / by Ona Russell.
    pages ; cm
  ISBN 978-1-63293-047-7 (softcover : acid-free paper)
  1. Nineteen twenties--Fiction. 2. Los Angeles (Calif.)--History--20th century--Fiction.
3. Political fiction. I. Title.
  PS3618.U765R85 2015
  813'.6--dc23
                              2014044950

WWW.SUNSTONEPRESS.COM
SUNSTONE PRESS / POST OFFICE BOX 2321 / SANTA FE, NM 87504-2321 /USA
(505) 988-4418 / ORDERS ONLY (800) 243-5644 / FAX (505) 988-1025

For Jude and Ines

"What sets worlds in motion is the interplay of differences, their attractions and repulsions."

—Octavio Paz

"Poor human nature, what horrible crimes have been committed in thy name!"

—Emma Goldman

Prologue
May 6, 1928

The imported silk frock hugged Rita's curves a bit too tightly, but she would only make a token appearance at the trial anyway. Tomorrow, when she would stay for the duration, she would choose something more sedate. She called for the chauffeur, tilted her hat, and turned off the Victrola.

Jack Fulton's clear falsetto lingered in the air as she waited for the car to pull up. "*In a little Spanish town it was on a night like this....*" She hummed along as if the song were still playing. Bittersweet lyrics, a dark melody that, as of late, reflected her own mood. Today, however, the whole piece sounded lighter, as if the minor key had yielded a note or two to its more optimistic relative. The doctor had given her a clean bill of health, the stock market was up, and Phillip was traveling, allowing her to go about her business without having to lie. True, the weather could have been better, but it hadn't prevented the detective from checking the grounds and, for the third time this month, assuring her that all was in order. No footprints, no sign of any trespassing on their two-acre, currently drenched, Beverly Hills property. "If I may, ma'am," he said before leaving, "I think you're just alone too much, trapped in this enormous place. It's no wonder you hear things."

Perhaps he was right. She *was* alone a lot, and the home was indeed enormous, a grand Tudor with cavernous rooms and tunnel-like hallways. So many things to creak and groan. The servants were around of course, but they resented her, and unless performing a specific task, stayed in their quarters. Who wouldn't be a little afraid? Who mightn't imagine they were being watched? Still, for now, the detective's words, like Fulton's voice, were comforting.

"Pershing Square?" the chauffeur said.

She nodded and scooted into the back of the new Rolls Royce. She affixed a cigarette to her gold-encased holder, lit up and puffed. With each exhalation, she felt more at ease, the sense of foreboding that had accompanied her for weeks diminished, though not entirely gone. "Drake, you didn't see anyone lurking about this morning, did you?"

"Lurking, madam?"

"You know what I mean. Anyone, anywhere, doing anything!"

"No, madam."

"You're sure?"

"Yes, madam."

She laughed a little. "I asked you the same thing earlier, didn't I?"

"Yes. But that's all right."

Understanding as always, Drake, a young college student at the new UCLA campus, was the one employee she trusted. She regretted that he only worked for them part-time, for he had a calming effect on her.

"Silly of me. You won't tell my husband about that, or...or about the police officer, will you?"

"My lips are sealed," he said, grinning boyishly into the rear view mirror.

"*Gracias*. I mean, thank you, Drake." Rita smiled and closed the glass partition. Everything was fine, she told herself. Fine. Rain pattered lightly on the car windows as she looked out at the elegant neighborhood where politicians, leaders of industry, actors, and, against all odds, Rita herself lived. Rita Bradford. Maiden name Fuentes. Poor. Mexican. Like her parents and all those before her, destined for a meager existence. No one would have believed it. She didn't quite believe it herself, although she'd been married to Phillip for eight years, since January 1920, the dawn of the new decade.

Poor, Mexican, but also beautiful. She reached for her mirror to be sure. *Sí. Hermosa.* Despite the passage of time, beautiful still, from all angles. It was that trait, that blessing from God that had changed her life. Black, waist-length hair, wide, symmetrical features and smooth, caramel skin that even in this flat, grey light, looked, as Phillip often said, good enough to eat. Many had admired her, but none as much as Phillip, who by chance had entered the Baja tailor shop where she worked. He was instantly smitten. Twenty years her senior, certainly not handsome, but kind and rich. Phil thought she was the loveliest woman in the world and wanted to show her off. He took her to restaurants and movies, bought her shoes worth more than her father's adobe and an emerald that he said matched her eyes. He offered her a way out, and she took it.

Not that it was easy. Beads of sweat formed on her forehead even now as she remembered those days. She patted off the sweat, wishing she could rid her herself as easily of the humiliation she still felt at the thought of Phil's friends, of their whispers and stares when they first found out about her. Suddenly they were busy, far too busy for a drink or certainly a dinner party. Phil even lost a few accounts back then. They might have understood a backstreet affair, but marriage? Phillip Bradford was of prime, Anglo stock, a purebred with a reputation and legacy to protect. What of his fortune? What if, heaven forbid, there were children?

But there were no children, and over time the resistance to Rita waned. People adjusted, accepted, and some even welcomed her into their circle. She smiled again and sank into the leather seat. They welcomed her, but only because she had consciously remade herself, adopting their hairstyles, attending their teas, employing their decorators. She joined their clubs, took up golf and hired other Mexicans to clean her toilets. She reflected back their own image. And she learned their language, so well that she even had come to think, as she was now, in English. In a word, she assimilated.

"What was that?" She banged on the glass.

"Madam?"

"Drake, the car made a strange noise, didn't it?"

"We hit a bump. Water splashed up, that's all."

She laughed, heartily this time. "I really *did* hear something then?"

"Yes," he said, with a chuckle.

Rita leaned back and thought as they passed one soggy palm tree after another. Assimilated. Well, not completely. She had indeed cultivated a public self to blend in. But underneath still lay a private being who continued to embrace her heritage and secretly found ways to express it. In stolen moments, she did things that connected her to her roots, mostly just wandering through the Mexican part of town, grabbing a bite from a food stand, listening to conversations on the street. Often she would wind up in a church and kneel with her brethren. Occasionally, however, as she was planning to do today, she would go further, meeting personally with someone of her own kind. A very special someone. She stretched out her freshly manicured hands and imagined them being held, caressed, kissed. These were the best moments, the ones that made everything else bearable. For years, she had lived this way, first with the father, then with the son. Now, with another. Managing two worlds, giving and getting. There'd been pain to be sure, but it was worth every minute.

Recently, however, her control was slipping. Since that first time a few months ago when she swore someone was following her. That's when it all started, wasn't it? She bit her lip and nodded. Yes. When she was on that walk and felt a presence; fleeting, but terrible. Who? Who was it? A shadow her husband said. Only a shadow. Her mind playing tricks. She tried to believe him, just as she had the detective. But it happened again, and again. And each time the fear grew. She was afraid still, even in this car, even with Drake's assurance.

It was this fear that was chipping away at her, allowing the self she concealed to intrude into her everyday life. Chip. First came the Spanish, bursts of her native tongue. *Dios mío. Por favor. Cuándo?* Simple words, but suddenly they were peppering her speech. She had tried, as one might do with obscenities, not to make such utterances in public, but they had a will of their own. Chip. And then the images, the stubborn flashes of memory. At the beauty parlor, in the middle of a card game, it could be anywhere. All would be normal, and then, there! A photograph, or, no, more like a vision: the Lady of Guadalupe, the towering crucifix in the humble village of her youth, her mother's braided hair. Worst of all, the fires, those fetid, blazing flames she had desperately tried to forget. Chip, chip, chip. She felt her breathing quicken.

"Usual time, madam?" Drake said, opening the door.

She jumped. "Huh? Oh, yes, I'll meet you here at five."

Rita jogged up the courthouse steps and took an empty chair in the back of the room. She searched for familiar faces. Uh huh. There was Charlie, Phillip's partner at the ad agency, who had just finalized that incredible deal with Sears and Roebuck. Since Phillip had been awarded Advertiser of the Year in '25 for his work with the Chamber of Commerce, Charlie had been itching for a prize of his own. Of course, both men shared and benefited from each other's achievements, but the Sears Catalogue put Charlie on even footing. Rita willed the heavy-set man to look at her. She smiled as he twirled his pudgy fingers in the air, offering her a silent but friendly gesture of hello. Down the row sat Joan, one of the high society women she played golf with. She caught Rita's gaze, too, and hunted around for a nearby vacancy. Fortunately, there were no seats. She shrugged and Rita shrugged back.

After a while, Rita eased her way out, leaving, for now, what Phillip said was history in the making, a trial to rival any other where money and corruption were involved. Right now she didn't care. Rain was still falling, but she was well covered. She headed south, hopped over a few puddles and was soon being welcomed at the small, ivy-covered hideaway. She searched the tables. Not there yet. The familiar aroma of freshly baked *conchas* warmed her, that perfect mingling of cinnamon, vanilla and butter. She ordered a coffee, picked up a magazine and pretended to read. Out the half-curtained window, drops turned to drizzle. A cozy, romantic sight that she was eager to share. She checked the clock. Late. She ordered another coffee and pretended to read some more. "Any messages for me?" she asked the hostess, who frowned and shook her head. An hour passed and then another. Not coming. Maybe something was wrong. Probably not. Either way, she couldn't call to find out.

She sat for a while more, sad and empty, feeling the beginning of a chill. She could sense movement around her, but her eyes glazed over. She stared without seeing, until something, some ominous shape forced her to blink. No! Impossible. Her mind playing tricks again. She rubbed her eyes, but it was still there. A jangling skeleton, the one her parents kept in the closet to celebrate the Day of the Dead. "No! Go away!" She bolted up, threw on her coat and ran out. And she kept running, her purse swaying on her wrist, her half-opened umbrella useless in her trembling hand, until the street where Drake would pick her up came into view. Thank God. The car was already there. She slowed her pace and caught her breath.

But then…. "What?" She spun around. "*Quién esta*? Who's there? *Oye! Quiénes?*"

1

May 7, 1928

"What is your occupation, Mr. Julian?"

"Oil and mine operator."

"Are you familiar with the corporation known as the Julian Petroleum Corporation?"

"I am."

"Did you have anything to do with the organization yourself of the corporation?"

"I had everything to do with it!"

It had been four months, but Sarah could still feel the sting of that impudent opening testimony. Sitting in this same courthouse, directly behind the prosecutors as she was now, she'd watched as nattily clad C. C. Julian strutted to the witness box and responded to the State's questions as if he had nothing to be ashamed of. As if he hadn't swindled countless souls out of their savings. The nerve of the man! And yet he still walked free, debauching at one club after another, unrepentant in his gleaming spats and Parisian ties.

Sarah twisted her three mismatched rings, pressing metal against flesh until her finger nearly bled. Another form of penance, she thought, wincing from the stinging pain this little habit of hers had increasingly produced. But she deserved it. Indeed, she had reproached herself nearly every day since Julian insiders began dumping their stock over a year ago. Overissue? She had barely known the meaning of the word, let alone contemplated the possibility that her investment was threatened. Intelligence is knowing one's limitations, and she had clearly exceeded hers. Even so, she could have forgiven herself if it really had been out of ignorance, if she'd gone in totally unsuspecting. But deep down, not even that deep, she had known. Her inner voice had warned her and she'd ignored it.

Why? She knew why. Because everyone else was against her, too. Mitchell, her lover. Tillie, her sister. Even Obee, her boss and dearest friend, a man who usually rallied to the female cause, thought this was going too far. Investing in stocks? In oil? In *California*? "I know you're unconventional, Sarah, but really, you must be mad!" Or going through the change, he thought but didn't say. This sort of risky business should be left to adventurers, gamblers, big shots—in other words, to men.

Sarah felt in her purse for her notebook, an old pad of paper really, that she brought to chronicle her reactions to the trial. She had never kept a diary or a journal, mostly because she wasn't all that interested in rehashing her own experiences. Moreover, although she was an avid reader, she had no talent for writing. Several unfinished stories and reams of doggerel were a testament to that. Even an accidental glimpse at the stuff, tucked away in the back of her underwear drawer where it belonged, made her skin crawl. So when a year ago the doctor suggested she document her feelings, she resisted, and indeed, had yet to obey.

Just now, however, she found herself scribbling. *Obee,* she wrote in a forward slant, the *O* towering above the rest. Obee. The Honorable O'Brien O'Donnell. A devoted public servant whose intentions, and usually actions, were good. That was one of the reasons she had developed feelings for him, unrequited as they had been, and why she had worked for him all these years, first as a junior officer, now as head of both the women's probate and juvenile courts. Unromantic but important jobs that were as much about listening as administration. Obee had trusted and respected her. That is certainly why she had stayed working for the judge, even after his personal failings had nearly cost Sarah her life.

Cost Me My Life she wrote, examining the melodramatic but nevertheless accurate phrase intently, almost scientifically, as if through a microscope. **Nearly**, she added in bold print. The operative word. The pen felt surprisingly comforting, cool and smooth between her tortured fingers. And as the doctor said, the black ink was giving shape to those invisible thoughts, those repetitive, microbe-like thoughts. Treatable, he had said. You just need to face what you've been through head on.

That's what the doctor meant, and, of course, she knew that. Feigning ignorance about the therapeutic value of writing was just to avoid doing it. She had in fact advised many of the people she counseled to do the same. But maybe she was ready. She picked up the pen again and started to doodle. A swirl, a line, a dot. A stick figure in a robe and cone shaped hat. She breathed in deeply, pressed the pen hard on the page and exhaled. *KKK.* She had formed the terrible letters. They stared back at her as she remembered the murderous hatred. The shootings and lynchings. The killers she helped put behind bars.

Yes, perhaps she was ready. She quickly sketched two more figures—her artistic skills even worse than her prose—nearly identical, both with curves and little half-marks for breasts. Twins, of a sort. When she thought back on those events, it was as if she were looking at someone who resembled and spoke like Sarah, but who was a distinct individual, with an entirely different personality. Inviting danger, risking bodily harm? No, that wasn't someone she recognized. Certainly her work had brought her in contact with criminals, but with the distance of a guide, mentor or observer. Though her position in the courts was valued, it wasn't because she went where others feared to tread.

She drew a dotted line from *Obee* to each of these figures and nodded. Obee had been connected to both, in some ways brought them to life. And that had deepened the bond Sarah had with him. But it also made her wary of his advice. She closed the notebook and thought. The fact that he had been against the Julian investment had indeed made her want to do it all the more. Besides, in this instance, the judge was simply wrong, or so she'd convinced herself. She couldn't trust him or her gadfly of a conscience. She had done her research. More women than ever were entering the market, and plenty had bought shares of Julian Pete. This wasn't just for the high rollers. Indeed, C. C. Julian himself encouraged small investors, and that opened the door to the so-called fairer sex.

Sarah twisted her rings again: her mother's thin cluster of marcasites, the gold-encircled garnet Obee gave her for her birthday, the sterling silver band she'd bought on a whim. They were part of her, these modest little jewels, expanding the shape and function of an otherwise average digit. Had she'd invested any more in C.C.'s scheme, however, she might have had to hock them.

C. C. Short for Courtney Chauncy. The name alone should have put everyone on alert. C.C. Of the people, for the people. He wanted everyone to get a cut of the pie. Show Standard Oil they weren't the only game in town. And some of the early returns had been astounding. Thirty dollars for each dollar invested. Oil was spouting up everywhere, faster than they could build the wells. Why should other women, many of whom had husbands, who didn't have siblings to support, get rich while she struggled to make ends meet? It wasn't as if she were investing the bank. Just that little extra she'd saved for a rainy day. Her sister, Tillie, would thank her for it when they could finally buy some new furniture.

Well, now it was pouring, in Los Angeles no less, and Sarah had nothing to show for it except soaking wet pumps. Not her old black ones, mind you, but her favorite red suede. She glanced around the packed courtroom at all the other duped souls. Men *and* women of all stripes. A goateed aristocrat in a once-elegant suit, a bejeweled, thick-wasted matron, a shrunken, fair-haired young couple that looked as if they hadn't slept in weeks. More. Many more. A generally somber, if not forlorn crowd, but at least most had the sense to bring umbrellas. *Angelenos*, as they called themselves, apparently knew that, contrary to popular belief, it indeed did rain in their divinely touched city.

"Oyez, oyez. The Superior Court of Los Angeles is in session. The Honorable Judge William Doran presiding. All rise."

Judge Doran marched to the bench. A clean-cut, muscular Republican with strong, regular features, he had, despite his politics, impressed her before with his confident judicial manner, calmly overruling an objection as if there were no other possibility. Then again, as Sarah knew all too well, looks could be deceiving. He must be tired, she thought, bored even, from the length of this thing. Of course, he hadn't presided during all those years of testimonies, hearings and near arrests, the scope of which Sarah had only recently come to appreciate. But four months was four months. Longer than a Toledo winter, and that was saying something.

The room quieted as Harold Davis, a nondescript member of the district attorney's office, stood and routinely called his first witness: "Theodore Rosen." Sarah stiffened. Dear old Ted. Not so old really, thirty-two, seven years younger than Sarah, with a soft, rounded face that belied his hard-hearted core. This was the man she was here to see, the reason she had, for the second time this year, boarded the California Limited from Toledo and headed for Los Angeles. The Annual Juvenile Courts Conference was a fortunate coincidence and what helped her persuade Obee to fund the venture. Admittedly she was eager to see Jean Shontz again, the keynote speaker. But even if she had to steal pennies from all those jars Tillie had hidden around the house, she would have found a way.

There he was. Ted Rosen, son of a family friend. Sarah reached for her notebook again. On a fresh page, she wrote his name in Hebrew-like lettering and drew a motley Star of David beside it. Some friend. Persuading her to invest in what he knew to be a criminal scheme. "Join our little Jewish pool, Sarah. Put in a hundred bucks and you'll take home a thousand." More than C. C. More even than Stan Lewis, who masterminded the overissue after taking over the company, it was Ted she blamed, taking hers and everyone else's money, giving fodder to anti-Semitic stereotypes. Prosecutor Asa Keyes, reputedly of questionable character himself, had tried, to the shock of even his own colleagues, to have the charges against Rosen dropped. But Judge Doran was no chump. He politely declined Keyes' outrageous request. As Ted took the oath, Sarah drilled her eyes into him, trying to pierce his flesh with her gaze.

"Your name, please."

"Theodore Rosen."

"Your address?"

"Four twelve South McCadden."

"Los Angeles?"

"That is right."

"Mr. Rosen, I am about to inquire of you about certain matters connected with and appertaining to the Julian Petroleum Corporation, Jack Bennett, Stan Lewis, yourself, and various other persons. Are you willing to tell us all you know about this matter?"

"I am, yes."

Sure you are, Sarah thought. All you know that won't incriminate you.

"You know Mr. Adolph Ramish, do you?"

"Yes, sir, I do."

"You first met him, I believe, in regard to any transactions of this kind along about October, nineteen twenty-five?"

"Yes, sir."

"And, briefly, your attention was called to the fact that the Julian Petroleum Corporation needed some financing, and you heard that maybe Mr. Ramish might be, through you, induced to help in that matter?"

Suavely sinister in his dark pinstriped suit, Ted closed his eyes and sat back, crafting the proper answer. Sarah glanced at the onlookers, including the elderly, gentile jury, and could almost hear the unspoken epithets: *Shylock, yid, kike*. She knew the words, and the sentiment they expressed, by heart. It was only this morning, in fact, that she'd overheard a conversation in the hotel lobby about Jack Bennett, whose real last name was Berman. "He's a bumptious young

Jew," said one man laughingly to another, "reminds me of a wharf rat that has just climbed out of the water."

Sarah shuddered. Berman, Ramish and Ted finagled the funding of this scheme. What exact part each played she wasn't sure and didn't much care. Greed was greed. What she did care about, however, was that all three were Jews. The majority of her people were ethical, compassionate and generous. But just try telling that to those waiting for a chance to prove the rule through the exception.

Ted finally responded. "No, not that the Julian Petroleum Corporation needed financing, that Stan Lewis and Jack Bennett wanted to know if I knew of any one or a number of people who could assist Lewis and Bennett in the control of the Julian Petroleum securities market."

"Market?"

"Yes, sir."

"Was that the way it was put to you at the time?"

"Yes, sir. That was three days after the break of the market from thirty some odd down to ten or fifteen dollars a share, on a Friday in October, nineteen twenty-five."

"And at that time the matter of financing the corporation had not yet come up?"

"No, sir."

"And you approached Mr. Ramish on that subject?"

"Yes, sir."

"And stated to him just as you say?"

"Yes, sir."

"And from that time, as regards that transaction, do you know anything of what transpired between Ramish and Bennett and Lewis?"

"No, sir."

The room stirred audibly with that remark. Sarah didn't believe him and neither did anyone else.

The judge lightly tapped his gavel. "Order. Mr. Davis, please continue."

"Mr. Rosen, when did you…?"

The defense, silent until now, stood. "Your Honor, may I approach?"

Doran raised an eyebrow. "Now?"

"Please. Yes, sir."

Judge Doran nodded. Sarah kept her eyes on Ted, who patted his carefully coiffed, wavy hair.

Doran conferred with the prosecutor, then motioned for Davis to join them. The three talked briefly. Something was up, Sarah thought, something not good. The attorneys returned to their tables and shuffled thieir papers but remained standing. The judge rose, and with characteristic aplomb, addressed the audience: "Ladies and gentlemen, due to an unexpected circumstance, court is dismissed until tomorrow morning at nine a.m. Thank you for your patience." He admonished the jury, stood and exited the sanctum.

"What the hell?" "You kiddin' me!" "A travesty, that's what this is!"

Sarah sympathized with the spectators' angry remarks. *Bullshit*, she wrote, almost without thinking, and returned the pad to her purse. She too was tired of the waiting, especially with Ted, the very person who got her into this mess, on the stand. And now another delay, for some trumped up reason no doubt. She was experienced enough in such matters to know that even an upset stomach or a forgotten anniversary was enough to halt the flow of justice.

∎∎∎

She inched her way to the open double doors, her feet sloshing in her still-drenched shoes. Umbrellas started to flip up around her, so she hunched over, preparing to do battle with the elements. But to Sarah's and everyone else's surprise, the rain had ceased. A brilliant sun was flirting behind puffy clouds, which floated in a blue sky nearly identical to the unnatural color in the postcards Ted's father had sent when he first moved to L.A. The air smelled distinctly sweet, a fragrant, post-rain mix of eucalyptus and lavender.

The collective mood lifted a bit as umbrellas lowered. A few smiles, even an occasional laugh echoed out, as people headed en masse down the concrete steps, shedding jackets and adjusting hats. Weather certainly could affect one's spirits, Sarah reflected, although she suspected that most would have still rather faced a blizzard than wait another day to see these crooks get their due.

Sarah leaned against a marble pillar that the sun was beginning to warm. The conference didn't start for a few days. Perhaps she would finally see Hollywood and Vine. She wasn't star struck, but she loved the movies and admired the people who made them. Except for Cecil B. DeMille, that is, who, with the help of insider information, was reported to have made a bloody fortune on his investment in Julian stock. Indeed, DeMille and other elites got out in time, while the masses were left to fend for themselves. Ironic, given C. C.'s claim to be a man of the people.

Ah, well. Sarah pulled out a mirror and checked her hair—the French twist was surprisingly intact. In this light, though, she could see every line on what many well-intentioned friends called her gracefully aging face. She reapplied her lipstick and snapped the compact closed. Better to look elsewhere.

She turned just in time to see a lithe beauty in a long, mink coat flick her cigarette into one of the palm tree planters that flanked the court's Gothic arch. Was she an ingénue waiting to be discovered, or had she already paid the price for some bit part nobody would notice? Was she another victim of C. C.'s get-rich scheme or one of its beneficiaries? Whichever, she'd clearly been in the city for a while because she seemed immune to the lure of the palm, indifferently using it as an ashtray. Sarah didn't know what it was exactly. The plant wasn't pretty in a conventional sense, with its disproportionate, spiny bark and sharp, shadeless leaves. Nothing like her comforting oak. Yet it moved her, made her think of exotic places, just as the Chamber of Commerce intended. The fact that most palms weren't even indigenous to the region only added to the mystique. She closed her eyes and inhaled deeply, suddenly glad that she had a free day. First, some new shoes. What was that store? Bullocks? Then, she'd explore, maybe even take a bus to the ocean. Or….

A soft tugging on her arm interrupted her planning.

"*Señora! Señora!*"

Sarah cocked her head at a young, bronze-skinned girl with troubled green eyes.

"*Señora,*" she said again in a low, desperate voice.

"Yes?"

A few inches shorter than Sarah, the girl looked up. As she did so, Sarah noticed the beginning of folds around her mouth. She was older, thirty-five maybe.

"*Te acuerdas de mí?*" She glanced around, gulping back tears.

Mexican, Sarah thought. Though she'd been to L.A. before, she was still becoming accustomed to seeing these people. Selling spicy foods on outdoor carts, cleaning hotel rooms, digging along the road. They were everywhere. Sarah flushed. How could she? How could she think like that? But she had been warned. And last time she had almost been robbed. She swallowed and clutched her handbag.

"*Te acuerdas de mí?* Remember me?" the woman said. "I just saw you in the courtroom. I recognized you. Remember me?"

Sarah studied her now. High cheekbones, thick, arched brows. Her hair was thick too, thick, black and swept up in a heavy bun. She appeared quite fashionable, with her herringbone suit and initialed red scarf tied at the neck. Sarah released her grip on the handbag.

"*Te acuerdas de mí?*" she said again. "Remember me?"

"What? Remember you?" Sarah looked harder and shook her head. "No, I'm sorry. I think you've confused me with someone else."

"No, no. I know you. Remember? We met at...."

The woman suddenly stopped. Something or someone caught her attention. Sarah tried to follow her gaze, but the glare from the now full sun intervened. She turned back. "Can I help you?"

"*Por favor.* I need...." She froze for a moment and then started to run, kicking off her heels before heading frantically toward the street. Sarah impulsively followed, but the woman was out of sight in seconds. A few bystanders seemed mildly curious, but didn't budge as Sarah leaned over to catch her breath. She straightened back up and walked to the corner. Trolleys rumbled by. Horns blasted. Cars screeched. She looked every which way, but all she could see was traffic, throngs of people and more than a few near collisions. She thought for a moment, and then dragged herself back to the courthouse steps where the woman's shoes lay upside down and motionless. She traced the fine patent leather, the delicate strap and brass button, the curved French heels. On the instep was written "Salvatore Ferragamo", and the number five, which she noted with a tinge of regret, were two sizes smaller than her own. She held one in each hand and found a police officer.

"Sir, please, I need to speak to you."

Sarah described the incident as best she could, but the starched uniform towering over her was unmoved.

"Go to headquarters, a few blocks up on Broadway, if you want," he said, motioning with his head. "I don't know what they can do for you though. Nothing's really happened." He leaned in and lowered his voice. "I'd forget about it, if I was you. And I'd throw those shoes out, too. Vermin. Filthy."

Sarah let the shoes fall to the ground, then instantly scolded herself again. How could she, when the same thing was so often said of her own people? She shot the cop what she hoped was a dirty look. But he probably was right on one score. What could she do? She wouldn't even know what to ask, what to say. This had been strange. But everything was a little strange in this town. Invented, artificial, staged. Sarah slid the shoes near a trashcan, straightened herself and headed for the bus stop. At the very least, the woman was mistaken, perhaps mentally disturbed. Who knew what was wrong with her?

So, back to the plan. Sarah would buy a pair of shoes, tour Hollywood, and then… she slowed her pace. Shoes. Buy a pair of shoes, and…no. She continued on. No, dammit! She didn't need this. But the look on the woman's face. And she seemed so certain. "Remember me?"

Sarah sighed. All right. The least she could do was go to headquarters, tell her story and be done with it. Leave it up to them. She dashed back, wrapped the shoes in her sweater—it was a ratty old thing anyway—and scurried in the direction of the station. It would take only a few minutes. Then she could enjoy the rest of the day with a clear conscience.

■■■

But suddenly there was no possibility of secrecy; literally all the world knew—for the telegraph and cable carried the news to the farthest corners of civilization. The greatest oil strike in the history of Southern California, the Prospect Hill field! The inside of the earth seemed to burst out through that hole; a roaring and rushing, as Niagara, and a black column shot up into the air, two hundred feet, two hundred and fifty—no one could say for sure—and came thundering down to earth as a mass of thick, black, slimy, slippery fluid.

Sarah marked her place and closed the heavy volume. Now *this* was writing. And what better book to read on this trip than *Oil!* Mitchell gave her the copy, signed by Upton Sinclair himself, last year just after its release. He hoped that since it was about the early years of the California oil boom, it would help put the whole Julian Pete mess into context, make her feel better about being conned. Some chance. She was only a few chapters into it, but she already could see the outlines of deception, the villainous personalities that were purportedly so similar to the real crooks. Sarah was suspicious of J. Arnold Ross in particular, the imposing oil speculator with the common touch. How will he use that gift, she wondered. For good or ill? His young son, Bunny, hints at the latter. When the boy asks his father why people don't take care of the poor, Ross gives an answer that probably shows his true colors: *It was a world you had to help yourself in.* The answer bothers Bunny too, and that was why Sarah was drawn to him. Even at his tender age, he questions his father's methods, wonders about social injustice. A soft, little bunny. No doubt he will suffer, she thought.

She clicked the switch on the table lamp, pulled up the cold sheet, and wrapped the thin blanket over her shoulders. The Portsmouth Hotel was decent but lacked those little extra comforts she liked. What a day. She exhaled and tried to fluff up the flimsy pillow. A flashing red light outside penetrated the room's half-opened, dusty Venetian blinds. She got out of bed to close them. Through the slivers of window, she could just make out to her right the looming, concrete Pershing Square Building that had housed the notorious Julian Petroleum offices. To her left shone the grand Biltmore Hotel, where she might be staying now had things gone differently. She yanked the blinds shut.

As she slid back into bed, her eye caught the shadow of a small pile in the corner of the room. She'd almost forgotten. The shoes. Still there. A symbol, silently calling out: "Remember me?" Not that Sarah hadn't tried to help. After purchasing some unadorned but dry heels for herself, she'd gone to police headquarters and told the story again. This time to one Officer Hodges, mentioning her own professional involvement with the courts. The ruddy-faced man was courteous but not encouraging.

"It sounds peculiar, I will admit," he'd said. "But I've got far too many real crimes to solve, know what I mean? We'll hold the shoes if you want, but I doubt anything will come of it."

Sarah should have given them over, but she couldn't bring herself to do it. She owed the woman something; what, she didn't yet know. So she tossed them, still wrapped in her sweater, into the paper bag the officer provided. She'd wait a few days, donate them to the Salvation Army if nothing else. She exited the polished marble building, and after wandering around Hollywood and Vine without seeing any movie stars, and devouring a thick, grilled steak at a lively restaurant called Musso and Frank, she returned to the hotel.

She was exhausted but her mind raced. She got up again and grabbed the silver flask that over the past couple of years had become regular company. One swig to guarantee sleep. That was the one doctor's order that she followed, Prohibition be damned. The amber liquid burned her throat deliciously, and soon she dropped off, dreaming of a monstrous palm tree with oily leaves and overripe fruit.

2

"Toast, juice and coffee," she said. After that dream, it was all she could stomach.

A tall beanpole with a wide smile took her order. "You got it, ma'am."

Sal's Diner, recommended by the hotel clerk, was nothing fancy. A few wooden tables and a drab, empty counter. But it was open. Sarah had risen before dawn, hoping to be one of the first in line at the courthouse. It was only 7:30 a.m. now. She had time, so she scooted off her stool and flagged down a passing newsboy. Probably nothing much on the trial today. And no doubt whatever there was would be biased. Of course all papers had a point of view, even if they professed otherwise. But in this case, the *Los Angeles Times* had a vested interest in the outcome. Like Sarah, they wanted to see Julian hang. But not because of his victims, not because of all the ruined lives. No, according to Mitchell, who had followed their reporting on this matter for years, the omnipotent reactionary owner, Harry Chandler, had feared the regulatory reform that could arise from the scandal. C. C. might be a cad, but his cultivation of the small investor and vocal contempt for corporate cronyism, specifically the kind from which the *Times* benefited, put Chandler's power in jeopardy. The situation was far more complicated of course, but that was the gist of it said Mitchell. As a journalist for the *Blade*, Mitchell had begged the paper to let him do a story on the matter. Not surprisingly, they declined, stating the lack of relevancy to Toledo as the reason. That the topic actually might strike a bit too close to home certainly had nothing to do with their decision.

Sarah recalled the headlines from the past few days. *HUNDRED JULIAN WITNESSES DUE; BITTER JULIAN BATTLE BEGUN; SPEED IN JULIAN TRIAL ORDERED.* That last one was a laugh. She put on her glasses and opened to the front page: *QUIZ DELAYS JULIAN TRIAL: TWO LECTURED BY JUDGE ON CHARGE OF TAMPERING.* Ah, so that's it, she said under her breath, and continued reading.

Charges by the defense that prospective jurymen were being tampered with halted the Julian Petroleum Corporation case yesterday morning. Two women were taken into Judge Doran's private chambers by Court Bailiff Bryant, where the Court questioned them at length concerning the accusations. One was called before the Court following a complaint made by three defense attorneys, who informed the Court that she was moving about the courtroom talking to jurymen and pointing out certain defendants to them. The woman, according to the attorneys who made the charges against her, was a heavy investor in the Julian Company. She informed the Court that her life savings, amounting to twenty-five thousand dollars, had been lost in the financial debacle that preceded the trial of ten men charged with causing the company's collapse by issuing and selling spurious stock. At the conclusion of the interrogation, Judge Doran declared both denied attempting to influence any jurymen. Court resumes this morning at nine a.m.

"Here you go, ma'am."

"Thank you," Sarah said, and sipped the juice tentatively, as if testing for poison, and read on.

TESTIMONY BY TED ROSEN CONTINUES TODAY. Prosecutor Asa Keyes promises sensational exposures—startling disclosures of stock manipulations which have heretofore not been made public are promised.

Really? Sarah couldn't wait. She took a bite of buttery toast and scanned a few other articles.

BROADWAY WORK HITS FAST PACE. The tearing down of buildings and the actual opening from Broadway to Pico Street may begin about September first.

Indeed, Sarah noticed it yesterday. New construction everywhere. A city on the rise.

More than seven hundred property owners whose land is to be taken for the street widening and who are defendants in the city's condemnation cases to acquire the land have been served with copies of the complaint.

Of course there were growing pains, Sarah thought. Progress always comes at a cost, usually to those who have the least to give.

GIPSY SMITH OPENS REVIVAL. Crowds which filled the First Methodist Church at Eighth and Hope Streets to capacity last week heard noted British evangelist Gipsy Smith on the opening day of his four weeks tour. Smith's topic was, 'What I understand as Revival.' He likened religious revival to the awakening of flowers in the spring.

Sarah grinned. This fellow should have seen the revival outside the Scopes trial. Not too many flowers there. More like weeds. There was so much of this stuff these days. Here in L.A., in fact, that anti-Semite Robert Shuler, who had his own self-righteous reasons for wanting to bring Julian down. A bigoted, big business messenger of God. And Aimee Semple McPherson, who disappeared in '26. Everyone thought she was dead. Some of her followers even committed suicide at the prospect! Then she turned up; she'd been shacking up with her lover. The hypocrisy was beyond belief.

A few more customers straggled in. Sarah swigged down the rest of her coffee, folded the paper and started to reach for her handbag but stopped when her eye caught a tiny headline on the back page. *PHILLIP BRADFORD'S WIFE FOUND DEAD.* She brought the paper closer and adjusted her glasses.

The body of thirty-six year-old Rita Bradford of 104 Crescent Drive, Beverly Hills was found last evening by a group of youngsters playing in a ravine off Marianna Street, an area popular with Chicanos. Cause of death is still unknown, but the coroner was quoted as saying that he observed neck bruising on the woman of Mexican descent. Mrs. Bradford's handbag, with two hundred dollars in cash, lay by her side. Her clothes were intact, except for a red scarf bearing her initials, found several yards away. Her husband, noted advertising executive Phillip Bradford, was in New York on a business trip and is said to be in shock.

Sarah's heart pounded. She reread the words: *Mexican descent. Red scarf. Initials.* She forced down the toast that stuck in her throat. No photograph accompanied the article. But the description. *Mexican. Thirty-six. Scarf. Red. Initials.* Could it be? The woman's words echoed in her ears: "Remember me?" But Sarah still didn't remember. And now this poor soul might be dead. *Neck. Bruising.* Someone must have been following her after all. Her fear was real.

Strangled. Strangled! No, Sarah thought, trying to calm herself. It didn't say that. Maybe the woman, Rita, had been ill. She had seemed confused. Took a walk and collapsed. Maybe it was just a coincidence. Maybe....

"Anything else?"

Sarah looked up unseeingly.

"Ma'am?"

"Oh, no. No, thank you. Check please."

She put down a fifty-cent piece. Her foot had gone to sleep, and she nearly fell over as she got up and shakily exited the restaurant. The air was fresh, but it had no clarifying effect. What to do. Officer Hodges would certainly be interested in those shoes now. The shoes! Yes, she'd take them to police headquarters immediately. She started back in the direction of the hotel. But the trial. She couldn't miss it. Not today, not with those "startling disclosures."

A man shook his head in disgust as he edged around her. "One way or the other, lady."

"Sorry," Sarah said, realizing she was standing paralyzed in the middle of the sidewalk. She took a step, but then stopped again. She had an obligation. Rita thought she knew her. But the shoes wouldn't help that now. They could wait until later, when court recessed. Yes, that was it. Sarah would do it then. She turned around and this time kept going until she reached the courthouse, in front of which a large, boisterous crowd had already gathered.

■■■

"Order!" Judge Doran slammed his gavel at the third catcall of the morning. "One more outburst, and I'll close these proceedings to the public." He gave the crowd a stern look and turned to the prosecutor. "Go on Counselor."

"Thank you, your Honor. Now, Mr. Rosen, what brought you back into connection with these people in regard to any loans or financing?"

"Lewis or Bennett, I don't recall which, asked me to come up to see them. This was in the middle of February, nineteen twenty-six."

"And you did?"

"Yes."

"Please summarize the conversation between Lewis, Bennett and yourself?"

Sarah listened for further audience unrest, but all heeded Doran's surprisingly heated warning. So he could get riled after all. Not that she didn't sympathize with the breach of court decorum. She would have liked to utter a few choice words herself. The prosecutor was examining Ted at an excruciatingly slow pace, and given yesterday's delay, the frustration remained palpable, if no longer audible. It was hard to keep the presumption of innocence in mind when one had been the victim of such obvious guilt.

Ted shifted in his seat. "They said that they were strangers in this city, had no financial connections, and that in view of the fact that I had lived in Los Angeles for approximately eight years and that they knew that I knew a number of people who had money, they wanted to know if I would not assist them. In consideration of any assistance that I would give them I was to receive a commission of five per cent; in other words five per cent on the amount of money raised."

"Did you make any loans or arrangements as they requested?"

"At the outset the only deals that were made were straight guarantees against loss. By that I mean this: I would have, using a fictitious name, Mr. John Jones, buy one thousand shares of stock at the market; if the market was fifteen dollars that would be fifteen thousand dollars. Jack Bennett would give him a letter reading about as follows: 'In consideration of your purchasing one thousand shares of stock at fifteen dollars per share, I do hereby agree to protect you and hold you harmless from any loss, which you may incur through the sale and purchase of this stock. If the market price of the stock is higher at the time that you desire to sell the same, I will pay you the market price for yours. And Jack Bennett would sign it...'"

Harmless from any loss? For Christ's sake, Sarah thought, what more did they need? Fifteen dollars, Fifteen thousand dollars. Details, only details. She shook her head. Of course, she was being ridiculous. Ted was proving his own guilt. His account was essential, and she had come to hear every word of it. But that was easier said than done. Although Sarah's finances were always in order—God knows, she couldn't leave paying the bills to her ne'er-do-well brother, Harry, let alone Tillie, who considered Sarah the man of the house—she was inherently bad, and therefore bored, with numbers. In her work at court, she had helped countless women, saved hundreds of marriages, but it was the quality not the quantity of the results that concerned her. Sarah tried, really tried to be otherwise. She wasn't proud of this weakness, and the fact that it was one often attributed to women in general made her fight it all the more. Investing in Julian

Pete was surely part of that fight. But in losing her money, she'd lost part of that battle too, a thought that stung again now, even as her mind glazed over at the dreary sound of those lifeless pecuniary terms.

Sarah would have had difficulty concentrating anyway, though. "Remember me?" She racked her brain. "Remember me?" But it was pointless. She forced herself to listen to the questioning.

"Speaking of the stock," the attorney said, "you mean Julian Petroleum Company stock?"

"Julian Petroleum preferred."

"Julian Petroleum preferred?"

"Yes, sir."

"And in further talks, unless otherwise specified, let us understand we mean Julian Petroleum preferred when we refer to stock."

Preferred? This didn't involve Sarah anyway. Common stock was all she could afford.

"You went to New York with Mr. Lewis after that, didn't you?"

"Yes, sir."

"Up to that time how many loans or transactions in the nature of loans, or these buys, as you have explained, had been made, approximately?"

"Oh, I don't know. I would say in the neighborhood of a hundred thousand or a hundred and fifty thousand."

"And did you have an arrangement or agreement with Bennett or Lewis in regard to your commissions for making these loans?"

"Verbally, only."

"Verbally only?"

"Yes."

A portly man seated next to Sarah, who had been swearing under his breath, tossed her an apologetic smile. She nodded in sympathy and turned back to the stand.

"And what was the amount of your commission?"

"Five per cent."

"With whom did you have that agreement?"

"With Jack Bennett and Stan Lewis."

"And during all your transactions, did this agreement for five per cent commission continue?"

"No, sir. On my return from New York, Mr. Lewis and Mr. Bennett felt that five per cent was too much, and they wanted to know if I would accept two and a half. I told them I would."

"And during the remainder of your transactions, did two and a half per cent govern all of them?"

"No, sir. It was, at a later date, cut down to one."

"At about what time was that cut to one per cent?"

"I would say in the month of October or November of nineteen twenty-six."

"Did you keep any record of the various transactions that you had in regard to this matter?"

"I kept no official records. I would keep a sort of a tickler system so as to be able to determine or know on each day what loans or what payments were coming due."

How very convenient, Sarah thought.

"When that had served its purpose would you destroy it?"

"I think that the first three or four sheets I turned over to Mr. Bennett and after that time I kept all of them."

"Where did you keep them?"

"Where?"

"Yes, where?"

"In my desk. Anybody could have seen them. I didn't even lock the thing."

Judge Doran tapped his gavel and pointed to the clock. "Counselors. We've already gone overtime. Let's break for lunch. Testimony will resume at one-thirty sharp."

Finally. Sarah watched Ted joke with his attorney as he casually left the stand. He didn't appear to be worried in the least. "Startling disclosure?" Right. She sighed, but her thoughts quickly turned to the task at hand. As the jury marched out, she eyed her path, adjusted her jacket, and in seconds had swerved her way through the lingering crowd.

3

The L.A. morgue. Not where Sarah imagined she would spend the afternoon. But after she retold her story to the only slightly more interested Officer Hodges, she agreed to his perfunctory request. It was already 3 p.m. and she was still thumbing through magazines in the waiting area. The trial would have to go on without her today.

She leaned back. The shoes were now in police custody. Not that they'd be in a hurry to investigate. Based on everything she'd seen thus far, the death of a Mexican woman would be a low priority. Although with her husband being white and apparently a prominent citizen, they might be forced to act if there were more evidence that pointed to a homicide.

She picked up a *Saturday Evening Post*. It was the March edition, featuring on its cover a nightmarish Pied Piper figure surrounded by equally creepy-looking animals celebrating the onset of spring. Sarah thumbed through and stopped on an excerpt of *Lost Ecstasy*, a new novel by Mary Roberts Rinehart, the recently dubbed Agatha Christie of the States. Sarah wasn't a fan of humorous mysteries, but this one didn't sound too funny:

Kay Dowling was used to luxury, expensive pleasures, and the gentlemen who could afford them. But when she accompanied her wealthy family to her late grandfather's ranch, it was ordinary Tom McNair who caught her eye. Then Tom was arrested for a not-so-ordinary murder, and Kay's life was turned upside-down. But she was determined to help Tom prove his innocence, even if she had to put her own life in danger to do it.

"Sarah Kaufman?"

Sarah dropped the magazine and gasped, startled by a somber, hospital-garbed figure appearing at the door. "This way," the man said, and without introduction, led her down the sterile hall. Their syncopated steps echoed in the cold silence.

If Sarah never had to visit one of these places again it would be too soon—one of Tillie's tired expressions, but it was true. Most of her work for the courts was life affirming—repairing marriages, rehabilitating juveniles, finding work for the unemployed. But then there were the suicides, the wives beaten to death, and worse, the children, who had no family to bury them. The first few times she had to identify a body, she trembled violently, got sick, thought she could never do it again. But eventually she learned to control her emotions. Or more accurately, was *able* to control them, because she didn't quite know how she did it. An unconscious mechanism of some sort. Self-protection, no doubt. The psyche was good at that. But whatever the source, she was grateful for it, because the calm that came over her in such instances allowed her to focus. And that is exactly what she did now as a gloved hand slid open the metal drawer and pulled back the white sheet.

"Well?"

Sarah took in the stiff, purplish features. Mouth, cheeks, hair. Bruising on the neck. She could just make it out. The striking eyes were closed for good, but there was no question. She looked at the corpse hard, again hoping to remember something in the stilled face. "Yes," she said dully. "That's her."

The man nodded, and then mutely escorted her out. Soon she was back at the police station. Officer Hodges lit a cigarette and rocked back in his worn chair. "Well ma'am." He smiled sheepishly. "We appreciate your help, but, uh, looks like we didn't need it after all."

"Oh?"

"Nope. Path report is in. Cause of death is heart attack."

"What?"

"Massive heart attack. Probably happened very quick."

"Heart attack? A woman of that age? What about the bruising?"

"Ma'am?"

"The bruising on the neck."

"I don't know. Probably when she fell."

"Are you sure?"

"Yep."

"Nothing else?" Sarah wondered how they could make these determinations so quickly. Medical history?

"See for yourself," he said, handing her the official yellow form.

Sarah read over it. "Huh. Well, that's that then," she said, standing and feeling something between confusion and relief. "Do you know why she was in that area? I read it was popular with Chicanos."

"Well, if you hadn't noticed, she was one of them, ma'am. Marianna's just a street. Residential mostly, with that ravine at the end. But there are a few shops nearby with junk from Mexico. Probably went for that. I've heard even some stars like it for the novelty."

"Ah."

"Oh, by the way. You can have these if you want." Officer Hodges reached under his desk, pulling out the bag with Rita's shoes. "Family doesn't want 'em."

"What? Are you sure about that?"

"Wouldn't say so if I wasn't. So you want 'em?"

Really? she thought. According to the paper, the husband was in shock. Maybe not even in town yet. "No, no. Why don't you donate them to…uh, on second thought, I think I will take them."

"Here you go. Now then, Miss Kaufman. I've got a lot of work to do," the officer said. "Like I told you before, real crimes to solve."

Sarah nodded.

"Oh," he said, "uh, you say you're here for the Pete trial?"

"That's right."

He snickered. "C. C.'ll get off. Trust me. Him and all his Jew friends. They know how to work the system."

Sarah flushed and glared at the grinning officer. His smile dropped as he searched her face.

"Oh, uh, I didn't mean nothin' really. Just a type, you know, a certain kind I'm talking about, uh…"

"Don't worry about it," Sarah said, grabbing the bag and marching out. "Ignorant pig," she said under her breath. "You're lucky my people don't eat you."

■■■

Bunny thought quickly. It was a delicate ethical question—whether you had a right to unlock somebody else's backdoor, so that a possible thief could get in! But of course it wasn't really a thief, if it was your aunt, and she would give it to you anyhow. But how could you know if the story was true? Well you could go out, like the fellow said, and if he was a thief you could grab him. What decided Bunny was the voice, which he liked; even before he laid eyes on Paul Watkins' face, Bunny felt the power in Paul Watkins' character, he was attracted by something deep and stirring and powerful.

Sarah closed the book and tapped on the yet unblemished leather bound cover. She liked this Bunny fellow. He was young, but she could tell he had the makings of a complex man. Someone who would know that determining right from wrong wasn't always clear-cut. This was a minor offense he was contemplating—stealing a little food. And Paul, whose friendship Bunny so desired, even promised he would pay his aunt back once he got a job. He just couldn't bear living with his strong-armed, evangelical father any longer, and Sarah couldn't blame him. Paul, like Bunny, was a thinker. Then again, it could be a turning point, a slippery slope leading to a life of crime. But Sarah didn't think that would be Bunny's lot. A line she'd read in the book yesterday convinced her: *Bunny could not understand—he never did succeed in understanding, all his lifelong, how people could fail to be interested in other people.*

Sarah glanced out the hotel window. Cloudy, and rain predicted again. A good day to be inside. She would go to the trial and try to remember why she came here. Whatever sleep she had gotten last night was filled with dreams of Rita. Away from the morgue, her emotions ran wild. Freud was right. The unconscious could not be suppressed. She awoke with a start several times, watching the woman's desperate expression transform into a stilled purple mask.

The images still floated in her head when a bellboy knocked, informing her that she had a call from a Mr. Mitchell Dobrinski. Sarah wondered why Mitchell hadn't called before now, even though he'd promised to wait for a few days. Patience was not his strong suit. She would have started to worry had he not contacted her soon, especially because he had been so interested in the trial. Since Scopes and all that horror in Tennessee, their relationship had, well, evolved. They saw each other regularly. They went out for dinner, to the movies, and back to Mitchell's apartment. Once in a while, he even came over for one of Tillie's home-cooked meals. It was a pleasant, comfortable arrangement. Mitchell once, and only once, had brought up marriage, but Sarah didn't see the point. She couldn't have children. Was he going to move in with her and her siblings? No. It wasn't practical. Besides, Sarah liked it the way it was— companionship, a little romance and, yes, sex. She smiled, still somewhat amazed that the thing she thought was lost to age had become an integral part of her life. When was the last time? Two weeks ago. She wished he were here now.

If she were staying at the Biltmore she'd have a phone in the room. She hurried downstairs, pulled off her earring and clutched the receiver. "Hello. Oh, Mitchell. It's good to hear your voice." Sarah checked the clock. "No, I still have a little time."

Mitchell asked her how the trial was going. "Slowly. You should see Ted strut around. It's downright obscene."

"Seen any movie stars?" he said.

"I'm not sure. A lot of glamorous people around here. But something strange enough to be in a movie has happened."

"Not again," he replied with a short laugh.

"I'm not kidding. Strange and tragic."

"Oh?"

"Tragic," she repeated, and then relayed the story about Rita. Her plea, her disappearance, her death. Heart attack, the coroner said. Probably due to a congenital problem, some vessel weakness because she was pretty young for this kind of event. And yet I don't believe it, Mitchell. It's so coincidental. Too coincidental. That girl looked afraid. And that bruising, and her scarf was found…"

"Sarah. You're getting carried away. You can't tell about those things and you know it," Mitchell said. "Do you really think someone would just leave a scarf they had used as a weapon?"

"All I know is that the scarf was off and the neck was bruised. That's pretty suspicious."

"It's possible, of course. But why would they rule her death a heart attack if it wasn't? Come on. Besides, there's nothing you can do about it."

"I don't know."

"What do you mean?"

"I don't know. I don't know what I mean."

"I hope you're not thinking of…"

"Of Jacob? How I didn't act soon enough? Dig deep enough? That I was the one person his mother trusted to save him? Is that what you were going to say?"

"Yes, Sarah. Yes, it was. You're still trying to make amends. Jacob was black, this woman, Mexican. Don't you see?"

"No, I don't. Race has nothing to do with it," Sarah said, holding back tears. But it had everything to do with what happened to Jacob, Sarah thought.

That, and her own inability to imagine the evil consequences of her good intentions.

"Sarah, I'm sorry."

"Never mind."

"All I'm saying is just be aware. Now tell me, was this woman from Mexico or just a Chicano?"

"She was married to an American, so I assume she was a citizen. But I don't know if she's a native. She spoke English with a little Spanish. Had a husky voice. Why?"

"Just trying to recall if you ever mentioned her to me, you know, without remembering, in passing or something."

"Not a chance. I can't even…" Sarah jolted. Wait a minute. That voice. That voice. Where? She'd heard it before. "Maybe…"

"What? Sarah?"

"Yeah, yes. I think…that might be…that just might be…"

"Sarah?"

"I remember, I remember now. It was here, right here in L.A. …"

4

Los Angeles, Summer 1922

arah inhaled deeply the fresh, citrus air once more before boarding the tour bus to the oil fields, nudged along by the stream of people behind her. Having arrived at the Pershing Square stop at 7 a.m., she never dreamed she'd have to vie for a seat. But oilmen knew how to throw a party, and it seemed all of Los Angeles was in a celebratory mood.

With streamers and banners flying, the overly-full vehicle began to wend its way through the city. Their destination was Santa Fe Springs, formerly a quiet suburb known for its curative waters, was only twelve miles southeast of downtown.

It should have been a relatively short ride. But the driver was apparently under orders to take a circuitous path past the mansions of the rich. In front of one after another he slowed, pointing out this or that feature. He hovered particularly at those of the oil barons, especially Edward Doheny's new French Gothic structure, which, though not complete, already looked like a small Versailles. Never mind that Doheny was implicated in the ongoing Teapot Dome scandal, where President Harding and Secretary of Interior Fall had leased Navy private oil reserves without competitive bidding. Or that his ex-wife killed herself by drinking battery acid when she learned of his marriage to a telephone operator, or that his partner's wife was recently murdered. The man was worth more than three hundred million. The implied message: invest and you, too, could have this. Sarah knew better, but enjoyed the hour-long detour nonetheless.

After nearly an hour and a half, they rumbled onto Telegraph Road, the center of Santa Fe Springs. Heretofore, the bus was filled with loud chatter, but at the sight of a huge white tent, everyone grew quiet. All eyes, including Sarah's, glanced left to right and back again, wondering at the circus-like structure and taking in the other midway activities. Barbeque carts and fiddle players, magazine stands and cigarette girls. Trucks carrying lumber and drilling equipment were everywhere, as were Mexican workers and roughnecks. The wild frontier, Sarah thought, including, though Prohibition was in full force, a red-painted wooden saloon.

Shielding her eyes from the glare, Sarah gazed out the window as the bus kept rolling along. Beyond the town, massive steel derricks squeezed together as far as the eye could see, appearing like hundreds of second-rate Eiffel towers. Although, as she recalled with a little chill, they were actually named for their resemblance to a type of gallows, named in turn after an English executioner, Thomas Derrick.

"And here is the site of the Alexander disaster," the driver said with a broad smile, as if this were a cause to cheer. "And over there, the Bell fire." Everyone knew what he was referring to, and they collectively responded with "oohs" and "ahs." Earlier in the year, drilling on the Alexander well had caused a massive explosion, covering acres in mud, ruining the derrick, and forcing the roughnecks to run for their lives. A month later, a drilling accident at one of Alphonso Bell's nearby wells sparked a huge gas fire that destroyed telephone poles and threatened his ranch home. Fortunately, no one was killed. Nor did it hurt Bell much. He had owned real estate here before discovering oil. And he was a celebrated tennis player, made even more famous by this sensational incident.

The bus stopped finally at an area where the derricks thinned out. A stretch of unproven land lay before them. Unproven, but promising given the strikes that had occurred all around it. This was where they wanted them to invest, on this hellish, barren property relieved by only a few scrawny bushes. Hard to believe this was the same state, let alone the same city, that Sarah had been swooning over since she arrived last week. Where were the palms? The wide, clean streets? The Garden of Eden she'd written home about? What she saw before her was harsh and fetid. Raped by industry, the underbelly of progress.

Everyone started to exit the bus, but Sarah remained seated. Suddenly she questioned her decision to take this little side trip. Jean Shontz, the person she had come to Los Angeles to meet, wouldn't find herself dead here, of that Sarah was sure. Jean was the first woman to fill the role of a judicial officer of the Los Angeles Superior Court, and had nearly won a run for the Superior Court Bench itself. Sarah felt a great kinship to her, hoping to implement some of her ideas in Toledo. She still carried around in her wallet that yellowed clipping from the 1918 *Times*:

Feminine pioneering in the realms sacred to masculinity teems with adventure, reeks of daring, and lays one open to fearful dissection and public analysis. Hence the announced candidacy of Miss Jean Shontz for the Superior Court Bench has created no end of a sensation, not only in local judicial circles, where her masculine confreres see their sacred citadel under attack, but among the women, who are enthralled by her courage.

Of course, Shontz didn't win, but Sarah viewed her attempt as a turning point, and counted herself among the enthralled.

Judge O'Donnell, being progressive when it came to women's rights and always looking to improve the court, arranged for the trip. And Shontz did not disappoint. She had a striking, serious face but was open and friendly. Fair-haired and slight, she was at once feminine and powerful. Sarah learned that in organizing the court over which she presided, Shontz had insured that the judge, clerk, reporter and bailiff were all women. The scope of the court included all cases in which girls were defendants, and cases where boys up to the age of nine years were concerned. Shontz wasn't technically a judge, but she wielded the influence of one.

"All out," the bus driver said. "I'm locking her up for a bit."

"Oh." Sarah grabbed her handbag and disembarked, remembering she was here for a reason. Because of Ted, to be exact. It was upon hearing about Sarah's trip from the Rosens that Ted, their son, had contacted her. This was a chance of a lifetime, he said. The Rosens were good people, close friends of the aunt who raised Sarah after both of her parents died young. They all hoped that she and Ted would one day get together, but the spoiled, smooth-talking financier was not her type and she was not his. He went for dumb, blond *shickses* with money. Still, he did know investments. And based on his family, Sarah presumed he was honest. So when he said that oil was a sure bet, she decided to at least check out the fields in which, so to speak, he put so much stock.

One of the tents with red, white and blue flags flying overhead was close to the derricks, and Sarah wandered over to it. A jovial, barrel-chested man welcomed her: "Come on in, ma'am. Can't make your fortune out here." She smiled and ventured inside to witness the spectacle. On a blackboard by the entrance were posted maps of the fields. Placards everywhere read: *Buy These Lots and Enjoy Independence for Life.* The huge, jammed space already smelled of sweat and popcorn, and was so near the roughnecks at work that she could hear the sound of the steam engines driving the drill. A brass band was assembled on the stage behind a dwarf in preacher's garb who was screeching into a microphone, no doubt to be heard over the drills: "I'm not gonna speak for much longer. You're here to claim your destiny, not listen to some long dissertation. But, as a man of the cloth, I'm telling you honestly that such opportunities in life are rare! And if you're smart, you'll take advantage of this one. In just a moment, the band will strike up, and there will be representatives of Harrison Oil for your service. You can buy a unit for as little as five dollars."

As if betraying a secret, he then whispered into the microphone, still loud enough to be heard of course: "I shouldn't say this, but you might twist their arms and even buy two for eight. Either way, you could make at least a hundred times that amount in return. We should bow our heads and thank the Great Lord for this opportunity we have. Amen."

The mesmerized crowd applauded wildly and began lining up to get in on the deal. Sarah had read one of Albert Atwood's pieces in the Saturday Evening Post describing the people who visited the tent show promotions as "a sad aggregation of humanity" who bore unmistakable signs of "ignorance and poverty." But that's not entirely what she observed. If one could judge by appearances, there were some very rich folks here, too. Men with expensive looking linen suits and gold-tipped canes, women with leather handbags and feathered hats she knew cost a pretty penny. And as far as intelligence, Ted told her that many doctors had invested huge amounts after being wooed at the tents.

Nonetheless, Sarah had no intention of turning over her money. Not today anyway. Because when Ted encouraged her to view the sites, it was primarily to appreciate the distinction between most speculators and C. C. Julian, the one with whom he wanted her to invest. C. C. didn't have a tent. He didn't want to waste anyone's time. And he supposedly didn't want to waste his money on such lavish ploys. Julian was no-nonsense, new to the scene, and new in his methods. He won his clients by word of mouth and direct newspaper ads, a few of which Ted thought so clever that he repeatedly recited them: "Faint Heart Ne'er Won a Lady Fair; A Promise Made is a Debt Unpaid;" and "Let Me Be Your Santa Claus This Next Xmas Eve." Sarah wasn't impressed. Besides, she said, they celebrated Chanukah.

Still, C. C. did seem to be true to his word. When soliciting investors for his first well right here in Santa Fe Springs, he claimed: "When you lay your Jack on the line with me you know exactly what you get and how you get it. I am here to give you the straight dope. Whether it is good or bad, I'll give you the lowdown always." And he did. When the well had trouble, he told investors exactly what was wrong. When it looked as if it might not go at all, he offered them chances to sell back their units. And when his wells finally burst forth, producing sixteen hundred barrels a day in well number one and twenty-four hundred in number two, he shared his glee with them: "If you happen to hold a ticket on me to win on this baby you are in the right church and in the right pew." He was developing a reputation for trustworthiness, and the city took notice. The *Los Angeles Examiner* praised him as an "experienced operator, not a promoter of the fly-by-night type." The *Times* said he was "one of the star producers of the Santa Fe Springs field." And even his competitors complimented his investors, saying they were "awake while others were asleep."

The next day, after a restless night herself, Sarah agreed to accompany Ted to the new Julian offices in the downtown Lowe's State Theater building. He met her outside her modest lodgings, clad from head to toe in powder blue, a color that accentuated the smarmy softness of his face. Together they walked two blocks north to the corner of Broadway and Seventh.

"Here we are," Ted said, rubbing his nail-bitten hands together.

Sarah followed him into a twelve-story red brick building. When they reached the fifth floor offices, Sarah thought of C. C.'s reputation for no frills. Obviously it wasn't lavishness per se that bothered him, for this space was surely lavish, with its mahogany paneled walls, Art Deco lamps and Oriental rugs.

A noisy line of people stretched out into the lushly carpeted hallway. Ted took her arm and guided her past the excited crowd into a huge conference room with a long marble table and leather chairs. About thirty people dressed to the hilt stood chatting and snacking on little sandwiches. Ted exchanged nods with a few of them, while escorting her to the man responsible for all the excitement. "Sarah, this is Mr. C. C. Julian. C. C., Miss Sarah Kaufman. She wants to join the party."

Sarah glared at Ted. She hadn't consented to anything yet.

C. C. extended a diamond-ringed, manicured hand, "Miss? Miss you said? I don't believe it. Somebody hasn't snatched you up yet?"

Sarah smiled thinly. But as he continued to tease her with obviously strategic compliments, she couldn't help but blush. C.C. was movie star handsome and used it to advantage. It was maddening that one could intellectually know such things and still be a sucker for them."

"Mr. Julian."

"Call me C. C."

"C. C. Ted has spoken a bit out of turn. I'm not a wealthy woman."

"Well, then you're in exactly the right place."

"Perhaps at the back of that line," Sarah said, pointing out the door.

"Now, now. You've got it all wrong. Those folks are as important as any. No one has money to burn. I've got my man Harry taking their orders because I arranged a little gathering in here for my personal friends. Since you're a friend of Ted's, you're a friend of mine. Come on, let me introduce you."

And that he did, to five doctors and their wives, four lawyers and theirs, and a few others whose occupation was just "business." Educated, rich and white, except for one of the women who, despite her dyed, blond hair, looked Mexican and spoke with an accent. "Nice to meet you," she said in a voice much huskier than her small frame would suggest. The exotic thirty or so year-old was married to one of the businessmen, an older, bearded, paunchy fellow with little, sharp teeth and a jagged scar on his cheek. Sarah took a double take at the incongruous pair. She soon forgot both of their names, but she did notice how the wife clung to her husband as he made the rounds. "Nice to meet you," she repeated. The juxtaposition of her hair—a good dye job, as Tillie would say—and brown skin was striking, especially against her green eyes. Sarah noticed those, too, because the woman glanced and smiled at her several times, probably in sympathy. Sarah felt and no doubt looked uncomfortable. She returned the gesture, and to her surprise, the woman let go of her husband's arm and approached. "You are alone?" she said.

"Yes, well, not exactly, with a friend."

"I don't understand all these things. Do you?"

"Yes, well, no, not really."

They both chuckled, experiencing a moment of camaraderie. Sarah told her she admired her dress, and she said the same about Sarah's hat. Sarah was about to get a little more personal, to ask about her husband, when that very man appeared, nodded politely and swooped his wife away. Soon they left the room altogether, but not before the woman glanced over her shoulder and smiled at Sarah again.

C. C. must have been observing. He caught Sarah's gaze and walked over to where she was contemplating her getaway. "Nice couple," he said. "Invested a bundle."

"Oh?"

"Absolutely. So, what do you think, Miss Sarah? Are you going to give yourself a chance for a better life?"

Sarah shrugged. "Uh, well…"

"You only live once," C. C. said, placing his strong hand familiarly on her shoulder.

He was right. Other women were doing it. And she wasn't getting any younger. Sarah glanced at Ted, who raised his thumb in an obnoxious gesture of support. That alone nearly made her turn on her heels. But all these people couldn't be wrong. Surely, they weren't all chumps.

"Well?"

She took in a deep breath and nodded. Minutes and a signature later, she had invested five hundred dollars of her hard-earned money. Five hundred dollars. One hundred dollars per unit, entitling her to a tiny percentage of whatever oil was produced in Julian "Well Number Two."

■■■

"Yes," Sarah said, although Mitchell had already hung up. "That's where I met Rita."

5

Mitchell hung up and stared at the phone. One minute Sarah was talking, the next she was gone, back in time, off in her own world. She said she would call him tonight. That remained to be seen. "Shit." He lit a cigarette. He was getting tired of this, too old for it. He never thought Sarah really looked for trouble, but now he was beginning to wonder. Every time she left town, which she did more and more these days, she seemed to find herself in the thick of some life and death drama. You would think that her near misses with the Klan would have soured her on such matters. Instead, she headed straight for them, as recklessly as she invested in Julian Pete, as frequently as she had started to refill that little flask.

He formed a nearly perfect smoke ring and sat back in his wine stained chair, a remnant of his drinking days. He of all people knew how one sip could lead to three, and he feared Sarah was on that road. And he did indeed think this latest matter was related to what happened in Tennessee. She was always looking for some way to undo it. That lynching left all of them reeling. She had found the killer of that professor, but in doing so, had stirred the pot, rustled the hornet's net, and got burned and bitten. It was deep in her, the feeling of responsibility to Jacob's mother. If she had just left things alone, maybe the police would have made discoveries on their own. The drinking soothed the pain, but it hadn't removed the guilt. It was always there, waiting for a chance at redemption.

The investment, however, was another matter. Maybe reckless wasn't exactly the right word. Thousands of others had done the same thing. Gullible was more accurate. Had he known Sarah when she fell for the scheme, he would have warned her about C. C. Mitchell had followed his career, along with many of those other vultures involved in the oil game. He knew a con man when he saw one. Not that she would have listened. Sarah was stubborn, strong-willed. Mitchell smiled. He'd never liked those traits in a woman, until he met Sarah. She had made him admire them. But left unchecked, they could turn on a person, male or female. Maybe it was her age. Like Mitchell, she felt the squeeze of time. She'd worked all her life, supporting her siblings. No husband, no children. Mitchell had tried to change all that, but, despite what she claimed to be her strong feelings for him, she would have none of it.

He walked over to the wide-open apartment window. Snow was in the air. He smashed out his cigarette on the sill and gazed into the frigid late afternoon. He wanted to feel Sarah's not-so-supple-body. Not so supple, but delightfully so. Imperfect, human. He picked up his camera, aimed at a hovering bird in the flat, slate sky. Click. What did Sarah say? A woman claimed to know her. A frightened woman. Hours later, dead. Right out of Hollywood. Fuck. This mindless corruption story he had to cover for the *Blade*. There was always corruption in Toledo. The Julian trial was big. Teapot Dome big. His boss was wrong. This wasn't just an L.A. matter. Mitchell should have insisted. He would have been there with Sarah now. He squinted out the window, raised his camera and shot again, imagining a burnt orange sun sinking into the Pacific.

6

Sarah rushed into the courtroom and took her seat, just in time to catch Ted cloyingly nod to the judge as questioning began.

"Mr. Rosen, you were on the stand the other day were you not?"

"Yes, sir."

"At that time did you have your rights explained to you, that anything you say here may be used against you in a future transaction?"

"Yes, sir."

"You understand that you have a right to refuse to testify at this time?"

"Yes, sir."

"Do you wish to tell anything else we may desire to know concerning the affairs of the Julian Petroleum Company or anything connected with it directly or indirectly?"

"Yes, sir."

He does, Sarah thought? We shall see. It was the connected part she was thinking about, but not in the manner that the prosecutor had in mind. She already knew that Ted was guilty of the stock swindle in every way possible. Deception, fraud, embezzlement, whatever. But was he also connected, directly, indirectly, or unknowingly perhaps, to Rita? Was C. C. himself? It was the hair, of course. That's what had tripped Sarah up. Rita had gone back to what presumably was her natural color. Yes, a defect could've caused a heart attack, but Sarah increasingly believed that terror had something to do with the woman's death. Terror and that bruising. She glanced up and saw Ted's mouth move but only heard Rita's shy, husky voice: "Nice to meet you." "Remember me?" She closed her eyes, envisioning C. C.'s luxurious surroundings, the chumps who had made them possible, and Rita, turning to Sarah, even then, for understanding.

"Mr. Rosen. Could you please go back and tell us something about your work prior to your involvement with Julian Pete?"

"Prior?"

"Yes, what kind of jobs did you hold?"

"Oh, a little bit of everything. Banking, investment, mostly. Before that I delivered newspapers on my bicycle!"

The attorney smiled. "I didn't mean that far back. Another question."

"When was your first contact with the Julian Petroleum Corporation?"

"Well, let me see…"

Sarah thought back again. Rita's husband was Phillip Bradford, the paper said. Now she vaguely recalled the name. But all those others at C. C.'s office. The rich ones. Doctors, lawyers. Sarah wished she could remember their names, too. Then again, what would it matter? Like Mitchell said, what would she do about it? What was there to do? If fear caused the attack, who would care? Certainly not the police. But Rita had come to her. Did she know something else about this stock business, something that had yet to surface?

The courtroom burst into laughter. She glanced at Ted, who by his self-satisfied expression must have cracked another stupid joke. Infuriating. Any laughing should be at, not with him. Sarah reached down and rubbed her foot. I guess everyone needs a little comic relief, she thought, even if it's proffered by the person who caused their grief. Her new shoes were making themselves known. She regarded the pointed toe, a flattering look despite the plainness of the rest, almost worth the pain. It would get better when the leather softened, but right now her feet needed to breath. She slipped them half-off and sighed.

"Again, sir, your first contact?"

"I had come up to the office of Julian Petroleum in twenty-four a number of times in connection with the sale of some wells Mr. Julian owned in Huntington Beach, and then some land at Costa Mesa or Newport, and the wells at Torrance."

"You invested in those wells and land?"

"Yes."

"And made money."

"Yes."

"How much?"

"I don't know."

No one was laughing now. Everyone in the audience knew exactly how much *they* had made… and lost.

"Order."

"You don't know?"

"No. I don't have a dime of it now anyway."

I'll bet, Sarah thought.

"Well, we'll be exploring this more I assure you."

Judge Doran tapped. "Okay, that's it for today. Gentlemen, remember my admonition. Court dismissed."

Sarah followed the crowd out, shuffling along with everyone else. She kept her gaze on the feet ahead of her. Wing tips, spats, French heels, all walking with common purpose. Poor Rita. She'd never walk again. Never wear those shoes that had made their way into Sarah's life. Sarah marched on, noticing that almost every pair ahead of her, worn by a woman that is, had a strap across the instep. All the rage these days. Rita's did, too. Enough already! But then she thought. The name of the shoe store was embossed on the underside, wasn't it? Yes. Maybe something there. At the very least, she might be able to get hers stretched. It was worth a try. She hobbled back to the hotel, grabbed the bag, and asked the clerk for directions.

■■■

A tinkling bell announced Sarah's entrance but no one seemed to notice. Several shoppers were milling about, examining the rows of temptingly displayed styles. The shop was small, but appeared popular.

"It's too tight," a man whispered to Sarah out of nowhere. "But she don't care." Although Sarah had yet to identify herself, the man said this as if he knew she wasn't a customer, as if she were a confidante rather than a stranger.

"I love them," the chubby woman gushed, the French pumps already indenting her swollen, pale flesh. "Ring me up, Sam."

The man, Sam apparently, winked at Sarah. "Whatever you say, Blanche." He pushed the sale key for what, Sarah soon learned, was the fourth time this morning. $3.95. "Not bad for a rainy Tuesday. Not bad at all," he said, after Blanche left. And there were still three prospects browsing the aisles. He checked to see if they wanted to try anything on. Not yet. Which meant he needed to keep his eye on them. If they raised their brows or slowed, certainly if they picked up one of the samples, he would gently pounce.

A ray of sunlight pierced through the dark, heavy clouds, illuminating the gold-painted sign on the storefront window: Kantor's, or s'rotnaK, reflected backwards, as it appeared now. Sam pointed, telling Sarah that it always gave him a bit of a thrill to see his family name. He had built the small Boyle Heights store from the ground up, and in five short years turned it into a footwear destination. Not only because of its "perfect fit" guarantee and fashionable styles, but because of Sam's discretion. Feet were a personal matter, he said, occasionally a source of pride, but more often cause for embarrassment. Mottled nails, rock-hard calluses, flat arches, you name it. But Sam never flinched.

"So, what *are* ya here for, ma'am?" he asked Sarah. "I know by the gleam of that patent leather that you don't need any shoes."

Sarah smiled. "No, you're right. Although I have to admit that you have some beauties in here."

"Nothing but the best. You a teacher?"

"In a way. How'd you know?"

"From Marvy's school? He get into trouble again?"

"Marvy?"

"My son, that little punk, what'd he do this time?"

"No, no. I'm not from the school. Mr. Kantor…"

Sam scanned the customers again. Before Sarah could complete her question, however, he bent down and asked her to remove her right shoe.

"Aha," he said standing. "Now I see. No pebble marks. Everyone that works at the school has 'em, with all that dirt and gravel everywhere." Feet told a kind of story, he explained. He said he could tell Sarah wasn't from around here, because her feet hadn't ever been tanned, for example, and that she had a desk job because her skin was smooth, except for the blisters from the newness of the leather. Maybe she worked for the government, probably used her mind more than her body.

You could say that again, Sarah thought, both impressed and depressed with this analysis. "So you're a *sole* reader."

"Ha. Yeah, I suppose so. Feet tell stories, like I said."

Sarah slowly nodded. She couldn't hope for more.

"But I keep them to myself," he said, as if reading her *mind*. "I measure 'em, analyze 'em and then shoehorn 'em back into hiding." That's why Sam could count more than a few movie stars among his customers, he said, puffing out his chest. Imagine how an admirer of some Hollywood bombshell would feel if he found out that the object of his desire had a bunion the size of an apple.

More sun seeped in. Two days of on-and-off rain. Unusual for L.A, Sam said. Back east, the heat, snow, rain, whatever the conditions lasted for weeks. Here most days were dry and sweet. He loved that. When he learned that Sarah was from Toledo, he offered his sympathies. He himself was from New York, he said. Brooklyn. That his store was on Brooklyn Avenue was all the reminder he needed of the place too, he said. In 1922, with a small savings, he packed up his family of four to start a new life and never looked back. His daughter, Bella, was sickly, and Southern California weather—today notwithstanding—offered hope. He had learned the shoe trade from his father, so when he found a shoe store for sale at a bargain, he felt the move was meant to be. His only disappointment, and it was a big one, was that Bella's health hadn't improved much. Sam shook his head and sighed. His daughter was a constant source of worry. He was a nervous man anyway, prone to anxiety and dark moods. The doctors didn't know what was wrong with her exactly. Hearing and sight trouble. He wiped his pale blue eyes. The routine of the store was a godsend, forcing him to focus on something else.

"Well, now, I don't know why I'm telling you all this," he said.

"It's okay. I'm used it." And she was. Sarah didn't need to tell people what she did for a living to gain their confidence. They sensed that she was a listener. Sometimes this was a good thing, sometimes exhausting, occasionally dangerous.

Sam glanced around and saw a young lady reach for a tie up boot. "Be right back, Miss…"

"Kaufman. Sarah Kaufman."

"Ah, that's why."

Sarah smiled.

Immediately Sam was at the woman's side. "Mr. Kantor, do you have these in a seven?"

"I think so. Let me check."

Sam was still in the storage room when a young boy, his black hair matted with sweat, burst into the store. "Dad, Dad!"

Sam quickly appeared, clenching his jaw. He handed the customer the boots and told her he would be right with her. "Damn kid. Marvy," he said, grabbing his shoulder, "how many times do I have to tell you. Not when I'm working. Go home!"

"But Dad! Old man Wolf's locked up. He's bangin' on the glass!"

"What are ya talkin' about? I'll bang you if you don't scat!" Sam raised his hand, but Marvy ducked and slid away.

"Dad! He's screamin', I'm telling ya."

Sarah watched as Sam stuck his head out the door, appearing to take in the landmarks, then glancing down toward Soto, the cross street where the bus had left her off. He muttered to himself something about a crowd gathered near the bank. "What's going on, Oscar?" he said to a man standing on the sidewalk. "Not a run, I hope."

"It's at Wolf's, not the bank. Al locked his father up again. You remember the last time, don't you, Sam? He does it to get sales. Pulls the outside alarm, the old man panics, folks go to check out the commotion, and there's Al with his goddamn dry goods yelling 'three for one!' Can't you hear the alarm?"

"Yeah, now I can. But I've got a store of my own to run. Been so busy, and Marvy's driving me crazy. His teacher dragged him here yesterday again for clowning around in class. I don't have time to wipe my ass let alone pay attention to such nonsense." He glanced at Sarah. "Pardon me, ma'am."

"Well, it's not like I don't work, Sam," Oscar said, "but look at the crowd. Maybe not a bad idea."

"Ach, go waaay," Sam said, drawing out the vowel, shaking his head. "So what is it that you want, anyway?" he said to Sarah in an irritated tone. "You're here for a reason, I take it."

"Yes, well, I don't know if you read about it, but a woman's body was found in a ravine yesterday."

"What?"

"I saw your store name on the woman's shoes. It's a long story, but I'm trying to find out more about her."

"You a cop, too? I wouldn't have guessed that!"

"No, no cop."

"Well, people die all the time," Sam said, heading back into the store, leading Marvy to a chair where he sat him down and told him to stay.

Sarah followed. "Mr. Kantor, there may be more to it."

"What do you mean?"

"I'm not certain this was a natural death."

"You said she wore mine, you sure?"

"Yes."

"How'd you get them?"

"That's what I want to talk to you about, sir."

Sam eyed her closely. "More to it? I don't want any trouble. I've got enough."

"I don't want any trouble either. But I would like to clear something up and you may be able to help me."

"Me? You sure you ain't a cop?"

"Promise."

Sam hesitated, then offered a tired smile. "If it weren't my shoes, and if you weren't a member of the tribe…but make it fast."

Sam kept watch on a remaining customer as Sarah recounted the events that led her to seek him out. He perked up when she explained the nature of her work, shook his head when she told him about her Julian stock, and frowned when she relayed her experience with and suspicions about Rita.

"Tsk tsk. Maybe you're wrong, Miss Kaufman."

"Sarah."

"Maybe you're wrong, Sarah. Maybe that gal just had a heart attack, you know, just like that."

"I hope I am. You may be able to help me prove that."

"How?"

"Well, by examining these shoes to begin with. By seeing if you remember anything at all about the purchase."

"Damn Mexicans," Sam said. "Always up to no good. Hot-tempered. And their kids are always up to no good, too. Married to a white fella you say? Bradford? No, I don't know anybody like that."

Sarah squirmed, feeling both offended and guilty.

"I like Mexicans, and they're Chicanos, Dad," Marvy piped in. He was still seated, juggling a pair of sneakers.

Sam got up, grabbed the shoes and covered his son's mouth. "Shush!"

Marvy yanked his father's hand away and smirked. The ten-year old boy's wide-set blue eyes, a younger version of his father's, twinkled at Sarah. Sam heaved a deep sigh and tousled his son's hair. "Healthy as a horse that kid." And a handful, he told Sarah. Wasn't fair with Bella so sick. Wasn't fair to Marvy either.

"You like greasers," Sam said, "but what about your friend Joe Reyes? Remember what you told me, about what he said during that crazy game you kids play?"

"He was just jokin' Dad, I told you that too!"

"All right, all right, Marvy. Now, you better go home. Mom'll be worrying about you. I'll be there soon."

"But Dad…"

"Now! Or I'll get the belt!"

●●●

Sarah leaned back in the worn lobby chair. *Oil!* She had just finished the chapter entitled "The Ranch." Bunny was growing up, learning the oil business from the bottom up; that is from the mechanics of drilling to his father's shady sales techniques. He was interested in the former, but troubled by the latter. A.J. Ross was gaining ground, accumulating investors and, as he was just about to do with Paul's family, conning people out of their oil-rich land. Sarah opened the book again and reread the passage.

> *'But listen, Dad; you'll pay Mr. Watkins a fair price!'*
>
> *'I'll pay him a land price, but I ain't a-goin' to pay him no oil price. In the first place, he'll maybe get suspicious and refuse to sell. He's got nothing to do with any oil that's here—it ain't been any use to him, and wouldn't be in a million years. And besides, what use could a poor feeble-minded old fellow like that make of oil-money?'*
>
> *'But we don't want to take advantage of him, Dad!'*
>
> *'I'll see that he don't suffer…'*
>
> *They walked on and Bunny began to unfold the elements of a moral problem that was to occupy him, off and on, for many years. Just what rights did the Watkins' have to the oil that lay underneath their ranch?*

Indeed, Sarah thought. And what rights will they have if and when they realize they've been cheated out of their money!

That remained to be seen. But fiction was fiction. Reality demanded her attention, and today it had not lived up to its promise, at least as Sam had depicted it. All he could tell from Rita's shoes was that her big toes were on the plump side, that she had high arches, and that she wore silk stockings, as he found a tiny piece of that fabric clinging to one of the straps. It was a story, yes, but without a plot. The shoe alone wasn't enough, he said. He needed the foot, he needed "flesh and bones." A vision of Rita's corpse flashed before Sarah's eyes as he spoke. Flesh and bones, already decomposing. She wondered for a moment if there was a way for Sam to view the body. Maybe then he could summon his full narrative skills. But she quickly discarded the idea. No one would agree to it, including, she surmised, Sam himself.

Sam couldn't recall anything at all about the sale. The shoe was a relatively old style, he said, but still very popular. And one of his most expensive. Ferragamo was the shoe designer to the stars. Sarah tried to jar his memory, describing Rita's hair, the kind of clothes she wore, how she spoke. What about her husband, the advertising mogul, Phillip Bradford? Maybe he had accompanied her. Sarah described him. But no. He'd sold so many of them, to whites, Negroes, Russians, Japs and yes, even to the Mexicans he so distrusted. Everyone needed shoes, he said, and business was business.

Sarah plopped on the bed, reached for the nearly empty flask that she had ditched under the nightstand and swigged. She needed to hunt down some more. She shook the last few drops onto her tongue and put the flask back into its unimaginative hiding place. No, as far as Rita went, Sam hadn't been of any help at all. When the hotel clerk had first told her how close Kantor's was she thought she was on to something. Perhaps a mysterious force had intervened to show her the way. She was susceptible to that kind of thinking. And not entirely without cause. Sarah really did seem to have more than her share of "unexplained" experiences. Even Obee acknowledged that. Dreams that had come true, thoughts of old friends who would suddenly appear out of nowhere, that sort of thing. No doubt they were coincidences, but there was a little part of Sarah that thought, even hoped, it might be something else, although what she didn't know.

The trip to Boyle Heights hadn't been a total loss, however. As it turned out, Sam had invested in oil stock, too. Everyone had, he said. Not Julian Pete, and not much. But he had a few buddies who had lost their shirts. "It's the little people like you and me that get the shaft," he said. "And the big ones, like your friend Rosen, that get off."

Sarah bristled, assuring him that Ted was definitely not her friend, and that she still held out hope that he'd go to jail."

"You don't know L.A.," Sam said, shaking his head. "You don't know what money can do in this town. And what the lack of it can't."

"I think I do!"

"Ha! Yeah, but I mean in politics, and to people, on every level."

"I work for a city," Sarah said. And I'm close to one of its best journalists. I know about graft, corruption. Toledo is no paradise."

Sam moistened his lips. "Well, I live here, and I bet I could tell you a thing or two. It's unique, has its own rules. And its own kind of snakes," he added grinning, obviously proud of his allusion.

"What kind of things? What rules? What snakes?" Sarah asked.

Sam said he would be happy to relay all the sordid details on one condition, that she'd agree to come for dinner at his home the following evening. His wife would make her a nice Jewish meal. Sarah forced a smile. She'd had enough Jewish meals to last a lifetime, and was, moreover, a little taken aback by the offer. Other than their common heritage, and the shoes, of course, they were strangers.

"Thank you, Mr. Kantor, but I, I don't think I can make it."

"Oh, sure you can."

"No, I…"

"Look, Miss. I'll be honest with you. I do have some information, things I'll bet that newsman of yours doesn't know. And Henrietta is a good cook. But I was also kind of hoping that you might spend a little time with Marvy, you know, give your professional opinion."

Sam was serious. He said he couldn't afford counseling, but he really was worried about the kid. Meeting Sarah seemed lucky. How often did one happen upon an expert on these matters? Marvy didn't listen, had a fresh mouth, and hung around with the wrong crowd. He was always getting into one mess or another. Sam couldn't control his son, and this is what made him so nervous. He just wanted to know: What was wrong with him? Was there hope?

Sarah smiled, this time easily. She was already fond of the boy. But she wouldn't jump to conclusions. Okay. She would go. It might be interesting after all. At the very least, it would be a relief to put her energy where it really could be of help.

Sarah checked the clock. Too late to call Mitchell. Besides, there was nothing to report. She turned off the light and sank into a deep, dreamless sleep.

7

Agua Caliente had not officially opened but that didn't stop Carlos Martinez from tossing a few newly minted hundred dollar chips over the pristine felt table. After all, he had invested in the resort, and if he wanted to pretend, here alone in the Gold Room, that he was a high roller, so be it. He picked up the chips, embossed on one side with a silhouette of the luxurious Mission- style casino, and on the other with the initials of its three founders: James Crofton, Wirt Bowman and Baron Long. *Gringos*. Fucking *gringos*. But they couldn't have pulled it off without Governor Rodriguez's complicity. Carlos spat with contempt. The honorable Abelardo Rodriquez, *jefe* of Baja California, purchased the property, enabling them to skirt the Mexican constitution's prohibition of foreign ownership of land near the borders. Bought and sold. *Traidor!* It wasn't enough that whites had stolen California from his people, turning natives like Carlos' grandmother into second-class citizens. Now they had come here, to Tijuana, bringing their own brand of conquest over the border, further lining their filthy rich pockets.

Carlos caught himself. Such feelings needed to be kept in check. One day things would be different. That, he vowed. It would take time. Step by step. He took in a long, deep breath and exhaled. For now, he would have to be patient and take comfort in the fact that finally, in some small way, he had his hand in the game.

He gazed at the ornate, gilded ceiling, with its intricate carvings and painted scenes from Greek mythology, and immediately fell back into ruminating. Why not Mexican myths? Why not Aztec figures? Yes, the hacienda architectural features paid small homage to his heritage, as did the Amerindian pattern in the dining room and other touches here and there. But he was talking about inspiration! Primitive forces, origins. What about a tribute to the plenty of *Quetzalcoatl*, the justice of *Tezcatlipoca*, or even the sin of *Nahua*? Indeed, sin would be appropriate in this place, represented, as it was with *Nahua*, as excrement.

Carlos half-smiled, brushing a speck off his white linen jacket. He looked up again. Still, the image was stunningly executed, and he had to admit that, in general, Agua Caliente's mix of styles and furnishings was appealing. Art Deco lines, Arabesque arches, European chandeliers, Roman-style columns. There was a kind of discombobulated beauty to it. And Carlos knew about beauty. He was a lover of it. In music, literature, art, not to mention as it manifested itself in the female form.

Ah, women. In that area Carlos was an expert. The numbers were too many to count, not to mention that lovely little *chica* waiting for him even now in the bungalow. But he was also a thinker, self-taught and proud of it. He'd read and studied the greats in every field, educating himself and disproving the greatest myth of all: that Mexicans and Chicanos like himself were basically a simple people, designed for manual labor. Not that he had anything against such work. He loved his brothers and sisters who cleaned and built, who toiled in the fields while their white bosses slept. Indeed, if things went according to plan, he would soon be celebrating a vast improvement in their conditions. No, it was the widely held belief that this was the *only* thing they were good at that burned his soul, not only because it was wrong, but because of how the powerful used it to justify their deeds.

Carlos thought back to his younger days. With his father dying at forty and no siblings to help out, he too had to work, leaving school far before he wanted to. But not laying bricks. He was determined, and despite the bigotry, despite the resistance he encountered at every turn, he made it in business, first as a clerk, then a bookkeeper and finally a manager. Now he owned those grocery stores in Boyle Heights, as well as his childhood home that his father could barely afford to rent. He wasn't about to let his mother down. At seventy-five, she lived there still, a testament to his resolve.

He lit the cigar that had been resting between his lips and exited the luxurious room in which the wealthiest guests would soon be betting with abandon. Boyle Heights, he thought. Sounded more like a fulminating wound than the melting pot it was, but no matter. It was the only place in L.A. that Carlos still felt at ease. Named for an Irishman, comprised today of Russians, Japanese and Chicanos, and, of course, the ever-present Jews, the Los Angeles neighborhood, so close to the city's rich and famous, was a world apart. There were dividing lines there to be sure, geographic, ethnic and religious. But economically everyone was in the same boat, struggling to make ends meet, and this joined them in common purpose. To a point. Tensions periodically surfaced among the groups, and he'd had his fair share of fights growing up, especially with the Jews. Not that he had anything inherently against that money-grubbing lot, or the others, but when push came to shove, he would do what he needed to and never look back. His once naive belief in the basic goodness of people had been tested too often, he thought, squelching a familiar image of burning houses, closing his ears to the echoes of suffering. Eventually, one had to choose sides.

As he walked through the Moorish halls of the ballroom, across the layered hardwood of the main casino, past the murals depicting sensuous flappers and toward the double-doors that led to the courtyard, he thanked his lucky stars again that the *gringos* had relied on the sale of public shares. He'd purchased as many as he could afford, mostly from what he'd earned from his Julian stock. He'd been lucky with that one too, getting out before the fall. The Tijuana pool had served him well, providing him with enough to keep his stores secure and his mother protected. Yes, he'd been lucky, and he would pay back that luck in spades.

"*Buenos días, señor.*" Carlos turned to see one of the staff, who even at this early hour was sweating from polishing the lobby's tile floor.

"Ah, *buenos días. Cómo estás…*Luis, *sí?*"

"*Sí.* Luis. You remember. I'm very well, sir. I see you're up with the birds as usual."

"Indeed. It's nice to enjoy the quiet while it lasts."

"I know."

"When did that go up?" Carlos asked, pointing to an over-sized curved mirror with a massive silver frame.

"Yesterday. Beautiful, no?"

Carlos bent his head toward the glittering new artifact. He smiled, regarding his image with matter-of-fact approval. A still strapping figure at fifty. Just five foot nine, but erect and broad shouldered. His silver hair was slicked back, exaggerating the ancestral cheekbones and wide-set, heavy-lidded dark eyes that women loved. Muscled but trim, Carlos also had not succumbed to the paunchy fate of most men his age. He smiled again. Was he vain? Perhaps. But not excessively so. He simply believed in acknowledging, respecting, and, when necessary, using what nature had given him. Still, he kept such things in perspective. He wouldn't escape the ravages of time forever. All the more reason to enjoy what he had while he could.

He moved closer and inspected himself from top to bottom. The white suit complemented his dark complexion. He tilted his head and smoothed the thin mustache that neatly crowned his full lips. Mmm. What delights they had tasted!

"*Señor?*"

"Oh yes, beautiful," Carlos said, sliding his hand over the frame. "Well, Luis, you're helping to create an incredible place here. But take it easy. The day is young."

"I'll try."

"*Hasta luego.*"

"*Adíos, señor.* Oh, the papers just arrived. Over there."

"*Gracias.*"

Carlos reluctantly grabbed a copy of the *Los Angeles Times* and walked out into the cool morning air. It irked him to patronize that rag, mainly because of its owner, Henry Chandler, a dictatorial racist with no scruples. The Spanish language *El Heraldo de Mexico* was his L.A. paper of choice, but one had to stay in front of the enemy.

The elaborate clock tower, surrounded by palms and brilliant green grass chimed. Eight o'clock; time to wake up Maria, one way or another. He tapped out his cigar and tossed a penny into the little brick wishing well before reaching for his reading glasses, the one sign of age he couldn't dispute.

As he headed toward the bungalow, he scanned the headlines: *TRAINLOAD OF WWI VETS TRANSPORTED TO OWENS VALLEY TO PATROL L.A. AQUEDUCT.*

"That fucker Mulholland," Carlos said aloud.

FIRST TALKIE, THE JAZZ SINGER, TO PREMIER AT GRAUMAN'S CHINESE; L.A. HAS HIGHEST NATIONAL SUICIDE RATE; TESTIMONY CONTINUES IN THE JULIAN PETE TRIAL.

Ay. Here he stopped. Suicide and stocks. Perhaps some effect and cause. Carlos didn't think that C. C. Julian had intended to be corrupt. Greed had just gotten the better of him. He wasn't so sure about Rosen and the other Jews. Funny how they're always around when money is involved. He also wasn't certain if Chandler himself hadn't caused Julian's fall, constantly publishing those villainous op-eds against him. Chandler and the stinking Chamber of Commerce whose ass Carlos had to kiss to get any notice, even though he had made a showpiece out of his markets. Chandler and the Chamber, creating their own news, their own version of L.A., their own history.

Maria. He needed Maria. He picked up his pace and prepared to toss the paper out in a nearby receptacle. "Trash in the trash," he muttered. But a final glance stopped him in his tracks.

Rita Bradford, wife of advertising mogul Phillip Bradford, will be laid to rest this week at Calvary Catholic Cemetery. She was thirty-six years old and died suddenly of a heart attack. Ligature marks noted initially have been deemed unrelated. Mr. Bradford is said to be in deep mourning and will receive no visitors. Relatives fear for his health.

Carlos steadied himself against the heavy trunk of a nearby tree as he reread the tiny article. "What?! *Qué?!*" He stared at the words, shaking his head. Gradually, he looked up and saw the freshly painted bungalow, tempting with its garden of rare specimens, not to mention the one exquisite flower blooming inside. So near, yet now.... "*Maldita sea!*" he shouted.

8

The Kantors' current home on Winter Street was their fourth residence in three years, each within a mile of the other, all within walking distance of the shoe store. They rented, Sam said, but the last move had been a step up, leaving a cramped apartment for the tidy two-bedroom cottage they now occupied. All the homes in the modest neighborhood were small and well kept, much like Sarah's in Toledo, except for the palm trees.

Familiar smells of roasted chicken and potatoes wafted out to the concrete porch where Sarah and Sam waited for Henrietta, his wife of fifteen years, to put the finishing touches on dinner. The weather had cleared, and Sam wanted to keep watch on Marvy who was playing ball in the street with some of his pals, or scamps, as Sam called them.

"So," Sam said.

Sarah sat facing him, his downward sloped blue eyes, etched with worry lines, darted from Sarah to Marvy. Sarah followed his glance just as his son threw a pitch, right down the middle. "Strike!" Marvy yelled.

"No way!" said the hitter.

"Bobby, what do you say?" Marvy said.

The umpire paused: "Strike!"

Marvy raised his fist and then prepared to wind up.

Sarah smiled. "Don't worry so much, Mr. Kantor. I think your boy is going to be okay."

"I hope you're right. We'll see. But enough of that for now. I said I would give you the scoop, as they say around here. And I keep my promises."

Sam began, and it soon became clear that the "scoop" had more to do with his theory about L.A. than it did with any secret facts for which she had thought she exchanged her services. Still, there was something to it. Since coming here, the city had grown, he said, so much so that he hardly recognized it from month to month. Every day, builders started at least fifty new homes. Just over the past year hundreds of office buildings had sprung up, schools, warehouses, apartments, and property prices had soared. This, Sam said, was good and bad; good because things felt continually renewed, offering the almost daily possibility of a fresh start. Bad, because nothing felt secure. Sam pointed to the floor. Not even the ground was stable, he said with a shivering gesture. "I gotta tell ya Sarah, the first time we felt one of those quakes, we nearly packed up and moved back to Brooklyn." Sarah shivered in sympathy. From what she'd seen of those photographs of San Francisco, that was one experience she could live without.

Then Sam said: "Now, here's the point I want to make. It's something I've thought long and hard about since I arrived in this place."

Sarah leaned in a bit, encouraging him to continue.

"Well…" He gave one quick look to Marvy. "You see…"

As Sarah listened, she understood Sam's somewhat disjointed but intriguing hypothesis to be this: that the rapid growth and accelerated building, coupled with the fine weather and even the constant threat of earthquakes contributed to the city's unique eccentricity, debauchery and rampant corruption. Why? Because in such a place, where everything is in flux, the old rules and conventions don't matter much. Why work for a living when you can gamble on the latest craze? Why stay inside and save for the future when rain was so scarce, when the sun was shining today and tomorrow and the next day? And if the earth, God forbid, could at any moment crack apart, why not indulge your whims, reinvent yourself, now? No wonder it was here where movies were made; the land itself was in continuous motion. Sam looked at Sarah thoughtfully. "Am I making myself clear?"

Sarah nodded slowly. Yes, he was. The land, the climate, the newness all shaping behavior and character. It made sense. She also was ashamed to admit that she was astonished by Sam's intelligence and by the fact that he took the time to contemplate such matters. With his work and anxieties over his children, she would have imagined he would have used his remaining energy for simpler things.

Mind you, Sam said, this didn't prevent him from loving the city. Los Angeles was fresh and sparkling, and business was good. But this feeling was tempered by the knowledge that there were forces at work, greedy, scheming, powerful forces like Henry Chandler and his banker buddies. Like Louis B. Mayer and some of the other studio heads. Like all the big oilmen; the really big oilmen, that is. Edward Doheny, for instance, who took that government bribe with impunity. Julian may be a brilliant con, he said, but he obviously never would have that kind of influence. Sarah interrupted, stating that Mayer had invested in Julian stock, but Sam said that was nothing. He was still one of the elite, right up there with Chandler. They were all intertwined, Sam said, and they could break you if they wanted. Then Sam drew in closer. "They buy their shoes from me. They joke around and treat me like a pal. But just you watch what would happen if I spoke out of turn, or tried to rise too far above my station. Whisper campaigns, arson, you name it. I've seen it with my own eyes. Happened to a friend of mine, although as you might guess, he could never prove it. L.A. is the land of dreams, within limits. Dream too big and you'll be in a nightmare. That's what makes this place different, Sarah," Sam said. "That's what your reporter friend doesn't know."

Sarah thought he was probably right. Mitchell wouldn't know this, nor for that matter, would anyone else who hadn't, well, walked in Sam's shoes. She started to tell Sam that when Henrietta called them to dinner. "Marvy," she yelled out in a thick Brooklyn accent. "Come on." Sam stood with his bulky arms folded as his son continued to play. He counted to three and threatened him with "the belt" before Marvy finally ambled toward them. Sarah resisted smiling. The kid was strong-willed, a good trait if harnessed for an equally good purpose. She briefly considered expressing her views on the inefficacy of corporal punishment but decided to wait until she gave Sam her full assessment, after she had the opportunity to fill in her increasingly optimistic but still superficial picture of the boy.

Sarah followed Sam into a small living room with a pink couch and matching chair, walnut tables accented with lace doilies and a few slightly tattered oriental rugs. The dining area was immediately attached, with a bay window that looked out to a stoop and the grassy backyards of other homes. Sarah took the chair Henrietta offered her, next to Marvy, who glanced at Sarah with a smirk that she interpreted as amused curiosity. "Mom's a great cook," he said.

Sarah nodded at the steaming dishes on the table. "It looks like it."

"Don't try to get on my good side, young man. You need to listen to your father," Henrietta said with soft eyes that belied her quasi-angry tone.

The juicy, browned chicken was cut up and centered on a flowered ceramic plate, with potatoes and buttered green beans arranged around it. Sarah's stomach growled. She was hungry too, and more receptive to Jewish food than she thought.

Sam passed around some yeast rolls and started gnawing on a chicken leg before Sarah had even decided which part of the bird she wanted. Marvy and Henrietta followed suit, so Sarah opted for a breast and dug in. As he buttered his roll, Sam asked Sarah if she'd heard about the time a few years back when her dear C. C. Julian decked Charlie Chaplin at the Café Petroushka.

"What? No, I haven't."

Henrietta, an ample, sweet, wide-faced woman with creamy skin, shot him a disapproving look. "Sam! Not in front of Marvy."

"Go waaay," he said, shooing her with his hand. He's all right."

"And you wonder why he misbehaves."

"I'm not gonna say anything that he hasn't heard. Besides, it's a lesson."

Marvy smirked again as he and Sarah waited for the story that Sarah hoped wasn't too risqué for young ears. Sarah was of the school that children should be informed, that teaching them compassion and the Golden Rule were more important than shielding them from the reality of life. But there were limits.

Sam said that the café was owned by a Russian princess, was very posh and catered to celebrities. The former chef for Czar Nicholas headed the kitchen. On the night in question, back in '22, he had made borsht for Jascha Heifetz among others. "Heifetz, I said," Sam repeated, glancing at Marvy with gritted teeth.

Marvy frowned. "I know, I know, Dad."

"You've got that damn violin but you never practice!"

Henrietta slapped her dimpled hand against the table. "Sam!"

"Come on, Dad," Marvy said. "I'll practice, I promise."

Sam shook his head. "Yeah, yeah. So anyway, some famous Russian author was there too, Duneav or Dunave, that fellow who could bend a dime between his fingers. And Charlie Chaplin. Chaplin was there with Mary Minter."

Sarah widened her eyes, partly involuntarily, partly on purpose. The mention of Minter was somewhat surprising, but Sarah also wanted Sam to know she was paying attention. Minter was an actress implicated in director William Desmond Taylor's murder. News of Taylor's untimely death had even made it into the *Blade*. Minter's involvement was never proven, but her career had never been the same either. Murder, Sarah said to herself, suddenly realizing that she hadn't thought of Rita all evening.

"Yes indeed, it was quite a night," Sam said. "As Julian passed by Chaplin's table, he bumped up against Minter, apparently on purpose. Chaplin warned C. C. to leave her alone, and that was that. Julian took a swipe at Chaplin, who ducked and then knocked Julian down. Then for whatever reason, the author hit C. C. too. Fighting just to fight," he said, looking at Marvy, who again was smirking. "They all have so much money, you'd think they'd have better things to do. Chaplin ended up with a bloody nose and Julian was pretty banged up. It was in all the papers. But I learned about it first hand because Chaplin came in the store the next day."

"To buy shoes?" Sarah said, her mind returning to Rita again.

"Yep. One of my best customers," the 'little tramp.'"

Sarah smiled. "I'm impressed Mr. Kantor."

"Sam," he said.

■■■

Henrietta offered her a slice of homemade yellow cake with pungent orange frosting, dotted with tiny pieces of candied peel. Sarah was stuffed, but accepted out of courtesy and then devoured it. Citrusy and perfectly baked. She would try to get the recipe for Tillie.

"So how do you like our Boyle Heights?" Henrietta asked.

"I've seen very little of it. But I like the feel."

"You should," Sam said. "This part is all Jewish. Very few places like it in the country. It's like an extended family."

"I did notice the store names on Brooklyn Avenue."

"Uh huh. A lot of Eastern European Jews settled here after escaping the pogroms, although now, you know, with Coolidge and those damn quotas, there aren't as many comin' in. A lot of 'em are going to Mexico I hear. Whew. I can't imagine that."

"Mexico, huh? Well the country must be welcoming then."

"I'd rather stay in Europe."

"Have you ever been to Mexico?"

"Nope. And I ain't going. I know what it's like from what I see here."

Sarah felt a little sick.

"Most Jews still speak Yiddish here, though. Not me. It's important to blend in, you know, be part of the mainstream."

Sarah nodded. Well, on that she agreed. She didn't even know the idiom, except for a few obscenities. She was proud of her heritage to be sure, but, as she told Tillie when her sister tried to make her feel guilty for abandoning the mother tongue, she wasn't from the Old World. Moreover, she couldn't abandon something she hadn't ever really known. She turned to Henrietta. "Please tell me a little more about the neighborhood," she said.

"Well, let me think. We've got some well-stocked grocery stores, you know. Oh and the Brooklyn Avenue Delicatessen always has fresh smoked cod. I make my own pickles, though, because theirs are too salty."

"Mom's pickles are great!" Marvy said.

"The best," Sam said, touching his wife's arm.

She smiled and continued. "Our little town also has a bathhouse, athletic club, and, of course, the Meralta Theater. I don't go to the movies much, but Marvy and Sam love it, mostly for the poly seeds."

Sam and Marvy chuckled in unison.

"What about my school?" Marvy said.

"What about it?"

"It's good, too."

"You're right, Marvy," Henrietta said, "Hollenbeck has an excellent reputation, but I'm surprised you'd bring it up, considering."

"Yeah, sometimes I act up, I know, but I like school!"

Henrietta raised a brow. "I'm glad to hear it."

"Do you ever go downtown?" Sarah said.

"Now and then. The P car, the same one you took here, leaves me off right on Broadway. Or I take the B to Main. I do enjoy window-shopping. I miss New York sometimes and that makes me feel better."

"There are some nice looking stores there."

"Oh yeah. I'll bet you like to shop, Sarah. I've been meaning to tell you how much I like your frock. That color of pink goes so well with your dark hair. Of course you have a lovely figure. I could never wear something so form-fitting, but you certainly can."

"Oh, sure you could, but thank you," Sarah said.

Henrietta rested her chin on her fists. "You know, now that I think about it, the best part of living here is that we genuinely like each other. God knows we each have our struggles. And some are luckier than others. But nobody's rich, and I think that's okay for most people. We put our relationships over money."

Sam nodded. "Yetta's right. We do. Part of it's because we're all we've got, the only ones we can really trust. We're working class stiffs, and, like I said before, the big shots want to keep it that way. But many wouldn't leave even if they could. It's a real community. Not that we don't argue, especially about politics. Boy, walk around here any summer evening you'll hear it. Most of us are Democrats, of course. But some are liberals, some radicals, some socialists and even communists, and everybody tries to convince the other of their position. I'm a union member myself, for whatever good it does, and I've done my fair share of *kvetching*. But at bottom, we're all very close."

"Sounds utopian," Sarah said, "certainly not like my neighborhood, where people keep to themselves." But she wondered: Did their camaraderie extend to other groups in the area? Boyle Heights, she had discovered, was unusually diverse. Indeed, the hotel clerk described it, with a hint of disgust, as "the melting pot of melting pots." But was it really? She lowered her tone. "Does your valuing of relationships apply to *everyone* in Boyle Heights?"

Henrietta was quiet.

"You mean to the other races?" Sam said.

"Uh huh."

Sam sat back in his chair. With two quick bites, he finished his cake and scraped up the remnants of the frosting. "You already know the answer to that question, I think, Sarah. Listen, some around here mingle, at workmen's meetings and so forth. I don't. I know, they're my customers, and sometimes I'm even theirs. I know that Mexicans, Chicanos, whatever you want to call them, probably picked the oranges in this frosting," he said, licking a tiny piece of peel off his fork. "And really, I don't have anything against them. You know, I don't wish them ill. But people are happier with their own kind. At least I am. Soto and Brooklyn, that's my people. South of Fourth and Soto, that's theirs. East of Evergreen, the Japs. Not too many Negroes anywhere but the Flats, which is mostly Russian. White Russians, who blame us, by the way, the Jews, for their revolution."

Sarah nodded. He knew his mind anyway.

"But then again," Sam said, "I was willing to help you with that woman, wasn't I? See there, I'm not a bigot. I would have helped if I could. What was her name?"

"Rita. Rita Bradford."

"Yeah, Rita. Hmm. Dammit, still wish I could remember something more about her."

"Sam," Henrietta said, "Marvy."

"All right, all right. But I do wish I could remember."

"Me too," Sarah said.

■■■

She thanked the Kantors and assured Sam that his son would be fine, although in reality one could never be absolutely certain. Sarah squinted at her watch. 6 p.m. The last streetcar left at nine. She gazed east, according to Sam, the direction of the ravine. Pretty far, Sam told her. A mile or so, down toward the river. And it could be dangerous. Lots of gangs fought there. But if she hurried she could make it back before dark.

Sarah knew all along that she would need to see the ravine, the site where Rita was found. Though voiceless, places spoke, occasionally even providing a clue. She'd learned that in Tennessee, where the discovery of a seemingly insignificant piece of glass led to a killer. She had hoped to have company on her journey, but Sam had not offered. He didn't want to get involved, he had said earlier, and she surmised that this was still the case.

He did, however, provide detailed directions. Up Winter to Mott, down Mott to Brooklyn. Strong delicatessen smells had mingled with cigar smoke as she marched west on Brooklyn past several clothing stores, an ice cream parlor and a pawnbroker's shop. Through the pawnbroker's window, Sarah observed two animated men who appeared to be haggling over a fur coat. Across the street she spotted the Meralta Theater, where a crowd was milling about. "The Mysterious Lady," a new spy film with Greta Garbo, flickered on the marquis.

At Soto she turned right and continued on a slight incline for nearly a mile. Shifting aromas wafted through windows: spicy, sharp, sweet. Pepper, onions, garlic. Seasonings and herbs she couldn't identify. She continued to sprint, despite the blisters on her heel—she'd forgotten to get the damn shoes stretched—stopping briefly at the gentle summit. In view was downtown, with the concrete, tiered, pointed tower of the nearly finished new city hall rising far above the other buildings. She had read that its unique shape had been inspired by an ancient Egyptian mausoleum. Interesting that the symbol of a young city would be modeled after a home for the dead. Then again, the Egyptians believed in reincarnation and soon the place would be alive with activity.

From the summit, down to the left, Sam had said.

Sarah scanned a wide region of dirt and pavement, peppered with run-down houses and a few tacky businesses. The setting sun cast everything in a sickly, yellow light. Past the Flats, she could just make out the banks of the Los Angeles River, a sickly thing itself. She had seen the river, if one could call it that, up close on her prior trip to the city. It was hard to believe that so much blood had been spilt for such a weak, brackish flow, and not that long ago.

She descended the hill, passing a ramshackle building that Sam said housed the Turkish baths. The Flats were basically there, between First and Fourth. Beyond that and west was Marianna Street.

Sarah walked straight ahead, turned right and right again past the now closed shops that the cop had mentioned, past empty lots and run-down houses, until she approached what she thought must be the ravine, or at least the general area where the papers said the body was found. It was not a crime scene, so there were no markers, no tape or rope to designate it as such. A nearby pack of rough -looking teens hunched together and smoking collectively eyed her but seemed neither troubled by nor interested in her presence.

She paced around the spot for a while, looking for something, anything. She inspected a yellow flowering shrub, a patch of grass, many varieties of weeds. She picked up a pebble and skidded it on the hard ground. It stopped abruptly, leaving a tiny trail of dust. She sighed. Nothing. No footprints. No blood. Not even a gum wrapper. No sign that a woman had taken her last breath on this unremarkable plot of land. Dirt and more dirt. Dust to dust.

How would Sarah herself leave this world? She had wondered this often, especially in the past few years when death had come so near. It could have easily happened by murder had Mitchell not prevented it. By a gunshot, perhaps, like the professor in Tennessee, or even a lynching. Well, that was unlikely, but certainly not impossible given her history with the Klan. But the real event would probably be far less dramatic. A fall on ice, a wrong turn, the flu. She had been one of the lucky ones in the deadly '17 epidemic, but would she be in the next?

She continued to ponder the grim possibilities as she slowly made her way back toward the bus stop. Her parents had both succumbed to TB, but at least they did so in the relative comfort of their own beds. Contemplating where one would pass one's final moments was as nearly terrible as thinking bout how it would happen. Surrounded by loved ones or completely alone? On a cold street or under a warm blanket? In the care of compassionate doctors or hung from a leafless tree? Or like Rita. By herself...or not.

Sarah boarded the bus thinking of that empty, sad place. It was dusk now, the sky dull blue with wisps of orange. Lights began to twinkle in the city as the bus rumbled toward town. Rita. A lovely name. Sam had said it with a Brooklyn accent, Riter. Not as pleasant of a sound. At dinner, they had in fact talked a little about names. It was Marvy who got it started. When Sam gave his blunt views on Mexicans, Marvy said that his dad would have liked his friend Joe if his last name wasn't Reyes.

"And maybe if he didn't say what he did!" Sam said. "Go ahead, tell Miss Kaufman about the game. Go ahead."

Marvy frowned. "Dodge ball," he said. "Throwin' a basketball as hard as we could at each other. See who's hurt the worst."

"Jeepers," Sarah said. "Is that fun?"

"Yeah."

"You like to hurt your friends?"

"Well, we're not really hurt all that bad. You know, it's like wrestling or something. Man stuff."

"Ah." Why boys liked this kind of thing was beyond Sarah, but she'd seen it enough to know that it was true. Poor Harry. He only had Sarah and Tillie growing up, only sisters to light the way. Maybe that's why he couldn't make it: he didn't have enough of the "man stuff."

"Dad doesn't mind dodge ball at all, do you, Dad?"

"Nope."

Sarah looked from father to son. "What did he mind, Marvy?"

"When Joe kinda broke the rules."

"How did he do that?"

"Well, a bunch of us were playin.' Joe has his buddies and I have mine, you know, but we all mix up when we get in the dodge ball circle. But this time Joe said something in Spanish to the Mexicans: *Mata todos Judiós!* He didn't think I'd understand, but I did. Kill all the Jews. He didn't mean kill really. Just hit."

"I see. Still, it must have bothered you, since you told your dad."

Sam nodded.

"I guess, a little. We'd never played one kind of kid against the other. I didn't get it."

"Do any of your Jewish friends ever say mean things to the Mexicans?"

"Yeah, sometimes. But we're all still friends...at school."

"That's good," Sarah said. "Best not to hold a grudge."

"*Only* at school," Sam said, obviously not thrilled with Sarah's remark. Tell Miss Kaufman about Franco Alcantar," Sam said. "Another Mexican."

"It not because he's Mexican, Dad. And besides he's Chicano and a friend of Joe's. They call him the "black widow" cause he's got really thick black hair that he wears high and slick. But he's got another name, too."

"You mean another nickname?" Sarah said.

"No. I mean another regular name. Ben Washington."

"Really? Did he make it up, or what?"

"I don't know, but some days he won't answer if the teacher calls him Franco. If he feels like Ben that day."

"He's nuts," Sam said.

Sarah couldn't help but laugh a little. "What does the teacher do?"

"Sometimes she just calls the next student. A couple of times she sent him to the principal for a spanking. But Franco just does it again. My mom thinks he wants attention."

Henrietta nodded. "Yes, I do."

"What do you think, Marvy?" Sarah said.

"I dunno. Maybe he just wants to be someone else."

The topic ended, but Sarah was thinking about it now. Not as it manifested in that particular case, which could be anything from a prank to psychosis, but the desire to be someone else in general. Everyone felt that now and then. Sarah certainly did. A married woman? A mother to be sure. A different name, too, one that opened rather than closed doors, one in which acceptance was a given rather than a fight. The biblical Sarah was a princess, the wife of Abraham. Sarah herself lacked that title, but she was a woman of high rank, at least within the Toledo court. And she was proud of that status. But occasionally she wouldn't mind changing places with a regular old Jane.

And what about Obee? O'Brien O'Donnell. Who better to be a judge than a descendent of Irish royalty? Yet there was a time that he longed to shed his honorable skin, a time he indeed tried to become a John Doe. Same for Mitchell, who told her that if some day he disappeared, she could find him in Tahiti living under the moniker of Mike Kodak, an allusion to the recognition he sought as a amateur photographer. And Rita? What did her name signify? Certainly had she known her fate, she would have changed it, her entire identity, in an instant.

9

arlos had reluctantly agreed to take the train to Tijuana, figuring Maria would be extra grateful if she got her way. He usually drove down, preferring the freedom to come and go as he liked. He should have stuck to his guns, for never had he needed his wheels more.

He'd paid for Maria's return ticket and made sure she was safely aboard, but he wasn't about to go that way himself. It had taken them seven goddamn hours to get down here, and that was fast by the usual standards. There were too many stops, and something always broke down. He thought about borrowing a car, but after asking around, discovered that one of the hotel workers was just leaving for L.A., due to some family emergency. So he'd hitched a ride with a man preoccupied with his own troubles, eager to get home. It couldn't have been better. Carlos had no desire for conversation, and over the past couple of hours, as the small truck sped north, neither of them said a word.

They had to be close to the city. Carlos was sitting in the rear, unable to see out. It was hot and dark, but that was fine. The conditions were fine. Fine for ruminating. He had been trying to squelch his fear, to come up with another answer. But all roads, this one included, led him back, back to the truth, back to the germ of the crime. For indeed, Carlos knew, knew better than anyone, the cause of Rita's death, no matter what the official story. The knot in his stomach tightened. Back. Further back, to the first day he met her in '25, when she came round the store looking for some Mexican spices. All dolled up, like a creature from another world next to his line-dried, working class customers. Carlos had been stocking the shelves when her bare, delicate ankles caught his eye. She was on her tiptoes, reaching for a bottle.

"May I help you," he said.

"Please," she said, in a sweet, recognizable accent. "I can't quite get that pepper."

Carlos handed her the item, taking in her exquisite features as he did so. She was a honey. Luminous green eyes, skin a little lighter than his own, lips that would rush a man to ecstasy. And that hint of tit, just peeking out of that blouse. Christ. One of his own, but…but, he thought, examining her more critically, dressed like a *gringo*. A rich *gringo*.

"Thank you," she said.

"It's okay, you can say *gracias* in here."

She giggled, huskily. *Gracias*, she said, her tongue seeming to enjoy the sensation.

"Anything else?"

It was the slight hesitation, the momentary blush that gave her away. Anything else? Oh, yes. Yes, she said without answering. But not just groceries, not only the foods of her native land. She needed the earth, the loam. She needed the seeds. But Carlos wasn't about to provide them, not with that rock on her finger. He'd tried that before and nearly got shot. There were enough loose, unattached beauties to last him a lifetime. She was tempting, but he couldn't risk it, not with the kind of plans he had, not with so many people depending on him.

He swore to himself, not this one. But that was before he discovered exactly who Rita was. It was her fourth or fifth trip to the store. By this time there was a familiarity to their encounters. Her face brightened when she saw Carlos, and he of course didn't mind the view, watching her stroke a melon, catching a whiff of her pricy perfume. That day she was there for tortillas, or so she said. After he wrapped them up for her, she hung around, searching in her handbag for a list she said she'd written up. A ruse. It was all a ruse. She still wanted those seeds.

They were standing in an aisle, baked goods on one side, produce on the other. She started to talk of Baja, of how much she missed it. One question led to another until she got to the topic of her husband, Phillip. Phillip Bradford. A kind man, really, she said. Kind but…Carlos must have heard Rita mention her last name before, but it only just then registered. He nearly toppled over a display of strawberry tarts, shocked as he was at his uncanny luck. In that moment, everything changed. He'd been waiting for a sign, a path, and there it was. He feigned ignorance of course. He was good at that. But destiny had arrived, ripening the green fruit before his very eyes. Finally, some settling of scores. And he would have fun doing it. Indeed, it was that very day that he took Rita to the little spot that became what she called "their" place. Week after week, and then, soon, she was his, in that seedy hotel room, where she said she was never happier.

"I'm not the unfaithful type by nature," she said, after he'd fucked her silly.

"I know, *chica*." And he did. Rita had a conscience, of a sort. She wasn't in it just for the sex. It was worse. She wanted love, the kind women dream about. Carlos knew that she was idealizing him, seeing him as a brown knight to the rescue. She was empty, miserable with her choices. She had sold her soul. She might have even divorced her husband had Carlos asked. But he didn't, and wasn't about to.

A year went by. She told Carlos that she lived for their meetings. And there were times, admittedly, that he felt some semblance of affection. But if he were kissing, or especially screwing her, and remembered, remembered who she was, he'd have to stop himself from smothering her with a pillow. Or squeezing her neck, squeezing the life out of her as all those poor families, those children who had coughed and shivered, retched and convulsed had had the life squeezed out of them.

"Carlos, we have something special, no?" she often said.

"So special," he said

"*Te amo*, Carlos."

"And I you, Rita."

She cried for joy, told him that she'd felt a part of herself had been missing, and that Carlos had restored it. It was as if she'd been a deflated balloon, all the air sucked out of her, and he'd blown her back up, expanding her, filling her, nourishing her with the right kind of oxygen.

"How long did you say?" he yelled to the driver.

"Twenty minutes."

Carlos took out his comb, ran it through his sweaty hair. He tightened the belt he had loosened and retied his shoes. Twenty minutes. Yeah, Rita had been happy, a balloon floating in the clouds. And that's when he did it, a stealth attack, a quick, lethal stab. "I've found someone else, *nena*." And he had. By then he was on to Sabrina, but he didn't tell Rita the name. Just someone. The name didn't matter. She wouldn't have heard anyway. "I found someone else." She screamed out, wailed, shriveled and fell to the ground. It was the next best thing to murder. Her pain was real. But minor in comparison to the other suffering, the ravaged bodies, the fires. In comparison, it was nothing, but by itself it was justice.

For a while Rita continued to stop by, begging Carlos to see her, to meet at "their" place. Once he agreed, and that was the day, the fateful day, that he brought Andrés. Carlos wanted the boy to see the damage. To learn. Rita was thrilled. She wrapped her arms around Carlos, kissed Andrés on the cheek. But Carlos wasn't there for any reunion. He was there to stick the knife in deeper, to warn her to never come to his store again. Then she sobbed, said she would kill herself. But Carlos knew she didn't have the courage for that. And she didn't. Little did she know, she didn't have to.

"We're here," the man said.

"Thanks," Carlos said, dusting himself off. He got out. The sky was leaden. He couldn't tell the time, felt a chill. He shook the driver's hand. "Good luck," he said, "with whatever it is."

"You, too, Mr. Martinez. You, too."

10

Sarah gazed at the sharp, glistening palms through the half-open taxi window. Nothing like the morning after a rain. The pervasive citrus scent had intensified, and the San Gabriel Mountains, muted until now, stood grandly etched against the cloudless sky. Despite a restless night, she had awakened at dawn and decided to take advantage of it. She would finally stop by the conference, which began with a breakfast meeting at 8 a.m., followed by Jean Shontz speaking on the topic of refereeing in the juvenile court. If Sarah attended nothing else, this talk should be worth the price of admission. Fortunately, the trial didn't resume until tomorrow, and she would be there, come hell or high water.

They were heading west on Wilshire Boulevard toward The Ambassador Hotel, host to the event. Sarah took in the passing sights with more than a little interest, not only because of the unique mix of homes, apartments and luxury shops, but because the road itself was named for native Ohioan, Gaylord Wilshire, who had just died last year. In 1895, Wilshire purchased a thirty-five acre barley field and filed subdivision papers announcing his plans to carve a magnificent wide boulevard. He never succeeded in that endeavor, but his vision was gradually becoming realized. The boulevard was indeed wide and had the potential of being magnificent, even though it was currently badly rutted.

Wilshire supposedly had been quite a character. To some he was a genius, possessing a great intellect and wit. To others he was a pompous fake. But it could not be denied that he was a charismatic businessman who obviously made his mark on Los Angeles. Even Obee, who, as a young lawyer, had met the man, had briefly fallen under his spell. With his arched brows, pointed goatee and fiery eyes, he was a "spitting image of Mephistopheles," Obee had said. "But I like him! A great conversationalist!" And it turned out that the man was as persuasive as the devil, convincing Obee and countless others to buy one of his crazy cure-all devices—a belt for dyspepsia in Obee's case—produced by his I-ON-A-CO firm. Electrically motored, it promised complete relief through some sort of balancing of positive and negative charges in the digestive system. It didn't work at all, however, and the American Medical Association eventually investigated and called Wilshire an "arch-quack." But people continued to flock to him for such products as well as advice.

Barley still sprouted up here and there along the boulevard, but the usually tough, full sprigs were scrawny and tired looking, as if acknowledging the inevitability of their surrender. Sarah turned around. The robust crop they had just passed was an exception. But it too looked out of place, situated as it was next to a restaurant shaped like a giant hat. The Brown Derby, the bold sign read. So Toledo wasn't alone in this sort of thing. The Proud Chicken was popular there not because of the food, which was mediocre at best, but because it was supposedly exciting to eat in a leg at the same time you were gnawing on one. She didn't get it. She could understand the appeal of such things to children, like Obee's little daughter Peggy, who squealed with delight at the mere mention of the place. But Obee, Mitchell and even Tillie, who never ate anything other than her own cooking, got a kick out of it as well. Perhaps Sarah was just too serious: that, or there really was no accounting for taste.

She adjusted the navy blue silk chemise Lena had sent her for her birthday. She always felt a little more stylish in clothes that her cousin selected, something she emphasized today by adding a pearl barrette to her French twist, deepening the kohl on her eyelids and darkening her lipstick. She even painted her short nails cherry red, which, while briefly lifting her spirits, ultimately reminded her of Rita, whose now colorless fingers no doubt once bore the popular hue.

Sarah breathed in the perfumed air. Never again to smell such a delicious aroma. Never to hear, see, taste, touch. She would probably never know the truth. But probability, she finally decided, after tossing and turning a good portion of the night, didn't spell defeat, at least not yet. Sarah might imagine another life, but right now she was who she was, the person to whom Rita had made that haunting appeal. So later today she would return to the police and tell her story again, and again if need be. She would tell it until one way or another she felt satisfied with the ending.

Another story, *Oil!*, was resting beside her. She smiled at it as if it were a companion. Gaylord Wilshire, she had learned, had also been a friend of Upton Sinclair's. Like Sinclair, he was a self-identified socialist, a little odd, given that he was also such a flamboyant entrepreneur. Of course Sinclair had his inconsistencies, too. Although he advocated for union rights and helped usher in reforms in the meatpacking industry with *The Jungle*, he apparently didn't want the burden of earning a living himself. Knowing Wilshire had money, he asked him to sponsor his writing for life. Wilshire declined, and the relationship soured. But the two continued to believe in and work for similar ideals, even if they didn't always live up to them.

Sarah was subject to motion sickness and reading even a paragraph in this swaying vehicle would turn her green. Still, she was glad she brought the half-finished novel along, not only because she might have an opportunity to snatch a few pages here and there, but for comfort and security. A book always provided this for her, a familiar place to turn one's thoughts. This was particularly true of *Oil!*, which was keeping her steady by confirming her own reality. Sarah wasn't much for maps, preferring to get a feel for an area without geographic precision—or maybe it was just that she wasn't very good at imagining a line as a road. But *Oil!* had become a kind of map to her. Not by directing her this way or that, but in expressing truths about the land, its resources and the men who abused them. The plot was fictional, but its lines had meaning, portraying the same human behaviors that had led Sarah to this particular place and time. Greed, deception, and naiveté, all part of the story: Bunny's, Sinclair's and her own.

She tightened her grip on it as the taxi swerved around a truck packed with Mexican laborers, undoubtedly on their way to the fields, whether of the orange or oil kind she couldn't tell.

■■■

The taxi turned into a long circular driveway lined with mature-looking palms and other exotic plants. "Here you are, ma'am."

"Ah, thank you," Sarah said, reaching for her change purse. Through the side window she observed an expansive lawn on which several golfers were practicing their swings. She hated those clownish outfits, the knee socks especially. She squinted to get a better view and felt her mouth drop just as a uniformed doorman helped her out of the car.

He smiled broadly, obviously reading her look. "It is what you think. That's Miss Pola Negri over there. She likes to walk her pet cheetah on the grounds."

"So I wasn't seeing things. Pola Negri the actress?"

"Uh huh."

"Doesn't she worry about getting in the way of a golf ball?"

"No, that's just a putting green. It's the golfers that should worry!"

Sarah laughed. "I guess so."

"That kind of thing is typical around here," he said, escorting Sarah to the elegant Art Deco lobby, which was already buzzing with activity.

Sarah signed in at the conference booth and was directed down a full-length windowed hall to an enormous convention auditorium with hundreds of brown velvet chairs, many of which were already occupied. Coffee and sweet rolls lay on white-cloth covered tables along one of the walls. Sarah helped herself to a cheese Danish and found a seat close to the podium. She put on her reading glasses and checked her watch. The program didn't begin for half an hour. There was time. She lay down her handbag and looked about. "What the…" She scanned the row, on the floor, under her chair. She rifled through her handbag, even though she knew it wasn't there. "Goddammit!" She apologized to the curious faces around her, pushed past the growing crowd and scurried back through the lobby. Out front were three parked taxis but none of the drivers was hers. Naturally. She described the avuncular man who had just dropped her off but no one could be sure. Maybe Charlie, they said, or Fred. Check with the cab company. They have a lost and found.

She'd check all right. But, rhatz! It was that cheetah. Don't these people have anything better to do? One woman dies on a piece of parched earth, alone and unnoticed. Another has every whim indulged, walking her zoo creature on a hotel lawn as if it were the most normal thing in the world. Sarah felt queasy, unbalanced. She could buy another copy of course. But this one was special, signed and personal. Well, so much for maps and all that. If she got lost, it was her own fault.

She heaved a deep sigh and headed back to the auditorium. On her way, she noticed a plaque stating that the site of the hotel had once been a dairy farm. She wished it still was. A regular old cow wouldn't have distracted her. She walked back down the hall, tried to clear her mind and reentered the room at the double doors marked "Exit Only."

11

"You have been sworn and testified before, Mr. MacKay?"

"Yes, sir."

"Your address."

"Seven forty-seven Title Insurance Building."

"I believe you also waived your constitutional right not to testify?"

"Yes, sir, I did."

"Getting down to one point at once, Mr. MacKay, the question of the knowledge of Mr. Ted Rosen that there was an overissue of stock; did you ever have any conversation with him on that subject?"

"Whether there was an overissue?"

"Yes."

"Yes, sir."

"Of preferred stock?"

"Of preferred stock."

"Yes, of preferred stock."

Yes, preferred stock! Sarah screamed to herself. All right already. Get on with it.

"Annoying, isn't it?"

Sarah turned to the low voice. "Sorry?" she said.

"Sometimes I think lawyers just like to hear themselves talk, even if it's the same thing over and over again."

"Ah, oh yes."

"I sensed your impatience."

Sarah nodded and turned back to the stand. Was she that obvious? She'd have to control herself.

She hoped that Ted would be testifying again, but apparently not, at least not this morning. This whole thing gave her a headache. So many people involved, so many tangled webs. There was no way to unravel it all, especially when she hardly understood the legal functioning of the market, let alone its criminal side. Still she was determined to see it through, at least until she knew Ted's fate.

Her determination, after all, had paid off yesterday. Not with her book, which was probably lost forever. The cab company did figure out that her driver had been one of their most trusted employees. Unfortunately, they didn't reach him until the end of the day, by which time at least fifty passengers had come and gone. He searched, but *Oil!*, other than that he had used to fill his tank, was nowhere to be found. Still, it wasn't the sort of object someone would normally steal, so they encouraged Sarah to keep checking. She would, but she didn't have much hope. No, she imagined that by now the precious copy was probably lying in some garbage heap after whoever took it realized that it didn't hold any secret cash.

Her visit to the police, however, went better than expected. On her way there, she practiced her lines, rehearsing what she would say. She would recite again all that had occurred, rationally and reasonably, but to someone other than Officer Hodges. Someone who might at the very least question the coincidence of Rita's terrified demeanor just prior to her untimely death. Initially, however, it seemed as if it would be another wasted trip. Indeed, she almost lost her nerve when she saw Officer Hodges himself manning the front desk. But she gathered her strength and waited for him to look up.

"Case is closed, little lady. Remember?"

"Yes," she said, "I know." She eyed the two other officers in the room. "May I speak to one of you?"

Officer Hodges knitted his sparse, yellowish brows. "I'm in charge and you're outta line."

The other men didn't budge.

"I just thought that if you didn't want to be bothered…"

"Did you hear me?"

"Okay, okay sir." She took a deep breath and tried to soften her expression. "Then can I just ask you one question?"

He stared at her unblinking. This was her chance, in earshot of the others. Precise, clear and succinct, Sarah. "You recall that I told you that Rita came to me the day of her death, that she felt threatened, that she flung off her shoes to run from that threat."

"You said a question!"

"Yes. I'm coming to that. I need to just explain a tiny bit."

Hodges kept staring.

"Well, it seems odd, very odd, that the family didn't want those shoes, the property of their loved one. I've worked in probate for years, and I'll tell you that's very odd indeed."

"What is your question?!"

The other officers snickered.

"You find this funny?" Officer Hodges said.

They shook their heads and turned back to whatever work they were pretending to do.

"Well?"

Sarah swallowed hard. "According to the papers, her husband wasn't even in town then. He had only just been informed of her death. Is that true?"

The man's red face puffed up. "This is ridiculous! Do you always believe everything you read in the papers? He didn't want the dirty shoes, and that's it. Question asked and answered. Now, stick to your own business and we'll do the same. And if you keep comin' round here, I'll arrest you for disturbing the peace."

He meant it, Sarah thought. He would like nothing better than to put her behind bars. So, she left. However, she was more determined than ever to keep investigating because now she was certain that he was hiding something. "Do you believe everything you read in the papers?" What did he mean by that? Had Mr. Bradford not really been away? Had he come back early? And if so, where was he at the time of his wife's death?

Sarah needed to find another way. And fate, it seemed, agreed. A few blocks from the station, a female voice called out to her: "Ma'am, ma'am, please, wait."

Sarah stopped and turned.

"Whew, you walk fast." The woman leaned over to catch her breath, her long tousle of red curls nearly touching the pavement. Gradually, she stood up: "I'm Paige Chastain," she labored out. "I was down the hall at headquarters just now. Heard you talkin' to Hodges."

"Oh?"

"Yeah, I know all about this case. About you, too, I mean about the shoes and your job and all that. I'm a kind of secretary. I've done the filing, typing, you know, that sort of thing, at the station for going on five years now."

Sarah offered her hand to the shapely, blue-eyed doll. Miss Chastain shook her hand vigorously and smiled with small, full lips. "What can I do for you?" Sarah said.

"Can we sit down for a minute?" She pointed to a bench and led the way, walking with a pronounced limp. "Polio," she said. "When I was a baby."

"I'm sorry," Sarah said with true sympathy. Tillie had a limp from the same cause, and the poor dear had suffered all her life because of it. It contributed to her being, well, the way she was.

"Oh, it's nothing. I just always mention it to get it out of the way."

"I understand."

"Well, like I said, I overheard your, uh, conversation. You know, I'm older than I look. Thirty-two."

Sarah didn't know what that had to do with anything, but, despite the heavy pancake covering her freckles, she did look younger. Pretty too, in a hard way for her age.

"I've been trying to get a break in Hollywood for years. Never worked out for me. Couldn't even get a role as a gimp. So I work for the cops and take voice lessons. Even get a gig now and then. Singing doesn't have an age limit, and you don't have to walk to do it. I'm pretty good, too, if I do say so myself."

Sarah smiled but sighed, signaling she wanted her to get to the point.

"Yes, well, anyway, I'd like to try and help you."

"Oh? How?"

"Yeah, strictly between us, though."

"How, what...?"

"Mind you, I wouldn't be doing anything illegal. I mean, it's really just my work. Files, phone calls, stuff like that. I'll just see what I can see."

"See what you can see about Rita, you mean? About her death?"

"Her murder, you mean."

Sarah sat up. "What?"

"Everyone knows she was killed. They don't say so, but they know. Those were ligature marks, sure enough. They all know that. But they'll write it off in their minds as a gang job. Rita went where she shouldn't have. She should've known better, that's what they'll think. Deserved it."

"Well, what...I mean, if that's the case, then...."

"It won't matter. Her husband said that she had a heart condition, and Rita's doctor supposedly confirmed it. The pathologist probably went along. It's murky, you know. I've seen it before. Too hard to prove. And she's Mexican. They'll let it go."

"But, that would mean that all of the departments colluded."

"Not overtly. It's just too complicated to pursue. She's Mexican, the husband is a pretty important fellow and he supports the theory. They'll let it go."

Sarah thought of Jacob. Was justice for Mexicans in L.A. like justice for Negroes in the South? She shouldn't be so shocked, and yet she was. "That's depressing," she said. "But there must be someone interested in the truth."

"I'm about as close as you'll get, without causing a riot."

Sarah shook her head. The corrupt and the powerful, making their own rules. This was a new city, but the story was old.

"Why you then, Paige? Why even try?"

"I think women should stick together, that's all. In Hollywood, boy, it's been rough. Women get the raw end of the deal all the time. And not just those with a defect, although the things I've had to do because of it…" Paige looked off into space, narrowing her eyes until they nearly disappeared. She turned back. "Yeah, I can't tell you the things I've had to do. Ha! I even tried rehabilitation, stretching the muscles. Excruciating. Like being on the rack.

"That's awful," Sarah said, thinking of Tillie.

"Well, we all have our cross to bear. But whenever a woman's treated unfairly, I get mad. I felt sorry for that Mexican gal, just for dying—those people have the deck stacked against them—and if you're Mexican and a dame, just like if you're a cripple, well, you don't much have a chance."

"I see," Sarah said, feeling both wary and hopeful.

"And, since you're a woman, who's concerned about another woman, and since they didn't treat you too well at headquarters either, well, I just want to help you out."

"I see."

"I can't promise anything, but I can at least sniff around for you."

"That's very generous. I wouldn't want you to get in any trouble though."

"Nah, I won't. They don't know what I'm doing half the time anyway. As long as I keep singing, they won't suspect a thing."

"Singing?"

"I told you. I want to be…. Oh, ha-ha. Not like that. I'm no snitch about anything. No, I mean really singing. Practicing songs. They don't ever stop me either. I think they kinda like it. *Sometimes I wonder why I spend the lonely nights, dreaming of a song, the memory haunts my reverie, and I am once again with you…*"

" 'Stardust,' " Sarah said. "Beautiful, though it always makes me feel a little lonely."

"That's what music does. Makes you feel things."

Sarah nodded, thinking back to that night in Tennessee, when she and Mitchell were listening to that jazz band. They felt things then all right.

"You have a lovely voice, Paige." She was being honest. It was smooth, velvety, the kind that makes men swoon. "I'm envious. I can't carry a tune."

"Ah well, now we can't be good at everything. If I remember right, you got a pretty good job there, Sarah."

"Pretty good. Well," Sarah said, "Thank you for this. I appreciate anything you can find out."

They agreed that it was better for Paige to contact Sarah, which she said she would do whether she learned anything or not. "Just one word of advice," Paige said before parting, "I wouldn't come around to headquarters anymore. Hodges has a direct line to the Chief. Meaning he doesn't just work for the guy. They're tight, you know. And the Chief makes Hodges look like a lamb. Together, they could make your life miserable."

Sam had told Sarah a little about L.A.'s chief of police. In bed with Chandler, big oil, and a real anti-Semite. As if Hodges wasn't a real one. "I'll take it."

"Good. But again, no promises."

"Okay," Sarah said, feeling a weight had been lifted. She'd been right. Probably. Rita *had* been murdered. Probably. And finally, someone was willing to help. Someone with compassion, interest, and access. Today, it definitely paid to be one of Adam's ribs. Had she not been afraid of offending any dogs, she would have belted out a melody herself.

Sarah shifted in her chair as the attorney continued: "When I say overissue, I mean over six hundred thousand shares of preferred stock and over six hundred thousand shares of common, but going more particularly to the preferred?"

"Yes, sir."

"When was the first conversation you had?"

"The end of April."

"Where was that conversation?"

"That conversation was in his office, as I recall it."

"Well, that was after the stock had been taken off the market?"

"No, that was the last day of April. The stock was taken off the market on the seventh of May."

Sarah stretched. It was going to be a long day.

"He was close to Motley Flint, you know."

Sarah turned again to the voice.

"He's all mixed up with this, maybe one of the worst."

Sarah nodded again and turned back. She didn't need a narration. Maybe she should move.

"I'm sorry," he said. "I talk too much. I've been so burned by this thing, I guess I'm just looking for sympathy."

Sarah turned again, seeing the man's face for the first time. Distinguished yet rugged. Handsome, she thought, quite handsome. Spaniard, Mexican? She thought of Rita, and Marvy. Chicano. "Empathy is all I've got. I'm here for the same reason you are, I think. But I do want to pay attention."

"Of course," he said, covering his mouth in "speak no evil" fashion.

Sarah smiled.

"Tell me more about the conversation," the attorney said.

"The conversation—I will have to go back. On the twenty-third of April, the final deal between California Eastern and Julian Petroleum was effected, and on the next day we went to the Corporation Commission. Mr. Lewis had his books owing to him some six million and some odd dollars. He stated: 'There have been so many rumors around here that there is an overissue I want to protect it.'"

"When you said overissue, you meant over six hundred thousand dollars?"

"That is what I was talking about then. And he said that there was 'absolutely no overissue.' Then we went out to Senator Flint's house."

Sarah glanced to her side. The man grinned.

"He came out there on Sunday night, May first, and Senator Flint told him that one of the officials of the company had the day before told him that there was a very substantial overissue, in his opinion, and Lewis said that it was a 'damn lie,' using his language, that he wanted to be faced with any individual who would state such a thing. Senator Flint said, 'Well, you will be at the proper time.'"

Judge Dornan tapped his gavel. "Counsel, chambers please."

What now? As the room grew noisy, Sarah waited for the man to start talking again, but he fooled her, sitting quietly with his large, masculine hands outstretched on his knees. Without her glasses the image was blurred, but she couldn't miss the thick gold band on his left ring finger. Etched and embedded with a round pale stone it comforted her. Married, she thought. Good. "Flint?" she said, surprised to hear her own voice.

He turned his heavy-lidded, dark eyes toward her. His silver hair was thick, straight and slicked back. She guessed him to be her age, plus or minus a few years, but she couldn't be sure. He exuded a vitality that was hard to quantify.

"Senator Flint is the brother of Motley," he said. "The senator is not such a bad fellow. But Motley. His name fits him."

"Yes, I've heard. He's one of the big bankers. Organized the Million Dollar Pool, didn't he?"

"*Ay, sí, sí.* I mean yes. Spanish is my first line of defense when I get aggravated. I'm Carlos by the way, Carlos Martinez."

"Sarah Kaufman."

"*Mucho gusto*, Sarah Kaufman."

Sarah smiled. "Still aggravated?"

"No. I use it when I'm happy, too. Lose much, if you don't mind me asking?"

"Enough," Sarah said.

"I lost more than enough, money I had saved for my mother," he said, shaking his head.

"I'm sorry."

"Oh well, many lost much more. And I recovered. What pool were you in?"

"A Jewish pool. Not *the* Jewish pool. A smaller one."

"Yes, I assumed so. Your name, I mean."

"Ah."

"I admire your people."

"Oh?"

"Oh, yes. So intelligent. And attractive, I might add."

Sarah blushed. "Not everyone thinks so."

"Well I do," Carlos said. "My wife was Jewish. She died a year ago. You remind me a little of her."

"I'm sorry," she said, certain that she was now beet red.

"Thank you." He looked away. "That may be why I'm confiding in you. I don't usually do this. I hope you don't mind."

"No, not at all," she said honestly. First Sam and now this fellow. She could set up shop here.

While they waited for court to resume, Carlos told her more. That he was a full-fledged Chicano, born and raised in Los Angeles. That he unfortunately had no children. That he had been part of the Tijuana pool, which, rather than an exclusively Mexican group as the name suggested, included wealthy L.A. Main Street pawnbrokers as well as Tijuana concessionaires. That is how Carlos got involved with it. He owned some grocery stores and provided delicacies to a few shops on the other side of the border. In fact, he said the pool was organized by Mendel Silberberg, a prominent L.A. attorney. Silberberg had purchased over six hundred thousand dollars of stock, made a bundle and, unlike Carlos, got out before the crash.

Silberberg wasn't at fault, though, he said. Lewis, Berman, Rosen, Ramish, and of course, at first, C. C. himself, pulled the strings. Sarah knew that. Who she didn't know as much about was Motley Flint, to whom Carlos attributed much of the blame. Flint, he said with disgust, was one of those fellows that the gods smile down on for no apparent reason. Tall, flashy, larger than life. From Colonial stock. His ancestors came, saw and conquered. And so did Motley. Born in Massachusetts, raised in San Francisco, he invested in Los Angeles real estate, and along with his brother got involved in Republican politics. After that, everything went his way. Postmaster, banker, hobnobbing with the movie moguls and financing their projects. One of the city's leading boosters. And he was, as Sarah said, instrumental in the formation of the "Million Dollar Pool," which was backed by the company's stock. That pool delivered a huge profit for its investors. One month after its liquidation, Julian Pete collapsed.

"I'm certain that Flint and a few others knowingly bled the stock while thousands lost their life savings," Carlos said. He narrowed his black eyes. "*Cabrón!*"

"I don't know what that means but it doesn't sound good."

"No, not a nice word, Sarah, but fitting. It's the same old story, the rich getting richer, and pardon me," he said, "but especially when they're white. I'm sure you understand, being an outsider yourself."

Sarah nodded.

"Flint fled the U.S. when the stocks collapsed. He lives in Paris now. But mark my words, he'll be extradited when all is said and done."

"I hope you're right," Sarah said, glad at least that Flint wasn't another, as Sam put it, "member of the tribe." She had winced at the name Silberberg and was relieved when Carlos exonerated him. Carlos appeared to be an extremely enlightened man, not the kind to generalize at all. Indeed, he married a Jew! So intriguing. She wondered about the woman, wondered in what way Sarah reminded him of her. No doubt his own minority status contributed to him being so tolerant. She could learn a thing or two from him.

They turned as the judge took the bench and McKay was ordered back to the stand. His testimony took up where it left off.

"Now, go back a bit. You had a meeting on March twenty-second, in Motley Flint's office, pursuant to a call issued by you, did you not?"

"Yes, sir."

"Was Lewis up there at the time?"

"Yes, sir."

"Was he questioned?"

"Well, I presume he was. I had so many meetings with him I am not sure, but I imagine he was."

"Now, at this meeting there was no discussion of over six hundred thousand dollars being issued?"

"Oh, none whatever."

"Lewis was not confronted with that question?"

"Not with that. The main argument was whether it was more than four hundred eighty-six thousand."

"So he made no statement at that time about over six hundred thousand?"

Sarah whispered to Carlos: "How many times do you think they are going to go over this figure?"

Carlos put his fingers to his lips and smiled. "Shhh."

"No sir, he did not."

"No partial admission?"

"No partial admission, no sir. And from his actions at the time he was notified of the overissue, I thought he was going to drop dead."

"When was that?"

"That was in the late afternoon of the day before it went off the stock exchange. That was the late afternoon of May sixth. Kottemann, the accountant advised him."

"And you were present?"

"Yes, sir, I was present."

"And Kottemann at that time stated what?"

"He had just completed his audit of the preferred stock, and he told him that it was three million six hundred shares, and the first remark that Lewis said, 'My God, Bill, it can't be true!' 'Well, it is,' he said. And he said, 'Those goddamned Jews have double-crossed me.' Those were the first words he said. And he went down on his face and turned deathly white and shook all over. I thought he was going to die from apoplexy."

Sarah nearly died of the same thing at hearing this. A shock wave traveled through her, and she, along with a few others in the room, let out an involuntary groan.

Judge Doran slammed his gavel. "Order!"

Carlos touched her shoulder. "Don't let it get to you. They've got to blame someone."

"I know," she said.

"Now, Mr. McKay, you are just repeating what Lewis said, correct?"

"Correct."

"From his appearance you don't think he could possibly have been 'putting it over?'"

"I don't think so, unless he is the best actor I ever saw."

"When did you first hear any rumor that there was overissue of Julian Petroleum stock?"

"I don't remember exactly. Someone brought it up at a meeting, saying that he heard on the street that there is an overissue."

"Was Lewis there?"

"Yes."

"What did he say?"

"He said it was absolutely untrue. He said, 'The goddamned brokers are the ones saying this.' He said, 'they are trying to drive the market down to ruin me.'"

"Well, we are getting near the close," said Shelley. "I want to get another witness today. You're excused."

The bailiff pointed to the clock, signaling to the judge that it was noon. Doran nodded, tapped his gavel and announced that court was dismissed until 2 p.m.

Carlos stood up. "You need some fresh air," he said to Sarah.

Sarah raised her eyes as he adjusted his grey striped tie. Well-dressed, but understated she thought. And those shoulders. He must lift weights. "No. I think I'm going to sit here for a while."

"Ah, come on."

"No, really."

"But I have an idea."

She shook her head.

"Don't you even want to know what it is?"

She did want to know. But she shouldn't. There were things to think about, matters to attend to. Somber matters. Already more than she could handle with only a week left before she was due to go home. And those words were still ringing in her head. "Damn Jews." As if she needed any reminding that even in paradise, anti-Semitism was alive and well. Carlos seemed to understand that, better than most people. She thought of Mitchell with a twinge of guilt. He understood too, of course. On the other hand, her stomach was growling. "Does it involve food?"

"*Sí*," he said, "and I know just the place."

12

His idea, and just the place, was *La Mision Café* on Spring Street, just a few blocks from the courthouse. Since Consuelo de Bonzo had opened it a few years ago, it had grown in popularity, especially amongst the Mexican immigrants of whom Consuelo herself was one of the most notable. The restaurant was doing so well that she had plans to relocate and expand, Carlos said, on what was currently a muddy and unpaved alley.

"Why there?" Sarah said.

"Why there indeed. I'll tell you all about it, over the best enchiladas this side of the border."

Sarah half-smiled, hoping her uninitiated stomach could handle it. She'd never even tried a tortilla, let alone one filled with strange ingredients and slathered with some mysterious sauce. But upon entering the cheerful room, she suddenly felt adventurous, ready to even suffer a little heartburn if it came down to it. After all, she'd survived Tillie's stuffed cabbage, and she couldn't identify much of what was in that either.

Flowered table clothes covered fifteen or so old wooden tables, all but one of which were occupied. Strings of dried chilies and colorful *piñatas* hung from the ceiling. A Victrola was playing mariachi music, lending to the overall festive atmosphere. "Let's grab it," Carlos said, leading her to the tiny remaining spot near the kitchen. He pulled out her chair, and she squeezed in, having barely enough room to cross her legs. Carlos fit his broad frame into the even tighter space across from her by turning his chair sideways and leaning against the wall.

She glanced around, noticing the mostly swarthy patrons devouring their indigenous fare, which, Carlos said, was authentic, unlike that of some of the other joints in town. This was the only place that didn't water down the flavors to accommodate the bland, Anglo palate.

Sarah frowned. "Oh, goody."

"Ha-ha. You're not Anglo, Sarah. You're ethnic, a Jew, used to different tastes. You'll see what I mean."

Different? Well, she supposed so. Tillie's cooking was indeed that. If aroma was any indication, however, he might be right. Scents she'd caught wafting from the city's outdoor carts were rich and concentrated in here, bringing to mind color and touch as well as smell: red, warm and earthy. Carlos closed his eyes and inhaled as if reading her mind. "Delicious," he said, tapping along with the pleasing, horn-heavy sound. She thought he was about to burst into song as well, but instead loudly called out: "Dolores, *eh* Dolores, *mi amor, dónde estás?*"

In seconds, a short, round woman with a long graying braid sprang through the swinging metal door. She wiped her small dark hands on her stained apron and hugged Carlos warmly. "Oh, *Carlito!*"

A brief conversation in Spanish ensued, which Carlos afterward translated. "Carlos dear, how are you? Very well. How's the business? Great. Another white girl, sweetie?"

Sarah raised her eyebrow at that comment, but Carlos explained. Consuelo used to do the cooking, but last year had become so involved with other projects that she handed the reins over to Dolores, her former helper. Dolores was a close friend of Carlos' mother and desperately wanted him to marry her daughter. That was twenty-five years ago but she'd been giving him a hard time ever since. "I intended to marry one of my own," Carlos said, "but you can't choose who you fall in love with, *verdad?* True?"

Sarah was glad he didn't wait for her to answer that question. Instead, he said that he told Dolores that Sarah was very nice and just a friend. "*Dos enchiladas especial*," he then said to the woman. She nodded as he whispered something into her tiny pierced ear.

"I told her to go easy on you. She knows that I like mine *con mucho picante*. Authentic is one thing, but it doesn't have to burn your throat to be the real deal."

Sarah nodded gratefully. "Graceias."

"*Gracias*," he said.

"Grawcias."

Carlos laughed, his dark eyes glistening like melted chocolate. He reached out and touched her arm. "Good try," he said.

Sarah wasn't sure if the tone was encouraging or condescending. Either way, she was embarrassed. "So, back to the muddy alley," she said.

"Yes. Olvera Street."

"Olvera? I think I walked by it. A sign read that Chaplin did some filming there."

"Yes, that's it. He turned one of the run-down buildings into an orphanage in "The Kid.""

"It did look pretty neglected."

"To say the least. But it won't be for long. And God knows, it shouldn't be. Carlos sank further back into the wall and sipped water from the icy glass that a Valentino look-alike waiter had just set down. "L.A. was settled by Mexicans, of course, *pobladores*, we call them. Forty-four to be exact. Just forty-four, and half were children! They founded the plaza right near the train station." He gazed intensely through the restaurant window, as if the past lay visible on the other side. "*El Pueblo de la Reina de Los Angeles*," he said, drawing out each word, it seemed, both to relish the original name and teach Sarah a little more Spanish. "Adobe houses, churches, stores, all conceived and built with their own hands. They created a water system, tilled the land and turned the region into a self-sustaining community. A Mexican community. But then came the Gold Rush, and the war with America. That changed everything. The invasion of Texas by Polk and his relentless quest toward the Pacific. Manifest Destiny. Ha! What a blasphemous interpretation of the divine."

Sarah nodded. She was no fan of Polk either, or of his self-righteous belief that God preordained western land for Anglo Americans. He was a Democrat, but that's when Democrats were more like Republicans. Seize the territories and expand slavery at the same time. That was his goal and it was blasphemous indeed. "But," she said, recalling a discussion she'd had with Obee on this very topic, "Anglos are not alone in their arrogance or appetite for conquest."

He pursed his lips and appeared to ponder the thought. "True. Civilizations arise from one group oppressing, invading, and killing off another. Go back far enough and everyone is guilty."

"Even you?"

"If by me you mean the Mexicans, sure. I'm of Spanish descent, and we've done a number on the Indians, who of course were both here and in Mexico before us. Deplorable. Rule of capture in reverse."

"Huh?"

"You know, rule of capture. Whoever gets the resource first has the rights to it."

"Ah, right. Oil."

"Yeah, oil and gas and water, even game. The law, you know, and one of the reasons our friend C. C. built so many wells. Wanted to get all the oil out before anyone else. He knew that if even one drop seeped into another's land, he could lose it all. If the owner had enough smarts to claim it, that is."

"So the 'in reverse' part is that Indians had the right to the resources but the Spanish didn't care, didn't honor that idea."

"Yeah. It's not exact. But a short-cut way of describing the injustice. The Spanish *capturing* the Indians, by the way, was particularly ugly since so many of us are of mixed race, *mestizos* ourselves. But then during the war some of the tribes joined forces with the Yankees and helped defeat us, so they got their licks. I guess it's a matter of degree. Some groups have just had more than their fair share. And we ultimately defend our own anyway."

Indeed, Sarah thought. If she had to choose, she'd side with the Jews. After all, they'd been oppressed, invaded and killed by just about everyone. Talk about more than a fair share. Talk about guilt. You could go back there, too. Way back to the beginning when Jews were blamed for the killing of Christ. That started it all. But why? Even if it were true, why would something that occurred thousands of years ago doom the entire race for eternity, especially since Jesus was a Jew whose death was supposedly necessary for salvation? It made absolutely no sense, except to provide a ready-made scapegoat for society's ills. She remembered reading about Martin Luther in particular, who at first encouraged embracing the Jews because he understood that they were of the lineage of Christ. But when business soured and the Jews wouldn't convert, he turned on them with vehemence, telling his followers to burn their synagogues, destroy their homes and, the line that stuck with Sarah the most, basically do anything that would rid the world of "this insufferable devilish burden."

She sighed. Yes, the Jews have suffered. But Mexicans had endured much, too, apparently more than she knew. Defying manners, which Tillie always said she lacked anyway, she leaned her bony elbows on the table and said: "So tell me about your side."

"About how our land was stolen, how the *Californios*, the rancheros, lost everything, how the culture was destroyed, the architecture ravaged? Ah well, you know how it turned out. Still, we gave them a run for their money, right here in Los Angeles too. As you can imagine, the locals were devastated when that holier-than-thou Commodore Stockton marched into the city accompanied by a brass band playing "Yankee Doodle," and especially when his soldiers occupied

Governor Pico's home." Carlos gritted his teeth. "Can you imagine? Pico had fled to Mexico to summon support. He was a hero to us, the last Mexican governor of California. 'What are we to do then?' Pico said. 'Shall we remain supine, while these daring strangers are displacing us? Shall these incursions go on unchecked, until we shall become strangers in our own land?' Brilliant. But when the lieutenant left in charge turned out to be abusive, hundreds rose up and forced him out. Stockton eventually regrouped and won of course, but that battle was one of our shining moments." He nodded, his eyes tearing up a little. "My grandfather fought in that battle. He was killed, dying for a cause greater than himself."

Carlos squinted tightly, as if with enough physical effort, he could actually see the last gasp, the final event that reshaped history and took his grandfather's life. Sarah herself must have appeared that way on occasion, when she tried to imagine her parents huddled together on the packed ship from Germany, coming to America for a better life. She had heard the story so often that she almost felt she had been there too. A better life. They achieved that goal to some extent, building a successful clothing business from the ground up. And even though they both died young, they had earned enough to help Sarah's aunt provide for Sarah and her siblings. Still, as Sarah knew all too well, they were never entirely free from the prejudice they sought to escape, that was really at the heart of their decision to uproot. It was her mother who had pushed for the move, her aunt said, feeling increasingly uneasy about the future of German Jews. She had always complained about the little persecutions, a whisper here, a look there. But as the years passed, she started to notice an increase in both the quantity and viciousness of such incidents. Then, in the late 1800s, she encountered a new word. Just a word, coined by a German journalist named Wilhelm Mahr. But that was enough to begin a two-year campaign to persuade her husband to make the journey. The word was anti-Semitism, and Mahr invented it because he felt he needed a more scientific, more benign term to define the growing political movement that was centered upon hatred of Jews. He needed to replace *Juden-hass*.

Why? her mother wondered. Why was a benign term, a technical term needed? Needed for what? Why not continue to call it what it was? There was something frightful in this, something sinister, and she didn't want to wait around to find out what it might be. She and Sarah's father wanted to have children. Jewish children, proud of their heritage, free to worship without fear. So where else but America? Sarah sighed. Where else indeed. Things were of course better here in that regard. But her mother learned the hard way that better was not perfect. And wouldn't she be disheartened to learn that anti-Semitism was on the rise and on display, this very day in the Los Angeles halls of justice.

A land of contradictions, that's what it was. Carlos knew this too, as she did, first-hand. "Are you Catholic, Carlos?"

"Yes."

"Religious?"

"Not particularly. I like the traditions, the rituals. But, uh, I'm, you know, a modern man."

"Was your wife religious?"

"My wife?"

"Was she a practicing Jew?"

"She, uh, no. Not really. But it didn't matter to me. Love is the thing. If we'd had children though I think she would have converted."

Of course, *she* would convert. Sarah thought of Luther, but let it pass. "What was her name, Carlos?"

Carlos stretched his hand silently, examining his ring. Without her glasses, Sarah could just make out a design carved into the gold, an intricate blend of swirls and horizontal lines.

"Carlos?"

"Rachel, her name was Rachel. But, now, let me tell you about Olvera Street, eh?"

■■■

The food arrived in what seemed to be the nick of time. Carlos clearly didn't want to talk about his wife anymore. It probably was still difficult for him. Sarah could understand that. Besides, he'd already answered her question. About religion that is, as well as about how they would have negotiated the subject had it become an issue. Or at least how he hoped they would've. Sarah fought a slight, admittedly ridiculous impulse to press him on the matter. She had only just met the man and knew nothing at all about Rachel other than the fact that Sarah reminded Carlos of her. Yet perhaps that is why she felt annoyed that he assumed she would have abandoned her faith. Even though Sarah didn't really practice her religion either, she wouldn't convert if her life depended on it, if for no other reason than to honor the struggles of her ancestors.

She cut into the sizzling, stuffed tortilla, releasing a rich scent of corn, tomato and something that smelled a little, though not unpleasantly, of body odor. Cumin, Carlos said, in response to her question about it, an ancient spice that flavored most Mexican cuisine. She blew on the bite-sized morsel, twisting a gooey string of melted cheese around her fork and slowly tasted. Carlos raised his brows and mouthed, "Well?" Unfamiliar, foreign, startling in a way. But all and all, good. He smiled as she chewed and nodded.

After sampling his own plate, which he deemed *perfecto*, Carlos finally began to explain the significance of that worn-down path on the north side of the plaza. His voice caught now and then as he spoke, although whether this was due to emotion or the green chili peppers that he nearly swallowed whole she wasn't sure. But by the end, she understood that Olvera Street was as much a cultural symbol as an actual place. Named for Augustin Olvera, the first superior court judge of the city, the street was once part of the thriving civic life to which Olvera greatly contributed. Carlos obviously felt a deep connection to the man, who, like his grandfather, fought the Yankees during the war. Indeed, to Carlos, Olvera was a hero because he stayed true to his roots even while achieving great success, purchasing an adobe in the plaza where he both lived and held court proceedings.

"Was he married?" Sarah asked, although she didn't know why.

"Oh yes, and he married well, the daughter of Don Santiago Arguello, who owned the lands south of the border. Ah yes. A marriage for the ages. And you, Sarah? You didn't tell me. Are you married?"

"What? Oh, no, no. Too busy for that."

Carlos grew silent for a moment and smiled. He strummed his fingers on the table. "Hmm."

"What?"

"You said, hmm."

"I did? Huh. Must be getting old. Anyway, by the time of Olvera's death, in eighteen seventy-six, I think it was, the plaza had been changed, you know according to Anglo tastes, and the street, which ultimately bore his name, was dilapidated. After that, the plaza became kind of famous, a gathering place for all kinds of disenfranchised groups, the working poor, Japanese, Chinese and Mexicans, too. But gone was the Mexican feel, the influence, the blood and bones."

Carlos took another few bites before continuing. With his index finger, he motioned for Sarah to come closer. "You know what would make this food even better?" He reached in his pocket, revealing a miniature booze bottle. She felt the blood rush to her face, as if she herself had been discovered. "Tequila," he said. "Nectar of the Aztec gods. We call this little vessel a *ponchita.*"

Sarah darted a quick look around the room.

"Don't worry," he said. "No one in here cares."

"None for me."

"Oh, come on. Ever tried it?"

"Nope, and I'm not going to start."

"You've come this far. It's not a real *Mexicana* experience without it. Don't tell me you're a Lemonade Lucy."

"No, not anymore. But…"

"Enough said. Just try a sip. Believe me."

She sighed and glanced around again to be sure. That booze was illegal had little to do with it. Obviously, some laws were meant to be broken. But not in public, not in the afternoon. Plus, there was so much bad hooch these days, some of which the government itself had tainted. Countless people had died from the stuff. And who knew if Carlos was, well, healthy? Germs could linger in the crevices of that ponchyeeta, or however the hell you pronounced it. And Carlos' germs were, well, of a kind she hadn't been exposed to before. They were…. She started to think "Mexican" and stopped herself. "Okay, she said, but just one. I don't want to go back to the trial with liquor on my breath."

Carlos grinned and watched her take a swig. She tried to look awkward, as if she hadn't perfected the art. "Whew! That's strong!"

"Delectable, though, no?"

A familiar heat fanned out through her body, a little more intensely than usual but with the same soothing effect. "Not bad."

"Another?"

"Absolutely not."

"All right. Have it your way." He took a long drink and sat back.

Sarah checked her watch. The modern, unscratched face reminded her that the Hamilton was a recent gift from Mitchell. "Jeepers," she said, "we've only got ten minutes."

"Enough time for me to tell you the rest, the good news, about Olvera Street. You know, I've blamed the *gringos* for much. But ironically, it's a white woman, the whitest of white, that we have to thank for what Olvera is going to become. There's a brand of Anglo women who think it's their duty to Americanize us, meaning to teach us not to be the lazy sons of bitches they think we are. Home-schoolers, they call themselves, trying to show us, especially our wives, who they think are more trainable, the light. But that's not the case here. If it hadn't been for this woman, our history in this city would have been entirely lost. Ever heard of Christine Sterling?"

"I don't think so."

"You will. One day everyone will. She's from the north, San Francisco. No ties to L.A., no Mexican background. But she's a tough, smart dame with a conscience. After moving here with her husband, she took a special interest in the old plaza, thought its poor condition was an injustice to its heritage. To its Mexican heritage. She was passionate about the issue. Of course, some say her fervor was self-serving, that it had to do with the Mexican artists in vogue, you know Diego Rivera, Orozco, and all those Latin lovers on the screen. Her husband is in the movie business. Still, what she has done…"

Carlos dropped his head. When he looked up, tears had filled his eyes again. "Excuse me," he said. Not very *machismo*. Must be the booze."

Sarah instinctively reached out and touched his hand, her own rings clicking against the shimmering gem that had symbolized his past union to another woman not of his background. With all his people had suffered at the hands of whites, Carlos didn't seem to generalize about them, at least where females were concerned. "It's okay," she said, staring unwittingly at his ring. "It's good to express your feelings."

"Moonstone," he said, clutching her fingers.

She flinched but didn't pull back. "Ah."

"It supposedly has healing properties. Keeps you young."

"I think it's working," she said, wondering where she got the nerve.

He smiled, gently released her hand and continued. "Christine, I call her that because she encourages everyone to do so, one day came across a condemned sign on an old adobe belonging to Don Francisco Avila, a prominent ranchero who served as mayor of Los Angeles. Unfit for human habitation, the sign read, by reason of unsanitary conditions. Signed by the current L.A. mayor, George Cryer, another holier-than-thou corrupt politician passing himself off as a vice stopper. Unsanitary, dirty. They always say that about my people, eh?"

Germs, Sarah thought, averting her eyes.

"Anyway, Christine saw the sign and that was it. It inspired her to go on a one-woman campaign to preserve the adobe and turn Olvera Street into a Mexican marketplace. And God bless her, she succeeded, even getting that bastard Chandler on board. In a few years, her dream will be realized. Quaint and romanticized probably, but at least a living tribute. Consuelo's will be one of the first businesses to open there. Her sister Rita will soon follow, with a jewelry store."

Rita, Sarah thought. Maybe.... "By the way," she said, "the name Rita reminds me. You must have heard about the death of a woman of that name. Rita Bradford?"

"Hmm. Bradford? Ah, oh, I think so, yes. On Marianna? Yes. A shame."

"Did you know her? Her family? She lived in Beverly Hills, I think."

"Ha! No, no. I didn't. Don't know many people from that end of town. And you know, Sarah, just because someone's Mexican doesn't mean I'd know them," he said with a harsh laugh.

"I know."

"Of course you do. I'm sorry. Why are you asking?"

Sarah sighed. "Oh, it's a long story, and we really have to go."

"Well, how 'bout you tell me about it as we walk back."

"That's all right. I don't think it will do any good."

"Can't hurt. And I'd like to hear it, really."

Carlos said his good-byes to Dolores and paid the bill, refusing to go Dutch. Sarah followed Carlos outside, re-pinning her hair as she went. He shut the door behind them and stopped under the awning. "One for the road?" he said, reaching for the bottle again. "It will help you tell your story better."

"It's not a pleasant tale."

"All the more reason."

"Perhaps you're right," she said, accepting the offer and drinking this time with the gusto and finesse of an expert.

13

After a little more tequila, Sarah grew relaxed and, as Carlos predicted, loquacious. She told him everything, from Rita seeking her out at the courthouse, to Sarah's recollection of their first encounter at the Julian offices, to her unproved but persistent suspicions that the woman's death was more than a coincidence. She described Officer's Hodges' response to her questions, how his initial apathy had quickly turned to anger, and how she believed his bigotry to be at the core of both reactions. The only part Sarah withheld was her meeting Paige, respecting their agreement to keep their communication, all of it, private.

Well, that was not entirely true. She also neglected to mention her own current struggle against the kind of bias that Hodges exhibited in its most extreme form. How her own, what else could she call it, but her fear of Mexicans, might be contributing just a tad to her unwillingness to let the matter go, how she wanted to prove to herself that she could conquer such ignorant thoughts. But why bring it up when Carlos himself was helping to rid her of them?

As Sarah knew from experience, the best way to begin to overcome prejudice was to spend time with individuals from the group to which such sentiment was directed. She didn't plan it, of course, but she was doing just that and already feeling the broadening effects. Carlos was Mexican or Mexican-American, Chicano as he preferred to say, but beyond the surface of color and habits, he was a man. Caring, intelligent, compassionate. Attractive too. More so than many white men she knew, including Mitchell, whose disheveled, oversized puppy-dog image was endearing by comparison. She winced at that thought, but it didn't stop her from continuing to check off the ways Carlos was indeed a superior being. He valued his family, was a successful businessman, well read, and, contrary to the unsanitary stereotype he himself invoked, immaculate; his nails clipped and clean, his silvery hair perfectly groomed, his teeth intact and white.

Sarah was also impressed with how intently Carlos listened to her narration of the events involving Rita. If that was an ethnic trait, it was one the entire white population should adopt, men in particular. Indeed, he listened as if each detail had personal significance, nodding appropriately, questioning when he wanted to hear more. No, he didn't know Rita, he said, nor her husband, whose description in the *Times* as an advertising "mogul" Carlos doubted since he knew the heads of the big ad agencies in town. He agreed that Mr. Bradford's alleged disinterest in his wife's shoes seemed odd, and he certainly didn't doubt Sarah's experiences in the probate court. But a shocked and grieving man might act strange, he said. After all, they're just shoes. Carlos himself packed away Rachel's belongings the day she died because it was too painful to look at them. That Rita was Mexican was naturally of particular interest to him, however, as was the racist attitude of the police. "Bastards," he said, clenching his jaw. "Don't get your hopes up. They won't lift a finger where a *pachuca* is concerned."

He admired Sarah's efforts, though. A little like Christine Sterling, he said, putting herself on the line for someone from an entirely other race. "*Muy generosa.*" So generous, that it was only fair that he would return the favor. He didn't know the Bradfords, but someone he knew probably did. In fact, he said he felt it incumbent upon himself to look into the matter. Rita was a compatriot after all.

Sarah was grateful, to say the least. Now there were two on her side.

"Shall we drink to it?" he said. "I think there are a few drops left in this thing."

At that point, it would have been silly to say no, so she didn't. She felt tipsy but encouraged as she and Carlos found their place in the courthouse.

■■■

"I call Henry Smithfield to the stand."

Who the "I" was Sarah wasn't sure, other than a member of the prosecution team. There were so many attorneys coming and going in this case that she wondered whether they had a consistent strategy, or, for that matter, even knew each other. If she didn't know any better, she'd think that they were simply auditioning for a part.

"What time did you go to work for the Julian Petroleum Corporation?"

"May first, nineteen twenty-five."

"And your duties were somewhat—you call it the personnel department, somewhat in the nature of detective work, was it not?"

"Yes, sir, I was manager of the personnel."

"You know Stan Lewis?"

"Yes, sir."

"Jack Bennett?"

"Yes, sir."

"And did you know that was not his true name, that his name was Jacob Berman?"

"Yes, sir."

"Was Bennett working for the Julian Petroleum Corporation when you first went with it?"

"I met him there. I believe he was working for them."

"From that time on was he around the offices all the time?"

"Yes, sir."

"When you first went to the offices in the Pershing Square building, in which office was Jack Bennett working at that time? Go over to the diagram please and show us."

"He had no particular office."

"And where was the transfer department at that time?"

"Room nine seventeen, I believe."

Sarah tried to make out the room. Where was it?

"Was that opposite the elevator?"

Sarah remembered. The room opposite the elevator. That's where they entered. That's where she met Rita. And her husband, whose scarred cheek she could envision now perfectly.

"Yes, sir."

"Was that afterwards moved, the transfer office?"

"I do not believe so."

Sarah felt herself nodding off. Room nine zero seven or nine zero eight. Southeast corner.

"When you went up there, was Ted Rosen around the offices at that time?"

She suddenly perked up.

"No, sir."

"About what time did he come there?"

"I believe it would be around January, nineteen twenty-six."

"And did he have a desk up there from that time on?"

"Yes, sir."

"Was that in room nine twelve?"

"Yes, sir."

"Rosen testified earlier that he kept some of the records in his desk. Did you see him do that?"

"No, sir."

"Where did he keep them, as far as you could see?"

"In a briefcase."

"Did he bring that briefcase with him to the office each morning?"

"Yes, sir."

"And take it away at night?"

"Yes, sir."

"And as far as you could see, he took any paper that he wanted out of that and put the papers back into it and took them away with him at night?"

"Yes, sir."

"Never using the desk for the purpose of putting any of his papers in?"

"No, sir."

Ted was briefly called back on the stand to answer Smithfield's claim. It seemed like a minor point in comparison to other issues, but the attorney demonstrated that Ted had something to hide. Not only by obsessively holding on to his papers, but by lying about it. "You said earlier that you left papers in your desk. Anybody could see them." Ted refuted Smithfield's assertion, saying that he was the one who was lying, but for the first time he looked visibly shaken. His body seemed to shrink, fold in upon itself. He was all suit, his oversized swanky clothes only emphasizing the smallness of the man.

Judge Doran tapped the gavel as Ted slowly rose. "Court dismissed."

The effects of the booze were wearing off, leaving Sarah tired, a little queasy but also exhilarated. No matter Ted's ultimate fate, this was a victory.

•••

Perhaps Sarah should have just stayed in that night, savored the moment with a hot bath and a good night's sleep. But Carlos convinced her, with very little difficulty, that a celebration was in order. Not only for seeing Rosen squirm, but because they had met, because the gods had seen it fit to bring them together. And this time, she could choose the restaurant.

It was 4:30 p.m. when court ended. He would pick her up at 7:00. She could take a short nap and dress, which she did with only a few minutes to spare. In that time, she memorialized her afternoon through a quick entry in her notebook: *Enchiladas, Olvera Street, Tequila. Rule of Capture: "Whoever gets to the resource first has the rights to it"—Carlos Martinez.*

She was glad she brought her flattering, drop-waist black dress. But she frowned at herself in the mirror. Not flattering enough. She darkened her lipstick and headed downstairs where Carlos was waiting in his car, a brand-new Model A. His stores must indeed be doing well, she thought, as he sprang around, opened the door and offered his hand as she slid into the cool leather seat. "You look lovely, Sarah. So where to?"

Sarah hesitated. Why not? She felt a little giddy. "The Brown Derby."

Three hours later they were still there, lingering with the eighty or so other customers. The place was rather plain inside, a plain old hat with booths hugging the walls and a counter encircling the service area. But the food was excellent. Sarah ordered the Cobb salad, a savory mix of chopped meats and vegetables, tossed at the table with their tangy homemade Old Fashioned French Dressing. The menu said that the manager, Robert Cobb, invented the dish, and since the opening nine months ago, it had become one of their most popular.

The tables were low, allowing patrons to see and been seen. Everyone in the place resembled a celebrity, although there wasn't anyone in particular Sarah recognized. Still, she and Carlos were enjoying the view and each other's company. Over silky caramel custard, she told him more about her job, about her family, even a little about Mitchell, which didn't seem to bother him in the least. He spoke mostly about his grocery stores, how he tried to keep up with all the latest tastes and offer "the best products at the best prices." Overhearing one of the customers mention the first "talkie," however, due out this very year, he turned to the movies. Naturally, like everyone else, he was anxiously awaiting the debut. But he wondered what would become of the Mexican actors and actresses in this new age. Lupe Velez, the Mexican born beauty, married to Johnny Weissmueller who came to fame in the Douglas Fairbanks' adventure last year, "The Gaucho"; Dolores del Rio, the first Mexican actress to achieve international stardom in "Resurrection"; Ramon Novarro, Del Rio's heartthrob in "Caramouch" and a major role in "Ben-Hur"; Gilbert Roland who stared with Clara Bow in "The Plastic Age." Carlos smiled. "Did you know that Roland was going to become a bullfighter like his father?"

Sarah shook her head. She knew these names but never thought much about their heritage. "Quite a switch."

"Maybe not. Hollywood can kill you, too."

"Ha. I suppose you're right."

Carlos was proud to see his compatriots on screen, even in stereotypical roles. Yet he feared that giving voice to the faces, an accented sound to the silence, might turn some fans against them.

They also talked more about Rita, about the tragedy and strangeness of the thing. Carlos sat pensively, listening; listening so hard that his somewhat pointed ears appeared to twist like those of a dog trying to make sense out of a new command. He tried again to think if he had seen her, heard of Phillip Bradford, somewhere, anywhere, but came up dry.

The Derby was of course near the Ambassador, site of the conference. When Carlos learned that Sarah hadn't even peeked into the Cocoanut Grove, the hotel's famous nightclub for celebrity watching, he insisted they do so before turning in. She wondered for a second if that was wise, given that she might run in to a colleague, but concluded there would be nothing wrong in that anyway. Sarah wasn't married, nor did she owe anyone an explanation. So an hour later they were doing the Charleston to the Jacques Renard Orchestra's rousing version of "You Went Away Too Far and Stayed Away Too Long." Renard's actual name was Jacob Stavinksi, Carlos said, as he led her to the lavish, crowded dance floor. Born in Russia and raised in Philadelphia, Stavinski was a classically trained Jew who changed his style and identity. A French jazz musician would no doubt have more commercial success, Sarah thought, regarding the animated, Semitic-looking conductor both with empathy and contempt.

If Carlos had not already impressed her, his easy sense of rhythm would have done the job. Sarah loved to dance, and wasn't bad at it. Learning new moves was challenging but interpreting the music in this way, becoming part of it in a sense, was liberating. Usually, however, this was a sport she engaged in alone, just she and the Victrola letting loose in her living room. And even then, she had to be cautious because it troubled Tillie to see her respectable sister in what she called such a "primitive state." Moreover, the only time Mitchell had been persuaded to give it a whirl was when he was tight. So he said, anyway, because he had been sober since she had met him. He was too self-conscious, he confessed, and felt it too unbefitting to a man of his size and, now, his age.

Carlos had no such inhibition. He swung his strong legs and muscular arms in perfect syncopated time. The Charleston could look jerky in a less coordinated man, but Carlos was smooth. He seemed comfortable, and that made Sarah feel the same even though the floor was so packed that one misstep could have sent her flying into another dancer's backside.

Surrounding them was a sea of scarlet-clothed tables with glamorous patrons squeezed together, smoking and laughing. Sarah searched in vain for a famous face but nevertheless enjoyed the stage-like spectacle; the sequins, the gold, the flasks that appeared and disappeared with almost illusory speed. Flowing, gauzy curtains, intricate Moroccan tiles and huge artificial palms completed the set. Sarah indeed felt as if she were in a play, or better yet, a moving picture, since out of the corner of her eye she thought she finally saw a star, Joan Crawford, no less, who Carlos said was a regular. Much to her disappointment, however, the sultry party girl turned out to be just another lookalike. Crawford was known for partaking in the club's weekly Charleston contest, and Sarah had been willing her to appear even though the contest wasn't for three days. Sarah thought Crawford wonderfully talented, and hoped to see if she was as beautiful, and as short, in person as reported.

"You Went Away Too Far, and Stayed Away Too Long." The scolding song title reminded Sarah of Mitchell, of how he might very well respond if she extended her trip just a little, as she was beginning to contemplate. It also made her recall that jazz lounge in Tennessee where he reprimanded her for leading him on. It was a pivotal moment in their relationship. That night they made love for the first time, and she had felt more alive than she had in years. For a brief moment she felt guilty, displaced, indeed too far away from all she knew. But only for a moment. She shook off the memory and focused on the present.

This had nothing to do with Mitchell, she thought, as the music slowed and the lights dimmed. Carlos drew Sarah close. "*Who Am I?*" the vocalist crooned. "*Who am I to ever expect you'd care…. You're so sweet… Still it's nice pretending that you're mine.*" Carlos held her tighter and she leaned her head on his shoulder Hollywood style, aware of the affectation even as she was actually enjoying the sensation. "Who Am I?" Carlos whispered. "*Quién soy?*"

After several more dances, Carlos excused himself, while Sarah stood half-listening to the band, nervously welcoming what was inevitably to come. Had she been younger, or even had she met Carlos before Mitchell, she would likely have been running for the exit. She might not even have been aware of the subtle and not so subtle signs of desire that manifested themselves over the course of the evening. But Mitchell had reminded her that she was a flesh and blood woman still capable of physical pleasure. And experience had made her more confident. Certainly, she still was self-conscious about the toll time had taken on her body. But she was no longer willing to let that stop her. The trick was to not think too much. The whiskey that Carlos brought for the occasion would no doubt help in that regard.

Carlos soon returned with a calm, certain look, linked his arm through hers and headed back toward the main hotel. Only once along the way did she question her decision, and then only because of the consequences of her poor judgment in the Julian matter. God knows she was capable of making a mistake. But that also made her think of Rita, and how short life was. Too short to let a blunder in one thing prevent her from doing another. And so she entered the shimmery, gilded lift with a free mind.

"*Cinco, por favor,*" Carlos said.

The young Chicano elevator operator smiled appreciatively, held out his white-gloved hand and scanned the lobby for other guests. With no takers, he closed the doors, sealing the deal.

14

The sun filtered through the lightly woven draperies with a director's flair, spotlighting the room's elegant furniture, softening the image Sarah saw reflected back at her in the curved metal lamp near the kingly bed.

She lay on her side, staring at the younger-looking female face. Something like herself; softened, yes, but a little distorted too, lengthened and off-center. She sat up and leaned against the plush, quilted headboard. "So it wasn't my imagination," she said aloud, spotting the glass carafe of coffee whose rich fragrance she had incorporated into a shapeless dream. Coffee and an abundant breakfast tray replete with a long-stemmed red rose. Right next to where she had hastily spread out her dress the night before. Very nice. She smiled. A real gentleman.

A gentleman, she thought, as she took a bite of toast. But not gentle. Adept, but not gentle. Passionate, but not gentle. Insistent. The opposite of Mitchell. Carlos knew what he wanted, took it, and left her more satisfied than she thought possible. There was a moment when she had felt a little uneasy, when insistence bordered on something coarser. But he never crossed that boundary. She closed her eyes and relived the excitement, the sure touch of his hands, the black eyes that gleamed at her in the dark.

She sipped the strong brew. No words either. Carlos was determined but quiet, hardly uttering a sound. She felt conspicuous when she couldn't stifle a little moan. But afterwards, he did speak, saying that he believed in the fate of their meeting and that he must see her again. And soon. Tomorrow. Sarah was glad about that. Very glad. But she was also a tad concerned. Not about getting hurt. She knew that was a possibility. Not about Mitchell, although she should be. And certainly not about getting pregnant, for the doctors told her that was no longer possible. But about...she hated to admit...diseases. Now alert with caffeine and in the clear light of day, she wondered. Yesterday she was worried about sharing a drink; last night she'd shared the ultimate intimacy. A shot of adrenaline raced through her, causing her heart to flutter. Jesus, Sarah! She took a couple of deep breaths. That such concerns had never even entered her mind with Mitchell was a sure sign that she wasn't over her prejudice. That, and pure stupidity, since she had counseled so many girls on the potential health risks of promiscuity, no matter the race, religion or culture.

She opened the drapes and gazed out at the hotel's immaculate grounds, being tended to already by workers who no doubt shared Carlos' bloodline. Healthy, strong men. Men whose ancestors fought till the end. Men who endured, who were still here despite attempts to cast them as lazy and dirty, as inferior beings. Dammit. She would be fine. God willing.

It was only 8 a.m., time to return to her hotel and clean up before court. She had known Carlos would be gone before she awakened, even though his earthy smell still lingered on the billowy sheets. Last night, he told her that he had to leave early to buy produce downtown. He promised to pay the bill and leave her money for a cab. She could leave discreetly. Again, a gentleman. She threw on her dress, grabbed the cash and sprinted toward the exit.

■■■

It wasn't until after the trial, during which the defense tried to reframe Ted's lie as a mere lapse in memory, that she finally checked for messages. There were two. The first from Mitchell: *It's cold here*, Mitchell's read. *The sound of your voice would warm me up.* She heaved a deep sigh. Later, she said to herself. Later. The second was from Paige. Sarah raced to the phone, her hands shaking as she dialed the number.

"Hello."

"Hello, Paige?"

"Ah, I was wondering when you'd call."

"Yes. I've been tied up," Sarah said. "I was surprised to hear from you so soon."

"I'll bet. I'm kind of surprised myself. I found out something that might interest you."

"Yes?"

"Mr. Bradford."

"Yes?"

"Well," she said, lowering her voice, "he's been spotted in Tijuana. At the new hotel, Agua Caliente. Luxurious, they say. With a casino, golf course. He was seen by the pool. Alone, taking in some sun. And he's got a reservation at a bungalow for a month."

"What's that? Really? Casino? Uh, well, hmm. How did you find this out? How do you know about his reservation?"

"Listen, sweetie, I didn't tell you I'd reveal my sources. That could get me into trouble. Just remember where I work."

"Oh, yeah, sure, of course. But, well, what about Rita? I thought Mr. Bradford was in mourning. What about the funeral? Surely he'd…"

"Just passing along the information. I don't know from nothin' about these other things. But thought you might, well, it's pretty easy to get down there from here."

"Tijuana?! Mexico? Oh, no, no. No, that's taking it too far."

"It's up to you."

"Isn't it dangerous?"

"Certain areas are, like everywhere. I've been several times and I'm in one piece. But, again, it's up to you, of course."

"Yeah. Well, it's certainly intriguing that he's there. I mean if it's really him."

"One thing I can tell you. I trust my source."

"I didn't mean…."

"Sure, I'll keep checking."

"Anymore said about murder, about the ligature marks and all that?"

"I'm afraid not. They know it, but they've closed the book."

"God. Well, thank you, Paige. Thank you very much."

"Okay. Good-bye then, Sar…."

"Uh, Paige?"

"Yeah?"

"You're really confident in, uh, this 'source?'"

"That's what I said. And I gotta tell you, I went out on a bit of a limb for this. And that's saying something coming from a cripple."

Sarah laughed a little. "And I appreciate it. Believe me. Would I, would I need a passport?"

"Passport? Nah. Silly nuisance. Ha-ha. Nobody needs one to go to Tijuana. But listen, don't feel pressured, honey. Just letting you know, like I said I would."

"Right. Well, I'll think about it."

"Sure, sure. I've got a singing gig tonight, but, uh, you could reach me at this number tomorrow evening, I mean if you want to talk about it or anything. I'm house-sitting for a few days."

Sarah slowly hung up and pushed open the glass doors. A squat woman in a silver fringed flapper outfit had apparently been waiting to use the phone. She frowned at Sarah, pointed to her watch and grunted. Sarah shrugged. God. Tijuana? She wasn't about to go there. Wild, she'd heard. Gomorrah. But Bradford supposedly had a reservation at a fancy hotel. Say that was true. How would she approach him? What would she ask? Hey, remember me? Stocks, C. C. Julian? The one who talked to your wife? "Remember me? *Te acuerdas de mi?*"

Anyway, what if he decided to leave, was already gone? Then again, if he really was there, it might be a unique opportunity. It might be, well, a perfect place, away from L.A. He'd be freer to talk. Maybe he really would remember Sarah. Still, why in the hell was he there? Was this his way of mourning? Carlos said it. People behave differently. Then again, he might have had something to do with Rita's death himself. In a way, he was the one who shut the investigation down. Even if she did have a heart condition, wouldn't he want to know the cause of those marks on her neck? If he loved his wife, wouldn't he want the cops to pursue all angles? Anything was possible. Including the fact that there was nothing to discover, that all of this was a waste of time brought on by an active imagination and a coincidental encounter.

She was beat. She put her hands in her coat pockets and felt a rumpled piece of paper. Shit. Mitchell. She turned back but the booth was still occupied. The woman shook her head, and her fringe, at Sarah. "No way," she mouthed. I guess she'll be awhile Sarah said to herself, even if it's just to prove a point.

Sarah closed the door of her room and collapsed on the bed, wishing she had her book. Was she really considering this? Her involvement in those matters in Ohio and Tennessee were random, but also deadly. In playing detective, she had put her life on the line, twice. Why in the world would she do it again? And yet, she had never felt more alive than during those times. Not happy, but alive. The searching for clues, the taking of chances, the challenge of putting her rusty mind to new purpose. She had learned then that solving a crime was really just an extension of her work, helping people who had taken a wrong turn. Some of it was terrifying, some ugly, some tragic. But in the end, she had, just as she did in court, helped put something right.

There was no question that Sarah had a sense, an intuition when something, or someone, was a little off. Not everyone possessed that trait. Even with the stocks, it was because she'd ignored it that she'd gotten into trouble. So

Tijuana. Could she help put something right by going there? It was close, easy to get to, Paige said. But alone? She didn't know the language, culture, anything. She'd only just had her first enchilada! She should forget it. Focus on the trial, the conference, and this, this…Carlos. That should be enough. Mitchell. Jesus. What would he think?

She twisted her rings, her thumb and little finger getting more into the act than usual. If Tillie were here, she'd smack Sarah's hand to keep it still. Maybe Paige will come up with another lead, she thought. Maybe…hmm. Carlos. I wonder. She sat staring at the dark ceiling. Carlos. She turned on her side and pulled up the sheets, which felt even chintzier than before. The Ambassador had spoiled her for good. She closed her eyes, but then snapped them back open, where, with no story or booze to lull her to sleep, they remained for most of the night.

15

The driver had tried to swerve around the deep rut but missed. The truck took a direct hit, wobbling precipitously. "Whoa! Hang on! Sorry," he said. Carlos sat unfazed, waving to the workers who called out his name. He'd been thrown about before, countless times. One didn't expect a smooth ride in the middle of the Imperial Valley, let alone on a dusty road bordering one of the region's many orange groves. Oranges, lemons, grapefruit. And that was just the citrus. Acres of other crops too, more everyday.

And who worked in these fields? Mexicans, of course! The old, familiar story. Rich, white property owners, dark-skinned laborers. Some would call it ingenuity, what the developers did. Rerouting a river, building canals and aqueducts, transforming dry river sediment into vast, aerable land. These fellows were smart all right. Like William Mulholland with the Owens Valley, they studied the Colorado, its twists and turns and figured out how to bend it to their will. Not without a fight, however, from both nature and man. In Mulholland's case, he and his cronies dissembled their way to water rights, knowingly underestimating how much water L.A. required and how much would need to be diverted. But the Owens Valley farmers eventually caught on, opening sluice gates, wrecking the infrastructure in protest. Carlos admired their spunk. Their tactics forced Mulholland to negotiate an agreement with them. If only it had ended there. But once a scoundrel always a scoundrel. Just this March, just a couple of months ago, Mulholland certified the St. Francis dam's safety, and twelve hours later it failed, flooding towns and killing hundreds. He should have been buried along with them.

Water. Water was at the crux of it all here, too. The Imperial Valley was originally a seabed, revealed after eons of erosion, eruptions and time. Carlos gazed up at the towering purple mountains surrounding the flat terrain. His mother didn't believe any of it. Catholic through and through, no room for doubt. Damn church wanted it that way. Keep its brown folk down. Bow to Rome and procreate.

That Kaufman broad had asked him if he was devout. Hmm. For being so smart, she was certainly gullible. He offered her some blather about loving the traditions, the rituals. Her eyes had gleamed in sympathy. Kindred spirit, she no doubt thought. It had worked, almost too well. Ha! Boy did his mother hate the Jews, and for reasons purer than his own. For Carlos, it was their habits. The money issue, of course, but mostly it was their whining and weakness. Their brains were big, but their bodies were soft. Who ever knew a Jewish soldier? Still, some he could do business with if it served his purpose. He smiled. Some he could even fuck, for a higher cause. But for his mother it was different. They killed her god and that was that. Poor mama. He loved her so. But she was simple, the stereotype fulfilled, perfect prey for the Vatican.

Some of the developers may have privately accepted the scientific explanation of the Valley's origins but their publicists targeted the true believers too, those who took the Bible as fact. One in particular, Holt, something Holt, promoted the region as the Egyptian delta of the United States, with the Colorado serving as its Nile. He suggested that irrigation and cultivation of the desert was akin to Moses and his followers going down into Egypt. The activity was, in other words, divinely sanctioned, preordained.

Maybe Holt's first name was Judas, Carlos thought, because it turned out that he knew that the Colorado was subject to seasonal flooding, that it was only during such times that the Valley was naturally green. Land sold all right, and developers were happy. But in the drought years, when it was dry as a bone, farmers were furious and sales dwindled. What they needed was more water. More of the Nile to keep the biblical vision alive. So they engineered a route, cut into the river left and right. But in doing so, they forgot that there could be too much of a good thing. They forgot about Noah. Water poured into the valley, flooding everything, turning a depression in the earth, a sink geologists called it, into a sea. They built levees that were breeched, aqueducts that silted over, dams that were ineffective. Now all of this would have been just another episode of *gringo* folly if it weren't for greed. To Carlos, greed was behind it all, an unquenchable desire for power and profit. Another version of manifest destiny coupled with the belief that there would always be a steady supply of Mexicans to do the dirty work, and for a very low wage.

Not only that. One of the canals cut right into Mexico itself, illegally and on the cheap. Three or four miles into Mexico and then back into the Imperial Valley. Locals were understandably outraged. Again whites were screwing them, this time on their own land, stealing their water. And then there was Henry

Chandler. He and his syndicate, the worst of all. It made Carlos' blood boil just to think of it. Early in the century, Chandler owned land in Baja. He too found a way to skirt the Mexican constitution. He wanted in on the irrigation game, and in Mexico. But just to throw salt in the wound, he hired Coolies, Chinese, to do the labor. *Cabrón!* Anything to humiliate his people. His people, who, despite it all, would still risk everything to do the *gringos'* backbreaking, mind-numbing work.

Carlos squinted at the hunched-over figures. *Sí,* they knew. Knew that wages in Mexico were even worse, that all the American bosses had to do was offer a little more and they'd keep coming. Not enough to provide them with a decent life. Not because they believed in their inherent value as human beings. But because his people came cheap and weren't built for anything else.

He lit a cigarette, his third of the day and his usual limit. Today might be an exception. They certainly had succeeded, he thought, scanning the vast crop. Taming, twisting, subverting nature until now crops thrived. Here one could almost turn water into wine. But there would be a cost. There would be a cost if Carlos had anything to do with it, that is. Much of the produce that was grown here he sold in his own stores. Harvested by his ethnic kin who certainly did their job and needed the money. But they would not be at the whites' mercy forever.

He smashed the butt on the side of the flatbed, hopped off and headed down the familiar path, kicking the artificially wetted soil, admiring the neat rows of bushy green trees still ripe with fruit. Late in the season, but it had been an unusual year. The fruit would be harvested and sent to market by the end of the week.

"There's a beauty," he said, licking his lips. Deep in color, unmarred. Perfection. A navel, of course. He plucked, peeled and stuck the thick rind in his shirt pocket. Carlos liked to munch on the white pith, both for the biting flavor and the vitamins he believed were concentrated there. Indeed, he attributed his virility in part to consuming the substance several times a week. The other part, well, a fortune of birth.

He continued for nearly a half mile, his destination growing closer with each plump and juicy section. He popped the sixth and final one in his mouth, wiped his hands on his pants and reached for the doorknob. But he pulled back when he heard raised voices through the open window.

"We must do it. For the sake of our cause!"

"I say we don't. I say *I* don't! I've got a family. I can't be taking chances like this."

"You want to work yourself to death? With no rights? No recourse? This is *for* your family, for all of our families!"

"You do what you want. You're not going to pressure me!"

"Ernesto, calm down."

"Take your hand off me!"

"Hey, hey...."

"I said, leave me alone!"

Bodies shifted, everyone talking at once, tempers audibly rising. Carlos flung open the door. "*Bastante*! Enough!"

The men stopped in their tracks and retreated. "Enough," Carlos said. No one is going to be forced to do anything. He looked sympathetically at the young man with the clenched jaw. "I think Ernesto will go along when he understands the stakes."

"No, Carlos," the man said. "I respect you, you know I do. But I've made up my mind. I waited to tell you myself. I'm out."

"Ernesto. *Amigo*. Wait. After you hear everything, you can decide. Okay?"

"What else is there to hear? If it had just been the union, that would have been one thing. But this other business. That's where I draw the line."

"This other business, as you put it, is just a bit of insurance, so that we will be taken seriously. And a little payback. Rule of capture, *recuerdas*? You know what for. No physical harm will be done. I guarantee that."

"How can you? What if we're caught?"

Carlos met his worried eyes with a steady gaze. "Trust me, please."

Ernesto looked down and shook his head. "*No sé.* I don't know."

Carlos turned to the others. "Get back to the fields now."

The men simultaneously frowned and mouthed, "*Qué?*"

"I'm sorry, Carlos said. "We have to postpone. We'll meet again in a few days. Something has come up. Something personal."

The men, their twenty-year old, broad, dark faces reminding Carlos of himself at their age, still looked perplexed. One said: "*Qué pasa*, Carlos?"

"Personal," I said. "Now please, go." Except Ernesto. Stay for a minute, will you?"

The rest trudged out, their boots thumping extra loudly on the planked wooden floor. Carlos heard annoyance in that sound, but it couldn't be helped. They'd get over it.

"Sit down," Carlos said, pointing to a rotted-out bench. Ernesto obliged, folding his hands on the makeshift table around which so much debate had given rise to a plan that was finally coming to fruition. "*Nito*, we've met here for months, at our peril. And you know how much I admire you, you in particular. Your careful thought, intelligence, willingness to take risks. This is not the time to let up. In a matter of days the union will be official. *Confederación de Uniones Obreras de Mexicanas*! Do you understand what that means?"

"Do I understand? Of course I do. We'll finally have a voice, and eventually, power. Eventually, Carlos. The union is committed to equalizing the rights of American and Mexican workers. But within the law, within the legal framework of the United States!"

"And you think I'm against that?"

"Well..."

Carlos shook his head and sighed. "You know that the Mexican government will only allow us to do so much. You know the consulate is deeply connected to the CUOM, that they will set the parameters. It's in the manifesto: "No radicals.""

"So?"

"So? Our progress will be excruciatingly slow. We might even be more constrained than we are now. Think about housing, the 'pickers' cabins, like this very dump. Rows and rows of them. In camps, *colonias*, villages, they say. More like prisons. You really think we can bargain for something better without a warning, without a bit of extra pressure? You know what the *gringos* believe. That we are simple, content with the barest of necessities. Sunshine and a little running water and we'll live happily ever after. The bosses aren't worried. They think our organizing is quaint. Now listen, *Nito*. I'm all for the union, you know that. I'm a representative for Christ's sake! But to have them respect us, truly respect us, they need to know that we are made of stronger stuff. That we won't be satisfied with whatever meager bone they choose to throw us."

"So break the law?" Ernesto said. "This scheme is crazy, against our own interests. We've clawed and scrapped to get to this point. It's not the time to rock the boat."

"That's where you're wrong. We should rock the boat until the wind is in our sails." He smiled thinly. Ernesto didn't look amused. "Remember, *Nito*, remember what they did," Carlos said in a somber tone, spreading out his fingers on the rough table, his ring glimmering against the dull wood.

Ernesto silently stared at Carlos' hands. Then Carlos said, "let's talk more on Thursday, okay? I'm already late for…for this personal matter. Please, don't say no, not yet anyway."

Ernesto sighed and nodded slowly. "Okay, Thursday. Everything all right?" Carlos exhaled. "Yes. Fine. *Gracias, mi amigo. Muchas gracias.*"

Carlos watched Ernesto leave, picked up the salt shaker on the table and threw a few grains over his shoulder. Then he hurried out and retraced his steps. Once back on the truck, he motioned to the driver who, after reaching the main road, sped, as fast as the cumbersome heap could, east.

▪▪▪

Another problem, Carlos thought, as the truck continued on, passing other groves, other crops. He lit another cigarette as they approached the California Eve Citrus billboard, with the Mary Pickford look-alike reaching for an orange while suggestively straddling a wall. Carlos usually threw the image a kiss but he wasn't in the mood. Too many problems. He could manage the Jewess, he thought, but Ernesto could be trouble. Carlos asked for the man's trust, but could Carlos trust him? *Ay*. Well, at least he had bought some time. He sat back, leaning his brawny arms on the large suitcase he had filled with food, toiletries and, of course, cash. Why now? Why, goddammit! Just when they were on the verge of success, when they were about to begin to reap what they had so arduously sown?

How long had they been planning? It seemed like an eternity, but it was really less than a year. "California Eve," "Have One," and especially the almighty "Sunkist." *Mexicanas* had picked for all of them, for decades the unsung and unorganized labor behind the company slogans, campaigns and bounty. But the union was, as he told Ernesto, a double-edged sword. The Mexican government would be watching like a hawk. Its motives were not pure. With the U. S. economy teetering as it was, Mexican officials were worried about repatriation as much as the rights of their overworked and underpaid citizens. Indeed, the union would not be independent, and that's why the deed had to be done now, while the structure was still loose. Justice could not move forward without it. After that, Carlos could rest. After that the law could have its say.

Admittedly, the union would be a huge step forward, an idea whose time was long overdue. The organizing had begun in L.A. but quickly spread, like a wondrous new religion, like a disease, the *gringos* no doubt would say. Carlos wished he could have been a fly on the wall when Mayor Cryer, staunch opponent of the Industrial Workers of the World, first heard the news. He recalled word for word what that crook said at his 1921 swearing-in ceremony: "In this day of 'isms' and I.W.W. agitation, every enemy of our flag and country and institutions is carrying on this insidious propaganda of destruction, and it is, therefore, very necessary and proper that the forces of law and order should be alive, awake, and on guard." By "isms," he of course meant the ones beginning with "commun" and "social," which he didn't have the interest or brains to distinguish from one another. And by "agitation" he meant seeking a formal means of addressing grievances. How satisfyingly ironic. The law-loving Cryer had proven to be so corrupt that even the *Times*, who originally had been a strong supporter, changed their tune, admitting just last year that the mayor was totally controlled by Kent Parrot, the city's political boss. Everyone knew that Parrot really ran the city, the L.A. Police Department in particular: he and the criminals comprising "The City Hall Gang." They'll soon dirty up that sparkling new building, Carlos thought, although in truth he wouldn't want it too clean anyway. There were benefits to this local version of Tammany.

The gnarled purple cactus came into view. It wasn't far now. Carlos lit up again, his gut churning at the prospect of what awaited him. This was priority number one. He had to get the situation under control before he could give the men the final go-ahead. Except for Ernesto, they were certainly ready. More than ready, never failing to answer the call, gathering come hell or high water in that shit hole the bosses reluctantly allowed them to use when they had nowhere else to go. Which was often, huddled together on the cold, hard floor. Southern plantation owners did right by their slaves in comparison.

Carlos smiled, marveling at his own ingenuity. It was actually some of those slaves who had inspired him to hold meetings in the place. He had heard the stories about the Negro songs, the lyrics with hidden codes, escape plots that were hatched in earshot of their masters. Why not apply the same principle? Meet in the light of day, right under their noses. After all, the bosses liked Carlos. Well perhaps *like* wasn't the right word. Begrudgingly accepted. He was a storeowner, one of the smarter of the species. An entrepreneur! He would never side with the workers, a belief that Carlos had carefully nurtured. Indeed, he was so convincing that they encouraged his visits, believing he would help keep the boys in line. Well, if you insist. Ha! Idiots. Seeing only what they wanted, only what their narrow minds could imagine.

■■■

The abandoned adobe ten miles farther east was something Carlos discovered on his own and kept to himself. After meetings, he would sometimes come here to think and of course replenish the stash of liquor that he stored in a nook so well hidden not even Al Capone could have found it. This place wasn't any more habitable than the one he'd just left, but it didn't bear the *gringo* stench. *Californios* had built it and therefore, to Carlos, it was a second home. He put down the suitcase. "Andrés?" His voice echoed in the nearly empty, darkening space. "Andrés! *Dónde estás?*"

Silence.

"Come on. Don't joke." Carlos stomped into the only other room, where he kept a candle and a few blankets. The heavy air was still. "Andrés!"

He heard footsteps outside and drew a sigh of relief. "Andrés, Andrés…. Oh."

It was only Don. "Where is he?" Carlos said.

"He left."

"*Qué?* What do you mean?"

"He's gone. Gone away."

"Where?"

"*No sé.* I don't know, Carlos."

"When?!"

Don averted his gaze. "This morning."

"Fool! I told you to keep him here. To lock him in if you had to!"

"I tried, *mijo*. Believe me. But you know Andrés. Here, he left this for you."

Carlos snatched the envelope from his uncle's trembling hand and tore it open. His eyes scanned the childish writing. "Oh no. No, no, no!"

"I'm sorry," Don said.

"Sorry? Do you know what this means?"

Don nodded, his already watery eyes tearing up.

Carlos glared at the old man but sighed. "Never mind." He dropped down to the dirt floor and leaned his head in his lap. "Get me a drink, will you?"

Don shuffled to the nook and returned with a *ponchita* of Cuervo from the new Jalisco shipment. Carlos gulped down enough to dull his senses. Thank God for the blue agave. A symbol of his people. Tough, sweet, of the land. *Salud!* He closed his eyes and felt Don cover him with a blanket.

The tequila worked its power, allowing him to float untroubled between one world and another. He felt himself nod off and didn't fight it. Deep, deeper. For a while he was at peace. But then, suddenly, he surfaced and was there again. Wandering, for years it seemed, through the smoldering ashes of burned-out houses. Again the antiseptic stink and anguished cries. Again the charred dead rats. Suddenly he was there, on that hellish street where it all began

16

S arah paced outside the courtroom, debating whether she would stay for the afternoon testimony. For the last two days, the witnesses had been peripheral figures in the scandal, uninteresting and tedious, reciting dates and times with nothing much to show for it and certainly not enough to take her mind off the fact that Carlos seemed to have disappeared. All those words about fate and needing to see her. Was it really just talk? Initially, she thought they'd simply crossed wires. But forty-eight hours later, reality was starting to creep in. Could it be that she had given herself too freely? Did the old adage "easy come, easy go" really apply to a woman of her age? She was angry, with Carlos for pretending to care and herself for caring that he didn't.

The crowd started to file in. No. She couldn't stomach it. Not today. Carlos gone. Nothing from Paige. She needed a distraction. She hailed a cab and directed the driver to the Grauman's Chinese Theater, which had just opened last year. She'd read a profile on its owner, Sid Grauman, in The Film Yearbook, a magazine she found in the hotel lobby. Grauman was far from Oriental. Indeed, he was a Jew from that faraway place of Indianapolis. The article said he came to California after accompanying his father to Alaska, where he was hoping to strike it rich in the Klondike Gold Rush. Looking for an easy way to make money no doubt, like someone else Sarah knew. The father didn't have any more luck than Sarah in that regard, but Sid earned a fortune in that wilderness as a performer. Eventually he moved to San Francisco and then Los Angeles, where he built the Million Dollar Theater in 1918 and then the Egyptian in '22. It didn't say how he came up with his exotic ideas, but he was obviously creative and resourceful. He even had to obtain permission from the U.S. government to import his Chinese building materials and artifacts, quite an accomplishment for a nice Jewish boy from Indiana.

Sarah kept hoping that her book would magically appear in one of countless taxis rides she had taken since losing the damn thing but all she found were tissues, cigarette butts and, as she just realized reaching for her handbag, chewed gum. Fortunately the sticky glob came off in one piece, and she tossed it out the window, onto a lonely strip of pavement on Hollywood Boulevard.

Lonely. That was a strange way to describe this bustling street of dreams. But it appeared that way now. Or perhaps Sarah was simply imposing her own feelings onto the space. A version of Freud's theory of projection, which she'd witnessed so often in her work. Especially with the couples she counseled. A husband blames his wife for being indifferent when it is actually he who has lost interest. The one advantage with an inanimate object, however, is that it can't protest. The pavement's lonely. The end.

They arrived at the theater in no time. Sarah scooted out of the cab and gazed up at the giant red pagoda with its prehistoric curved wings. There were carved dragons too, a huge hovering mother and smaller babies, two "Heaven Dog" sculptures, which a plaque said warded off evil spirits, and a gleaming copper roof. She strolled around a bit, examining the elaborate designs and of course the celebrity handprints that were becoming so famous. She'd read that they weren't part of Grauman's original plan. Norma Talmadge had been hanging around while some cement was being poured and inadvertently stepped into a still wet section. She was very apologetic but Grauman saw the potential. Since then many celebrities, including Mary Pickford, Douglas Fairbanks, Norma Shearer and Pola Negri, of all people, had left their mark. Sarah crouched down and placed her right hand into the outline of Negri's. Almost a perfect fit. She searched for some cheetah paws but to no avail.

What caught Sarah's attention more than any of it, however, was the movie listed on the marquis. "The Trail of '98." Sarah hadn't heard of it, but the name of the actress struck her: Dolores Del Rio. Carlos had mentioned Del Rio with pride, one of his culture's own. Sarah had never seen any of Del Rio's films but was pretty sure she had been in "What Price Glory" as well as "Resurrection," the one that made her a star. Del Rio was a sensual beauty, with black hair and dark eyes; hot-blooded, the critics said, a female Valentino. Despite her name, however, Sarah had never really thought of Del Rio as Mexican, probably because she was fair skinned. But then she hadn't ever really thought of Mexicans at all. Rita and Carlos, both gone but not soon forgotten, had changed all that, and now, discovering that she was in time for the matinee, she would view the woman from a more informed if tormented perspective.

She bought her ticket and a five-cent bag of popcorn from one of the outdoor vendors. Elaborately costumed ushers escorted her into the lobby, which was as dramatic as the exterior, with enormous red and gold pillars, murals of pastoral Chinese scenes, and huge, glittering chandeliers. A female mannequin of a Chinese goddess quietly stood watch in a corner. One of the ushers told Sarah that she could rub it for good luck, which she gladly did. She then pushed the black lacquered doors, which opened into the enormous auditorium filled with thousands of green leather seats, most of which were empty, another huge, spidery chandelier and glowing oriental lanterns. She took a center seat, midway down one of the red-carpeted aisles.

The "Prologue" was already in full swing. Grauman had invented these "shows before the show," live vaudevillian performances that were thematically linked to the movie. Sarah munched on a few kernels and inspected the props on stage, a mountain scene with a sign reading: *Gold, Thisaway*. A man dressed like a miner was running around in circles looking high and low for the precious metal, prompting a laugh here and there from the audience. Sarah didn't go in much for this sort of thing, but now she had an idea what the movie was about. Coincidental, given Grauman's background.

Fifteen minutes passed, then thirty. She wished she had a drink, and not just water, although with these fantastical sights, nightmares would surely have followed any booze. Finally the tiresome skit concluded. The lights dimmed, curtains drew back, revealing the vast, blank screen. And then, life! Marching music, not one of Sarah's favorites, introduced the main players: Del Rio, Ralph Forbes and Karl Dane. A star indeed, with top billing. Directed by Clarence Brown. Sarah settled back and read the caption as throngs of excited would-be passengers waited on a wind-swept shore: "On July 14th, 1897, a boat sailed into San Francisco Harbor to upset the world..."

17

"Western Union?"

"That's who you called."

"I'd like to send a message."

"Go on."

What's this woman's problem? Mitchell thought. At another time, he'd tell her where she could go all right. "Sarah. I've been trying to reach you. Stop. I convinced the old man to let me cover a week of the trial. Stop. I'll be there in four days. Stay where you are. Mitchell."

"Is that it?"

Mitchell thought. Love, Mitchell…?

"Sir?"

"Yes. That'll do."

"Where to?"

"Portsmouth Hotel, Los Angeles."

Mitchell hung up the phone with renewed confidence and purpose. He had finally found the angle that made Stephen's lip twitch, a habit that, even if he claimed otherwise, revealed his boss's interest. Mitchell discovered through a wire service report that one of the upcoming prosecution witnesses was an investor from Ohio. Not small time like Sarah, but a millionaire banker, a man of inherited wealth who had made a loan to the Julian Company and suffered such a huge loss that he was forced to sell his main home. As soon as Mitchell learned that the man would testify, he knew he had something. His boss would want the story not because the victim was an Ohioan per se, but because he was a rich Ohioan who had fallen prey to a get-even-richer scheme. Stephen would never admit it, but he took pleasure in the hardships of others, especially if they had money. Suddenly the Julian trial was not so irrelevant to Toledo after all. Indeed, after Mitchell made his pitch, Stephen wasted no time deciding: "What are you waiting for? Get going!" So tomorrow Mitchell would be boarding an afternoon train for Los Angeles.

That Sarah hadn't responded to his latest phone call made Stephen's change of heart all the more welcome. She was either purposefully ignoring him or had gotten herself in too deep with this woman's death. Either way, she needed him. She'd resist at first, of course, but he was used to that. Eventually, she'd come around. At least that's what he kept telling himself as he hurried home to pack.

18

A darkening, smudgy sky softened the transition from the imaginary to the real world. The air was cool. Sarah buttoned her sweater, took a last look at the now blindingly lit pagoda, and flagged a cab.

"See the movie?" the driver asked.

"Uh huh."

"How was it?"

"Entertaining," she said, in earnest. More than Sarah had initially thought it would be when the second caption read: "Gold!" Adventure tales usually bored her. That the plot did indeed involve the Klondike Gold Rush added a layer of interest, however, since Grauman must have experienced some of what was represented, especially the challenging physical environments which were quite realistically portrayed. But it was the story of human relationships that drew her in, particularly the love triangle between Del Rio, Forbes and Dane. Del Rio, simultaneously virginal and seductive, Forbes the poor, fair-haired lover, Dane, the rich lecher intent on conquest. Shakespearean almost in its unfolding, with Del Rio exchanging her innocence for a hot meal, Forbes succumbing to the siren call of wealth, and Dane getting everything he wanted, only to burn to death at the end. Entertaining to say the least.

As for Del Rio, Sarah forgot about her ethnicity almost immediately. Best laid plans and all that. And it wasn't just her complexion. Except for her dark hair and eyes, Del Rio bore none of the typical features of her race. Well, at least as Sarah had always thought of them. Like Rita's, that is, before the mask of death had blotted them out. Death, the great leveler, Sarah thought, recalling the blank sameness in the faces of the dead she had witnessed over the years. Del Rio's appearance was, however, perhaps why she had been embraced by American audiences, her delicate chin and straight nose suggesting a common heritage somewhere down the line. Carlos, who throughout the film Sarah kept associating with Dane, said it remained to be seen whether her popularity would survive the talkies, which everyone believed would soon supplant the current form. But for now, she was just foreign enough, exotic and familiar at the same time. And she was superb at playing the object of male desire, no doubt because she really was.

"What was the plot?" the driver asked.

"Plot? Oh, the usual. People wanting something for nothing," she said. "Gold in this case." Liquid gold in Sarah's. It really was the same story, she thought.

"Worth seeing?"

"Yes, I think so," she said as her hotel came into view.

"Here you go."

"One second," Sarah said, searching.

"What'ya looking for, ma'am?"

"A book."

"Huh?"

"*Oil!*"

"What? You batty?"

"A little, but never mind," she said, handing him a dollar. "Keep the change."

19

"Mr. Parsons, you were secretary of the Los Angeles Stock Exchange in nineteen twenty-six and nineteen twenty-seven?"

"Part of that time."

"Part of that time, yes. Now, Mr. Parsons, were you familiar with the records of the Los Angeles Stock Exchange in May, nineteen twenty-seven when the Julian stock was taken off the board?"

"Not particularly."

"Did you know what they consisted of?"

"Beg pardon?"

"Do you know what the records consisted of?"

"Why, certain record books that were made on the rostrum."

Sarah shook her head. Parsons sounded slightly incoherent. Stocky, with a fixed down-turned expression, he resembled a bulldog, although the breed would probably take offense at that comparison. Maybe that's why District Attorney Davis was treating him with kid gloves.

"Certain record books made of the transactions in Julian stock and other securities; is that correct?"

"Yes."

"These record books you speak about showed the name of the broker selling the stock and the certificate numbers did they not, and the date sold?"

"No."

"Well, you had some records of that, did you not?"

"The clearing house had some records regarding the number of certificates, yes."

At last, Sarah thought. An affirmative statement.

"That is what I am speaking about, the clearing house, Mr. Parsons, yes. Mr. Courtney has testified those records have been destroyed, here yesterday, and I call your attention—I mean you probably discussed it with him. When were they destroyed?"

"I don't know."

"Did you destroy them?"

"No."

"Did you authorize them to be destroyed?"

"No."

"Had nothing to do with the manner in which they were destroyed?"

"No."

Right, Sarah thought. She was tired, so tired of the lies. In this matter, and all the rest. But she was not going to let her mind wander. She had sworn that to herself this morning.

"Did you consult with the district attorney regarding the destroying of these records before they were destroyed?"

"No."

"Did you receive—did you or did you not receive a letter from the receivers asking that any and all records pertaining to Julian transactions be retained in order that certain civil litigation might be conducted?"

"No."

"Did not receive such a letter?"

"No."

"Have you now any records of the—do you know who it was that destroyed the records?"

No, Sarah mouthed, of course not.

"No."

"Do you know the manner in which they were destroyed?"

"No."

"Your official daily bulletins, transactions in Julian stock, you are familiar with the official bulletins?"

"Yes."

"Did you have anything to do with compiling the data contained in the official bulletins from the records of the Exchange?"

"No."

"Do you know whether they are correct or not?"

"No."

"Do you know who would know whether they would be correct, of the Los Angeles Stock Exchange?"

"The man in charge of the printing of the bulletin."

Sarah moaned, along with everyone else. Grauman should use this testimony in one of his Preludes, Sarah thought. Much funnier. She didn't know if she could take much more.

Judge Doran tapped lightly. "Order."

"Who was that man?"

"I think it was the Reeves Printing Company, but I am not sure about that."

"I didn't know a company was a man."

Sarah froze. That comment didn't come from the stand. It was spoken softly from someone right behind her. A familiar voice. She fought the impulse to turn around.

"So far as furnishing the data on which they print this information?"

"I don't know."

"You do not know the employee or the person with the responsibility of correctly setting up bulletins of the transactions?"

"No."

"And you were secretary of the Exchange during that period of time?"

"Yes."

"That is all."

Judge Doran looked to the prosecution. "Any questions?"

"Sarah."

Shit. Now she couldn't pretend. She craned her neck just enough to acknowledge his presence.

"I'm sorry, Sarah. I can explain," Carlos whispered.

"No need."

"Please."

"I'm trying to pay attention here."

"After court, then. Please."

She should agree. Act like it's no big deal. For Christ's sake, she was an adult. She turned and nodded.

"Thanks," Carlos mouthed, and leaned back in his chair.

Doran asked again. "Any questions?"

"I have one," said Mr. Swafield, a studious member of the prosecution she had not yet encountered.

"Mr. Parsons, do you know of a rule which has been adopted by the Los Angeles Stock Exchange requiring the destruction of clearing house records at the expiration of sixty days?"

"There is such a rule."

"You are familiar with that rule, are you?"

"Well, to the extent that I know there is such a rule; I am not in touch with it."

"Do you know when that rule was enacted?"

"No."

"Was there such a rule prior to May sixth, nineteen twenty-seven?"

"That I couldn't say."

"Don't you know that rule has been enacted since the so-called Julian crash?"

"No."

"You don't know that?"

"No."

"Do you know that it has not been enacted since that crash?"

"No."

"Were you secretary at that time?"

"What time?"

"May, nineteen twenty-seven."

"I think I was."

"Doesn't the secretary have charge of the compilation of the rules of the L.A. Stock Exchange?"

"Not necessarily, no."

"Who does?"

"The assistant secretary generally attends to all that matter."

"The assistant secretary is assistant to the secretary, is he not?"

"He is."

"Works under the supervision of the secretary?"

"Not necessarily."

"You have at the present time a book of printed rules of the L.A. Stock Exchange, which includes the rule which I have referred to about the destruction of records?"

"I couldn't say as to that."

"Does not the L. A. Stock Exchange have any authenticated record of its rules?"

"It has its by-laws, yes, sir."

"I am speaking of the rules."

"I believe it has its rules, yes, same thing."

"Are the by-laws and the rules identical?"

"Practically, as I understand it."

"You are not the secretary at the present time."

"No."

"That is all."

■■■

The crowd shuffled out, their tired steps voicing the same disgusted view. Parsons was either the most incompetent secretary in the history of the Exchange or, like those who profited from his actions, a bold-faced, unapologetic liar. Bets were heavy on the latter. Doesn't know the rules? Doesn't remember what he destroyed, had destroyed, when he was in office? Sarah could feel the growing collective fatigue, the cynicism and downright despair. They all were liars, all corrupt. Probably the attorneys too, maybe even the good judge himself.

Carlos took her arm. They walked silently until reaching an outdoor bench. He sat down and motioned for her to do the same.

"You must think me a cad."

"I don't think anything."

"*That*, I know isn't true."

"Well, let's put it this way, whatever I think doesn't matter. We're not children. Things happen."

"Yes, they do. And something did. Something urgent. I had to go out of town unexpectedly. I've been driving for hours," he said, running his hand through his matted hair. "I stopped by your hotel and left a note just in case you weren't here."

"Again, you don't owe me an explanation."

"I don't owe it to you, but I want you to believe that it couldn't be helped. I should have called but I was too distracted by the situation. I'm not free to talk about it other than to say it was related to my work."

Carlos sounded sincere. He held her gaze with bloodshot eyes. Still, it seemed a little strange, given his occupation. What could possibly be so urgent for a grocery store owner, and why so far away?

"I see by your expression that you're skeptical."

"Not really, and it doesn't matter anyway."

"It matters to me," he said, taking her hand.

Sarah started to pull away but he tightened his grasp. "Okay," he said. "I'm going to tell you something. But afterwards, you must promise not to ask me anymore about it."

"I don't even know what it is."

"Please."

Sarah felt a little alarmed but nodded.

"The truth is, I had to attend to some very important negotiations, involving rights for some of my employees. Rights. Workers' rights. *Comprendes?*" He raised his brows, waiting for a response.

Rights? Workers? Sarah thought of Sam, a union member he said. And *Oil!*. When she lost the book, the roughnecks were just beginning to organize, with Bunny increasingly on their side. Why was it the carpenters were working only eight hours? Paul had asked him. Because they were organized all over the country. One couldn't get a lot of good carpenters on any other terms. But the oil workers were poorly organized, so there was a two-shift arrangement, an "inhuman thing," he said. Since the chapter title was "Strike," Sarah assumed that was about to change. She herself had supported such efforts for workers in Toledo's glass industry, in all trades in fact where labor could be taken advantage of. A cause she believed in, and she understood the need for secrecy. She did indeed comprehend, wishing all of Spanish translated so easily. Suddenly Carlos' absence made a bit more sense. "I see," she said.

"I'll feel much better if you'd say you believe me."

"Why shouldn't I?"

"Does that mean that you do?"

She nodded. "Yes." She didn't say that she was also greatly relieved.

His face relaxed. "I'm glad. Very glad. *Amigos?*"

Somehow their fingers were now locked. His ring shone only dimly at this angle, a trace reminder of the past, long ago light from a distant star. "*Amigos,*" she said.

▪▪▪

Sarah knew where they would end up. That is, she knew it would be in bed. She hoped for a repeat performance at the Ambassador. But given where they had decided to go the next day, her hotel had made the most sense. And the truth was that the shabby room hadn't really mattered. In fact, although it made her a little uneasy to acknowledge, their lovemaking, if that's what it was, had been deeper, more intense, without the softening influences of all that luxury.

After that, anything seemed possible. Even Tijuana. They had gone out for dinner, ordered juicy, rare fillets and swigged another *ponchita* of tequila, the thick, smoky taste of which was growing on her. The restaurant was right in Pershing Square, an invitingly quiet place, with worn but comfortable private booths. The misunderstanding behind them, conversation soon flowed. Sarah filled Carlos in about the trial and her visit to Grauman's, the movie, Del Rio. Carlos told her about a new kind of orange, a hybrid that he wanted to start carrying in his stores. And then he said: "So tell me, I've been wondering, any progress with, uh, with the woman, I'm sorry, I can't recall her.... Oh yes, Rita. I've been so preoccupied I've been unable to look into it."

"No. Well, actually, sort of."

"What do you mean?"

"Nothing. I don't want to bother you."

"No, please, go ahead."

So she did, explaining that, according to an anonymous source, Phillip Bradford was in Tijuana, at the new Agua Caliente Resort. "I assume you've heard of it," she asked.

"Who hasn't?"

"Me."

"Well, all of L.A. has been waiting for it to open, especially Hollywood. I think Chaplin has already been there. No Volstead and all that. Anonymous source, you say? "You sure you didn't read that in a novel?"

"The source is real," she snapped. "But I promised."

"*Ay*, of course. Sorry. Must just be this town. So much fiction floating around."

She smiled. "It's okay. I admit it sounds a bit too mysterious."

"I admire your loyalty to whoever the person is," he said. "Shows you can be trusted."

He was thinking about the union matter, she knew. Sarah could keep a secret. "Yes, I can."

"The question is, can the source be trusted?"

She nodded, recalling Paige's limp. So much like Tillie's. "Yes. But it would have been crazy to go on my own. First I'd have had to find the man, and that might be the easy part, all in a foreign environment. Probably a goose chase, wilder than normal."

"You're smart. Not fit for a lady unaccompanied there."

"That's what I thought."

"Hmm."

"Hmm?"

"You said he rented a room for a month?"

"Supposedly."

"So he's likely still there."

"Uh huh."

"Well, there's one way to find out. And I could use a break."

"Meaning what?" she said, already knowing. It was exactly what she had considered, what she thought about asking Carlos before he disappeared.

"You were granted another week or so off, weren't you, Sarah?"

"Yes."

"And the trial, it will still be there when you get back."

She sighed. "Yes."

"Well then. You have nothing to lose."

"That's quite a statement, considering my luck at investing."

"We're not there to gamble, I mean at the casino."

"That's for sure." She thought for a moment, and then said: "I've never been out of the country, you know. I always thought the first time would be Paris."

"Fate has other plans."

"Maybe so."

"Look, Sarah, like everyone else, I naturally want to see this place. After all, it's in Mexico! But to explore it with you, to serve as your guide and, let's face it, bodyguard if need be, that would give me much satisfaction."

"And Rita. That's the reason, the only real reason, for going," Sarah said.

"Of course. That goes without saying. And I could be of great help in that regard." Carlos averted his eyes. "Forgive my enthusiasm for other things. It's just been so long since I've, I've felt that way."

"I'm flattered," Sarah said, understating the actual thrill that comment elicited.

"Well then?"

"Well then, okay, if you're sure."

He leaned in and gave her a soft peck. "I've never been surer of anything."

20

The brightness of the lobby at this early hour boded well for the travel day ahead. It was only 7 a.m. but Sarah could already feel the sun warming the empty room. She rang the front desk bell, with Carlos by her side.

"Will you be returning, Miss Kaufman?" The double-chinned, formal but usually pleasant clerk frowned.

"Yes, but I'm not sure of the exact date."

"Well, I can't hold a room based on that," he hissed.

"I understand," Sarah said, trying to ignore the spittle clinging to the corner of his mouth. "I'll just have to hope that one is available. What do I owe?"

He handed her the bill. "Oh, you have a couple of messages. "One from Mr. Carlos Martinez. That's you, ain't it?" he said, barely glancing at Carlos.

"Yes, I was here yesterday," Carlos said.

"I remember," he said, still frowning. The other, from Ohio again."

Sarah took the envelopes, unsealed the one from Carlos and read. She smiled. It was exactly as he said. But Mitchell. She still hadn't called him. She slipped his note in her handbag.

"Aren't you even going to look?" Carlos said.

"No. I know what it says."

"That's the way. Good girl."

She nodded, but good was not the word that came to Sarah's mind.

•••

In search of clues, facts, truth. That's what Sarah thought as they headed south, on a road she had never traveled. "The Road to Hell," locals called it, a moniker that should have concerned her but didn't. Last night, while Carlos left to pick up some clothes, she took a bath, packed her suitcase and waited. For Carlos, but also for signs of inner rebellion. A tightness in her chest, the beginnings of a headache, something that would serve as a warning. But her little voice was quiet, approving in its silence. Even her rings were still, her tortured fingers getting a much-needed break. She was nervous to be sure, but not conflicted. She needed to go for Rita, wanted to go for herself. She was on a mission, preordained perhaps.

Carlos handed her the map, not a book but the real thing, a tangle of lines, numbers and mostly Spanish names that traced the path from Los Angeles to Tijuana. 164, 205, 210. San Pedro, Corona, La Jolla. Parallel swirls denoted the Pacific Ocean, along which they were now driving. "You can follow our progress," he said.

She smiled, but fortunately he didn't need her to recite directions. Neither her brain nor stomach would permit it. She neatly folded the accordion-like document and placed it on the dashboard. "Thanks, I'd rather just take in the view."

They drove in silence for at least an hour, no mention of the previous night's passion or what it might mean. They could have been strangers, which they nearly were. Sarah stared at the vast sea, mesmerized by its deep, sapphire hue. With rivers and lakes as her usual reference point, she couldn't help but be awestruck by this seemingly endless body of water. In Ohio, she and Mitchell often picnicked near the banks of the Maumee. It was a pleasing setting, with lush trees and thick grasses picturesquely framing the steady flow that wound its way through the heart of Toledo. It was easy to see to the other side. Bridges could take you there in minutes. The scene was contained, reassuring. What she looked upon now had no visible limits. It was sublime, but a little disquieting.

She glanced at Carlos who appeared to have no such thoughts. He was concentrating on the Model Ts and As, and all manner of jalopies streaming passed on the narrow, curved highway. One false move and they'd be goners. Think about something else, she told herself. Think about Rita, which she did until the sound of a distant train roused them both.

"Be glad we're not taking that lumbering caboose," he said.

"I don't mind a slower pace."

"It's fine if you don't have to get anywhere. Speaking of that, I better get some gas or we won't either. There's a station up ahead."

He turned off the 210 and pulled into a small lot with a bold sign that read: *Lightning*. He drove up behind a maroon Chrysler Imperial idling at the one of the pumps. "You won't believe who owns this place," he said.

"Mother Nature?"

"Ha! More like Hades. Our dear old friend, C. C.

"What!"

"Uh, huh. His stations are scattered all around. One of his most lucrative ventures. Lewis was behind the idea."

"Jeez, you really want to give those crooks any more money?"

"Well, it's either that or walk the rest of the way."

A perky attendant peeked in the window. "Nice machine," he said. "Fill it up?"

"Please."

"*Lightning* is what exactly?" Sarah said.

Carlos turned, leaned in and kissed her, open mouthed, then licked her lips with his tongue. "That," he said.

Sarah felt the charge down to her toes. So they knew each other after all. She looked at him with what she knew were glassy eyes. "Powerful stuff," she said.

"Indeed."

"But seriously, what is it?"

"Ethyl," he said. Ethyl mixed with gasoline. Makes cars run faster. Faster and cleaner. Gets better mileage, too. Standard Oil manufactured the stuff, but Julian was the first to bring it out west. Pretty expensive process, though, so it makes everyone wonder how the company could afford it."

"Our investments helped, no doubt," Sarah said, feeling the tank guzzle the witches' brew.

They drove on, stopped at a little stand for sandwiches, and drove some more. Sarah dozed now and then. She was drifting off again when Carlos announced that they had reached San Diego. Sarah shook herself awake and took in a low, sleepy skyline, interrupted by the graceful, fourteen-story El Cortez Hotel that Carlos said was only a year old. "El Cortez," Carlos said. Named for a Spaniard, built in the Spanish tradition, designed by *gringos*. "Haven't been there yet either but I hear it is quite inviting. Gardens and fountains, very relaxing they say. El Cortez, San Diego, Coronado. Spanish is everywhere, Sarah. More than you've probably heard in a lifetime, eh?"

"Yes, but remember I'm from Toledo!"

Carlos grinned. "Ha, that's right. Toledo," he said, with the correct Spanish pronunciation.

"A lot of Jews lived in Toledo…Spain that is. And they co-existed there for quite a while with Christians and Muslims," Sarah said, suddenly remembering that little coincidence.

"Before they were expelled."

Sarah nodded. Right. One of any number of diasporas. Everywhere they went, kicked out. But as Sarah knew, Jews weren't without their own prejudices, even within their own kind. The swarthier Sephardics from Spain, Portugal and some parts of Asia were considered by many Ashkenazis—those, like Sarah, whose ancestors came from Western and Central Europe—to be second-class citizens; boorish and less intelligent. How could one legitimately argue against anti-Semitism if one harbored such views? She glanced at Carlos who had started to accelerate. The car in front of them was barely moving and he'd apparently had enough. She looked the other way. But wasn't her reaction to Mexicans, the one she'd been fighting since she arrived in Los Angeles, a version of such sentiment? Color. That was the thing, the common thread. Even some Negroes favored the lighter skinned among them. It made no sense. Herman Melville wrote in *Moby Dick*, which Sarah slogged her way through in school, that white could be evil. Indeed, it was the whiteness of the whale that appalled the crew. There was nothing inherently good or bad in one shade or another, she thought, touching Carlos' dark, strong arm.

He smiled and pointed to a large airfield. On a nearby billboard was a picture of The Spirit of St. Louis.

"Lindbergh's plane was constructed in this city, wasn't it?" Sarah said.

"Uh huh."

"I hear he's no friend of the Jews."

"Probably couldn't get any financing from them."

"I hope you're kidding," Sarah said.

"Ha-ha. Of course. Still, his flight to Paris was amazing."

"Yeah, I'll give him that."

"Aviation is big in this town. And the navy. A lot of history here. You might have heard about the Wobblies' protest downtown in nineteen twelve. The International Workers Union in quiet, little conservative San Diego. Nearly five thousand people showed up. Emma Goldman herself was there, and her lover, uh, Ben Reitman. *Your* people."

Sarah smirked. "Kidding again, I take it. My people, and your late wife's."

"What's that?"

"Your late wife, Jewish."

"Oh, right. I guess I shouldn't joke with you on this topic."

"Could I with you?"

"Depends where we were. If we were in bed, for instance, you could say anything you wanted."

Sarah smiled, but didn't let it drop. "No, really."

"Well, if I knew it was in good fun, yes. But Goldman and Reitman were anarchists, that's my objection to them. I've got my gripes with this country, and I'm obviously for unions, but I'm still a capitalist."

"I see."

"Hey, Sarah. Come on."

"No really, I do," she said. One could certainly dislike the activities of a particular Jew—Ted Rosen, for instance—without hating the whole damn race, which Carlos clearly did not. She was however, surprised that he brought up the topic of unions, given his admonition to not ask about his own involvement with them. Perhaps he was paving the way to tell her more. At the very least, the comment showed that the situation was on his mind. How could it not be?

Traffic slowed. Carlos lit a cigarette and leaned back. "Yes, quite a history, San Diego," he said as if to himself. "Cabrillo claiming the land for Spain, two decades under Mexican rule, the eighteen fifty-eight hurricane. History, that's the way it's usually told, Sarah, one thing after another, when really it's a jumble. Somebody puts events in order, makes sense of them, arbitrarily decides who and what are important."

"You're quite a thinker."

"When your story is not told, or told badly, or unfairly, you think, whether you want to or not."

"Indeed."

They picked up speed again. Carlos highlighted the city's offerings: the Point Loma Lighthouse, the Spreckles Theater—the first poured concrete theater west of the Mississippi, he said, built to commemorate the opening of the Panama Canal, and Balboa Park, site of the 1915 Pan American Exposition nearby. Did Sarah want to stop and see anything? There were some lovely sights. The buildings at the park were spectacular, the harbor, the first mission in California: "Basilica San Diego de Alcalá."

"In that order?" she said.

He turned to Sarah, keeping his left hand on the steering wheel. "Well done," he said, pushing back a strand of her hair. "We all have to choose, don't we? One thing in front of the other. No other way to communicate. No other way to live. Sanely, that is. So, you want to stop?"

"Some other time," she said. "Phillip Bradford is waiting. I have to choose, too."

■■■

Ocean and mountains. Palms and pine. Unexpected in their proximity, striking in their contrast. Sarah had witnessed them all in a single, five-hour journey. There were orange groves too along the way, fecund and ripe, waiting to flavor a cake, nourish a child, quench a thirst. And over a ridge, oil wells: grinding steel, blackening the earth, yet pumping to a kind of natural rhythm. For whatever reason, because of Carlos, or because the other Sarah was in control, even these mechanical monstrosities that had cost her so dearly seemed to belong in the landscape today. Function over form. Breathing energy into the world. Oranges and oil.

No, Sarah wasn't herself. Or perhaps she was more herself than ever. As they pressed on, ever closer to the border, she was being replaced, atom for atom, by her more adventurous twin. She sat upright, filled with determination and excitement as the checkpoint, a small wooden structure flanked by two billowing flags, the Stars and Stripes and its tri-colored counterpart, came into view. They stopped and waited for their turn. Name, reason for trip, a brief check of the car. All acceptable. They got the go-ahead and crossed with barely a nod from the guard. Crossed from the U.S. to Mexico over a boundary that was heavy with meaning but that the land itself didn't recognize. Before she knew it they were there, in less time than it took to drive from one side of the Maumee to the other. And there was no difference. If she straddled the line separating one country from the other, she'd kick up the same dirt.

No difference. Except, Sarah thought, except for those poor beggars with their tattered clothes and strange wares, pleading with *por favors*. And those crowded shanties on the hill, painted in bright colors but looking so miserable. No difference, except for this unpaved road, the foreign signs…. Why was her heart pounding? The window was open but there wasn't enough air. They passed an abandoned car and a hunched figure on a rickety cart and donkey.

"You okay, Sarah?"

"What's that?"

"You seem tense."

"No, no I'm fine," she said, lying. Tense. Yes, suddenly she was tense. Very tense. Dammit. The little voice, the other twin, making all sorts of noise when it was already too late. She twisted her rings madly. She had to fight, push it away. Breathe deeply. In and out. Temporary. It was only temporary. But just to play it safe she closed her eyes, as if they were heading directly into an oncoming car. And she kept them closed for what seemed like an eternity, but was really only six miles from the border. Kept them closed until she heard Carlos say: "Here we are: Agua Caliente."

21

inally. The conductor announced their arrival in Los Angeles. What with the engine trouble in Chicago and that screaming baby, Mitchell had actually considered turning back. He probably would have if the delay had gone on any longer. As it was, five days had passed since they'd pulled out of Toledo. The Ohio witness was due to testify tomorrow. Enough time to check into the hotel, shower, and take Sarah to bed. The last in particular.

He hailed a cab. Each night on the train, he'd fallen asleep envisioning his destination, or rather, hoping how his time there would unfold. In his mind's eye he painted a canvas; an abstract in the vibrant, primary colors he always associated with this part of the country. He wrote an award-winning article, took masterful photographs of the new city hall, the Santa Monica pier, the Hollywoodland sign. He shed layers of heavy clothes, felt the balmy air warm his pale, winter skin. And he saw Sarah too, smiling in one of her silky frocks, surprising him at the station. But imagining didn't make it so. Indeed, today L.A. looked muted and dull. The sky was grey. And Sarah was nowhere in sight.

Not at the station, and worse, not at the hotel. Not there at all. Checked out the clerk said. Checked out? "Yes, a few days ago. With a man, too. Mexican."

Mitchell thought he misheard. "What do mean, *with* a man?"

"Together," if you know what I mean. Came down the elevator arm in arm. Disgusting."

Mitchell shook his head, certain the clerk was mistaken.

"Dark hair, five foot six, brown eyes. Attractive, in a Jewish sort of way?" the clerk said.

Mitchell glared at the white trash that had just described Sarah to a tee, the backhanded compliment notwithstanding. Attractive in a Jewish sort of way. At another time, he wouldn't have let that pass. But he was too shocked. Together? Arm in arm? It didn't make sense, but he felt like he'd been hit in the gut.

"She left with him all right. But said she was coming back."

"Do you know where she…where they were going?"

"No, but it certainly wasn't in protest."

"I see." Mitchell took in a deep breath, steadying himself on the desk. "Could you tell me if she received my messages? From Toledo?"

"Oh yeah, she got 'em."

He sighed. "All right. Well, can I have my key, please?"

"I'll have the porter take your bags up."

"No. I'd prefer to do it, if you don't mind."

"Okay, here you go. Fellow's name was Carlos, by the way."

"Carlos. Carlos what?"

"Don't know. Garcia, Flores, one of those types."

You're a type too, Mitchell thought. But I don't have the energy to tell you what kind. Somehow he found his way to his room. He put down his bags and sat on the hard bed, staring into space. *That's* why she hadn't answered? She met someone? Incredible. Almost laughable. Sarah had so often told Mitchell that she couldn't imagine being with another man, that they were so lucky to have found each other at this stage in their lives. She declined his marriage offer not because she didn't love him, but because it just wasn't practical. But now he wondered. Maybe she just didn't feel it, had never felt it. He'd been through this kind of thing with other women. But never, he thought, with Sarah. She wasn't beautiful, wasn't young. It even took him awhile to fall for her. He'd idealized all the others, and always got burned. But Sarah grew on him. A real human being. Not a poem, not a painting. She breathed, got the flu, but could be trusted. What a damned fool he was.

He lied down and instantly fell asleep. When he awoke, it was dark. For a second he didn't know where he was, hoped he'd been dreaming. But reality soon came flooding in. He checked the clock: 8 p.m. He'd come all this way. For what? He didn't give a fuck about the trial. He needed to get out. He turned on the light and saw the room for the first time. Almost fit for a traveling salesman. Not that he cared much about such things. Sarah did, though. Or so he'd always thought. Who knew what the hell she felt about anything.

Mitchell showered and reached for his razor. His face was either rough or rougher. By the time he shaved one side, stubbles appeared on the other. He checked himself in the mirror. True to form. God, he was a hairy brute. Looked awful. Six foot two but stooped over like an old man. He straightened his back, which was aching from that miserable berth. His strong jaw looked weak, his nose bumpier and longer than usual. Perhaps it was the downcast expression.

He forced a smile but it only made matters worse. He dressed, combed his unruly grey curls, a few of which immediately sprouted back out, grabbed one of his cameras and headed for the lobby, which had filled with a raucous crowd. The clerk nodded as he walked silently past the front desk and out through the revolving glass door. It was a nod of pity, Mitchell thought, a nod to what was, for all intents and purposes, a cuckold. Coming from this idiot, it most probably was a bigoted gesture too, one in which ethnicity—Mexican, Jewish and maybe even Mitchell's own Polish heritage (his last name of Dobrinski could leave no room for doubt) made the situation all the more abhorrent to him.

It was, however, Carlos' Mexican identity that Mitchell himself was pondering as he lumbered aimlessly around Pershing Square, a grass park anchoring the growing downtown businesses. Pockets of fog made the already unseasonably cool air colder. He buttoned his thin cotton jacket, which did almost nothing to warm him up. Mexican, he thought, like that dead woman. There must be a connection. Sarah was poking around, asking questions, met this guy in the process. Perhaps he knew something. In which case, she wouldn't let it, or him, go until she discovered what. She was unrelenting in such things, obsessive even since Jacob. Mitchell perked up a bit, felt a sliver of hope. The idea of Sarah bargaining, trading information for sex, was too ridiculous to entertain. But she certainly wasn't beyond pushing the boundaries a little if the cause were just. He smirked, recalling the time she feigned interest in Toledo politician John O'Dwyer. O'Dwyer was unethical, but ultimately innocent of attempting to blackmail the judge, which Sarah's convincing performance helped to reveal. And she even came on to the great H. L. Mencken, in an effort to learn more about the murder of that professor. So why not again? There was a precedent. Indeed, she might very well have asked this Carlos fellow to her room for nobler purposes. A drink, conversation. Perhaps a little squeeze. But nothing more, and certainly not true affection. No doubt they were on the trail of some sort of evidence now, which was worrisome enough. That clerk clearly misinterpreted the nature of their relationship, incapable as he was of seeing beneath the surface of things.

Well, it was a possibility anyway, enough to give Mitchell the beginnings of an appetite. Through the fog, which seemed to be thickening by the minute, street lamps shone murkily, and he could just make out a flashing silver image of a fork and knife. He started in that direction, taking a path through the park. A few feet away stood a granite monument, covered in dew. He moved in closer, took his glasses from his pocket and read that the figure commemorated a California infantryman in the Spanish-American War. He had seen it on a former trip to L.A., but then it was sunny, and the warrior, who now regarded him with ghostly sorrow, looked benign, almost happy. Mitchell attached the flash to his camera, focused the lens and clicked.

Nearby was another sculpture, a life-size bronze of a doughboy, flanked by two old cannons. He took a few shots of it, as well as of an ornate three-tiered fountain surrounded by cherubs. These objects too appeared more somber in this atmosphere. And a little creepy, as if they might suddenly come to life. Mitchell shivered and picked up his pace. Ahead was the restaurant, a fish place, he realized, with a welcome glow and a sign announcing the daily special as New England clam chowder. He entered a small cheery space decorated in nautical style and was seated immediately.

The chowder was good, not too milky. He lit a cigarette, sat back and regarded the various customers. A mother and son at one table, a group of bluestockings at another, and behind them several young men, with that certain look. Ah yes. Pershing Square did have a reputation. Mitchell couldn't care less. Live and let live. For a brief spell he was the aloof urban spectator, or, in the language of one of his favorite poets, Baudelaire, the *flaneur*. But that didn't last. How could it with that couple in the corner? Staring into each other's eyes. So clichéd. A parody of romance. And yet Mitchell wanted what they had, wanted it desperately. The woman had dark hair, too. Wore it up like Sarah's. Caressing that man's homely face. Shit. Who was Mitchell kidding? Sarah was with that Carlos, in exactly the way the clerk described.

He threw his napkin on the table and asked for the check. He wasn't about to go back yet. All he would do is wallow in self-pity. So he walked. Walked and walked, ending up in a seedy part of town. And he was glad. Anyone could photograph tourist attractions. Here was some grit, something to sink his teeth into. He shot, one after another: broken windows, a mangy, maybe rabid, dog, a rotting orange. He walked on, feeling his creative juices flowing. There, next to that ramshackle flat was a church, a mission of some sort. The massive doors, open. Inside were the hungry, the down and out, the lost. On the roof, a chipped, white painted cross tilted to one side. Perfect. He stooped down and widened the aperture. It would be jake to play with that cross, superimpose it on....

"Hey, honey."

Mitchell gasped. The sultry voice was close. Very close, and belonging to those two shapely legs wrapped in beige silk. He ran his eyes up to the visible knees, to the hips, narrow waist, full chest, vanilla neck. A girl, streetwalker no doubt, smoking through a studded cigarette holder and smiling down at him with pouty red lips. "What ya doin, honey?"

Mitchell pushed himself up. "Taking photos."

"Wow, you're tall."

"Go on, get out of here," Mitchell said, shaking himself.

"Nice camera."

"Thanks. Now scram."

"You sure you don't want a little fun? Looks like you could use it."

Mitchell shook his head. It had been years since he'd gone that route, and then only a few times, when things were really black. The girl was petite and young. Soft blond curls fell on her dress. "Aren't you cold?" he said. "Why don't you go home? You shouldn't be doing this."

"We all gotta earn a living, buddy. If it's not you, it'll be someone else."

"Well, go find him then."

"Whatever you say." She started to leave, her peep-toe heels clicking on the pavement. An image of Sarah flashed in his head. With another man, giving herself over, enjoying it.

"Hey," he called out. "Wait a minute."

The girl stopped.

Why not, Mitchell thought. Why goddamn not. "What's your name?"

She turned slowly and smiled. "My real one?"

"Whichever."

"Ida."

Mitchell swallowed hard. "Know anywhere to get a drink, Ida?"

"Of course," she said. "Follow me."

22

arlos got word that Ernesto had relented. The operation was on. And there was even more pressing news. A lead. A very good lead on Andrés. Both demanded his immediate presence.

What was he going to do now? He finally had this nuisance of a woman where he wanted: occupied and out of the way. It had taken some work. She had grown uneasy at the border, so much so that Carlos feared she would change her mind. But she relaxed at the sight of Agua Caliente, where everything was shiny and new, with many reassuring *gringos* milling about. She had also been greatly relieved to learn that Mr. Bradford was in fact a guest. The faith in her source had been rewarded. The man rarely left his bungalow, the staff said, and gave strict orders not to be disturbed. But at least he was there.

The fact that Bradford demanded privacy was, Sarah said, understandable. He was in mourning, or perhaps in hiding, since she viewed him as a suspect in what she was certain was Rita's murder. Why she was so certain Carlos didn't know, but trying to dissuade her could only lead to trouble. She was a curious sort, and would surely press him to explain. Better to go along. At least here he could contain the threat.

Despite the challenge, Sarah was optimistic. Bradford had to go out occasionally, she said, otherwise he wouldn't have been recognized in the first place. But three days had passed and thus far no luck. She had crept around every bungalow, followed bellmen and waiters, pretended to lounge by the pool. She'd asked other guests whether they had seen a wizened American with a jagged scar. A friend of hers, she claimed. And she lingered at the gambling tables, scrutinizing each player, so much so that one of them accused her of trying to read his cards. Carlos was of course the perfect helpmate in this quest. He translated, offered sympathy and kept watch. More than that. He alleviated her frustration, provided a physical release. Repeatedly.

That part of the deal was in fact becoming slightly problematic. This nosey little Jewess, it turned out, was pretty good in bed, each time better than the last. She had loosened up considerably since their initial encounter, letting him know what she liked and giving back in spades. And he was enjoying it, more than he should. That article he'd read in Liberty magazine might have had something to it. Tijuana, it said, "nudges something quite profound in the American psyche, that crossing the border was like playing hooky from the world's greatest supervisor of morals—Uncle Sam." It indeed seemed to nudge something in Sarah's psyche, and the fact that she was a Jew made it all the more notable. *Mujeres Judías* had a reputation for being cold, frigid even. In the past few days, Sarah was anything but. She was no movie star to be sure. A few wrinkles, some lax skin here and there, a long nose, of course. Her hair, though, was thick like Carlos liked it, and her eyes were dark, with a depth that occasionally made him wonder if she knew all along that he was lying. Her body wasn't bad either for a woman her age. Trim but shapely, with nice round breasts. Probably because she was childless. Well-proportioned. But it wasn't just the physical thing. No, and that was the real danger. She was getting to him in other ways, making him begin to regret a little what he had done and what he might yet have to do.

The first hint of this, moreover, came not after sex, when he might have felt kindly to any *zorra* worth her price, but during the car ride down. Sarah had been a surprisingly pleasant passenger, meaning she was relatively quiet. Not a lot of idle chatter, which was good because it allowed Carlos to think about his next moves. Naturally she was intelligent, too. Whatever their faults, one couldn't accuse the Jews of a low IQ. So when she did talk, it was mostly thoughtful, challenging even, as when she offered that sharp little retort to his comment about history. He had smiled then, genuinely, appreciating her quickness and courage to take him on—a brief emotion that he had to speed up to drive away.

But the feeling resurfaced, and last night came to a head. After another fruitless search for the illusive Mr. Bradford, Carlos convinced Sarah to take a break. She needed to see more of Tijuana, he said, bring a few souvenirs back home. *Avenida Revolución*, the center of town, was just the place. There she could buy anything for a song: necklaces strung out of seashells, brightly colored *serapes*, little horses fashioned from the long arms of a Tule cactus. No elegance. This was down and dirty. She'd have to buck up, but that was part of the fun. Without hesitation, Sarah agreed. She was game, she said, willing and indeed enthusiastic. And Carlos found that attractive. The attitude, and suddenly, he realized, Sarah herself.

Just a street, six blocks or so, with narrow, jumbled alleyways and modest stores and stalls jutting off on each side. They ambled along with all the other tourists, sampling a *torta*, watching a cockfight, from which Sarah ultimately turned away, trying on *sombreros*. After a couple of hours they wound up at Caesar's, where they sat at the carved, mahogany bar. In contrast to most of the other local joints, Caesar's was a stylish place with beveled wall mirrors reflecting a happy crowd in various stages of inebriation. For Americans, this was becoming a mandatory stop, a nostalgic reminder of the time before Volstead. In the mirror Carlos could see the busy tables, the waiters delivering aromatic dishes, and more than anything, the open chinking of glasses. His eyes rested on a cheerful couple, glowing with obvious affection for one another. It took him a second to realize that it was actually he and Sarah whose image had drawn his attention. Indeed, it was his own smile he'd caught in the mirror and she who warmly returned it. He saw himself notice that her hair was a bit out of place, and that she was flushed from the mescal, a more potent and fiery version of tequila. He looked again as they sampled the lemony salad dressing that was becoming all the rage, the one that the restaurant's owner, Caesar Cardini invented. He watched them clap as the waiter tossed the lettuce right in front of them, a dramatic flair that complimented the deliciously biting flavor. And he witnessed their intimate toast, to finding Mr. Bradford, and to life itself. "*Salud!*" "*L'Chaim!*"

This had to stop, Carlos thought. He could not let sentiment of any kind interfere. There was far too much at stake. He had to remember that despite Sarah's good intentions, despite the fact that she was actually trying to find justice for one of his own, she posed a serious threat. A Jew was a Jew he repeated to himself, even after they'd had passionate sex again that night. "A Jew was a Jew," he said, though admittedly with weakened conviction.

He continued to visualize that phrase, though, as they sat down for lunch at the hotel dining room, the lavish space in which only weeks earlier he had wandered alone, the future at his feet. At that time, the hardwood floors were pristine, yet unmarred by human activity. But that was then. Today, grease, water and heels had already left their marks. And today Carlos needed to be clear-eyed, absolutely in charge of his emotions in handling the ensuing conversation. Transparency, honesty, concern for her well being. Sarah must believe that Carlos was the embodiment of all three. Supplying more details about the union should help, he thought. She was sympathetic to labor. It was risky, but he had no choice. She would need a good reason for his departure, not to mention her staying on without him, and he couldn't very well provide the one in which she herself was unwittingly involved.

Luis nodded to him from across the room as they were seated near a mural of a nude woman chasing two hunting dogs. Fortunately, Carlos had managed to enlist the young staff member as soon as they had arrived at the hotel. Of course, Luis didn't exactly know the truth either. Carlos had simply said that he preferred that Sarah not know his acquaintance with, and, of course, investment in, Agua Caliente. He was testing her, Carlos said, to see if it was Carlos or his money she was after.

Luis had smiled. "*Por supuesto*. Of course." But, with all due respect, *señor* Martinez, she's not your usual type, eh?"

Carlos nodded. "She has her talents."

"Ah, I see."

They both sniggered, and then Carlos said, handing Luis a few *pesos*: "Let the others in on it, too, okay, *amigo?*"

Luis had obliged. He'd acted as if Carlos was just another guest, and so did everyone else who otherwise would have greeted him with almost filial recognition. Carlos would need to be far more inventive, however, if he required Luis' services for more nefarious deeds. He hoped, sincerely hoped, that that would not be necessary.

23

Mitchell scribbled a description. *Balding, heavy-set. Tortoise shell glasses riding low on a ski-jump nose. Dark suit, checkered vest stretched to the breaking point. Combative, entitled.*

"Please state your name."

"Ronald Bishop."

"Address?"

"Address? That's some question, given this swindle has cost me one of my homes!"

"You do currently live somewhere, though, do you not?"

"Yes."

"Please just provide that address."

"Two ten Lamont. Waynesfield, Ohio."

"Thank you. Now, please tell the jury about how you got involved with the Julian Petroleum Company."

"I was conned into providing a loan."

"Why do you say conned?"

"I was told that everything was in very good shape and perfectly safe, and it was operating good, and it was on a wonderful foundation and all that—and that, obviously wasn't true."

"Objection. Hearsay, Your Honor."

Mitchell wrote again. *Edgy voice.*

"Overruled. Go on, Mr. Bishop."

"You had a vast sum of money in there, didn't you?"

"Objection. Leading your Honor."

"Sustained."

"How much did you loan them?"

"Fifty-thousand dollars. Fifty goddamn thousand dollars!"

Judge Doran raised his hand. "Watch your language," he said calmly, as if he were ordering a meal instead of admonishing a witness. He was just as Sarah described him.

"So you were getting pretty nervous over it when conditions didn't suit you?"

"Yes, sir."

"Didn't suit you at all?"

"Didn't suit me at all, because I didn't like those articles he was getting out in the paid press all the time."

"And you wanted a little bit closer information than you were getting."

"Yes. They would never let me in on the inside."

Poor fellow, Mitchell thought, actually feeling a little sorry for him. Anybody who would loan that much to such a shady character deserved some pity. Stephen would be pleased. *Ronald Bishop: A Cautionary Tale,* Mitchell wrote, then turned to a clean page in his notebook where he scribbled his own name. *Mitchell Dobrinksi.* Subtitle? *Lucky Bastard.* His head pounded, but he was indeed lucky to have escaped the evening with only a hangover. Not on the street. Not in some ditch where he thought he might end up after partying with such a questionable crowd. He'd made it back to the hotel on his own accord, too, his camera intact. Looped, after all these years. But he gave himself some slack. An anomaly. A moment of understandable weakness. There would be no more booze. As for the girl, however, that he didn't regret that a bit.

"And you had a friend, Mr. Rosen?"

Mitchell sat up. Rosen?

"It was the father."

"Yes, Ted's father. The father would visit my office because I got into the Julian business through that father."

"You were friends of the father?"

"Yes. Theodore Senior."

Mitchell was stunned. Rosen? That, Mitchell didn't expect. Certainly it was possible, given that Ted was from Ohio. But the father! Sarah would be shocked, if she still gave a damn.

"And with all that money in there, in the Julian Company, you wanted Mr. Rosen with you; that was what you wanted, wasn't it?"

"No, sir."

"And so as to get Mr. Ted Rosen in there you worked around through his father, I suppose?"

"What the hell are you talking about?"

The judge tapped his gavel. "Just answer the question."

"I don't know who got him in there."

"Well, he was in there for your benefit, wasn't he? You expected to get information out of him, didn't you?"

"Surely; well, I expected to get it from somebody."

"You expected to get information out of him because you put him in there, didn't you?"

"Objection! Badgering the witness, your Honor."

"Sustained."

"To your mind, then, why was Ted Rosen there?"

"I would always ask, 'What is Ted doing over there?' He would always tell me he was there for protecting me and all his friends."

"He was there protecting your interests, wasn't he?"

"Yes, supposed to be."

"Supposed to be?"

"Yes, sir."

"Therefore, you were instrumental in getting him in there?"

"No, I won't say that."

Mitchell rubbed his temples. In there, in there, in there. In where! This didn't help his head. He presumed the prosecutor was trying to link Bishop to Rosen to show that the Ohioan knew ahead of time about the stock manipulation. That would make the story even juicier. But he wished they'd get on with it. Mitchell needed a smoke. And coffee, lots of coffee. He checked the clock. 11:45. Soon.

"You won't say that?"

"No, because I never suggested him being in there."

"Well, you wanted somebody to look after your interests, didn't you?"

"No, no."

"Not at all?"

"No."

"Even with your fifty thousand dollars?"

"No sir; that was a surprise to me. That was a surprise when I learned he was in there."

The judge audibly sighed and motioned to the bailiff who then announced the noon break. He seemed to want to get *out* of there as much as Mitchell, who pushed toward the exit and was lighting a cigarette before most of the other spectators had even realized that court was recessed. Clear skies. No rain, no fog.

He smelled coffee, and followed the scent to a stand where he bought a large cup and a ham sandwich. He found a bench, and jotted down a few questions while his impressions were fresh, sipping, munching and puffing alternately.

Rosen. He wrote and circled the name. How well did Bishop know the father? What part, if any, did Senior have in the scheme? How many homes did Bishop possess? What was the value of the one he lost? Was our fellow Ohioan totally innocent, duped like all the rest, or did he enter knowingly into the conspiracy? Or did the truth lie somewhere in between?

He closed his notebook and tossed the remnants of lunch in the trash. Camera in hand, he scanned for shots. Granite, marble. Columns, steps, arches. Through the viewfinder he spotted a ragged figure with an easel and paints. Mitchell drew closer and observed the man's arthritic hands begin to fill in a sketch of the courthouse. Grey, white and dark blue. The brush strokes were heavy, as if reflecting the weight of the building's significance. It was a pretty good rendering, although the man did not look pleased with it. Indeed, his expression fell somewhere between solemnity and disgust. Mitchell understood that. Art, real art, wasn't easy. The best of it came from pain. Mitchell raised his camera to capture that truth, suspecting that these shots of Los Angeles would be some of his finest. He ambled past the courthouse, down Broadway toward Pershing Square and continued to shoot. A flock of dirty pigeons. A matron laboring toward the bus. On he walked, and before long found himself in the neighborhood where he'd ended up last night. In the light of day, it lacked the gloomy romance. Darkness had softened the scars, hidden the open wounds. Now, the unfiltered light sharpened bloodshot eyes, deepened the creases where makeup had caked.

He passed a whore who barely nodded, too bored, depressed or exhausted to conduct her trade. Beggars held out cups that stank of stale booze. Where had Ida taken him? He couldn't remember. He thought he recognized the dilapidated store front that led to the speakeasy. What was the password? Tease? Please? A long hall, winding steps. A laughing crowd. Jazz. Smoke. Dancing. One drink, and another. Not more than three, Mitchell was sure. Next, on to a much fancier place: The Rosslyn Hotel. Yeah, somehow they got there and were escorted down a marble tunnel to The Monterey Room, a dark, sultry bar in Spanish motif. Cactus and desert, and a sexy, raven-haired flamenco dancer painted on a wall. Mitchell's eyes were blurry then but he remembered now that he kept staring at the mural, associating the daring female image with that dead woman, and with Sarah. In a haze, he'd downed another drink and could have sworn he saw Douglas Fairbanks in a booth making time with a flapper. Then a hard bed, a warm body, the transfer of cash. A gin and tonic for the road. Gin and tonic. His favorite. He felt like one now. His throat was parched, his tongue, thick. He searched, seriously for a minute, and then stopped in his tracks. No! He shook himself. No. He turned and left.

There was still time. He headed back to the hotel. The clerk shook his head. Sarah was not there, had still not returned. Mitchell stood motionless in the lobby and thought. The phone booth was empty. It would be delicate. He didn't want to alarm the judge or, despite everything, get Sarah into trouble. In fact, as far as Mitchell knew, Obee wasn't aware that Mitchell had come to L.A. at all, and there was no immediate reason to tell him. But Mitchell needed to know.

Obee's secretary, Elaine, picked up. Yes, the judge was in his chambers. "You sound far away, Mr. Dobrinski," she said. On secret assignment, was Mitchell's response. Being a reporter had its advantages. Elaine transferred the call. "Mr. Dobrinksi calling, from parts unknown." Fortunately, Obee was due in court, so couldn't talk long. For the judge, however, that meant, in addition to the usual inquires and mild curiosity about Mitchell's location, a reference to Thorton Wilder being awarded the Pulitzer for "The Bridge at San Luis Rey," Mussolini banishing women's rights, and of course the Mud Hens lousy opening game.

As soon as there was a lull, Mitchell said, casually, as if as an after thought, "well, good talking to you, Obee. I know you have to go, but, oh, by the way, have you heard from Sarah?"

Sarah? Oh yes, he'd heard. Indeed. She was beaming, he said, sounded happier than he'd heard her in years. Seeing Rosen get grilled on the stand had been a tonic, he said. Some camaraderie too, you know, with all the others. Therapeutic. So much so, that Obee said he granted her request for another two weeks off. "Surely, you know that, Mitch," he said, before wishing him good luck with whatever story he was covering.

"Of course," Mitchell said. "Of course I do."

24

The rock patio was charming, ideal for a late lunch. Attached to the ornate dining room, it had a more casual ambiance and was fast becoming a favored place for people-watching, which, until yesterday, had been Sarah's continuous activity. There was the overdressed matron addicted to Panguingui, a card game that was similar to Rummy. Sarah had played it last night and nearly got hooked herself. At the next table was the young man with the white suit and ruby-studded cane. A character right out of *The Great Gatsby*. And further away, one of the many blonde bombshells who had been fluttering about since they'd arrived. Sarah observed them all eyeing each other with curiosity and envy. But with the sense of urgency gone, she released her gaze.

Instead, she browsed the surprisingly cosmopolitan menu. *French Field Salad. Whole Boned Rock Bass, Cold Lobster, Beef Tenderloin Slice en Cassolette, Potatoes Gratin*. Ah, and oh, yes. *Tortillas Enchiladas de Pavo estilo de la Casa, Colache de Calabaza, Frijoles Refritos*. She sounded out the Spanish to herself and then read the English: *Homemade Turkey Enchiladas with Mexican Squash and Fried Beans*. The only Mexican dish. Something for every taste bud. She leaned back and breathed. There was no rush. No rush at all. Carlos wouldn't be back for at least two days, maybe three. And she had finally located Bradford's bungalow. Now was the time to relax and mentally prepare.

Agua Caliente was certainly not a bad place to wait, if she didn't let herself think too much. The luxury and architecture made it easy to imagine she was in France, Greece or even the Italian Riviera, as if she really had any clue about those parts of the world either. But when they'd gone into the town the other day, she was disabused of any such flights of fancy. Here was Tijuana. Impoverished, seedy, dangerous. Dark and desperate. Prostitutes and food carts openly vying for business.

As they approached *Avenida Revolución*, the main street where misfortune and debauchery were concentrated, she could feel her heart start to race, as it had when they first crossed the border. Whoring was certainly not unique to Mexico. Nor was poverty or any other unlucky human circumstance. Toledo had its fair share of all of it. But here everything seemed worse, coupled as it was with the unfamiliarity of place, the strangeness of language, the difference in color. So again the fear rose. Again Sarah wanted to run. But again she didn't. And this time she kept her eyes open. Open to the squalor, but also to the smiles, the warmth, the appreciation, when she bought, for less than a cup of coffee, a few souvenirs. She opened her eyes and eventually the anxiety eased. And then she saw beauty too, in the finely woven sweaters, the carved dolls, the plaited hair of the female vendors, who, Carlos said, were far younger than their weary faces appeared. She listened to the strings of the strolling Mariachis. She devoured a Caesar salad. And she advanced from tequila to mescal, an achievement made possible by her growing tolerance for Mexican hooch and the urging of other Americans in the bars.

Carlos had reserved a lovely bungalow, with creeping vines and a bird's eye view of the recently christened golf course. A warm rain shower here and there, but otherwise the days had been clear and balmy. She thought of his strong arms, blushed at how often they'd made love, at how free she'd become with him. No expectations. No promises. But if this wasn't the real thing, she didn't know what was.

Nothing indicated this more to Sarah than when Carlos confided in her again about the Mexican workers' union. As he spoke, she listened, feeling privileged, and in some sense, not deserving. She had made progress but was still struggling with her attitude toward his people. So odd, so troubling, given her feelings for Carlos himself. It was entirely illogical. Certainly she had never responded with such wariness to Negroes, for whose equality in Toledo she had worked tirelessly. Still, she believed that she was winning this struggle, one Mexican, or Chicano, at a time.

It had been the end of another disappointing but beautiful day. Carlos pulled her close, as was becoming his habit. "I need to tell you something," he said. "I'm afraid what you might do, but I have no choice." In love with someone else, Sarah thought. Married! Instead he said that the Mexican workers in California were on the verge of attaining independence, of having a union all their own. But also, that there were powerful, opposing forces that would do anything to prevent it. The battle lines were drawn and things were heating up. What heating up meant exactly he still didn't say, but Carlos was needed to keep up the pressure and ensure the rights of labor. And he was needed now, not far from here, just over the border and inland. So he was asking, begging Sarah in fact, to stay at the hotel until he returned. She could take the train back if she wanted, of course, but he hoped she would wait. If she didn't spot Bradford while he was gone, he would redouble his efforts to help. "Please," he said. "It would mean the world to me."

Mean the world? How could she not, when he posed it that way? Despite the trial, about which she had begun to feel a little guilty, she hardly gave his request a second thought. It would be another challenge. Alone in Mexico. Alone, but so long as she didn't venture beyond the hotel, with all the comforts of home. And then some. So she agreed, and when she did, Carlos kissed her and presented her with a pretty little handkerchief, crocheted by his mother and once belonging to Rachel. It was one of the most meaningful gifts Sarah had ever received.

Phillip Bradford. That of course was the most important reason to stay at that point. She indeed had not located him and had begun to think she never would. She had looked everywhere and at everyone. She had even followed waiters with room trays, hoping to catch a glimpse as he signed a bill, or came out for a breath of fresh air. But that was futile. Guest rooms occupied only a small portion of the hotel proper. The rest were the bungalows that were peppered throughout the vast property. Could she really hope to be at the right place at the right time?

She wracked her brain and considered the old ploy that she'd read about in Agatha Christie, Conan Doyle, and maybe even Poe. When detectives wanted to secretly learn the identity of a hotel guest, they'd check the register when no one was looking. So Sarah lingered in the lobby, waiting for the right moment. But it never came, primarily because the register was always locked away, not conveniently lying about as writers often portrayed it. However, soon something happened that also could have come from a novel, but this time the idea worked. Worked so well that she wondered if some external force, some *deux ex machina*, had not been somehow involved.

She had been on her way to The Plunge, a crystal clear, opulent pool imbedded with cobalt blue tiles and framed by palms, umbrellas, and tables and chairs. She did not intend to swim and thus would have never dressed for the occasion had she not wanted to examine the crowd without appearing out of place. She had no bathing suit, so Carlos purchased one for her, a black-and-white striped, scooped-neck little number with a thigh-length skirt that in Ohio she could get arrested for wearing. Indeed, back there, more than six inches above the knee and a woman could be put in the slammer. But maybe that wasn't such a bad idea for someone Sarah's age. How could she have let Carlos convince her that this thing was flattering? It emphasized all the wrong parts: her long arms, small breasts, fleshy rear end. And the color and pattern intensified her pastiness. Her skin was a light olive, but much of it had not seen the sun in months. She checked the mirror, full length no less, and slipped on a terrycloth robe that she had no plans to take off.

Carlos had already left for California when Sarah finally made her way down the meandering path that led to the pool. It was very warm, perhaps enough to force Bradford out of hibernation. She was thinking about what she would say if that lucky event were to finally occur when she heard a woman yelling outside one of the bungalows. It was an American woman, and as Sarah grew closer, she could hear the ugliness of the words. "It's noon, and my room has not been cleaned! What are you people paid for anyway?!"

The poor maid to whom the remarks were addressed looked confused and apologetic, but clearly did not understand. The American didn't seem to care. She continued to chastise and demean the girl. Sarah nearly gagged. This was too close to home. That sense of superiority. Wasn't that part of what Sarah was fighting in herself? She was about to intervene when another maid who spoke English appeared with a notebook. "*Señora,*" the woman said calmly. "I am the housekeeping manager. Here is our list. Every day we check off the rooms that have been cleaned. See here? Williams. Bungalow fifteen. Yours has been checked."

"I don't care what the list says. You made a mistake. My room is filthy!"

"Okay, *Señora.* We're sorry. We'll fix it for you."

"You better. I'll be out of here in ten minutes." She turned, went inside and slammed her door.

Sarah shook her head and continued on, passing more palms, an unearthly flowering cactus, and the brick wishing well near the casino. She reached for a penny. Williams. Fifteen. Name and number. Hmm. What if? Indeed. What if? Not very noble, she thought. But it could be the answer. That old ends justifying the means thing. She tossed in the coin and flew back to her bungalow. Off came the robe and, happily, the bathing suit. She rumpled the sheets, wetted the towels, and scattered some crumbs of a sandwich she was planning to eat at the Plunge on the bathroom floor. She dressed, waited an hour, and then placed a call to housekeeping, demanding that the manager come to her room with information about the cleaning schedule.

The woman, whose nametag read Esperanza, arrived in no time. She must have thought she was in a nightmare, as Sarah repeated with slight variation the complaint she'd overheard earlier. As before, Esperanza, hefty and graying but with youthful dimples, displayed the list. There was a check by Martinez. Seventeen. Sarah leaned in her head. "May I see?" she said, taking the notebook from her. "Well, well. It does appear you're right," Sarah said.

Esperanza exhaled.

"But look at these sheets. And if you peek in the bathroom," Sarah said, "you'll see what I mean there, too. Perhaps the maid was just in too much of a hurry. If you wouldn't mind just straightening up in there a bit, I'll let it go."

Her mouth fell slightly open, but she quickly recovered. "Of course, *Señora.*"

As soon as Sarah heard the faucet run, she scanned the list, flitting from one page to another. No, no, no. The water stopped. Towels were being hung. And then. Eureka! There it was, on the last page: Bradford. Twenty-five. Check. She blinked, not quite believing her eyes. Bradford. Twenty-five.* An asterisk. Sarah dropped her gaze to the bottom of the sheet. *Día de por medio. Seis de la mañana.* "What the hell?"

"*Sí, señora?*"

"Oh, nothing. Actually, uh, that's fine," Sarah said. "I'm sorry I had to call you here. Thank you."

"What? Are you sure?"

"Yes, yes. Here," Sarah said, handing her a few pesos, more than she probably earned in a week. "For your trouble."

Her black eyes widened. Sarah liked her heavy brows. The thin, fashionable trend in the States had gotten out of control. Women were plucking their hairs to extinction. "*Gracias,*" she said, in a tone somewhere between a statement and a question. "*Muchas gracias.* If there is anything else I can do for you...."

"Well, uh, there is one thing. You know, I'm trying to learn Spanish, and, uh, I shouldn't have of course, but I was sort of absent-mindedly thumbing through your list here and, well, just wondering, what does this mean?"

Esperanza half-smiled. "That's private information, ma'am."

"I know," she said, staring at the woman. "Please. It is so very important."

There was a long silence, during which Esperanza looked Sarah up and down. "Every other day. Six a.m.," Esperanza finally said. "But you didn't hear it from me."

Sarah nodded and touched her shoulder. "Thank you."

Sarah watched her leave, made sure she was out of sight then headed directly to bungalow twenty-five. Not a particularly secluded setting. The blinds were drawn. She straightened herself and knocked on the door. No answer. She knocked again and waited. Nothing. She came and went the rest of the day but to no avail. So it would have to be then, the next scheduled room cleaning. The day after tomorrow. Six a.m. Up with the birds. Carlos might even be back. The opportunity she'd been waiting for.

"So what will you have, *señora?*"

"Sarah ran her eyes over the menu one last time. They fell on an item she had missed the first go around. Indeed, something for everyone. "I'll have the special," she said. "Chicken soup, with matzoth balls."

25

His mother would have knelt and thanked the Virgin Mary. Carlos just knocked wood, and even then only in his mind. But he was still grateful. Everything so far had gone according to plan. They had bought the salt, two tons of it in fifty-pound sacks, and not all from one seller. They'd spread the purchases around to avoid arousing suspicion. Then, they had carted the sacks to an abandoned barn—there were many of them in the valley—and stored them there, fortunately close to their destination. The next step, renting the four horse-driven water trucks, had been trickier. Such vehicles were not typically used to haul water around the valley anymore, as the irrigation canals were fairly effective. But now and then spots went dry, so some were kept to distribute extra water when needed. Still, they couldn't take chances. Each truck had to be rented individually, from proprietors who ideally didn't know each other. Tricky indeed. But not impossible. Ernesto had taken charge of the operation, delegating the task to four of his most trusted comrades. Good Ernesto. Once he decided, he had given it his all. If Carlos had anything to say about it, the man would be rewarded with a key position in the union.

After securing the trucks, it was relatively easy to fill them. Deming pumps were ubiquitous. All it required was a little manpower, of which they had no shortage. Carlos lit a cigarette and thought. Those trucks were really nothing more than huge, barrel-shaped wagons. Hoops of steel barely held the wooden staves together. Yet to him, they were a thing of beauty, of potential, of power. Especially now, because mixed with each truck's five hundred gallons of water were millions of tiny white crystals. Banal in themselves, delicious sprinkled on eggs. But a weapon in the right hands. So, it was not surprising that the boys had treated the stuff with such reverence. As if performing a baptism, they had cradled the bags and blessed them before dumping the precious contents into the water. Water, which currently was ten times saltier than the sea.

With all that accomplished, they had reached the final stage, releasing the mix into one of the minor canals that fed Rochester's newest orange grove. Situated deep in the Inland Empire, the crop was small in comparison to the rest of their many properties. But it was young and therefore vulnerable. By next week, those saplings would start to look puny. In a couple of months, they'd be done for. Carlos frowned. Nasty business, that part of it. He hated wrecking the soil, killing the delicate shoots. They didn't deserve it. But there was no other way. Appeals to fairness and reason had failed. The only saving grace was that nature would ultimately right itself. Unlike men, who often needed other men to force them to do the right thing.

And Rochester Farms was in particular need of such action. It was a lucrative enterprise. The owners had become rich on Mexican labor and aimed to compete with the biggest players in the citrus industry. Yet they were also among the most vehement in their opposition to the union, threatening their workers with permanent banishment and implying much worse. Some who worked there said they feared for their lives and even that of their families. Thus, despite paltry wages and miserable living conditions, most of them would have nothing to do with the union. Carlos understood their position. He also realized that this little act of subterfuge could backfire, that the innocent could be blamed. But he and the other top organizers hoped to avoid that by claiming responsibility themselves. Not as individuals. Rather, they would identify themselves generally as Friends of the CUOM, declaring their support of the union and willingness to disrupt business should Rochester Farms and its ilk continue its smear and intimidation campaign. Of course, Rochester would do everything in its power to discover their identities, enlist all the bullies in the Empire. But the fact that so many of the growers viewed Carlos in particular as an ally would, he hoped, keep them off the scent. For a while at least. Until the union was a done deal.

Carlos stood watch by the head of the trail. Probably not necessary, but it paid to be safe. He could hear the rattling of the barrels, the clip-clop of the horses. It shouldn't take long. He sat down on the dirt and lit another cigarette. He exhaled and followed the plume as it dispersed in the clear night air. A star appeared overhead. One became two. Another and another. The longer he gazed, the more emerged, as if the mere act of looking were creative in itself. There was the Big Dipper, or was it? He traced the dots of light but kept losing the image. The constellations, when he could locate them, were reassuring. Something permanent in this slippery world. As for the myths associated with them, that was another matter. All cultures, including his own, read their fates in the skies. Prophecies and personalities. Garbage. All he knew was that he was born November twenty-first. That supposedly made him a Scorpio, and everyone who believed in such things pitied him for it. Still, one couldn't help wondering. Wondering about everything, except what he was doing right now. Of this he had no doubts. *Yo soy yo y mis circunstancias*, as the Spanish philosopher Ortega y Gasset wrote. "I am myself and my circumstances." Carlos took a deep drag. In the face of a meaningless universe, one must acknowledge that truth and make the most of it.

"Carlos! *Ven aquí!*"

Carlos jumped up.

"Carlos!"

"*Qué pasa!*"

"*Ven aquí!* Come here!"

"*Qué?* What is it?," he said, sprinting toward Ernesto's voice and the ruckus that followed. He stopped in his tracks. "Jesus. Shit!" One of the lead wagon's wheels had come off, leaving the barrel dangerously listing and the other wagons nearly colliding with one another. Several of the boys were leaning on the thing, struggling to hold it up. "*Imbéciles!* Can't you do anything without me?" A lantern lit up their terrified faces. Sweat already dripped off of them even though it couldn't have been more than fifty degrees.

Carlos sighed. "It's all right. Not your fault. You just gave me a start," he said, looking at Ernesto. He ordered the men to stay put and not panic. "There's a wheel jack, right?"

"*Sí,*" Ernesto said.

"Good, then we're okay."

The wheel had rolled several yards. He and Ernesto lifted the rickety but heavy object and rested it near the wagon. They found the giant lug that had come loose and got to work. It could have been worse. After much grunting and heaving, they succeeded in getting the wheel back on with only a few splinters to show for it. They tightened the lug extra hard and checked all the others.

"Done," Carlos said.

The boys clapped. One of them pulled out a *ponchita* and started to pass it around. Carlos grabbed it out of his hands. "Not now! We've gotta stay sharp. Get going!"

The horses snorted and neighed as if in agreement. Carlos watched the wagons continue down the path toward the canal and returned to his watch. His heart was pounding. He felt his wrist until his pulse slowed and then sat down crossed-legged and gazed back up at the sky. The Big Dipper, still there, clearly now, and the Little one, too. The same stars were shining over Agua Caliente, where Sarah was hopefully not getting into any trouble. She had agreed to stay, willingly. So far so good.

Soon there were noises. But the sound was coming toward him this time. Carlos got on his feet. His pulse quickened again as he went to meet the wagons. Ah. He could hear the shift, the lightness of their steps. Success. He and Ernesto embraced. Then they all stood silently for a moment, some in actual prayer. Like the gates of heaven, the valves had opened, Ernesto said, and the trucks had emptied in a matter of minutes. The equivalent of fifteen thousand gallons of seawater, flowing into the channel.

It was not yet dawn. Carlos returned the *ponchita* to its owner.

"*Ahora?*" the man asked.

"*Sí, ahora.* Now we can toast."

"To, to…to the rule of capture," Ernesto said, beaming at Carlos.

Carlos smiled and nodded. He was right about Ernesto.

They shared one celebratory swig before scattering. By mid morning, the boys would be in the fields, the trucks and horses back at their farms. Everyone and everything back in place. As for Carlos, he would be at a ranchero in Calexico, where Andrés was supposedly holed up. He was driving there now. "Please," he said to no one, "let it be so." The road was empty, a sliver of sun in the East. His tires crunched on the gravel road. He stopped the car, got out and pissed. *Yo soy yo y mis circunstancias.* Make the most of it. Yes, he had lived by that code. The problem was, he had taught Andrés to do the same.

26

itchell's usually iron stomach churned. What was the world coming to? Theft he could forgive, arson he could understand. Even murder in some instances could be explained. But the harming of children was a different animal. No way to account for it. No category to put it into. He straightened the paper and reread the lines.

> *A reported sighting of nine year-old Walter Collins, who disappeared from his Mt. Washington area home in March, occurred Tuesday afternoon at a Glendale gas station. The station owner said he saw the boy in the back seat of a car, wrapped in newspaper with only his head showing. He described the man driving the car as 'foreign-looking.' With the memory of the December kidnapping and dismemberment of twelve year-old Marion Parker still fresh, the LAPD is putting all of its resources into this investigation.*

Fortunately, they'd caught the Parker killer, William Hickman. Called himself "The Fox." Everyone else called him a monster and breathed a sigh of relief when he was sentenced to death. But then, only months later, the Collins boy. In the same city. Was there something in the water here? Did the place itself, with all of its pretense and shattered dreams, inspire such insanity? One was tempted to believe so, if for no other reason than to have something to blame. Mitchell flipped the page.

> *The body of twenty-five-year-old, Sabrina Johnson, an aspiring movie actress, was found early yesterday morning on an empty lot on Pomeroy Street. The woman's roommate said that Miss Johnson failed to come home after auditioning for a movie. Officer Hodges of the LAPD stated that foul play might have been involved, but provided no details.*

Tragic, Mitchell thought, but at least more typical. He folded the paper under his arm and returned to the courtroom where his fellow Ohioan was back on the stand.

"Mr. Bishop, you said that you were surprised to discover that someone on the inside was looking after your interests, even though you invested fifty-thousand dollars."

"That's right."

The prosecutor smiled. "That strains credulity, sir."

"Objection!"

"Sustained."

"Okay. Well how did you expect to get information out of Ted Rosen unless he got some information on the inside? You knew he would get it for you, didn't you?"

"I didn't have to have the inside information."

"You wanted it, didn't you?"

"I did afterwards, while he was in there, yes."

"You didn't want it before, while you were nervous about your loan?"

"That was not before. I was not nervous about the money at all until just about the time the bank got in. I was never nervous before that time."

Well, you should have been, Mitchell thought. Just as everyone else should have, including Sarah. He surveyed the packed room again, hoping once more that he'd turn and she'd be there. A number of women nearly fit Sarah's description, but something was always a little off. Curls where there should have been waves, lines where there should have been curves, taller, fuller, thinner. This goddamn city. Yeah. It was L.A.'s fault for that, too.

"That was about September, nineteen twenty-six?"

"Somewhere around August or September, yes sir."

"You felt then, at that time, that there was considerable stock circulating around, didn't you?"

"No, it was not that so much as it was that they—I would try and ascertain why there was this much stock and they would always tell me the brokers were selling short, they can't deliver."

"You saw that that was delivered, didn't you?"

"I didn't know. I never watched it."

"You knew when the market was operating that somebody was delivering, didn't you?"

"I never watched it! I'm telling you, you're trying to make me admit something. I'm a victim. I'm a victim!" Bishop yanked at his tie. His face was crimson.

The prosecutor leaned toward him. "Calm down, sir."

"Don't tell me to calm down! God, it's hot in here. I can't breathe, I can't breathe!" He clutched his chest and doubled over.

Judge Doran stood and pointed at the bailiff. "Empty the courtroom and get the medic."

A flurry of activity followed. In minutes reporters were swarming and the crowd was hustled outside. Everyone waited. In about a half hour, the bailiff came out and said that Mr. Bishop would be okay. However, his testimony would not resume until the following Tuesday. He was suffering from nervous exhaustion and needed a few days to recuperate. In the meantime, the trial would proceed tomorrow, Wednesday, with other witnesses.

Immediately opinions flew. "I told you he was strange. "The guy's faking!" "Got something to hide." "Guilty as sin."

Mitchell wasn't sure what to make of the breakdown. It seemed real enough, but who knew? In any case, it would be a juicy addition to his story. Moreover, after hearing of the incident, Stephen would no doubt demand that he stay in Los Angeles until Bishop recovered. And that was fortunate, because Mitchell had decided not to leave without knowing for sure anyway. About where he stood with Sarah, but first, whether she was safe. Sarah's need to discover the truth about that woman's death was one thing. But mixed with a new romance and perhaps more than a little booze, well, anything was possible. Kidnappings, mutilations, bodies in empty lots. Of course, everyone was vulnerable when it came to love, and though it vexed him to think so, she may very well be under its spell. Even so, her silence was entirely out of character. Even if she'd eloped, Mitchell would have expected some word. No, he couldn't just lick his wounds and go home. He needed time to find out, and Mr. Bishop unwittingly had obliged.

Sarah had been to the cops. Mitchell would go there too, see if they'd heard from her again. He'd push the hotel clerk for more details. A comment she may have made, anything else he could recall about the man she left with. Mitchell was a reporter for Christ's sake. He shouldn't take no for an answer. In the end, if he humiliated himself, so be it. He'd regret it more if something happened and his pride had prevented him from discovering just what in the goddamn hell it was.

27

The white, gauzy trousers were not a smart choice. Dirt was already clinging to the wide cuff, and the thin fabric offered scant protection from the chilly air. Sarah shivered, but didn't budge from her hiding place behind a squat palm with an unusually wide trunk. It was 6 a.m., and the maid was due any minute.

It was a miracle she was here at all, given the kind of night she'd had. No sleep. No sleep at all. Naturally, she was nervous. So much depended on the success of her plan. Mr. Bradford would be taken off guard. He'd be shocked, angry, slam the door in her face. Sarah had rehearsed the possibilities. But she was determined. She would learn the truth about Rita, or at least come away with a piece of the puzzle. Yet, as nerve-wracking as the prospect of this moment was, it wasn't the cause of the insomnia or the torment that accompanied it. It should have been, but it wasn't. She wondered even now if she'd heard right, if the whole incident wasn't some alcohol induced illusion. But no. Esperanza confirmed it. Confirmed that Sarah had been duped and deceived, a victim of her own stupidity again. And maybe even worse. A pawn perhaps, in some scheme that would make the Julian debacle pale in comparison.

The evening, which now seemed so very long ago, had begun on a high note. Carlos had sent a message: *All is well. Be back tomorrow afternoon. Love, Carlos.* She had read and reread the words, unable to prevent a smile. He was on his way. In good spirits, mission accomplished, it would seem. Love. Love, Carlos. He didn't have to say that. She immediately caught herself. Hanging on a salutation so common as to be meaningless. But just as quickly she turned back, back to the word. Love. The use was not declarative, but it was a statement. Love Carlos. Yes, she thought she might.

Given her morning task, she had planned to turn in early. But suddenly she wasn't tired. And with only soup for lunch, she was ravenous, in the mood for a good meal. She slipped into her midnight blue frock, added some pearls and long, white gloves. There was color in her cheeks and not from powder or the sun. Her heels, the same plain pair she had purchased in L.A., clicked on the moonlit path. She listened to the cheerful sound. The sound of a woman walking toward the future, alive with anticipation. She stopped for a moment and thought, with sadness and a twinge of guilt, of those other shoes, yet in her possession, stilled on the courtroom steps. "Tomorrow," she said into the fragrant night air.

The dining room was nearly full, the lightning sunburst chandeliers illuminating the domed, muraled ceilings. Tables encircled the glossy parquet floor where, although it was still early and the band subdued, a few decked out couples were dancing. Later, if the past few nights were an example, the floor would swell to capacity and vibrate with a primal, marimba beat.

"Table, *señorita?*"

The heavy, tuxedoed maitre d' extended his gloved hand.

Sarah smiled. "*Sí, gracias.*"

"*Muy bien,*" he said, twisting his thick, handlebar mustache. "Someone so lovely should not be unescorted," he said. "Where is your…your friend?"

Referring to her as *señorita* was enough. He was overdoing the flattery. And there was something she didn't like about his tone when he asked about Carlos. "Is it against the law for a woman to dine on her own?"

"Nothing is against the law here, my dear. This way," he said, leading her toward a single table wedged in between two larger parties. She followed, returning a few nods as she passed.

As he pulled out her chair, Sarah turned and said: "I'm sorry. I don't know why I barked at you. Mr. Martinez will be back tomorrow."

"Ah. No need to apologize. Perhaps you would like a drink."

"Yes, that would be lovely. Tequila…. No make it whiskey. A double."

He bowed and left.

Sarah dropped her shoulders and exhaled. It was natural that she should be a little on edge. The drink would help. She divided her gaze between the food being served at the next table and the dancers, who, she just realized by their matching outfits, were here to entertain. She watched as the men twirled their partners in sync, not a step out of place. They started another maneuver, but the aromas drew her attention back to the table and ultimately to the elegant menu, which, with the exception of a photograph of the hotel entrance, bore no hint whatsoever of its Mexican location.

Table d'Hote Dinner. $2.50. That was all she could see without her glasses. Dammit. She'd switched handbags. She held the menu at a distance and squinted. *Jam? Crumb?*

"May I help?"

Sarah looked up. It was one of the waiters, a short, wisp of a man with round cheeks and a toothy smile. Now that's service, she thought. "Yes, please."

He read with impeccable pronunciation and took her order as she chose from the options:

"Japanese Crab Flake Cocktail or Supreme of Grapefruit *au Duboneet.*"

"Crab."

"Lamb *Veloute Leishman* or Essence of Clams *en Tasse.*"

"Lamb."

"Stuffed Fresh Lobster, Live Soft Shell Crabs, or Steak."

"Steak."

"And, madam," he said, that comes with Potatoes *Demi* French, Braised Swiss Chard with Marrow, Salad *Caprice.*"

"Fine."

"And Biscuit *Glacee Tortoni,* fancy wafers for dessert."

"That will be fine. Thank you."

Sarah turned back to the dancers but felt the waiter still hovering over her. She grinned. "Don't tell me there's more?"

"No," he said, his tone suddenly serious. He glanced around, furtively, she thought, and then leaned in and whispered. "Don't trust him."

She twisted her head. "Excuse me?"

"*Señor* Martinez."

"Carlos? What do you mean?"

He leaned in closer. "You're not the first woman he's brought here."

Sarah sat silently for a moment, trying to make sense of the comment. "What's that...?"

Just then, the maitre d' swooped in with her drink, nearly tipping it over as he abruptly set it down. He glared at the waiter. "Raul, *qué pasa?* What are you doing here? This isn't your station."

The little fellow laughed nervously. "Of course. I was helping the *señorita* with the menu and forgot myself."

"Give me the order, and get back to your customers. I'll hand it over to Nico."

The waiter, Raul, did as he was told. "Very sorry," he said to Sarah, and quickly disappeared.

"Now it is my turn to apologize," the maitre d' said. These waiters were trained to never make such mistakes. I hope he wasn't…wasn't bothering you."

Sarah forced a smile. "Not at all."

"You're very generous. *Gracias*, madam. Enjoy your drink."

He bowed again, leaving Sarah to her own darkening confusion. She sat for several minutes unseeingly, sipping, then gulping down the whiskey. Not to be trusted? Here? Here, in this hotel, where he said he'd never been? With another woman! More than one, Raul seem to suggest. She couldn't take it all in. One question only led to another. My God. She tried to stay calm.

She shook herself and started to get up, but her legs wouldn't hold. She nearly fell but managed to bolster herself on the chair.

"Oh dear. You all right, honey?"

The gentle voice belonged to a buxom American seated directly behind her.

"Yes, thank you," she said limply.

"Come on, now," the woman said, "sit down."

Sarah obeyed and turned to see a genuinely concerned, maternal face. She swallowed the lump in her throat. "A little too much to drink."

The woman craned her neck, surveyed Sarah's table and then touched her shoulder. "Not good on an empty stomach."

Sarah was silent.

"Oh, now, forgive me. I'm always butting in."

"No, no," Sarah said. "I'm sorry. You're right. My food is on the way."

"Are you alone? Would you like to join us?"

"Yes, do!" someone chimed in. "Join us!"

Sarah smiled gratefully at the fellow and at the other several pairs of friendly eyes. Feeling her own well up, she thanked them for the offer but declined. "I'm waiting for someone," she said.

"Okay, but we're here if you change your mind."

Sarah nodded, turned back and wiped her tears. What nice people, she thought. Normal people. Happy people. The brief exchange with them reminded her of home, of family and friends. Tillie and Harry. Obee. Mitchell. More tears. A sea of them if she allowed it. But she couldn't. Not yet. She wiped her eyes again and tried to focus.

The crab cocktail arrived. Just minutes before she would have devoured it.

Now the sight of that poor creature's delicate flesh turned her stomach. But she squeezed some lemon on it, picked her way through and took a few bites of the courses that followed. Objectively, she could tell that the food was good; her taste buds were working but the signal to the brain had shorted out. She lay down her napkin and carefully stood. Yes, the energy had helped. She straightened her back and wended her way through the tables in the direction that Raul had headed. Lamb was being carved, booze was flowing, and everywhere people laughed. Others were dancing now, the warmth from their bodies literally heating the place up.

She leaned on a vacant chair and searched for the waiter. After a few minutes, she spotted him exiting the kitchen with a tray full of drinks. She watched as he delivered the order and then called out: "Raul!"

He turned. His eyes widened and he shook his head "Not now," he mouthed. But she fixed her gaze on him and didn't budge. He looked all about, put down the tray on a counter and motioned to the patio. In seconds, they were face to face in the cool air. "Do you know where the barber shop is?" he said, breathing fast.

"No."

"To the left and down the hall from the lobby. Meet me there at eleven thirty."

"Why there?"

"I'm filling in for the janitor. We can talk privately."

"Can't you just tell me..."

"No, later," he said, and dashed off.

Sarah squinted at her watch. 9 p.m. She sighed, perhaps the deepest sigh she had ever drawn, and returned to her table, where the glace was melting. She spooned up a little of the rich, eggy vanilla. She still couldn't taste anything, but the texture was soothing.

"Feeling better?"

Sarah turned again. "Yes," she said.

The woman leaned in. "Your make-up is a little smeared, my dear. Here, let me get it." She took out a handkerchief and patted underneath Sarah's eyes. "There."

Sarah smiled. "You are so kind. Thank you."

"Don't mention it. I'm Marge, by the way."

"Sarah."

Sarah thought for a moment. "Is the offer still on? My friend was held up. I have a little time to kill."

"Absolutely! Make room everyone!"

Thus, Sarah spent the next two hours in blessedly lively company. Twelve long-time friends from Connecticut, all in the manufacturing business, all boating enthusiasts, despite the loss of a beloved comrade on the Titanic. Wealthy, white, Protestant. *Goyim*, her sister would say. But they were in no way as reserved or prissy as that term suggested. Just the opposite, in fact, warm and somewhat bawdy. Sarah gave them only the barest of details about her stay, although she did tell them about her Julian investment, for which they were both admiring and sympathetic. Basically, they kept her distracted, which is exactly what she'd hoped when she decided to tag along. Anything to stop her from thinking. They joked. They drank. They coaxed her into the casino where, amidst the glittering high rollers and chips worth thousands, she won ten dollars playing Panguingui. And they even persuaded her to join them in a group rumba.

When the time came to leave, she was, if not in better spirits, at least worn out enough to take the edge off the pain. She hugged Marge. "I can't tell you how much I needed this," she said.

"I'm glad."

They wished each other well and exchanged addresses, even though Sarah knew she would never see her or any of the rest of them again.

•••

Sarah peered through the locked, beveled glass door. Raul was there, sweeping, a lone figure amidst the opulent leather chairs and porcelain sinks. She tapped lightly. He leaned his broom against the wall and let her in. "Back here," he said, leading her through a tiled archway to a narrow supply room where combs and scissors soaking in disinfectant lined white metal shelves. It was an odd, slightly macabre setting for a talk of this nature, the antiseptic smell reminiscent of a doctor's office.

"Okay, now please," Sarah said, actually feeling a little like a patient, one who already knew the news was bad but was waiting for the official diagnosis.

And so Raul began, repeating his original claim that Carlos was not a stranger to the hotel, but indeed had stayed there often before its opening, each time with a different woman. Moreover, he told Sarah that Carlos had even invested a little in the place, anticipating her question of how he had gotten early access.

Raul, in fact, anticipated nearly all of her questions. How did Raul know all this? Everyone knew, he said. Carlos was friendly—and generous—with the staff. They returned the favor by agreeing to his request, whispered from one employee to another, that they pretend not to recognize him. Had Carlos ever asked this of them before? Not that Raul was aware of, but of course the hotel hadn't been open very long, and they just assumed that he had his reasons. Why then did Raul tell Sarah?

Here Raul stopped. His round features sharpened. "Because," he said, "because one of the women Carlos brought here was my nineteen year-old sister."

Sarah stifled a gasp. Her hands were moist, too slippery for her rings to do any good. "Your sister," she just said.

"A child really."

"I hope, I mean, not against her will?"

"No. Not against her will, but he took advantage of her innocence."

Sarah felt briefly relieved. Everything was relative. "I see."

"But I didn't just tell you to get even. Believe it or not, I also felt sorry for you. You seem like a nice person, older, different from the others. I thought you had a right to know, and I have to admit, I feel a weight off my shoulders."

Sarah felt numb, but somehow she was talking. "What happens to you if I confront Carlos?"

"If? I assumed you would."

Sarah didn't respond. She didn't know what she would do.

"Even if you don't," Raul said, "I'm probably done for. Pedro, the maitre d', suspects something. You saw him. He and Carlos are tight. *Amigos,* you know?"

Sarah nodded.

"I knew the risk. I like it here, but I can get other work."

"You're brave. I appreciate it."

They both stood silently for a few moments.

"Well, you should go. I do have to close up," Raul finally said, escorting her back into the shop. "I'm not fired yet. Will you be all right?"

"Yeah," she said, not at all certain that she would be. She shuffled toward the exit. The Moroccan look of the tiles reminded her of that night at The

Coconut Grove, and that of The Brown Derby, and that of all the rest. She held on to the doorknob and braced herself. "By the way," she said, her back to Raul, "do you know anything about, about Carlos' wife?"

"Wife?" he said, with a short laugh. "Which one?"

■■■

Before anything else, Sarah needed confirmation, and so at that late hour, exhausted and near the end of her rope, she somehow found her way to the employee housing and pleaded with the night watchman to wake Esperanza. Sarah was her friend, she said, and it was important. A matter of life and death, her shrill voice must have implied, for the man quickly obliged.

In a few minutes, Esperanza appeared in her robe and curlers. "*Sí, señora?*" she said, yawning and squinting. At the mention of Carlos, however, her eyes sprang open. She stiffened and raised her hands as Sarah started to explain. "No," she said, "no, no."

"No, what?" Sarah said.

"I can't talk to you about that," she said, and started to leave.

"Okay, then don't talk."

"What?" Esperanza said, slowing but still facing away.

"Please," Sarah said, "you're the only person I can trust. As one woman to another, if what I asked you is true, just look at me. I promise, no one will ever know. No one," she repeated.

Sarah waited, for what seemed like an eternity, and held her breath. And then, finally, Esperanza stopped, glanced at Sarah over her shoulder, and walked off.

Sarah didn't know which was worse. The deception itself or forcing others to participate in it. Why Sarah? Why in the world would a man like Carlos go to this much trouble? Why would he chance it? For sex, when he obviously had his pick of the litter? Nothing made sense. Raul also said that Carlos told the staff he was testing Sarah to see if she wanted him for himself or his money. How could they believe such a ridiculous claim? Unless, perhaps, he also told them she was a Jew. Some of his remarks that she'd let pass now made her wonder. Wonder about everything, including whether he'd actually been married to Rachel. Was she *one* of the wives? Did Sarah really remind him of her, or did he invent that story on the spot when Sarah told him her name?

Sarah shifted her position. Her knees ached, and she could barely keep her eyes open. But her mind was still racing, now with a question more disturbing than any of the rest. Had Carlos ever had any real interest in Rita? Or, could it possibly be that he was very interested in her. More than he should be. Did he somehow, some way, know something about her death? About her murder?

Sarah ripped off a palm leaf, like a child lashing out at the nearest object in reach. It didn't make sense, of course, and yet, the coincidence could not be dismissed. One by one, she began to peel away the leaf's spindly fibers. The pointed ends were sharp. She fingered them and then tore them to shreds.

Of all the places in the world. Rita's husband, here, in the exact location where Carlos was a regular, where indeed he was part owner. And a foreign location at that, where U.S. laws didn't apply. Sarah thought back to the trial, to their first encounter and tried to recall whether there was anything that Carlos said, or did, that would have connected him to Rita. No, no she didn't think so. It was Sarah who brought the topic up, she who asked the questions, solicited his help. And it was chance that seated them together in the courtroom. Chance. They met by chance. Or…or had they?

Steps! Sarah had missed the maid's arrival. The woman must have taken the back route. Sarah raised herself a little and peered around the tree. The door opened. She was still determined, perhaps more so, but needed to be extra cautious, to keep in mind the possibility of Carlos' involvement. She strained to see. Yes, an older man. The features were not clear from here, but the general outline, yes. He let the maid in and Sarah dashed over just as the door shut. She twisted the knob. Locked. She straightened herself and knocked. No answer. She knocked again.

A male voice bellowed out. "*Si?*"

"Mr. Bradford? Mr. Bradford. Please, I need to speak with you. About your wife."

"What's that? Go away!"

Sarah pounded her fist.

"I'll call the police!" the man said.

"Please, I mean no harm."

Nothing.

She ran around to the side and tried to peek in through a window, but all the shades were drawn. She dashed back and knocked again. Still no sound. She put her ear to the door, but just then it yanked open, sending Sarah sailing into a shirtless, hairy chest. She pulled back and exhaled. "I'm so sorry," she said, now looking up at the face that had so eluded her. Craggy yes. Grey. A bit stooped, like she remembered Bradford to be. She searched the features. Yes, yes. But wait. No. No scar. No scar! And no, the nose didn't match. Not as old, either. No, no!

"So what do you want?" the man said, revealing large white instead of sharp, little teeth. "Who sent you?"

She felt weak. Her back was wringing wet. "Is, is your name Phillip Bradford?" she said.

"Bradford's my last name."

And now Sarah detected a British accent.

"But I'm Timothy." He sniggered. "But you know that, don't you, dear? And you also know that I have no wife. Now, who in the hell sent you?"

"Sent me?"

Another man, much younger, slinked in beside him and nuzzled his curly blonde head on Timothy's shoulder. "Are we found out then? One of the maids give us away? They don't approve, forbidden in their religion, you know." He nuzzled closer. "Just as well, my love."

Sarah dropped her jaw. "I…I…. I'm sorry," she said. "I'm so sorry. I've…. I've made a mistake."

"Obviously," the younger man said.

"So you're not from one of the papers?" this Mr. Bradford said.

"Papers?" Sarah said. "Papers? No, no. No papers. I, I…I…." Their faces suddenly blurred. She felt herself fall, slowly, as if in a dream. Then everything went black.

28

By the time Carlos reached the *ranchero*, Andrés was gone. Again! Carlos nearly wrung his friend Sol's neck at the news. Don was one thing. An old man. Weak. Feeble almost. But Sol was young and strong. Not to mention clever. If he couldn't make Andrés stay by force, he should have been able to by craft. And yet, even as Carlos spoke those words, cursing and bellowing threats he would never carry out, he knew that it wasn't quite true. If his son was in that crazed state of mind, no one could stop him, including Carlos himself.

Carlos flicked his cigarette out the car window and pushed on the gas. Poor Andrés. Since a little child, he'd been subject to those fits or spells or whatever they were. Periods when he was agitated, fearful and, worst of all, unreachable. They could last for hours or even days, and he usually knew when they were coming because his senses would become unbearably acute. The sound of a buzzing fly, the glare of the sun, the tousling of his hair, each could make him scream out in agony. Usually, at the first hint of it, he would barricade himself in his room. But sometimes he would escape, hide out in some secluded spot near the river or in the hills. Carlos had tried everything to keep him from leaving. Punishments, rewards, bribes. None of it worked. Even threatening to commit him to an asylum or turn him in to the police, neither of which Carlos could ever really bring himself to do, had no effect. If his son wanted to go, he would find a way. The heightening of his senses seemed to extend to his strength and will.

The sun was directly overhead, a massive fireball in the cloudless sky. Heat rose from the road in thick, dusty waves. Carlos nodded at the border cop, a pie-faced *gringo* who reminded him of one of the many doctors he had taken Andrés to over the years. Like all the rest of them, stumped by the symptoms, although Carlos was certain they all would have tried harder had his boy been white. Physically, of course, they could find nothing wrong. Andrés was a perfect specimen, a taller, lankier version of Carlos himself. Those same chiseled features and penetrating, black eyes. Moreover, during most of the appointments, he would seem fine. Open, communicative and intelligent, the way he was when not plagued by his demons. Indeed, much of the time, he was a sweet and loving boy who excelled at both school and sports. And despite his condition, which on more than one occasion had kept him from class for a week, his teachers adored him. So too, especially now at twenty-two, did the girls. He was after all his father's son.

Carlos turned down the winding road that led to Agua Caliente. His head was pounding, his muscles cramping from fatigue. Only a few more miles. It was Andrés' mother, Rosa, that whore who took off when the boy was only three, who Carlos blamed. Indeed, before that, Andrés was a normal kid, a little shy perhaps, but not any more so than Carlos himself was at his age. Rosa didn't even say good-bye. *Dónde está mi mamá?* Where is my mother? *Dónde estás?* Andrés kept asking. *Dónde?* It broke Carlos' heart. Whore! *Puta!*

At first Carlos told Andrés that she was on a trip. But then when it was clear that she would never return, he said she was dead. He thought it would be easier that way. Six months later, Andrés showed the first signs of his ailment. It was during a light rain. Hardly enough to wet the ground. Carlos was reading by a fire, listening to the drops softly pattering on the roof. Suddenly Andrés started running through the house, holding his ears. "Hurt! Andrés said. "Hurt!" Carlos was terrified. He tried talking to the boy to figure out the cause, but Andrés was inconsolable. Only later did he realize that it was the sound of the rain. So sweet and gentle, but to Andrés like the buzzing of a thousand bees. From then on, the symptoms ebbed and flowed but always grew worse in the summer, the time of year Rosa had left.

Thank God for his own mother. He smiled at the thought of her. Taking care of Andrés while Carlos worked, and even while he played. And after Rosa, man did Carlos play. Two more marriages and dozens of flings. Calm, accepting and patient. Always understanding even when she didn't really understand. Such small shoulders, but never a complaint. Without her, Andrés, and indeed Carlos, would have been lost. And it was only a few hours ago that she had come to the rescue again. Indirectly, unknowingly, but no less powerfully. At his time of need, again.

Carlos was still smiling as Agua Caliente's chime tower came into view. He would have never imagined it. Naturally, he had been in the darkest of moods. The success of the previous night, even getting word that the boys had made it back without incident, only barely registered. What did any of it matter if Andrés was gone, gone and in trouble? But then, like an angel from heaven, his mother's voice. On the other end of the phone, calling the *ranchero* just as Carlos was about to drive away. She had been trying to reach him. Tried everywhere.

Andrés was home. Home! Sick with a virus, his mother said, but home. Not dangerous, but the boy felt pretty bad.

Those words washed over Carlos like a cool mountain spring. Yes, the doctor had been there. No, not *that* doctor, the other one, the Chicano fellow who just graduated. Such a nice young man. The bug was going around, he told his mother. Lasted about a week. He'd be all right if he rested. Fluids. Soup. No, not the flu, or at least not a deadly one.

She talked and talked, and Carlos let her go on until she talked herself out. The only thing that mattered was that Andrés was home. At one point his mother asked why Carlos was laughing. Did he hear her correctly? His boy was sick! In his body, his mother said, making sure Carlos understood that the illness wasn't the usual. "*Sí, Mama,*" Carlos said. "But you have assured me he will get well. And how could he not? He is with you, and that makes me happy."

His mother laughed a little herself, but urged Carlos to come home. His son needed him. Carlos assured her that he would. And sooner than she might have hoped. Tonight, in fact. He would be there tonight. But let it be a surprise, he said. "Whatever you do mama, don't tell the boy I'm coming."

"Why not," she said, "he asked for you."

"Asked for me?" Carlos was surprised and a little relieved, but couldn't chance it. "Please, just keep it to yourself for now, Mama, okay?"

Carlos leapt out of the car and motioned to one of the attendants. "Clean her up, will you?" he said, handing the man some coins.

Carlos needed a cleaning up too, a shower and a shave before telling Sarah she needed to pack, immediately. He stopped by the bar on the way to the locker room. The bartender, Ruben, was drying a glass. "*Cerveza, por favor.*"

Ruben looked up. His eyes widened, but he didn't move.

"Ruben. *Cerveza,*" I said. "And pronto."

"*Sí Sí.* Sorry. *Un momento.*"

"What do you mean, *un momento,* he called out, as the man scurried toward the restaurant. "What the devil? Ah, Pedro," he said, seeing the maitre d', with Ruben by his side, rushing toward him. Both men were frowning."

"Hey, what do you have to do to get a drink around here?" Carlos said.

Pedro put his hand on Carlos' shoulder. "You haven't heard, then?"

"Heard? Heard what?"

"Come, *amigo,* sit down."

29

arah leaned her head against the stained blind. The throbbing had not entirely subsided, and it helped to take the pressure off the side that had broken the fall. Carlos had told the truth about one thing, anyway: the train was slow. Slow, dirty and aggravating. They had been rumbling along for over an hour already and hadn't even crossed the border yet. Fortunately, her car was only about half full and very quiet. Everyone seemed exhausted, recuperating from one debauchery or another, she imagined.

She was traveling on a section of the "Impossible Railroad," so called because of the brutal terrain through which the tracks had been carved. The SD&A ran inland to El Centro, where, after a short stop, she would board the Southern Pacific to L.A. The route was far out of the way, but it was her only option if she wanted to be gone before Carlos arrived. Besides, she needed the rest and time to think.

She closed her eyes and slept. When she awoke, giant sliced rocks and a few scattered shrubs indicated that they had made some progress. She raised her head. Better. Her neck and back, though, were soaking wet. Shadows flickered over the dusty, leather seats, but offered no relief from what she gradually realized was sweltering heat. The conductor, a tall, stately black man, walked by and smiled.

"Sir, please, where are we?" Sarah said.

The man chuckled. "A little farther than we were the last time you asked."

Sarah frowned. "Last time?"

"Well, sort of. You were talking in your sleep, I think that's what you said."

"Oh! Well, what did you answer?"

"Carizzo Gorge. Some pretty spectacular scenery, but a little warm, huh?"

"Indeed."

"Won't cool off much until you head west. We'll be at your stop soon."

"Ah, thank you."

He tipped his hat and continued on down the carpeted aisle.

Talking in her sleep? She'd have to watch that. She touched the lump on her head. Not that big, but sore. She blankly noticed the car's shabbiness, flipped through the pages of a fashion magazine that someone had left, and then stared into space. The events of the past twenty-four hours swirled around in her mind. Disturbingly, painfully, but in no particular order.

That wouldn't do. She needed to recall them with precision, just as they'd happened. To place them in time and space and see if there was a pattern. In her handbag was her tablet. Perhaps a real use for it after all. She reached for the smooshed thing, as well as a Mexican flag pen that she had planned to give her brother Harry for a souvenir, and her glasses.

The train veered to the right, over what looked like a dangerous precipice, but they were still in the gorge. Deeper into it, if the dimming light was any indication. Sarah opened the pad and glanced at her prior scribbles. Two Sarahs. What crap. The whole idea, let alone the silly figures, made her cringe. She scratched them out with the pen, so hard and for so long that she had to shake out her now cramped as well as calloused fingers. She didn't know who she was. She thought she'd had some kind of epiphany, some deep insight. Bah! There wasn't one or two or three or any neat, new way to think about herself anymore. She was a mess. Splintered, fragmented, in pieces.

She gulped back tears, which was becoming a common practice, and turned to a blank, wrinkled page. *The Deauville of the Americas,* she wrote, quoting what one of the fellows in that group last night had dubbed Agua Caliente. Since Sarah was the only one among them who'd never been to Deauville, he explained that it was a French seaside resort catering to the upper crust. With a racetrack, such as Agua Caliente would soon have, a grand casino and exquisite accommodations. And of course, gourmet food and the finest wines in the world. "Read Proust's *A Remembrance of Things Past,* and you'll know Deauville," he said, assuming that she hadn't read it. Which she hadn't. But then again, neither had he. When Sarah pressed him for details, all he could offer up was that he'd heard that Proust had set part of his newly published tome there and that the story was about the unreliable nature of memory.

Indeed. That's why Sarah was writing her memories down now, before they became even more jumbled than they already were. And what she remembered at the moment was that phrase "The Road to Hell." She wrote that down too. Whoever coined that expression about the journey to Tijuana had been right, at least as far as Sarah was concerned. Hell, that's what the last twenty-four hours had been.

Escorted to table by maitre d' (Pedro)—suspicious comments
Waiter, Raul, warns me: "Don't trust Carlos"
Raul later (in barbershop) explains: Carlos' marriages, dalliances, including
Raul's young sister! Investor in the hotel, enlisted staff in scheme to keep me in
the dark
Housekeeper, Esperanza, confirms the account
I confront Mr. Bradford, who turned out to be…

Now this requires some detail, Sarah thought. The pen felt a bit easier in her hand. She turned the page and switched to a loose script.

I didn't learn who Timothy Bradford was until after being examined in the infirmary. I had passed out for only a few seconds, but because I hit my head, he and his friend insisted that I be checked. It was there, after I briefly summarized the mix-up and assured him of no other motive for my spying, that he explained the reason for his seclusion. He didn't have to, but witnessing first-hand my level of distress and believing, as I told him, that I was not the judgmental sort, he did.

He told me that he was a singer, well known and beloved in England. I was ashamed to say I'd never heard of him, but he assured me that I wasn't alone—he couldn't claim an international following. In recent months, there had been rumors about his romantic affiliations, so he'd taken a holiday, to a place he thought would be safe, until they died down. But the damned press had followed him, he said. The press and all sorts of other nosey folks (he in fact suggested that perhaps among them was the person from whom I had gotten my information, that they had confused one Bradford with another). A couple of hours by the pool was all he needed to figure that out. He wasn't about to make it easy for them, though, and thus the decision to go into hiding. As for himself, he didn't care a wit. He was a "bugger," he said, plain and simple. It had taken him years to face it, but once he had, he never looked back. But he feared for his children, who were prominent citizens in their own right. He had been married many years ago, and a daughter and son were what he called the "fortunate result." He loved them dearly, and didn't want his behavior, which, in addition to being stigmatized was still illegal, to affect them. "We are the country that sent Oscar Wilde to prison, you know," he said.

Yes, I did know, I said, and I was sympathetic, having been through that whole episode with Obee and Ken. I thanked him for his help, and we wished each other luck.

And then, after the doctor said I was fit to travel, I bought a ticket and got the hell out of there, got the hell out of Hell without leaving Carlos a word.

Sarah removed her glasses and sank back into the seat. She felt the lump again, confirming that it was really there, and squinted at her writing. So, she could string a few sentences together, coherently if not artistically. But a pattern? No, other than her own stupidity. And what now? What was she to do? Go home. That was her impulse. Get back to work, to her family. The trial no longer held any interest. Damn trial, damn courtroom, damn oil! She was weary, so weary. But it would be hard to live with the fact that she had gone through all of this for nothing. No, not for nothing. For degradation, humiliation. That's all she would be taking with her, that and a few cheap trinkets. And yet, if she continued on with her investigation, such as it was, she was back to square one. She had no clue of Phillip Bradford's whereabouts and surmised that, as Timothy suggested, whoever had told Paige that he was at Agua Caliente had simply been wrong. Some young, ambitious dick, no doubt, eager to be of service. With the name Bradford, and Timothy being rather old, it was certainly possible, especially if someone wanted it to be so. Like Sarah herself.

Moreover, if she continued on, and even if she didn't, she would also have to accept that Carlos was simply a cad. It almost would have been easier to think she had been part of some elaborate scheme, even if it meant that he had been involved with Rita's death. At least then there would have been a logic to it, however demented it might have been. But sometimes a cigar is just a cigar, as Freud said. Agua Caliente was a coincidence that Carlos merely exploited. Probably because the whole thing was like a game to him. A sleight of hand. He spun his roulette wheel, and Sarah just happened to come up. A little diversion to take his mind off the union business, if that was even true. She wouldn't try to find out. If she continued, she would avoid the trial and find a new hotel. She need not see the man ever again.

She inhaled deeply, as if she'd been cooped up in a dungeon and someone had just opened a window. There would have to be phone calls of course. As soon as she arrived. First, to Paige, second to Obee, third to Tillie, and then, if she could summon the courage, to Mitchell. She returned the tablet to her handbag.

They entered a tunnel, a long, dark rickety passage that could quicken the breath of even someone without claustrophobia. But finally the proverbial light emerged and soon thereafter the conductor announced their arrival in El Centro. Sarah gathered her things, smoothed her hair, and felt the lump once more. Her head hurt, her heart was broken, her soul tortured, but she was lucky to have gotten out of this thing. If the game was indeed roulette, the wheel had spun ever so slightly back in her favor.

30

Carlos shot up, raised the wooden chair over his head and launched it against the wall, missing the bold Diego Rivera print by inches. The force was enough, however, to shatter the glass protecting it and rattle the bottles lining the bar's shelves. As for the plaster taking the direct hit, it crumbled to the floor. Carlos glared at the two dazed men. "That's nothing compared to what I'm going to do to Raul! Where is the bastard?"

"I don't know," Pedro said, shaking his head.

"What do mean, you don't know? He works here, doesn't he?"

"Carlos, please, cool down. There are guests."

Carlos looked around. "I don't see any. And what if there are? I don't give a damn!"

"Think of the owners."

"I am one of the fucking owners!"

"Carlos...."

"*Ay*, leave me alone," he said, jerking his shoulder loose from Pedro's meaty hand.

"Please, wait...."

"And clean this stuff up!" Carlos said, storming out.

He searched the restaurant, the casino, the pool. Stuck his head in the locker room, the barbershop and the steam bath. "*Dónde está* Raul?" He pressed every worker he could find, grabbing a busboy, who snickered at the question, by the collar. "You think this is funny?"

"No," the fellow quickly answered and lowered his head.

They all, in fact, lowered their heads, probably hoping to escape a blow. And they shrugged. No one seemed to know their unfortunate colleague's whereabouts.

Carlos stopped at the wishing well and leaned over, breathing heavily. From his vantage point, he could see the bottom half of a shapely woman approaching. She tossed in a coin and uttered some magic words to help her win. Carlos groaned. She turned to the sound.

"Pig," she said, and made a fast exit, her round buttocks jiggling against her clingy dress.

Carlos lacked the will to react. For a while, he just sat on his haunches, recovering his breath.

"*Estás bien?*"

He glanced up. It was Luis. "Do I *look* okay?! You heard, I assume."

"Yes, I'm sorry, *Señor* Martinez."

"Do you know where Raul is?" he said, standing. He felt the fury subsiding, despite himself. One could only hold on to something like that for so long.

"His shift starts at five."

"Ah. I guess no one wanted to tell me. Doesn't matter. I'll wait," he said, thinking that it would only take a few minutes to knock out the son of a bitch. "In the meantime, I'm going to see the hiring manager. Raul will be gone by tomorrow." One way or another, he said to himself.

"If I may, *señor*, perhaps if you were talk to him...."

"No!"

"*Señor*, I don't know what got into Raul. He's a good man. Maybe something happened at home. He must have not been thinking straight. I'm sure he could explain."

"Luis, I know you mean well. But I suspect this was a personal vendetta, and I intend to make him pay. Listen, do you really think I asked you all to lie just for a piece of ass? And an old Jew one at that?"

Luis' eyes bugged out, and as soon as Carlos spoke those words, he felt a little shocked himself. Certainly, that is how he originally would have characterized Sarah, but his feelings had changed, somewhat. And yet, it was safer to keep thinking of her that way. Safer all around. "There are other reasons that I cannot go into," he said.

"Oh, I see."

"Now, go. I'll keep in mind what you said."

■■■

After receiving the assurance that Raul would indeed be fired, Carlos had returned to the bungalow. He hoped to find a note, or something, anything that hinted at Sarah's plans. But she left without a trace, as if she'd never been there at all. The only thing he knew was that she had taken the train. At first that sounded promising. The old steam engine often had problems, was delayed frequently, sometimes for hours. If that were the case, Carlos could intercept

Sarah at one of the stops, talk to her, make up something again, kidnap her if he had to. But he checked and the damn thing was on time.

Carlos showered and packed. He apologized to Pedro and gave him cash, under the table, of course, to have the wall fixed, ASAP. The fewer people who knew about his outburst the better. He ate a sandwich and went to the casino, played a little black jack to give himself focus. If he allowed himself to think too much about Sarah on the loose, he could do damage again. When it came to Raul, he didn't mind if he did, but it behooved him to keep the hotel in one piece.

Carlos seated himself with a bird's eye view of the lobby's front doors. It was through them, he was told, that Raul always entered the building. The square clock hanging over the check-in counter read 4:45. Due any minute. Carlos examined each of the guests, most dressed to the nines, as they came and went. Beautiful and rich people who at the moment annoyed him to no end.

4:50. A large group of extra large Americans waddled through the door. They looked like overly corn-fed Midwesterners except for their high fashion attire. They were dripping money even if their shirts and dresses were busting at the seams. Carlos would have liked to punch them in the mouth, so he made for the other side of the room, where he could still observe the entrance. "Come on," he said under his breath.

"Another murder! What's L.A. coming to?"

Carlos glanced at the speaker, a luscious blond sharing a loveseat with an even more luscious brunette.

"What's that?" the brunette said.

"This paper says that a young actress was found dead on an empty lot on Pomeroy Street."

"God."

"I know! Scary."

Carlos stiffened for a second then fixed his gaze back on the entrance. "Come *on*."

"Sabrina Johnson, that's the poor girl's name. Oh, and it says she was strangled!"

Carlos spun around. "What did you say!"

Both girls jumped. "Excuse me?" the blond said.

"Let me see that!" he said, grabbing the paper out of her hand.

"What's wrong with you? Don't you have any manners!"

"I'll get the manager!" the brunette said, standing.

Carlos scanned the lines, his eyes moving at breakneck speed:

The investigation has begun into the May eighteenth murder of Sabrina Johnson, found dead on an empty lot on Pomeroy Street. The coroner listed the cause of death as strangulation.

Two days ago, Carlos thought. No. No! *Dios.* He smashed the paper under his arm and ran out through the Spanish archway, down the concrete steps and over the patch of grass that led to the driveway. "Get my car, now!" he said, and waited for what seemed like hours for it to appear. Finally! He jumped in and started off, but the path was filled with oblivious bystanders. "*Ándele*! Get moving!" he called out, but they dawdled as if they had all the time in the world. He gritted his teeth until the path cleared. Then he checked his rearview mirror. There he caught a glimpse of a young waiter tidying his jacket as he ambled toward the entrance. Raul. Carlos put the car in reverse but then stopped. He thought for a moment, banged on the steering wheel and switched back to first gear. "Fuck!" he said, and drove off.

31

"You noticed that, didn't you?"

"What is that?"

"You noticed that was done?"

"Yes, sir."

"That they issued stock?"

"Yes, sir."

"In fictitious names, and as far as you saw, there was no transfer?"

"Yes, sir."

"Did you ever hear any conversation up there about stock being turned in to be canceled and not canceled, but resold?"

"No, sir."

Mitchell copied every word of this exchange between Prosecutor Shelley and one Harold McKay, a trustee and manager of one of the bank pools who had been called back to the stand for the third time. The two men were a study in contrasts, with Shelley being tall and serious and McKay short and jovial. Indeed, McKay seemed perpetually amused, preceding each answer with a piggish snort. This appeared to have no effect whatsoever on Shelley, but Judge Doran finally asked the man if he had a problem. McKay snorted again, and said no. Whether he was just enjoying himself or had some sort of nervous tick was difficult to say, but he kept on doing it. Mitchell would have to weave this bit of comic relief into his article.

Word had it that Ohioan Ronald Bishop might be back by the end of the week. Mitchell hoped not. Let the man get some more rest. This testimony was heating up, and he was glad for the required focus. Still, he might not have been able to concentrate at all had he not had that meeting a while ago with the officer. Officer Hodges.

Mitchell had played it just right. He had called the station and spoken to the secretary, telling her that he was an Ohio journalist covering the trial. He wanted law enforcement's point of view, would appreciate an interview with the person in charge. She conveyed the message and Hodges agreed on the spot, proving Mitchell's theory that ego is the reporter's best friend. Mitchell wasn't sure what the man would do had he initially revealed the real reason for the visit. According to her own account, Sarah had not made a favorable impression and vice versa.

And indeed, the welcoming smile dropped when Mitchell mentioned Sarah's name. But he quickly recovered, took a breath and extended his hand. "Pretty tricky there, fella. You reporters do have your ways. So what about the little lady?"

"Well," he said, "I know she came here with questions about a woman's death, uh, the name was Rita, Rita something."

The officer, a heavy-set man with a drinker's nose and a slight metallic odor, folded his arms. "Uh, huh. Rita Bradford. Sad case. Died pretty young. But that Sarah, friend of yours, is she?"

"Friend, yes."

"Smart gal. But she got it into her head that there was foul play and wouldn't let it drop."

"Yeah, well she told me that there were some strange occurrences."

"Strange, if you're looking for strange. Mrs. Bradford thought she knew Sarah, so what? Mistakes like that happen every day. And the woman seemed upset. Lots of people get upset, especially at that trial. But Rita Bradford died of natural causes, pure and simple. I know your Sarah meant well, but she's got one helluva imagination. And, I hope you don't mind me saying so, but she's a bit too big for her own britches," he said, winking.

Mitchell played along. "Oh yes, that's Sarah."

The man released his arms and smiled again, revealing brownish, mangled teeth. "So, how can I help you?"

Mitchell quickly came to the point, telling him that Sarah was needed back home but that he couldn't find her. She'd checked out of her hotel and was last seen with some Mexican, or Chicano fellow named Carlos.

Hodges small eyes narrowed. "And?"

"And, I'm worried about her, I mean...."

"Oh, you don't have to tell me why you're worried. I told her not to waste her time on those types. I mean, Mrs. Bradford was a little different of course, seeing who her husband is and all, but still. You see?"

"Oh yes, I see." Quite well, Mitchell thought. "But, I'm still worried."

"Of course. We'll see what we can do. "Paige," he said, take down the details and get someone on it, will you?"

The secretary had been listening. Mitchell had caught her eyes a few times. Pretty eyes at that, if a little overly made up. "Yes, sir."

Mitchell provided a description as the officer looked on, adding a few observations of his own. "Heavy walk, kinda loud, and uh, a hook nose," wouldn't you say?

"*You* could say that," Mitchell said. I would say determined walk, resonant voice, aquiline nose.

Hodges reddened but offered no retraction. Paige wrote down every word, and then twisted her pencil around one of the red curls that framed her face. "Is that it, Mr. Dob..."

"Mitchell," he said.

"Is that it, Mitchell?"

"For now."

"Okay, Paige," the officer said, "get to it."

The woman rose from her chair and, Mitchell noticed, limped away. Sweet gal, he thought, just as she turned and smiled.

"Well, thank you, officer. I appreciate your help."

"It's my job. But, uh, since you're here, you sure you don't want that interview?"

Mitchell smirked. "Some other time maybe. But since I *am* here, and, as you suggested, possess a reporter's, um, instinct, is there any chance, any chance at all, that Mrs. Bradford's death could have been...."

"No. Don't push your luck, Mitch. You're at The Portsmouth, right? We'll be in touch."

"Okay." I won't push it, he thought, not yet. At least now the wheels were in motion. Someone other than himself was looking for Sarah, and the officer, however repugnant his views, knew Mitchell wouldn't let the matter drop.

▪▪▪

The attorney paced and then turned to the jury as he asked the next question. "Approximately how often, if you can estimate it, during the whole time you were up there and Rosen was there, did you hear Bennett say in Rosen's presence, "say to Harris, issue me some certificates in street names?"

"Possibly half a dozen times."

"And approximately how many times, can you remember Rosen say to Harris, "Issue me stock in street names.""

"Several times."

Mitchell jotted down the tentative title of an article: "*The Oily Streets of L.A.*" He would work on it tonight after dining with James, the bigoted hotel clerk who Mitchell also thought wise to befriend. This morning James stated that he couldn't recall anything else about Sarah other than what he'd already said. But he nevertheless accepted Mitchell's invitation. A free meal is a free meal, especially when accompanied by the promise of a flattering portrayal of the hotel in one of Mitchell's columns. It would go over well with the management, and Mitchell had the feeling it might also help to improve the man's memory, especially over a secret whiskey or two.

"Do you know any of the names of the streets?"

"Names? Let me see."

Madison, Mitchell thought, an image of his own street, where he'd been living since God knows when, coming to mind. An avenue actually, Madison ran through the heart of Toledo. Since Mitchell first moved there, the vacant lots had all but disappeared, and Art Deco high-rises were rapidly replacing deteriorating nineteenth-century stores. The wide pavement bustled at all hours of the day, but it lacked humanity, the warmth of family bonds. Just the opposite of Fulton, the street where Sarah lived. Quiet and orderly, narrow and tree-lined, to Mitchell it nevertheless seemed full of life. Sarah's siblings often drove her to distraction, but he envied the familiarity and sense of belonging that he experienced, second-hand, whenever he visited their modest little home. Not only did it increase his desire for a more permanent arrangement, but it also stirred memories of his youth. Before his parents died, before he became so cynical about the world, before he started, and stopped, drinking.

Maybe Tillie had heard from Sarah, he thought. Maybe he should…

"Normal."

"Normal?"

"Yeah, Normal."

"This act was anything but normal," the prosecutor said.

"You asked me the name of the street. That's the only one I can remember. Normal Street."

Mitchell wrote the word: *Normal*. A normal, old street. Did such a thing exist in L.A.? The orange-scented Pershing, the famous Hollywood and Vine, the unnamed alley where he met Ida. Ida, the streetwalker. Jesus. Nothing normal there. And that street where they found that young girl. Palm? Palmer? Palmeroy. Murdered, the papers now said. Strangled.

"Did you ever hear Rosen say simply, 'Issue me stock,' without saying any street name?"

"Yes sir."

"How many times?"

"Several times."

"Did Rosen at those times say, 'Bennett says to issue this stock,' or did he simply say, 'Issue this stock?'"

"He would simply say, 'Issue this stock.'"

Mitchell copied this last response and then wrote: *McKay's testimony suggests that Theodore Rosen was a key player in the Julian scheme, high in the chain of command. But it remains to be seen if this witness will help the prosecution drive a nail in the coffin, or whether Rosen is so wily and well connected that he will escape before the lid is even closed.*

"Thank you, Mr. McKay. That's all today."

Judge Doran tapped his gavel. "And that's all for us, too, today, ladies and gentlemen. Court dismissed."

Mitchell sat and thought for a moment as the room stirred and the sluggish departing began. The registering of fictitious names was routine of course, legally required when the name of a business wasn't the same as the individuals who owned it. But in this shady world of backdoor deals and secret accounts, where share prices were inflated and stocks were knowingly overissued, those names were conveniently employed to shield the identity of those involved. At least that's what Mitchell assumed Shelley was getting at. "Hmm," he grunted and got up.

It was only 3:00 p.m., warm and sunny. Mitchell wanted to call Hodges, but it hadn't even been twenty-four hours. Not the way to please, and pleasing the cop was prudent for the time being. Instead, he hopped the P Car and got off on the corner of Wilshire and Western. All this talk about streets reminded him that he'd been wanting to see if it really was the "busiest intersection in the world," as the L.A. boosters claimed. He removed his new Leica thirty-five millimeter from his pocket and swung his jacket over his shoulder. What a beauty this camera was, with its black and gold finery. And so compact, almost fit in his hand. But that also made him deathly afraid of losing it. This was the first time he'd used it here in L.A., and he prayed it wouldn't be his last.

Directly across from him was a row of fancy shops with striped awnings and evenly spaced palms. They were housed in an ornate building called the McKinley, from which mostly fashionable women were coming and going. He turned, tuned, focused, and clicked. To the left was an Oriental art gallery, and to the right, in the distance, a massive dome under construction. Irrefutable was the density of cars. If that's what the description referred to, then it wasn't an exaggeration. Chaos. Bumper to bumper, in every direction. Motionless, except for the idling and steady flow of filthy exhaust.

He took several shots and then called it a day. He returned to the hotel, where again no messages awaited him. But his frustration didn't end there. The dinner with James was fruitless, a waste of time and money. The food was lousy, and the booze did nothing to loosen the man's tongue, other than to free him to tell a few sloppy jokes. Mitchell couldn't make any headway on his article either, despite the compelling material. Sleep, that's what he needed. But when he closed his eyes, all he could see was Sarah, bound and gagged, or sick, or rolling around in another's man's bed. He tossed and turned for an hour before giving up. And giving in. Actually, Sarah hadn't been quite all he could see. Behind her image peered another female form, one whose soft reality was only a short walk away. He dressed and was there, on that crummy little alley, in minutes. But, ha! Ida was a goddamn working girl, as if he didn't know. And she was booked. A friend offered herself, even suggested someone else when he didn't seem interested, but Mitchell passed. It wasn't so much sex he wanted. No, that was a lie. He wanted sex, but with someone he knew, so to speak.

He started back. He could sleep now, maybe. But he was thirsty. That small hovel over there, the one in disrepair with the "Closed" sign. Such simple lines. So soothing. He knew a speakeasy when he saw one. Unobtrusive, vacant, invisible to the casual observer. Ah, yes. The old pull. The return of the enemy. The one he thought he'd conquered, until the other night. At least he wasn't dumb enough to think he could have just one. If he walked through the door now, he was done for. He drew closer. Silence, but his finely tuned ears could hear the laughs, the tinkling of glass. Someone approached, started to knock but then saw him milling about and left. The excitement rose. Still outside, he breathed in the perfume, feeling intoxicated already. He knew he should do battle, but he longed with every fiber of his being to surrender.

32

Sarah climbed the five sets of stairs that led to her tiny cubicle at the Hotel Figueroa. The place wasn't far from the Portsmouth, but was an entirely different species. Built by the Y.W.C.A., it catered to professional women and their families. She had contemplated staying here in the first place, but had opted for the Portsmouth because it was a bit closer to the courthouse. But now she didn't care a damn about that, and the Figueroa had a number of things going for it. First, it was cheap, all she really could afford given that she had exceeded her allotment for the conference. Second, the top nine of its eleven floors were women only, a godsend in her current state of mind. And third, though newer and cleaner than the Portsmouth, it was bare bones, unadorned and uncluttered, the right kind of space in which to think. Indeed, the glitz of Agua Caliente and even the luxury of the Ambassador, which had previously so impressed her, seemed repulsive. So too did the possibility of running into Carlos, which staying here made remote.

Attached to the hotel was a gym and lounge, neither of which Sarah would go near. The gym because she would get enough exercise going up and down the stairs, and the lounge because she had no interest in socializing. Fortunately, the hotel wasn't exclusive, meaning Jews were welcome despite its association with the Y. "Can't say the same about some other establishments around here," Mrs. Parks, the kindly clerk with a giant, amber cross dangling from her neck, said when Sarah asked about their policy. "No, we don't believe that Christ would want us to discriminate. Love thy neighbor, you know. But, uh, Miss, Miss *Kaufman*, if you have the time, I'd sure like to tell you about the 'good news.'"

Sarah thanked her for the offer but declined. That Jesus had supposedly died for Sarah's sins was in fact old news, and she had long since decided that if failing to accept this nice Jewish boy as her savior doomed her to hell, so be it. She'd rather burn with her relatives than rejoice with strangers.

She unlocked the door and threw the hotel's complimentary copy of the *Times* on the bed. The milk she'd purchased earlier had soured, which was disappointing since she had just bought some stale cookies to go with it. But it was too much effort to return to the store. She'd settle for water, with a drop of that whiskey she'd refilled her flask with in Tijuana. She kicked off her shoes, reached for her notebook and placed it on the small desk in the corner of the room. She would write, continue to record. The act was becoming easier, almost something to look forward to. She mixed her drink in a paper cup and ripped open the bakery bag. She switched on a lamp, put on her glasses, and titled a clean page: "*Stymied.*"

I arrived late yesterday afternoon. On approach to Central Station, I observed, with a strange kind of melancholic relief, the outlines of the city, especially the towering City Hall, chiseled against the sky's orangey glow. The Southern Pacific had been on time, the car fancier than SD&A, but the ride was still slow and long. I disembarked, exited the grand, white-stuccoed building and immediately hailed a cab. On the way to the hotel, we passed the courthouse, and I slinked down in the seat, wanting neither to see nor be seen.

Maybe I wasn't damned after all because my prayer that the Figueroa would have rooms was answered. I checked in, undressed and fell into a dead sleep, not waking until morning. I might have slept all the next day had not a bright sunbeam streamed in through the tiny, square window. I squinted and rubbed my eyes. The austerity of the room, coupled with this almost mystical light made me wonder for a moment if I had in fact crossed over and was in some holding cell, waiting for judgment. But then I came to, hit by the rush of reality and the awareness that I was hungry.

Sarah reached into the bag and pulled out a snickerdoodle. She had been unconsciously picking at a chocolate wafer, as she noticed a trail of dark crumbs on the page. She blew them off, bit into the new cinnamony treat and washed it down with a swig of the contraband. Much tastier than milk would have been. She wiped her hands on a towel and continued.

I opened my suitcase. All my clothes, save one checked skirt and a flowered blouse, were dirty. As I gathered the rest to be washed, my eyes fell upon Rita's shoes in the bottom of the case, fine and delicate, the thin strap and little brass button, the curved French heel, the black patent leather. I picked them up, fingered the soft insert, traced the gold lettering with the designer's name, Salvatore Ferragamo, the size five. It was the first time I had really examined them. Exquisitely crafted, with faint, almost invisible silk cross-stitching along the sides.

I turned one of them over. "Kantor's." I smiled at the thought of Marvy and the kindness of the couple, but then remembered their intolerance too, a version of what I observed at Agua Caliente, where guests felt superior to the people in whose land they were visitors. A version of my own feelings as well, feelings that had been tested beyond anything I thought possible. I gently laid the shoes on the floor and tried slipping my feet into them. Even with the smoothness of my stockings, the toe pinched and my heels hung over the backs at least two inches. I was no Cinderella, but like a child playing dress up, I tried to walk, walk in Rita's shoes. But the reality didn't work any better than the metaphor. The best I could do was scoot. So I put them away and dressed, leaving the room clothed but mismatched.

Sarah stood and stretched. She poured another drink with a little more hooch this time. Her words were flowing, whether in good form or bad, she now didn't much care. She felt as if she'd been bound by a corset, the laces of which were finally loosening.

It was early. I found a diner, stuffed myself with griddlecakes, and delivered my clothes to a nearby laundry. I then returned to my room, which, despite its lack of adornments, had a phone, perhaps because the place was filled with women, who, as men are so quick to point out, like to talk. In any case, it was lucky. I removed my earring and first dialed the number Paige had given me. I was hoping that even if Paige wasn't there, her friend could relay a message. But there was no answer. I tried several more times before deciding to chance the station.

The voice that picked up was female, but not the one I'd hoped for. It was a woman filling in for Paige, who was out sick. Went home with a fever yesterday, she said. Half the Force was down with it. Bad bug. Then she laughed. "The only good news is that criminals aren't immune from the thing. May I take a message?"

"I don't suppose you could give me her home phone number?"

"I'm afraid not."

"No, no message." I said, feeling my luck quickly diminishing.

I then called Obee. I was afraid he'd hear my anxious tone and be worried. But he was involved in a demanding case and actually seemed impatient with me." You gonna stay there forever?" he said.

I told him that Elaine would cover for me, that it was very important I remain a little longer, that I would naturally pay my own expenses. He agreed, but said that if I didn't resolve whatever it was by the end of the month, in other words in two weeks, that my job was in jeopardy. I was stunned! Never, in all the years I'd worked for him, did he ever make such a threat. But after the shock wore off, I realized how irresponsible I must seem. What did I expect? I promised that I would return by then, at which point he softened a little and told me he'd heard from Mitchell. I held my breath, thought I might throw up on the spot, until he said that Mitchell had been assigned a story and was already on it. Top secret. Couldn't provide any details. And then Obee said: "He wanted to know if I'd heard from you of course, Sarah, and I said that I had and reassured him that all was well. Was I right? Is all well?" At that point, I drew a huge sigh of relief. Mitchell was on assignment. It bought me some time with him. "Yes, Obee, all is well."

I then called Tillie, who screamed and cried like a mother who was both furious and relieved to know her child was safe.

Sarah chewed on her pencil, read through the text and nodded. The words blurred a little from the booze, but she was satisfied with the telling. There was nothing to do now but wait, wait for Paige to get well and try to avoid getting sick herself. She would take a bath, read the paper and skip dinner entirely.

Her watch read 4:30 p.m. She started to undress, glancing up at the far wall as she shimmied off her skirt. She hadn't noticed it before but there, leaning against an otherwise empty shelf, was a small crucifix. She went over and examined the carved figure, head slumped, hair flowing, limbs nailed. Not surprising, she supposed, but a reminder that she was in enemy territory. Yes, the hosts were nice enough, but proselytizing was never far away, in this case, only a few inches. She recalled once staying overnight at a friend's house where a far more imposing such replica hung over the bed. Although Sarah was young, she remembered wondering if the parents had intentionally assigned her that room, either to punish or convert her.

She started to unbutton the blouse, one eye on a man who in life was a carpenter and advocate for the poor. And, a rabbi. Friday. It was Friday, Friday evening. Perhaps she didn't just have to sit around and wait. She quickly redid the buttons, pulled up the skirt and checked herself in the mirror. A belt, that's what it needed. In the zipped pocket of her suitcase were two. She tried the brown but it was too dull and stiff. The black tie one was better. She looped it around her waist a few times and fashioned a loose bow. She checked the mirror again. Not chic, but presentable.

The cavernous new Sinai Temple was only about half full, putting the women's furs and jewels into stark relief. Sarah felt herself contract, slouch. Everyone dressed for *shul* of course, but here was an added flair. The Sabbath in Hollywood. Or to be more exact, on Fourth and New Hampshire Street, the so-called Mid-Wilshire district. When Sarah had looked up temples in Los Angeles, she decided on this one because of its more progressive customs, like the sexes sitting together, and, more importantly, its proximity to Beverly Hills, home to Phillip Bradford.

Sarah stood at the entrance, gazing up at the huge, Byzantine dome and multi-colored bricks. It was beautiful but a little dizzying. A young man with a red velvet *yarmulke* sitting high on his curly brown locks approached her. "Are you a member?"

"No. I'm visiting from Ohio. May I attend the service?"

"Of course. You're lucky tonight. Small crowd. Welcome. Please," he said, motioning for her to sit in one of the near-empty pews. Sarah selected one close to the exit because she didn't plan on staying long. Just enough to get a little comfort, a momentary feeling of belonging. The cantor's sonorous voice echoed out, leading the congregation in the singing of a familiar minor-keyed melody. She hummed along, not knowing or wanting to know the meaning. It was the ritual to which she responded. Hebrew to her was a moving vocalization of the mystery of existence. The words were powerful, as long as they remained illusive.

Sarah craned her neck to catch a glimpse of the rabbi. Not Jesus, she thought, but from here with certainly some resemblance. He uttered a prayer and then asked the crowd to rise for the viewing of the *Torah*. The curtain on the wooden cabinet was drawn, and there, ornamented in satin and gold, rested the holiest book of her people. In it were inscribed the tenants of Judaism. To Sarah it was a beautiful hieroglyph, an ancient artifact whose value was more literary than literal. Still the sight of it always stirred something in her, like the American flag to a patriot.

The rabbi uttered a few prayers and then told everyone to be seated. Men adjusted their *tallis*, the silky fringed shawls that adorned their shoulders, and women their minks.

"With our sacred text visible," the rabbi then said, "I wish tonight to discuss a concept that while not explicit to our teachings, is central to our faith, a concept that I ask you to take into your own hearts and practice in your lives.

Tikkun. Tikkun olam. You've heard it, but how many of you really know its meaning? *Tikkun olam.* Literally, to repair the world, by following God. Now, this is of course noble and good. A spiritual mandate. But my friends, *Tikkun*, I believe, is also a temporal imperative. To repair, to help fix the things that we know are wrong, not just with Jews, but with all of humanity. To fight injustice wherever we may find it."

Sarah leaned in. She knew the term, but it certainly seemed more relevant just now.

"We Jews know the importance of justice, since we have so often been without it. Because of our own suffering, we have been blessed with the ability to recognize the feeling in others. But recognition is not enough. It is our responsibility, our calling even, to help ease that suffering, to help rectify and repair, to fix what we can."

The cantor then led another song, but Sarah's mind remained on the message. *Tikkun.* Justice. Rectify, repair, fix. The following God part she didn't know. But she nevertheless folded her hands and prayed. Not to a man in white robes, but to some essence, outside or inside herself, to some principle of unity or wholeness, or perhaps to nothing at all. She prayed to repair herself, to rearrange the pieces, to fix and put right what she could. And she prayed for the strength to continue her quest, to seek justice for Rita, if there was any to be found.

The song ended and the curtain was closed. The rabbi spoke a little about current events, from Benito Mussolini's ending female suffrage in Italy, "a bad omen," he said, to the "Firedamp" explosion in the Mather, Pennsylvania coal mine, where hundreds died because of "a lack of regulation," and, then, closer to home, about the Julian trial. On this topic he simply said, "justice will be done."

From your lips to God's ears, Sarah thought, another one of Tillie's tired expressions that nevertheless seemed particularly appropriate. And then, as is a tradition in Jewish services, the rabbi asked the congregation to call out names of the sick, of relatives or friends in need of extra prayers. "I imagine," he said, "there will be more tonight than usual. So many down with this illness. Look around, how thin our attendance is! Now everyone take care. They say it's not the flu, but we don't want a repeat of nineteen-seventeen. Take precautions."

And then names flowed. "Saul!" "Mina!" "Leopold!"

Sarah took that opportunity to make her way out, but not before whispering, "Paige."

33

I t was twilight, the sky an eerie, reddish hue. Sarah hailed a cab and took out the newspaper clipping listing Rita's address from her pocket book. She had saved that first article, never imagining she would put it to this kind of use. Why the papers included such information was perplexing. Unethical, it seemed, if not illegal. When Sarah's own address appeared in the *Blade* a couple of times, she was outraged. Didn't this make it easier for curiosity seekers, not to mention potential burglars and kidnappers, to carry out their deeds? But for now she was glad for the practice.

"Where to?" the driver said.

"One-zero-four Crescent."

"Movie star?"

"No, I'm looking at, uh, the style of the house. Getting ideas."

"Now? It's near dark."

"Do you mind?"

He shrugged. "It's your money."

They drove up Wilshire and turned on Crescent, a winding, wide road dotted with new mansions. Sarah's knowledge of architecture was superficial, but she recognized in nearly every one they passed the Tudor influence. Vast empty land separated the properties, but the numerous for sale signs indicated that would not be the case for long. They soon reached the Bradford abode, also a Tudor, an expansive, brick two-story with young vines and a sprawling lawn. No lights were on, but a street lamp lit up the front.

"Here it is," the cabbie said. "Now what?"

Sarah asked him to drive by it slowly, turn around and do it again, and then again.

"Hey, this is a little queer," he said.

Sarah sighed. "Yeah, I know. Last time, I promise."

They drove by again. "Okay," she said, "you can go."

As they headed out, she turned. And just then, a house light switched on. "Stop!"

"Jesus, lady!"

"Sorry. Could you back up and wait here for a moment?"

"You're on the meter, but something about this ain't right."

"Thanks." Sarah jogged up a curved path to the set of stairs that led to lacquered double doors. On them hung two dying laurel wreaths with twisted black ribbons. She pulled the brass knocker, with an overwhelming feeling of déjà vu. Not that surprising, given her experience with the other Mr. Bradford. Doors. Everywhere doors that shut out the truth. The metaphor was too easy. But history was indeed repeating itself. No answer. She waited and rang the bell, a harmonious, sweet chime. Nothing. She rang it again, and this time there were footsteps. A suspicious eye regarded her through the peephole.

"Yes?"

"Oh, hello, uh, my name is Sarah Kaufman. I, I was a friend of Rita's. I'm wondering, is Mr. Bradford in?"

"What? No!"

"Do you know when he will be?"

"Mr. Bradford doesn't just meet with anyone," said the same woman. Now Sarah could hear an accent.

"Who is it?" a male voice then asked.

"I'm sorry to just show up, and at this hour," Sarah bellowed out. I'm a friend of Rita's, and I just wanted to talk to Mr. Bradford. I'm from out of town. I, I…"

The door opened. A Mexican woman in a black and white maid's outfit stood with one hand on her hip and the other on the knob. Sarah caught herself, again. Chicano, maybe, or something else. Either way, she didn't look happy. The young man towering over her, however, smiled. "Maybe I can help you, ma'am. I'm Drake, the chauffeur. "You said you were a friend of Mrs. Bradford's?"

"Yes."

"Go ahead," the man said to the maid. I'll take care of this."

The woman scowled and left. Drake, a pleasant-looking fellow with deep dimples, glanced out at the car. "That cab's waiting for you?"

"Yes."

"Where are you staying?"

"Downtown, at the Figueroa. I'm going home, back to Ohio, very soon. I was attending the Julian trial and heard about Mrs. Bradford's death."

"Ah. And you say you knew her?"

"Yes, we met some years ago."

"Hmm. Well, if you want, I could convey your message to Mr. Bradford. It's as close as you'll get to him. He's not seeing anyone. As you can imagine, his wife's passing came as an awful shock."

"Is he, is he here, at home?"

"No, and I'm afraid that's all I can say about that. But listen. If you want, I could drop you off. I've got to go that way to make some deliveries. We could talk about Mrs. Bradford, if you'd like."

"Oh. Uh, well, really? You sure?"

"Of course. You came all the way out here."

Sarah thought for only a second. She couldn't decline this offer. "Well, all right. Thank you."

She paid the cabbie and dashed back.

"Sarah, you said?"

"Yes."

"Come on in. He flicked on a light. Have a seat," he said, pointing to an exquisite burgundy couch. "I'll be just a minute."

Sarah sat quietly, trying to suppress her excitement and indeed anxiety over gaining entrance to the Bradford home. She ran her hand over the fine embroidered fabric and scanned the rest of the luxurious room, with its high ceilings, Mediterranean furniture and gold swag curtains. A massive stone fireplace served as the centerpiece, and Sarah tried to imagine it with a roaring fire. Her eyes drifted upward to a gilded framed oil painting. Rita! It was Rita! Sarah bounced up from the couch and approached the portrait. She put on her glasses. So realistic. And quite recently done, no doubt, for she appeared much as she did that day at the courthouse, all in red with her hair swept up. Except that here she was smiling, her green eyes unworried, her flawless neck unadorned. She was seated, her hands folded on her lap. Sarah cocked her head this way and that, examining the face, the clothes, the gently swirled background. She was alive here, and, from the looks of it, content.

"Sarah?"

"Oh, yes, sorry, I…"

"Is that how you remember her?" Drake said.

Sarah nodded. "Quite a likeness."

Drake came up beside her. He was very tall, with straight, slicked back auburn hair. From the side he looked no more than twelve. Freckled and hairless, with a peachy cheek. The only indicator that he was older was a bulging Adam's apple. "She was a beautiful woman," he said, shaking his head. "Had to endure so much."

Sarah turned to him. "Endure?"

"What?"

"You said she had so much to endure."

"Oh, yes. Well, you know, if you're her friend. Ready?"

No! she wanted to say. I'm not ready. I don't know. What did Rita have to endure? "Yes."

"After you."

34

arlos had already gone through a pack of Camels. The car ride home had been brutal. Heavy fog. Traffic as far as the eye could see. His throat burned, and he was coughing, but that didn't prevent him from pulling over at a roadside store and buying another pack. He needed the distraction. Every second he wasn't home was a second too long. If Carlos' mother let anything slip, his son might very well escape again, sick or not.

After another fifteen minutes or so, however, he started to make progress, just passing the town of Orange. It was 10 p.m., and the fog had lifted a bit. He could actually see the car in front of him now. At his current rate, he'd be home in an hour. He lit up again and tried to relax. How he approached Andrés would be crucial. Gently, calmly. No accusations. No shouting. Just questions. Simple, reasonable questions. And then he'd have to wait. Not force the issue. Patience. Give the boy all the time he needed.

He was on Highway 101, his car from this point divining the way on its own. Over the years he had witnessed the growth, the road's widening and sprouting of limbs, spreading out in all directions. But the way home was still straight ahead, past the bronze mission bells on El Camino Real, through the town of Whittier, final residence to Pio Pico, and on to Montebello, where the oil fields had blackened the once verdant, if artificially cultivated, land. Closer and closer.

Nearing the cutoff, he sat up. The light from the street lamps was diffused in the heavy air, like a distant, waning fire. A bitter taste rose in his mouth as he neared the neighborhood. *The* neighborhood, where the bodies were found. Rita on Marianna, Sabrina on Pomeroy. And before that. Way before. All the others. A graveyard. The odor still lingered. It would never disappear, forever embedded in the soil. He slowed as he passed those dead streets, only three miles from home. So close. Another block and everything he too held dear could have been lost, wiped away. Except for the stench of bigotry, which was permanent. Tears welled up in his eyes. He shook his head, banged the steering wheel again and sped off.

He arrived at his own street, quiet and dark, but alive. Alive with families.

Mothers and daughters. Fathers and sons. He hoped. The house lights were on. He parked and sat for a moment, fighting the impulse to run in and push his way through whatever blocked his path to Andrés' room. He needed to compose himself, so he sat and breathed, not moving a muscle until he saw his mother coming toward him.

"*Mijo*! What are you doing out here?" she said, her thin, white, waist-length hair hanging loose.

"Just getting my things, Mama."

"Leave them for now."

Her tiny, frail body looked even more diminutive in her oversized robe. "Okay," Carlos said, hugging her bony frame with affectionate restraint. He could not let her know the level of his concern. He kissed her cheek, and then took her weathered face in his hands. "Andrés?" he said softly, his legs almost giving out.

"He's sleeping."

"Ah, good." Sleeping? Sleeping! he thought. He wanted to jump for joy.

"*Sí*. Come, I've made some…."

"Don't tell me. *Albóndigas* soup, I hope?"

She nodded and leaned her head into Carlos' chest as they walked into the house. The warmth, the peace, if only momentary. No more than a cottage, really, with a living room, three tiny bedrooms, a kitchen and a bath, but his mother revered it, treated it like a sacred gift. She had adorned the plain furniture with Mexican blankets, the windows with handmade curtains and the walls with colorful plates and photographs. In her own room was a makeshift alter to Our Lady of Guadalupe. A figurine of the Virgin, gowned in teal and gold, surrounded by candles and a rosary. Over each bed in the immaculately clean house also hung a crucifix. Carlos let his mother do as she wished, believe as she wished. Yes, she was simple, a pawn of the Church. But if it comforted her to think that a woman could give birth without having sex, that a piece of wood could protect them, so be it. It was a small price to pay for the care she had given to Andrés. And for the aroma. Ah, the aroma. Tonight, cilantro, tomatoes and mint.

"Carlos! Carlos! Carlos!" Fernando, his mother's parakeet, shrieked out his name, fluttering in its cage.

"Hush!" Carlos said to the little green and yellow monster, but the bird kept on.

"Carlos! Carlos!"

"Hush up, I said!"

His mother frowned. "*Mijo*, he's just happy to see you."

"*Ay*, I know." Normally Carlos would shake the cage to silence him, but he didn't have the energy. "All right," he said. "*Hola*, Fernando."

"*Hola! Hola! Hola!*"

Carlos shook his head. He didn't know how his mother stood it. As soon she went to ready his meal, he inched open Andrés' door. He had to make sure. He tiptoed over to the bed and breathed a quiet sigh of relief. Yes, asleep. Such a handsome face. Long, dark lashes, full, etched lips. Even sweaty and disheveled, jet-black hair that no woman could resist running her hands through. And innocent. So very innocent looking. Carlos lightly touched his son's head, causing Andrés to twitch. He pulled back. Fever. "Tsk, tsk." The boy was really sick. Good, he thought.

Carlos sat at the kitchen table and gulped down a hearty bowl of the soup. The meatballs were tender and juicy, with just the right amount of rice. As usual, the balance of spices was perfect. His mother watched him eat. "What are we going to do with this kid?"

"What do mean, Mama?"

"He's too idle. That's why he's sick."

"Mama, he's sick because he caught a virus. But as soon as he's well, I've got a plan, a job for him, in Mexico."

"Mexico! Why there? Why not at the market?"

"I need him to handle the exports. He'll be fine."

"What are you talking about? Are you crazy? You know his problems."

"No more about it tonight. I'm bone tired."

"But...."

"No! You leave Andrés to me."

"After all I've done?"

"Yes, after all you've done. I know what's best for my son."

She looked at him with a pained expression as he got up and went to bed. But it couldn't be helped. How could he tell her that he needed to get Andrés out of the country? As soon as possible. And for good.

■■■

Carlos woke with a start. The sun was already high, streaming in at a sharp angle. He jumped out of bed and peered into his son's room. Andrés was up! Drinking some tea. "Hey there, fella." Carlos said.

"Hi, Pop."

"How are you feeling?"

"Not great," Andrés said in a hoarse voice. His eyes were watery and bloodshot.

"Son, do you feel well enough to talk?"

"Sure, Pop."

Carlos sat down on the bed just as his mother came in with a tray. "You see, he's better," she said. "Here, boy, eat up."

"Mama, could you leave us for a few minutes?"

She furrowed her brow. "Why?"

"I just want to speak to my son, alone."

"All right, but don't upset him. He needs his rest." Then she whispered in his ear. "No talk of Mexico."

Carlos nodded but said nothing. He watched her leave and then turned to Andrés. "So, tell me, what've you been up to?"

"Up to? Oh, hanging out with Jimmy."

"Where?"

"Around. The Flats. And…and around. The usual places. Jimmy got sick first. That's how I got it I guess."

"What else?"

"I've been practicing the guitar, and reading."

"Reading? What?"

"Actually, some of those stories you told me about, from the *Estridentismo* writers, the Stridentists, Pop." He coughed, blew his nose, and continued. "I've been remembering what you told me about their art, how you said it was a product of the Revolution. That it was about new forms and political action. Vela especially. I read his "*Le Señorita Etcétera*." Read it many times. You're right, Pop. He's a great author."

Vela, Carlos thought. Shit. Why did he tell Andrés about him? And *that* story. Why did it have to be *that* story? "Your fever sure hasn't affected your memory."

"If I lived in Mexico, I could be part of that movement, Pop."

"Mexico!" Carlos looked at his son, trying not to reveal anything. Could it be that Andrés might actually go there willingly? "Doing what?"

"Composing music, maybe. Chopin to the electric chair!"

"Andrés. You know those slogans are just exaggerations. Chopin and folk music can coexist. So can turkey *mole* and pheasant under glass. I don't know," he said. "I've changed my mind about that group a little. Tradition isn't so bad."

"Whose tradition?"

"Smart ass."

Andrés laughed and then had a coughing fit. When it ended he said: "You've been a good teacher, Pop."

"Hmm."

A brief silence ensued, and then Carlos said: "Andrés, I've been very worried about you."

Andrés averted his gaze. "I know."

"Had any spells?"

"I guess."

"You guess?"

"I don't know. You know, sometimes I'm not sure. But Pop, I'm sorry I left. I know you said to stay."

Carlos braced himself. "That's okay," he said, patting Andrés' tightly muscled arm. His skin was still very warm. "But, uh, why did you, son? You know, I just had a little job for you at the store. I needed some help, that's all. Why didn't you wait?"

His son now turned away completely, facing the wall.

"Andrés?"

"I don't know."

"Hey, okay, don't worry. Here, your grandmother made you this toast. Let's share a little."

They each took a half and munched silently.

"Pop, I do need to tell you something," Andrés said, licking butter off his fingers.

Carlos stiffened, but kept munching. "Sure."

"It's, it's about girls. A girl. A woman."

"Yes?"

"I, I...."

"Go ahead. You can tell me anything."

His son looked away again. "I...."

"Andrés, please...."

"No, I can't. Not now. Pop, my head is pounding. I can hear my heart beat in my ears. Do you hear it!?"

"Stop it! You're just sick, boy."

"I *am* sick! I'm tired, too."

Carlos bit his lip and then forced himself to smile. "Listen," he said, removing the tray, "take a little snooze, and we'll talk later, *bien?*"

Andrés closed his eyes and lay back. "All right, Pop. All right."

Carlos tucked in the sheets and walked out. He closed the door and immediately headed for the jar hidden in the hall closet. He removed the key, tiptoed back and locked Andrés' door. Then he found his toolbox and removed the large screwdriver. He went outside and, as quietly as possible, jammed the window to Andrés' room, testing it several times to make sure that it would stay. Only after he was satisfied of its strength did he allow himself to ponder the dark meaning of his son's words, confirming unequivocally Carlos' suspicions

A girl! A woman! Both, Carlos thought. Both. And Vela. "*La Señorita Etcétera.*" About alienation from the self. But also, goddammit, from women. That narrator, yeah, he takes a lover, but views her as an object. "Nothing of her would remain with me," he says, "except the sensation of a Cubist portrait." Carlos had remembered that line because, admittedly, it had resonated with him. He had read the story after his wife left, when one hot *señorita* blurred into another. Sex, that's all they were good for, and even then, some better than others. He'd have been hard pressed to recall any of their features, except in the abstract. He blinked, however, as Sarah's face flashed before him quite clearly. Fuck, he thought, I still have to deal with her.

Near the window, on the side of the house, was a rose garden, bordered by a short adobe wall that Carlos had built himself. Weeds had sprouted up everywhere. Carlos knelt down and yanked several out. The roses were wilted, the surrounding shrubs dry and brittle. Tending the space was Andrés' responsibility, and he had clearly let it slide. If only that were the worst of his problems. Carlos should never have confided his vengeful thoughts, taken him to see Rita, introduced him to Sabrina. What was he thinking? He should have never recommended those books to him either, an impressionable, sensitive boy like Andrés. He took everything too literally. Carlos should just grab him now. Why wait? He'd be all right. Cover him with a blanket, get him out of here. Ask questions later. Yes. He would do it. As soon as he woke up. At least the stores were in good hands. Carlos had checked in with the managers, and all was in order.

He needed some coffee, black and strong. He went inside, took down his favorite mug from the shelf and poured it three quarters full. In his pocket was a *ponchita*, the contents of which he added until the mixture reached the brim. His mother was in the kitchen, standing with her hands on her hips, resuming where she left off. "It doesn't make sense, Carlos. Taking him to Mexico. What's wrong?"

"Nothing. Nothing is wrong. Make me some eggs, will you?"

"Carlos. What are you doing? You're not thinking straight. Who will he live with? Who will take care of him? You know he's not like other boys. I am an old woman. This will kill me!"

"Mama, enough!"

That silenced her for the moment, but Carlos knew that this was not the end of it. It didn't matter. She would adjust. She would have to. He would explain, something, somehow.

Butter sizzled as she beat the eggs. Carlos took a few swigs and gazed at his mother. She's right. This very well could kill her, he thought. The eggs hit the pan, just as someone banged on the front door. Fernando screeched out some nonsense as the banging escalated. Carlos got up and flung open the door. Two uniformed cops faced him. *Dios*, he thought. Andrés. They know.

"Carlos Martinez?"

"Yes?"

"We have a warrant for your arrest."

"For *my* arrest? Me? What? For what?!"

"Sabotage."

Carlos glared at them, at first confused and then relieved. He nearly laughed out loud. The irony. But quickly he realized the danger. "Sabotage? Of what?!"

"Don't play the dummy. Rochester Farms. The water supply. *Com...pren... do?*"

"It's *comprendes*, but I don't know what you're talking about."

"Well, you can tell that to the judge. We have a witness."

"Witness? I know about your witnesses."

"Get moving!"

"Carlos! Carlos! Carlos!" The bird went wild. His mother rushed in to the sounds. "What is this? What do you want here?" she said to the cops, wielding a spatula like a gun.

"Mama, I'll get this straightened out. Don't worry. But whatever you do, don't let Andrés leave! Do you hear me?"

"I knew something was wrong. What's this all about, Carlos?"

"It's nothing. They just want to round up some greasers. Need their daily quota."

"*Mijo!...*"

The officers handcuffed Carlos and pushed him outside. As they dragged him to the car, Carlos turned. "Mama, don't worry. But remember. Do *anything*, anything you can to make him stay. I'll be back before you know it."

35

arah poured herself another cup of coffee from the thermos she'd purchased on a whim. The café across the street had just filled it up, and they made a pretty good brew. She wanted to have the beverage in her room to ward off her cravings for hooch. The thermos kept it hot and plentiful.

She sipped, took a bite of a muffin the café claimed was its specialty, and replayed the previous, revelatory day, beginning with that strange ride back to the hotel with Drake:

"Were you close with Mrs. Bradford?" Drake said.

Sarah looked at Drake, the silhouette of his pug nose and Adam's apple. He had offered her the private backseat, an act of respect, she assumed, but that would have made talking difficult. She needed to maximize her time, so she opted for shotgun. "Not really. But I felt a kinship with her."

"How so?"

How so? Sarah suddenly wondered at the familiarity and, indeed, authority of this person. Drake told her that he was a student at UCLA and worked for the Bradfords part-time as a chauffeur. But he seemed much more than that. It was he, after all, who gave the maid the order to leave. It was dim of Sarah to not have considered this before. "May I ask *you* a question first?"

"You may."

"How long have you been working for the Bradfords?"

Drake's half-boy, half-man profile came into clearer focus as he turned onto the still bustling Wilshire Boulevard. He smiled. "A year. Why?"

"You just seem to be so caring, so involved."

"I am. The family has been very kind to me, taking me in, treating me as a son of sorts. They don't have any children, and my folks are in Nebraska, so it's kind of worked out. I mean, I don't live with them or anything, but they do little things for me. Buy me dinner sometimes, give me their throwaways. In return, I feel protective. You know, some people you just hit it off with. I cared a great deal about Mrs. Bradford. And, uh, I'm paid to be watchful."

"I see," she said, intrigued by this window into the relationship. Paid to be watchful. By whom? For whom? So he was indeed more than a chauffeur. Like a son, he said. He was old enough to be Rita's brother, or even more, but perhaps he had sparked her maternal instinct. A childless woman was susceptible to such things, as Sarah knew first hand.

"And you, Sarah?"

"I met Rita in the Julian offices. You know, C. C. Julian. The stock scandal and such. Mr. Julian was holding a party for investors."

"Ah. I don't really know much about that, only what I read about the trial."

"Yes, well, that's the strange thing. I actually saw Rita at the trial, at court, the day before she died."

Drake hit the brakes. Sarah jolted forward, nearly hitting her head on the dashboard.

"Oh, I'm so sorry," Drake said. "Are you okay?"

"Yeah, I think so," she said, relieved to have escaped another lump.

"I'm glad there was no one behind us. So you say you saw Mrs. Bradford? Did you talk to her?"

"Briefly."

"What, what did she say?"

Better not, Sarah thought. No. Better not. "Just hello, that it was nice to see me again."

Drake was silent, but Sarah thought she detected a sigh. Of relief? she wondered.

"I can see why reading about her death must have been so shocking," he finally said.

"Indeed."

"I'll see that Mr. Bradford hears of this. Maybe he'll see you."

"That's very kind of you, Drake. I would appreciate it," although something in his voice made her doubt his sincerity. Sarah wanted to ask so many questions. If Drake was like a son, he might know if Rita had been ill. Was the family really satisfied with the coroner's report? Did Rita have any enemies? Perhaps Mr. Bradford himself? Clearly, Drake knew something about the man's whereabouts. But she held her tongue. She didn't want him to become suspicious, whether she had cause to worry about that or not.

Sarah waited while he dropped off a package at a men's store, a return, he said, and another at a bank. Soon they would arrive at the hotel. She hadn't learned anything of substance, so she ventured: "Drake, what did you mean that Rita endured a lot? You said I'd know, but I don't. As I said, I wasn't that close."

"Oh yeah. I just meant all the stares, the snide remarks. The adjustments, in the early days of her marriage. She talked about it to me a lot. You know, being Mexican. It was hard on her. Beverly Hills is restricted. I mean, technically she's not allowed. Despite his position, Mr. Bradford had to really plead his case. Took time for people to accept her."

"You mean Mexicans aren't allowed in the whole of Beverly Hills?"

"Not unless they're hired hands."

"Even if they're citizens?"

"Nope. Neither are Negroes, or Jews."

"Jews?"

"They in particular."

"Really? Well, I broke the law then."

"I assumed so."

Sarah scowled at him in the blackness.

"Your name," he said.

"Oh."

Sarah trudged up the stairs. The night had proved interesting but not particularly enlightening. Except that now she thought that Mr. Bradford was perhaps somewhere close by. As for Drake, she wasn't at all sure about him. Just then, outside, when he'd come around and opened the car door, he held onto her arm a bit too tightly and said: "I'll tell Mr. Bradford about your visit. You leave, when? Wednesday? Shall I call you here if he wants to see you?"

Sarah had nodded and yanked out of his grasp. His hands were large, his fingers long. Could they possibly...? Ach. Not likely. A friend. A son. Still, his reaction was extreme. Slamming on the brakes like that. As if he were afraid of something.

She'd flicked on the light and locked the door. Her eyes fell immediately on the crucifix. "No Jews in Beverly Hills?" she said to it as if it were alive. "Well, you shouldn't be allowed in there either, then."

Her notebook lay open on the desk, waiting for the next entry. There was much to record, but she hadn't been in the mood. She glanced around the cubicle. "Ah, the rag," she said, on the bed where she'd left it. Something to relax her. She kicked off her shoes and grabbed her glasses. The lenses were scratched.

She needed some new ones, a different style, too. They still worked though, and that was unfortunate because plastered all over the front page was, what else, but articles about the Julian trial. Her first impulse was to skip to another section, but how could she resist that headline?: *OHIO MAN TO RETURN TO THE STAND.*

Ohio?

She'd read on, discovering that a Ronald Bishop from Waynesfield had been called as witness for the prosecution, having lost property and huge sums of money in the scheme. He'd had a nervous attack on the stand, but was due back in a few days. Sarah shook her head. "Well, I'll be damned. I'm not the only one." Then, more! The article summarized his testimony, stating that Bishop had been encouraged to loan the Julian company fifty-thousand dollars. By…by… Theodore Rosen Senior, Ted's father! One of the gentlest, and as far as she knew, most law-abiding men in the world. Indeed, Bishop claimed that Ted Senior had been the instigator. But the defense attorney had pushed Bishop. So what? he said. Everyone, both Rosens included, thought the company was in good shape. It was Bishop, the attorney said, who should be on trial, suggesting that he expected favors from Ted Junior for his investment. Wanted him to watch over it, and, the reporter implied, provide him with inside information. "Mr. Rosen wouldn't do that, and that's why you're here testifying against him, isn't it?" the article quoted. It was this charge that led to Mr. Bishop's collapse.

Sarah had read it again, twisting her rings, the old habit suspended for a bit but now painfully, comfortingly back. Ted's father? Impossible. Such a sweet man, a good soul. She remembered him taking her hands one day, grinning. "So many rings," he had said. "But where's the wedding band? Now if you and Ted would just…" Sarah had stopped him right there, repeating what she had said many times before, that it wasn't in the cards. "But you would make such beautiful children!" he'd said. The thought of that nauseated Sarah, but she smiled and told him she appreciated the compliment.

No. Ted Senior's involvement had to have been innocent. He loved his son, but wouldn't knowingly contribute to his corruption. But that made Sarah start to think again about the son, about Ted, the investment, Julian, and whether any of it had anything to do with Rita. It was after all at the courthouse where she appeared, where she pleaded, where she spent her last day. Of course, now Sarah had no other choice than to return to the trial. To do the very thing she swore she wouldn't do. She had to see this Mr. Bishop, on the stand, and off. And she'd have to do it cleverly, without being recognized by Carlos, should he show up.

She turned to an accompanying article, which quoted testimony by another victim. The reporter introduced it by saying: *And the suckers continue to mount…*

> 'You never had possession of that stock at all?'
> 'No sir, they never gave me any stock at all.'
> 'Did you receive the check for that stock?'
> 'No sir.'
> 'Who gave you the orders on that? Mr. Bennett'?
> 'Yes, sir.'
> 'That is your signature there?'
> 'Yes, sir.'
> 'That transaction took place on what day?'
> 'April thirtieth.'
> 'How long was that before Mr. Bennett disappeared?'
> 'Possibly two or three days, maybe longer.'

Suckers, indeed. Were the cops even looking for Bennett or Berman or whatever he might be going by now? She searched for other news. *FIFTY-ONE FROGS ENTER FIRST FROG JUMPING JUBILEE, AT ANGEL'S CAMP, CALIFORNIA.* Twain lives, she thought. Who actually does such things, though? Toledo was known as Frogtown, given that the city was built on a swamp. And the city liked its moniker. But she didn't know anyone who'd take the little critters this far.

AMERICAN FILM ACTRESS CLARA WILLIAMS DIES AT FORTY. After playing an immigrant's wife in "The Italian," Williams, from English stock, only played Latin women, her last such role being in "Carmen and the Klondike." She married and retired at thirty-one, dying last week in Los Angeles of a prolonged illness.

Sarah had seen Clara Williams in several films, but only then did she realize the typecasting, and Latin at that. "Forty famous frocks." That's what Sarah associated her with, the term some reporter had coined to describe her many gowns. Sarah thumbed through the pages. Another actress dead, but this one…

ASPIRING ACTRESS' DEATH RULED A HOMICIDE. *Twenty-two year old Sabrina Johnson, who was found on a vacant lot between Marianna and Pomeroy, was murdered, police say. Ligature marks were confirmed to be the result of strangulation. The young woman lived at the Hollywood Studio Club. The investigation is underway, but no suspects or motives have yet been discovered. Everyone at the Club and at the audition where she was last seen has been cleared. Johnson's roommate, Jill Sloan, was quoted as saying that Sabrina had been afraid of late, that she felt she was being followed. When asked what the girl might have been doing in that part of town, Jill said she didn't have a clue. "Poor thing. She didn't have a mean bone in her body."*

Her dead body, Sarah had thought, squinting until the text blurred, faded, dissolved. Except for those five words, stark and familiar, leaping off the page. *Ligature, strangulation, fear, followed, Marianna.* She'd pulled back from the paper, as if it were on fire. *Ligature, strangulation, fear, followed.* And *Marianna*, near the very street. In this case, an empty lot on Pomeroy. In Rita's, a ravine. If Sarah had any doubts about the cause of Rita's death, this article put them to rest. Surely this, out of all the maybes and possibilities, out of all the things that might or could be, surely this was not a coincidence. And surely others would agree. Phillip Bradford, Drake—did he already know?—even Hodges. Yes even, and most especially, Officer Hodges. If not, Sarah would make sure that he did, or somehow force him to acknowledge that he'd known from the beginning. But this time she would wait until she had something concrete. Something irrefutable that would connect Rita and Sabrina. Because they had to be connected, dying in the same way, perhaps for the same reason and by the same hand.

Revelatory. Yesterday had certainly been that. Sarah took a remaining bite of muffin and drained the thermos. Okay, she said to herself. Next stop: Hollywood Studio Club.

36

itchell nodded at his sober image in the mirror. He'd made it. Survived again. And all because of that young couple, stumbling out of the speakeasy. He had been ready to dive, one foot off the board, when he asked them for the password, the key to the bottom of the pool. The flapper had stared at him with unfocused eyes. "Sorry, fella. No can do. But here," she said, streaming a little of the booze in her flask on the pavement. "Drink up!" She and her lover staggered away, arm in arm, laughing. That hit Mitchell like a slap on the kisser. He could have easily found some other booze, but instead he left while he was still smarting and went to bed.

That was the day before yesterday. Since then, sleep had quieted his squawking crow's feet, cleared the whites of his eyes. If Sarah hadn't been tormenting his thoughts, he might even have appeared refreshed. But as it was, the downward slope of his already bent features counteracted any salubrious effect. He rubbed his heavy stubble and brushed on the thick lather he'd whipped up for the second time today. He shaved, slapped on some stinging lotion and already felt the beginning of growth.

As soon as he'd gotten up, he called Hodges. "We're working on it," the man said, and abruptly hung up. That was all Mitchell could handle. He immediately located a private investigator, a man whose ad he had by chance heard a few days ago on that miraculous invention, the radio. Radio. He was still amazed by it. Connecting people all over the country. Mitchell remembered the nationwide broadcast at the Scopes trial, the first of its kind. But lately the airwaves had been taken over by evangelists, hucksters and self-promoters. C. C. had used that route. But damn if it didn't work. Mitchell remembered the dick's ad because of the alliterative tag: professional, prompt and prudent.

Ray Sparks was his tough, sharp-sounding name, but it didn't match the man, who was short and fastidiously dressed and who spoke in an affected manner. Like Poirot, that little Belgian fop in those Agatha Christie novels Sarah read when she needed an escape. Still, Sparks had been in business for ten years and exuded confidence. To avoid unnecessary questions, Mitchell feigned the jealous husband. His wife had been missing, he said, and he thought she was having an affair. Could the detective help? Of course. The question was, did he have the time? He did some checking and then told Mitchell he could luckily work the case in. He took down all the information and promised a report in twenty-four hours, exactly when Ronald Bishop was scheduled to return to the stand.

In the meantime, Mitchell had landed quite a coup. It was his pretense to Hodges that gave him the idea. If a cop could fall for the interview story, why not someone else with presumably an even bigger ego, someone who might be relieved to have a respite from his personal tragedy, to have public attention redirected to something other than his wife's untimely death? It was a reporter Mitchell knew at the *L.A. Times*, a well-connected fellow known for his discretion and who just happened to owe Mitchell a favor, who brokered the deal, the meeting with Phillip Bradford that he was heading to now.

Sarah had told Mitchell about Bradford, the much older husband of Rita, whom she'd met at the Julian offices. His name had appeared in the L.A. papers nearly every day since Mitchell arrived, just a line or two stating that he was still in seclusion and that his agency, The Bradford Group, was temporarily closed for business. That seemed an extreme and financially irrational move to Mitchell, but perhaps it was just a ruse, a way to avoid the press. If that were the case, getting the interview was a long shot at best, but Mitchell had been optimistic. And motivated. If Bradford agreed, Mitchell would use all of his tricks to pry something loose from the man. Something that would help Sarah *when* she returned. A statement to allay her fears, or a slip of the tongue to confirm them. Either way, the interview could not hurt Mitchell's career, whatever he actually did with the material.

Mitchell told the *Times* reporter nothing about his personal interest in Bradford, of course, only that while covering the trial, he got the idea to do a piece about the growth of L.A. He was particularly interested, he said, in the city's politicians, financiers and boosters, the latter of which Bradford indeed was. Before pitching the story, Mitchell did a little research and discovered that The Bradford Group had been instrumental in attracting people to the city. Bradford had worked closely with the Chamber of Commerce to produce ads that would captivate and seduce, that promised a wealthier and especially healthier quality of life. Clean air and fertile land. Blue skies and warm sand. Fresh fruits and sanitary neighborhoods. Conditions that could cure anything from asthma to melancholy. *Hibernate Where You Are and Grow Old*, one of the ads read, *or Live Here and Grow Young!*

Mitchell's angle, and how he sold it, was a profile, the first in a series entitled "The Men Who Made Los Angeles." He promised to be sensitive to Bradford's loss, only mention his wife in the context of portraying the man's admirable traits. That Rita was of Mexican origin would make his persona more interesting, Mitchell said, his character more sympathetic. Yes, Mitchell said to the reporter, he was aware that no one had been granted an interview since Rita's death. But no one had presented Bradford with this kind of opportunity: to tell his story, recount his contributions to a journalist from out of state, with no local axe to grind. And it worked. More quickly than Mitchell would have thought. Perhaps the reporter had sweetened the deal. A promise to keep certain individuals off Bradford's back, or a scoop down the road, from Bradford's perspective, when he was ready. Certainly vanity must have played a part in the man's decision. He was old, no doubt thinking of his legacy. The ads would fade from memory; here was an opportunity for national recognition, a chance to go down in history.

The meeting was set for a few hours from now, but the drama had already begun. Bradford insisted that his whereabouts remain a secret, and that Mitchell therefore be taken blindfolded to where he was holed up. Only in L.A., Mitchell thought, as he waited on the corner of Figueroa and Third. He lit a cigarette and straightened his tie, keeping his eyes peeled for an old black Model T. Several cars matching the description passed by. In a few moments, one pulled over and stopped. Mitchell flicked his butt on the street and reached for the rusty handle. The driver raised his hand and mouthed, "Wait!" He jiggled himself out of the vehicle, keeping his hand in the air until he stood next to Mitchell. He was chubby, informally dressed, with a shock of black hair and matching full beard. "Name's Fred, he said in a squeaky voice. "Gotta pat you down."

Mitchell chuckled, the command and voice at odds. "You kidding?"

Fred didn't smile, so Mitchell raised his arms.

"I don't feel any guns," he said, as if he were telling Mitchell something he didn't know. He pulled out Mitchell's note pad and cigarettes from his inside pocket and replaced them. Then he fingered his camera. "I'm taking this for now," he said, fumbling and nearly dropping it.

"Hey, be careful with that!"

"Sorry."

"I wouldn't worry about me using it," Mitchell said. "I'll be blindfolded, won't I?"

"I'm still taking it. You can ask Mr. Bradford whether he approves of it later." He opened the car door, motioned for Mitchell to get in and ordered him to place a checkered cloth around his eyes. "Now tie it, he said, and tight." He checked the cloth's position, made a few adjustments and told Mitchell not to try any "funny business."

As the car pulled away, Mitchell felt his pulse beat in his temples, reverberate off the cloth. He could see nothing except swirling after images, but could smell the car's old leather and stale smoke. He asked if he could crank the window down a tad, received a positive grunt, and felt for the handle. Cool, fresh air blew in as they continued on a straight path for several miles. Here and there he'd get a whiff of something or other, exhaust, eucalyptus, grilled meat. Screeching cars, fleeting music, a ripple of street talk. Then they veered left, and soon started climbing, up several winding paths and then down, down, down, up again, and down. Mitchell tried to make conversation but to no avail. The breeze grew colder and the smells more intense. Fishy, salty. Ocean. Around several bends, up and down and then finally the car stopped on a gravely road. Yes, Mitchell could hear the crashing waves.

"Stay where you are," Fred said.

In a minute or two, the door opened and Mitchell was led inside, down a spiral staircase, through some sort of passageway and into a stuffy, cigar scented space. A door closed behind him.

"Okay," a low voice uttered, "you can pull it off."

Mitchell untied the cloth, squinted and blinked. The man who had spoken was seated. He was thin and frail, his white hair slicked back. He wore a blue velvet jacket over a grey turtleneck sweater. A bright lamp lit up his weathered, aristocratic face. His wiry brows were arched and a deep scar jagged down the entire length of the right side. He jutted his narrow chin out proudly, but there was pain in his yellowed, soupy eyes.

"Mr. Bradford," Mitchell said extending his hand.

"Sit," Bradford said, ignoring the gesture.

The chair offered was hard. The square, wood-paneled room was without ornament or windows. A couch, table and a few nondescript chairs were the extent of the furnishings. Other than knowing they were near the sea, there was nothing to give the location away. He could have been in a house, office, or even a film set.

"Shall we begin then?" Mitchell said, reaching for his notebook.

Bradford nodded, but then let out a little moan and grimaced. He held his gut, shooing Mitchell away when he offered assistance, even though he seemed to be struggling for breath. When the fit was over, he wiped his face with a rumpled handkerchief, removed a cigar from a canister and swished around a drink that lay on table. "So, I've been told you're a pretty serious writer, not one for gutter talk," he said.

Mitchell breathed. "I'd like to think that's true."

"Huh. I wonder. I was also told that you were trustworthy. That you respect your sources."

What the hell was he getting at? "As much as possible."

"I'd like a guarantee. I want you to sign this. It states you won't print or speak publically about me for one month."

"Well, the article won't come out before then anyway."

"Sign, or I'll call for the driver to take you back."

Mitchell took the document, clearly drawn up by a lawyer. He read and signed.

"Good," Bradford said, folding the paper and sticking it in his pocket. "Now, you agreed to this interview on the condition that my late wife stay out of it."

"Yes, sir. I said that I would only mention her with respect to your...."

"Yeah, I know what you said."

"Okay."

"I've changed my mind. I *want* to talk about her."

Mitchell squeezed his pencil. "Okay."

Bradford lit the cigar. Then with a great huff, he pushed himself up off the chair and circled the room, studying the barren walls. Mitchell sat frozen, eyeing him for what seemed like hours. With his back still to Mitchell, he finally said: "I want this to be included in the piece, with no gussying up."

Mitchell thought he was toying with him, building up to nothing. "I'm ready."

"I doubt it."

"You doubt what, sir?"

"That you're ready to hear what I am going to tell you."

"Well, you've certainly piqued my curiosity."

Bradford turned, half-smiling. "My wife, my wife Rita, was a whore."

Mitchell felt his eyes bug out. "You're right. I wasn't ready."

Bradford shuffled toward Mitchell until he hovered over him, close enough for Mitchell to see the web of veins on his mottled skin. "I should have listened. A greaser is a greaser. You can dress them up, teach them manners, you can even try to love them. But you can't change their blood. Their nasty ways. Their filth." He clutched his gut again, but continued to smile.

Mitchell just sat, immobilized. Come on man, he said to himself, where are your instincts. This is a goddamn gift. Make the most of it! "I assume you don't mind if I smoke."

Bradford offered him a match, his hand trembling.

Mitchell puffed and blew out a perfect smoke ring. "Why tell *me?*"

Bradford eased himself back down in the chair. "Timing."

"Just learn something?"

"No. I've known she screwed around for a while. Or at least I suspected it. But I'm damn fed up with the headlines. All that grieving husband bullshit. I'm not grieving. I'm celebrating! One less Mexican in the world."

Mitchell cringed, although he doubted Bradford was really celebrating. And he wondered too if he was as bigoted as his words. He married the woman, for Christ's sake. Blaming his wife's ethnicity for her dalliances, if indeed she'd had any, would be easier on the ego. Mitchell could relate. He'd like to believe that even the most virtuous of women would have trouble resisting the advances of a Latin lover. "I see," he said. "But Mr. Bradford, this, uh kind of changes the interview, doesn't it? I mean, I had a different impression. Would you really want me to print this?"

"Why not?"

"Don't you think this kind of statement could backfire? On your business, for example?"

"You think I give a damn about any of that? And anyway, no I don't. It'll probably improve it."

"Well, let me ask you another question," Mitchell said. "These are some pretty strong remarks. If they were made public, don't you think some might wonder, I mean, even just a little, about the cause of your wife's death?"

"Huh?"

"Well, I'm not a cop, but Jesus sir, it's not hard to imagine a motive."

"Ha-ha. You think I killed her?" He laughed again, catching his breath with a pained look. "Oh my dear boy, you're a naïve one. But I guess it shows that you really aren't from around here. Don't worry. No one gives a damn about a Mexican, alive or dead. Murdered or diseased. Man, I could tell you stories. Do you know that if I went to the cops and confessed, they would just shrug?"

Mitchell doubted that, even if Hodges were his confessor, but perhaps he wasn't far off.

"But don't be absurd. I didn't kill my wife, and neither did any one else. I told them so."

"You told who what?"

"Told the cops she had a heart defect."

"Did she?"

"I think lacking a heart qualifies. Why are you so interested, anyway?"

Better stop, Mitchell thought. "No reason."

"So you still want to do the profile?"

"Of course."

"And you'll include what I said about Rita?"

"If that's what you want. But I'm still confused. You say timing, but why not give it to the *Times*?"

"There are other papers in the city, you know. Don't want to show favoritism."

"I see," he said again, although he really didn't. What was that Conan Doyle quote Sarah often repeated: "Once you eliminate the impossible, whatever remains, however improbable must be the truth." Everything about this interview was improbable. It was the impossible he'd have to figure out. "So, let's begin at the beginning," he said. Where were you born?"

"Just a minute." Bradford reached in his pocket, pulled out some pills and swallowed them down with the drink. Then he cleared his throat. "Boston, I was born in Boston, Massachusetts."

He continued on for an hour, portraying a happy childhood, the only son of a doting mother and engineer father who instilled in him a strong work ethic. The family came to California when he was young and immediately got involved in Republican politics. His father was a self-made man, and Bradford followed suit, building his agency from the ground up. He likened himself to a character out of a Horatio Alger story, although he admitted that he was never really poor, nor particularly brave. A few times, Mitchell tried to steer the conversation to the history of the city, to its early inhabitants, to the Indians and more delicately, the Mexicans. But he would hear none of it. He believed in manifest destiny, now more than ever. He mentioned a few of his earlier campaigns, one for Goodyear Rubber, one for the stockyards, modeled after those in Chicago, another for Willis-Overland cars, all L.A. based industries that he helped to grow into huge moneymakers. He was most proud, however, of his work for the Chamber of Commerce, of the role his ads played in shaping the city's optimistic spirit. One in particular, a few years back, was his *pièce de résistance,* although due to the terms of the contract, he could provide no details. Just know, he said, that it saved the city.

"Saved the city?" Mitchell said. "Literally?"

Bradford gazed at the wall, as if it were the L.A. skyline. "Some say that advertising is a lie," he said. I say it is art. Magic, of a sort. It tells a story that with enough repetition becomes the truth. Some say it plays on people's fears. I say it speaks to their dreams, inspires a better quality of life. Boosterism. I know. Babbitt and all that. I'm not him, and I'm not dumb. The Communists say we don't read. Fuck 'em. I read, I just don't buy the premise. That's my response, and you can quote me on it."

"Hmm," Mitchell said, as he wrote. Complex fellow. He would have to dig through his cryptic answer later. "So why do you want to wait a month?"

"You haven't guessed?"

Mitchell shook his head.

"That's how long the doctors have given me."

"Wha...?"

"And remember. You signed that contract. Everything spoken here. What I just said, too. You've got some good material, but not a word until then."

"How long have you known?"

"A year. And no one else knows. Or knew. No one."

"I'm sorry to hear it."

"We all have to go."

"One more question?"

"Not about my health."

"Okay. Do you...do you know whom your wife was with? I mean, the man or, men?"

"Not important."

"But it could be."

"Why?"

"Well, I don't know, because...."

"Because you think one of them might have killed her?" His eyes narrowed. "Is that why you're here?! Is that what your visit is really about?" He tried to stand, but fell back in the chair. "Fred!"

"Sir, no...."

"Fred! Fred!"

The door swung open.

"Get this man out of here. Now!"

Mitchell had to think, think and talk fast. "Wait," he said. "Please, Mr. Bradford. I swear, I came for the profile, that's all. But reporters have instincts. It's my job to question. You took me on a detour, and I was just trying to follow the signs."

He didn't say anything, so Mitchell continued.

"Remember, I just arrived from Toledo, here for the trial. All I knew of your wife was what I read in the paper, that she died of a heart attack. It was your own words, sir, the bombshell you dropped that led me to even consider another possibility. You can see that, can't you?" Mitchell feigned his most sincere expression. He knew the look, head bent, unblinking, direct gaze. He'd mastered it, a necessary evil of the profession.

"Mr. Bradford?" Fred said.

"Never mind. Go back out for a minute."

"You sure, sir?"

"Yes, go!"

When the door closed, Bradford said: "Fred's a little thick. My usual driver is ill, with that bug, you know."

Mitchell nodded, feeling a twinge, but only a twinge, of guilt.

"All right. I'll buy your argument. But I don't know the names. Don't want to," Bradford said.

"How did you find out?"

"I have my ways."

Mitchell nodded again.

"But sex and murder are two very different things, Mitch."

"Usually. But one can lead to another."

"Only in Hollywood."

"Isn't that where we are, or at least very close?"

Bradford sniggered. "But even if it were true, I don't give a damn. It doesn't matter. Don't ya see? Nothing does."

Mitchell exchanged a long glance with the man. Bradford didn't do it, he thought. Yeah, he had a motive, but he was just too open about it. Unless of course that was a ploy, to somehow exonerate himself, posthumously. But if that were the case, why not fess up? He was going to die anyway. Still, if he was right about Rita, then Sarah might have been on to something. Improbable, but certainly not impossible that a lover had it in for her. He closed his note pad and returned it to its worn out home in his jacket. And then he remembered. "Ah! Mr. Bradford, before I go. Fred out there has my camera. I wonder. To accompany the profile. A picture or two?"

"Why not?" he said.

The lighting was poor, but Mitchell could do something about that in the dark room. He shot straight on, from the side and at an angle. He took a few with the man leaning on the table, his hand resting on his swollen knuckles. Through the viewfinder, he could see the illness, the halo of death. Sallow and gaunt, a cadaver in waiting. If, as Bradford claimed, advertising created truths, photographs revealed them. When Mitchell was done, he handed the camera back to Fred, who blindfolded him again. They started to leave, when Bradford called out: "Hey Mitch, you believe in God?"

"No, I'm sorry to say."

"Neither do I. You can include that in the article, too."

37

arah browsed the photographs that lined the Hollywood Studio Club's moss-green walls. A few showed the building under construction, but most were of the 1926 opening. Dedication ceremonies, dancing contests, and numerous celebrities, including Norma Talmadge, Mary Pickford, and aviatrix, Andree Peyre, who Sarah remembered from a stunt-flying exhibition Mitchell had covered. Mitchell had never been in a plane himself and, after witnessing Peyre's daredevil near misses, said he never would. Sarah hadn't flown either and wasn't in a hurry to do so, but she chided Mitchell nonetheless for his unmanly reluctance. She smirked, recalling that he'd responded by taking her to bed. God, if she only knew how simple things were then, how lucky she had been. Her eyes started to fill. Stop, she told herself. Stop.

A historical timeline traced the Club's origins to a 1910 gathering of young women in the basement of the public library who were trying to break into the movies. The librarian, Sarah read, had worried about their ability to practice their craft safely and thus instigated a public funding campaign. That led to the renting of a meeting hall, the purchase of an old house and finally to the building of the current three-story establishment.

Sarah was waiting for the receptionist to call her name. She had requested permission to speak to Jill Sloan, listed in the paper as Sabrina's roommate. Upon hearing of Sarah's arrival, the manager immediately appeared and called Sarah to her office. Given all the recent police activity, the elegant, aging beauty who oversaw the facility assumed Sarah was some sort of cop. When she learned she wasn't, she exhaled but then immediately stiffened. Who was Sarah then, and what did she want with the girl? Sarah was ready, however, concocting another story based on half-truths, using her job once again to her advantage. Specifically, she told the manager about her work with women, providing her court identification card and examples of her expertise. She recited the reasons she was in town, for the trial and the conference, adding that she was a friend of Jean Shontz. That elicited a nod and a smile. Every woman in L.A. knew who Jean was, the manager said, every informed woman, that is. Sarah then explained that she'd read of the tragedy involving Sabrina and thought she might be of some help. An event like this could be traumatic, she said, especially for those closest to the victim.

"Very thoughtful of you. Poor girl didn't have any family. Her mother died when she was just a child, and her father a couple of years ago. He was a doctor, here in L.A. Worked for the health department, I think. Didn't leave her a dime."

"This was like a family to her then," Sarah said.

The woman sniffed and wiped her eyes. "True, as it is for many of the darlings. You know the Club was established for their protection. They come to Hollywood with big dreams, but little money, live in cheap hotels and become vulnerable to, well, the elements. Some sell their bodies. Most go home, a few take their own lives. The rare one is *discovered*. This was supposed to be a safe haven. And it is for the most part. We are so very careful."

"You can't control everything."

"I know. But it is so terribly sad. And it's disconcerting, of course, to all the girls. Sabrina was very sweet. Always there in a pinch, home before curfew. Wasn't wild like some. Committed to her work. She'd only been here a couple of months, too. I just pray the police find whoever did it."

Thank you, Sarah thought, that information could be useful. "So, may I speak to Jill?"

"It's up to her, but I'll encourage it. You know, we could use more people like you in the world," she said, before inviting Sarah to look around while she checked to see if Jill was in.

Sarah winced at the deception. Still, it was for a good cause and not without some sincerity. Sarah did indeed believe that the girl might benefit from a talk, even if Sarah had her own motives for instigating it.

She glanced at the receptionist, who, writing with one hand and dialing the phone with other, seemed as if she might be a while. Sarah continued to wander about the central section of the building. There were two other connecting resident wings and a busy staircase in the middle. Above the entrance was a painted frieze flanked by two tall windows, which a few of the girls were currently washing. Dressed in loose frocks and aprons, they stood on various rungs of a ladder, creating quite a wholesome-looking scene. Behind a closed door nearby, Sarah heard muffled speech, perhaps the practicing of lines.

On a nearby wall hung a portrait of Julia Morgan, the architect who designed the building. A studious, bespectacled, almost grandmotherly figure. Sarah read the text under her name:

> *First woman to be accepted in the architecture department at l'École Nationale Supérieure des Beaux-Arts in Paris, first woman to be issued a license to practice architecture in California. Favors the Mediterranean style, including full-length arched windows, balconies with iron balustrades, and decorative brackets. Currently at work on a special project for William Randolph Hearst.*

That's no typical grandmother, Sarah thought, regarding her surroundings with greater interest. Yes, she could see the elements now. The style was indeed Mediterranean. She looked again at the windows and nodded. Full-length and arched. If she had the energy, she would examine the structure for the balconies, balustrades and brackets later.

"Miss Kaufman?"

Sarah snapped to the call. "You can meet with Jill in the room at the end of the hall," the receptionist said, pointing. "She'll be down in a minute."

"Ah, good. Thank you."

The room was empty, save for an old table and chairs. Sarah sat and twisted her rings. In a few minutes the door slid open.

"Hello."

"Jill?" Sarah said, extending her hand to a fair blonde in a terrycloth robe and furry slippers. Little spit curls framed her round face.

"Uh huh. Miss Kaufman?"

"Yes. But call me Sarah. I appreciate you agreeing to talk to me."

"I think it's supposed to be the other way around," she said. "Miss Lee said you might do me some good, that you're some kind of women's counselor."

"Yes, well, what helps you, helps me. Because if I can help you, then I've done my job. You see?"

"I guess," she said. She sat down and folded her arms "So?"

"So, is there anything you'd like to talk about?"

"Not really."

"Well, how about you tell me how you're feeling."

She sighed and pursed her pale lips.

"No pressure," Sarah said, "just anything that comes to mind."

"Tired. That's how I'm feeling. Tired of all the questions."

"And now I've just asked another."

"Ha-ha." She raised her round eyes. "Yeah. The cops never asked about my feelings though."

"No, I imagine not."

"Worst of all is that I don't know anything. I can't help them."

"It might not seem like it, Jill, but you never know. Even the tiniest detail could lead to something."

"Uh huh."

"What else do you feel?"

"Sad."

"Of course. You were roommates. Were you close?"

"Getting to be. Sabrina hadn't been here long. But, I liked her. Everyone did. You know, she was a good person. Didn't deserve this."

"No one deserves what happened to her."

"No."

"This may sound like a strange question, but do you feel guilty at all?"

"Guilty?"

"That happens sometimes. Even if there was nothing you could have done. You're alive, Sabrina's dead. The guilt isn't rational, but you can feel it just the same."

Jill sat, and slowly nodded. "You know, now that you put it like that, I think I do. Especially because she had this feeling of being followed, and I laughed. I mean she never saw anyone, just had a feeling. I should have taken her seriously."

"Well, you couldn't know now, could you? And that may have had nothing at all to do with what happened to her," Sarah said. "So, she never saw anyone?"

"No, never."

"Hmm."

"I'm scared, too. Yeah. That's the worst. Fear. Around every corner, you know. Until they find out who did it."

"That's understandable. And more rational, although you have to keep in mind that the chances of something happening to you are extremely remote."

"That's easy to say."

Sarah nodded. Here was her chance. "Of course. But Jill, the chances *are* remote, "unless…"

"Unless?"

"Unless you suspect someone. Someone Sabrina…knew perhaps."

Jill crossed her legs. "Do you remember what happened with Fatty Arbuckle?" she said in response.

"Huh?"

"Fatty Arbuckle. The comedian."

"Do *you* remember him, Jill? You seem too young."

"I'm nineteen. I was thirteen then. Hadn't thought about it until now."

"What about him?"

"I think he was guilty. You know of killing Virginia Rappe. I remember her name because it sounded a lot like what he did. Rape. Rape and murder. He was a funny guy, and so light on his feet. But he was a monster. The idea of it, killing her with his weight. Accidentally they said. He got away with it because he was a star."

Sarah wondered at the connection to Sabrina. "I don't know. The press ran with that one, you know. Yellow journalism, some said." Mitchell, she meant. "But why did you think of him?"

"Just because. Maybe it was someone like that. Some creep. A star even."

"Do you know of anyone, someone she might have dated?"

"Now you sound like a cop."

"I didn't mean to."

"She didn't date. In fact, I wondered if maybe she, you know, batted for the other side. Except…."

"Except?"

"Sabrina did mention a fella. Two actually. In passing. I don't know if she dated them or what, but one was older. Maybe that's why I thought of Fatty. Someone she used to see."

"Think, Jill. Do you remember anything more about them?"

She twisted her mouth and squinted. "Nope. Never came here or nothing. But one was definitely older, yeah. And…and maybe, not an American. Someone foreign. They both were, I think. Dark."

"Oh?" Sarah said.

"Hey, ma'am, you're turning red. You all right?"

"Oh my. Yes, it's just a flush, you know. Part of my age."

"Ah. That must be awful. I get pretty sick myself every month. Well, anyway that's all I can remember about it. Other than that, she was a nose to the grindstone kind a gal. I think she might have made it, too. She had that real talent. Gosh, that reminds me. I've gotta practice for an audition. Very tiny role, but it's something. The film's a whodunit, involving a kidnapping." She shook her head. "Jeez, too close to home."

"Did Sabrina get any parts?"

"Not yet, but she would have. God. Being dumped there like that. Who would do such a thing?"

"I don't know, Jill. Somebody very troubled. By the way, did you tell the police about these men? These foreign fellows?"

"No. Just thought of them. There's really nothing to tell."

"Well, you never know. I think you should mention it." Dark, that should get their attention, she thought.

"Okay. You know, I do feel a little better."

"Good. Talking helps. I'm staying at the Figueroa. Call me any time. I'll be in town a little while longer."

"Thanks."

Jill stood, and Sarah followed suit. They exited the room and headed back to the lobby. She didn't want to press her luck. Establish trust. Perhaps more would come out. Already there were things to pursue. That puzzle, that dark puzzle was taking an even darker shape. Darker and older. Mexican, Sarah thought, shivering at the possibility.

"Talk about foreigners," Jill whispered to Sarah.

A plain girl in even plainer clothes walked by. "She's a odd one. Studious, Russian, I think. A screenwriter. Her name is Ayn Rand. Not Ann. Ayn. I'm sorry to say that I don't like her."

"Oh?"

"She's a know-it-all. Snooty."

"Well, we can't like everyone."

"Yeah, I don't think she'd like me either. Too low class."

"Probably wouldn't like me either then, Jill. Good luck with your audition. I'd love to know how it turns out."

"I'll let you know, if you'd like."

"Do," Sarah said, knowing she wouldn't. "Oh, and please keep this conversation just between us."

"I will."

"And remember, try to keep things in perspective," she said. Now if Sarah could only take her own advice.

●●●

The way to do that, Sarah decided after returning to the hotel, was to record in her notebook what she had learned. To let facts, not emotions, speculations and jumping to conclusions dictate her thinking. But when she started to write, she realized that the facts were actually few. Rita and Sabrina? Both bodies found in the same area. Yes. A fact. Both afraid? Yes again. Of being followed? Likely, but only presumed with Rita. Ligature marks? Yes, but with Rita, the cause officially unknown. Other than that, the women were as different as night and day. One dark, one light; one young, one middle-aged; one married, one single; one rich, one, if not poor, certainly not wealthy like Rita. Sabrina's father was a doctor, the manager said, who didn't leave his daughter any money.

And then Philip Bradford. *Nothing*, she wrote. Indeed, even less than before. Still in seclusion, somewhere perhaps close by. Drake? Who knew? A strange reaction, a few questionable remarks. And the older "dark" man Sabrina used to date? Sarah had really stretched on that one, filling in the blank with: Mexican. A particular Mexican. No, a Chicano. Carlos. She wrote his name in capitals. *CARLOS*. Did she really believe that? And even more, that Carlos had known and in some way been involved in the *death* of both women? Yes, that's what kept creeping into her mind, with no evidence to back it up. No, she wouldn't even expect Hodges, who would surely jump at an opportunity to put a Mexican behind bars, to take that seriously.

And yet Sarah couldn't let the idea entirely go. Not until she spoke to Paige. About Tijuana of course, about how wrong her trusty contact had been, but also about the status of the investigation into Sabrina's murder. Given where she worked, Paige was in a perfect position to help Sarah determine once and for all if her vague suspicions had any basis in reality. Did the cops have any clues? Had anyone noted, privately perhaps, the similarities to Rita's death, to what Paige said they believed down deep was her murder? Would Jill follow through and tell them about the men in Sabrina's past? That, too, Paige could find out, as well as following the trail to which that detail might lead.

Now, the question was, would Paige be willing? That remained to be seen, but Sarah had cause to think so. Certainly the woman would be apologetic about Bradford and perhaps desirous to make amends. But also, Paige had sisterly feeling; we women have to stick together, she had said, the reason she had approached Sarah in the first place. And obviously she had few qualms about going around official channels in the pursuit of that idea. So with the murder of Sabrina, she would hopefully do what she could to help find the perpetrator. In any case, Sarah would know soon, because fortunately, Paige was due back at work tomorrow. Sarah had called the station again and was told that Paige would be there, but for only a half of the day. She was better, but still weak. Maybe Sarah should have screamed rather than whispered her name in temple, but something was better than nothing. Again Sarah was asked if she wanted to leave a message. And again she declined. She simply couldn't take the chance with Hodges lurking around. She would call at 10 a.m., an hour after Paige was due to arrive.

∎∎∎

The good news was that today the man from Ohio, Ronald Bishop, was due on the stand. Sarah was actually looking forward to his testimony. She would be doing what she had come here to do, her mind occupied with something other than murder. But even as she thought that, she realized it wasn't exactly true. Rita, Carlos, Ted, were all connected to the courthouse, all investors in Julian Pete, all part of that damned puzzle. Even Ted? It strained credulity, and yet she still couldn't toss out his piece either. And of course her disguise, or at least the alteration in her usual style, would remind her that this wasn't just another day at court.

She had gone to a second hand store and purchased a shapeless jersey dress, a size and half too big, a pair of oxfords and a felt hat with thick netting. No makeup either, and she combed her hair severely to the side. When she looked in the mirror, she could hardly see her face, let alone recognize herself, which was exactly what she wanted. Not conspicuous, just different. Plain. A little like that screenwriter at the Studio Club, Ayn Rand.

Still, her heart raced as she entered the sanctum. She darted a quick look around and exhaled. No Carlos. She took a seat in the middle of the room, where the rows were mostly filled. She wanted to be surrounded, although it wasn't as crowded today, perhaps due to the virus, perhaps because no one cared much about Ohio. Still, she would have imagined that the drama of Mr. Bishop's collapse would have piqued the usual morbid curiosity, a chance to witness a possible repeat performance.

A few more folks straggled in as the bailiff ordered everyone to rise. Judge Doran uncharacteristically lumbered to his chair. His face looked swollen. Perhaps he had the bug, too.

"The State calls Mr. Ronald Bishop to the stand."

Sarah lifted the netting halfway to observe her kinsman. Nondescript. Balding and pudgy, like any number of middle-aged men. He was sworn in and Judge Doran addressed him, in a voice that was in fact deep and hoarse. "I assume you are better, Mr. Bishop."

"Yes, your Honor."

"Good. Before we proceed, a reminder to the audience. Remember what I said yesterday about coughing. If you have a fit, please go outside. I would take my own advice, if I could."

That comment elicited some laughs and even a few coughs.

"Mr. Shelly?"

The prosecutor leaned on the witness box. "So Mr. Bishop, let's get to the point. When you said that you thought Mr. Rosen would be 'in there,' did you mean that you had expected favors, inside tips from him?"

"No," Mr. Bishop said calmly.

"Could you answer that question again?"

"I expected nothing at all from Mr. Rosen, other than a return on my money."

"Did you know anything about the overissue of stocks?"

"No. I simply made a loan, an investment, with the hopes of prospering. I don't think there is anything improper or illegal in that."

"Why did you get so upset the other day? "

"Because I felt that my integrity was being attacked. You can ask anyone. I am an honest businessman. I was taken in by crooks, like so many others."

"Forgive me, but such naivety doesn't mesh with someone as successful as you are. You're successful, aren't you?"

"Objection!"

"Overruled. You may answer the question."

"Yes, I've done all right. But we're all fallible."

Sarah wanted to clap. Thatta boy.

"Another question. Mr. Theodore Rosen, Senior. Do you think he knew about the overissue when he told you about the Julian Company?"

"Objection. Speculation, Your Honor."

"Sustained."

"Okay, let me put it this way. Did Senior ever say anything that would indicate he knew about the overissue?"

"No."

"And did Ted Junior ever provide you with any inside information?"

"No. Absolutely not."

"Okay. I think we have enough."

"Counsel?" the judge said, looking at the defense.

"He can go."

Bishop wiped his forehead and stepped down.

That's it? Dressed up only for that? Sarah thought. She watched him gather his things and start to exit the courtroom. Should she follow? Talk to him?

Shelley then stood. "Your Honor, I'd like to call Theodore Rosen back to the stand."

Sarah sat up. "What?"

The courtroom doors swung open and in walked Ted, dressed more sedately than she had ever seen. Sarah raised the netting again as she watched his sober steps. Well, she'd have to hear this. She sat back as he was sworn in, but out of the corner of her eye she spotted something that gave her a start. A jacket. The man wearing it was leaving, right behind Bishop. She turned completely around. Wha…? His back was to Sarah, but that jacket. That threadbare, corduroy jacket. With the patches. Not so unusual, but the left patch, stained like that. She gazed up at the sloped shoulders and the floppy grey curls. He pushed the courtroom door open and briefly glanced back. Sarah sucked in air, loudly, covered her gaped mouth with her hands. Her heart pounded. Mitchell!

She slunk down in her seat although he was already gone.

"You all right, ma'am? Ma'am?"

"Oh, yes. Yes," she said to whoever was sitting next to her. She scooted back up. How had Mitchell gotten here? Bishop. Was *he* Mitchell's secret assignment? God. She had to get out, and fast. No! She should stay. Stay right here. Don't budge.

"Mr. Rosen." She heard the prosecutor, but his voice was distant and bubbly, as if she were listening to it under water. "Do you know Mr. Ronald Bishop?"

"Yes, I know Ronnie."

Mitchell. Mitchell! Here!

"Ronnie? That sounds pretty familiar. How well did you know him?"

"Well enough."

"Well enough to let him in on the overissue?"

"Objection, your Honor! Mr. Rosen never admitted knowing anything about that."

"Sustained."

Mitchell. Sarah wished she could object.

"What do you mean by well enough, then, Mr. Rosen?"

"My father introduced us. If he was okay with him, he was okay by me."

"Well, then, did your father know about the overissue?"

"Objection!"

"Don't you attack my father!" Ted screamed. "You can say anything you want about me. But not about him. He didn't know anything!"

A member of the defense shot up, shushing Ted with a burning gaze. "Your Honor, please, I need to speak to my client, privately."

"Please do. Strike Mr. Rosen's last remark from the record," Doran said with a cough. "We'll take a ten minute break."

Sarah sat immobilized. Only her eyes moved, enough to catch the smirk on Shelly's face. Ted had just as good as confessed. His father didn't know *anything*. What *anything*? Sarah tried to smile but the muscles didn't work.

Ten minutes. She couldn't bear it. She glanced at her watch, the one that Mitchell had given her. Maybe he'd come back. Probably. She turned to the doors. She couldn't think, but she felt her legs move, felt herself walking out of the building. Then she saw herself check all around and rush to a cab. Only when she was safely in her room, door locked, blinds drawn, did she feel somewhat back in her body. But that was of little comfort. She tore off her ridiculous clothes—what a waste, an ironic waste—and fell onto the bed where she lay staring at the ceiling. Mitchell. How? Where? He must have gone to the Portsmouth. He must have. When? How long? She thought of her coat pocket, bolted up and found the rumpled, still unread message. The answers, of course. But now they didn't matter. He was here. She glanced at her notebook. If there were ever a cause to write…but she didn't have the strength. So she just lay back on the bed and agonized over her dwindling options.

38

Mitchell was torn. He of course wanted to stay for Ted Rosen, who was unexpectedly called back to the stand. But he couldn't let the chance to interview Ronald Bishop pass. Bishop had been dismissed, his own return to the witness box quick and anticlimactic. A few questions and the whole thing was over. He'd again denied having any knowledge of the overissue or of expecting any shady favors. But this time he spoke flatly, plainly, his emotions completely in check. And he seemed to still have trust in Ted's father. Mitchell needed to confirm that, among other things. A quote or two would go a long way with Stephen.

Mitchell called out to Bishop, who was springing down the courtroom steps. The man couldn't get away from the place fast enough and initially waved him off. But when Mitchell managed to get out that he was a reporter for the *Blade*, Bishop stopped and asked Mitchell to a lunch, a very early lunch since it was only 10:30 a.m. They went to a nearby café that Mitchell had been to before and both ordered a cheese hamburger.

Bishop turned out to be a pleasant fellow, something that would disappoint his boss. He told Mitchell how his "attack" on the stand, though mortifying, had put things into perspective. He'd lost money. A lot of it. But he still had more than most, and he'd learned from the experience. He wouldn't make the same mistake again. Yes, he said, before Mitchell even asked. He was telling the truth. He had known nothing about the scheme. The only thing he was guilty of was being a fool. As for Ted Rosen, he could rot in hell. But Ted Senior? He was indeed certain of his innocence.

Mitchell asked how Bishop had come to know the man. He said he met him at a business meeting in Cincinnati ten years ago. Rosen owned several clothing stores and was attempting to expand to Waynesfield. That never materialized, he said, but they had stayed in touch, and when Bishop asked if he knew of any good investments, Rosen told him about Julian Pete. He said his son worked for C. C., and that he thought it was a good deal. No pressure, no promises. But why, after all that had happened, did he believe the father's hands were clean? Because, he said, Ted Senior had a reputation for honesty. He had been instrumental in establishing a watchdog committee for the Ohio business community, to protect the average Joe from predators, ironically like Julian. "You get me?" he said. "He's one of the good guys. He is utterly devastated by this situation. I can tell you that because I talked to him before coming out here. He was in tears, apologized profusely. He still couldn't believe that his son was knowingly involved. But he said that if proven guilty, he'd want him to receive the full force of the law."

Mitchell nodded. That's the man Sarah knew, he thought. Perhaps he really was an innocent bystander.

They talked a bit more about Ohio, Bishop's properties, his family, and the Mud Hens, who were having a miserable season. They finished their burgers, which were good and greasy, and shook hands. Mitchell didn't have his camera, but Bishop said he could mail him a photograph. "It's poor quality, taken when I was young, with hair. Is that okay?" Mitchell smiled, gave Bishop the address and wished him a safe trip.

He lit a cigarette and considered returning to court, but instead headed to the P.I. It had been twenty-four hours and then some. The only reason the Rosens mattered to Mitchell at all was because of Sarah. Probably Senior was in the clear. But who cared if Sarah wasn't? The office was close. Just around that corner. He remembered those Spanish tiles and the waterless fountain. He squashed out his cigarette and jogged up the office stairs.

"So?" Michell said, after Sparks offered him a seat.

He twisted his mustache and smiled, seeming to enjoy the suspense. "I have information."

Mitchell froze. He almost didn't want to know. "Well?"

"Your Sarah Kaufman has recently been in Tijuana."

Mitchell shot up. "Where!?"

"Tijuana. Mexico. You've heard of it, haven't you?"

Mitchell sneered. "Of course. How do you know, though? Are you certain?"

"How do I know? You hired me for that purpose, didn't you?"

Mitchell sat back down. "Go on."

"A woman with that name purchased a train ticket to Los Angeles from the Agua Caliente depot a few days ago." He leaned back and clasped his manicured hands on his paunch. "We checked with the Southern Pacific and the conductor confirmed that a woman matching the description you provided was on the train."

"*Agua caliente*? Hot water. Fitting."

"Agua Caliente. The resort. The new gambling resort, just south of the border."

"Oh." Gambling? Mitchell thought. Well, yeah, maybe so. Could be. With Carlos. Mitchell was relieved. She was alive it would seem. But he couldn't prevent the anger from welling up. If he were alone, he'd spit. Or put his fist through the wall.

The dick was silent. He raised his brows.

"I'm impressed," Mitchell said. "What now?"

"It'll cost you more."

Mitchell thought for a moment, but then nodded. He had to be sure.

"I've got my best man on this. If she's in L.A., we'll find her. Give me another twenty-four."

Mitchell heaved a deep sigh as he headed down the stairs, one heavy step after another. His back was in knots, usually a sign of rain. But the sky was clear. He kicked a rock and kept kicking it as he headed back toward the courthouse. Until he lost it, until it careened out of his path, and he stopped. What the hell. He'd gotten what he needed from Bishop. Fuck the trial. He could write the piece in his sleep. Tijuana? Jesus Christ. He lit another cigarette and thought of Bradford. Poor guy, probably dead by now. Where the devil were they that night? Not that Mitchell really cared, but the thought of those waves made him remember how much he loved the sea, the way it drew him in, altered his perspective. He didn't get to the beach often enough, and hardly ever to the Pacific. Twenty-four hours. He had time.

He found his way to a bus station and bought a ticket to Santa Monica. No camera, dammit, but he'd make do. He'd stroll on the pier. He'd hunt for shells and watch the bathing beauties. If the water was warm enough, or even if it wasn't, he'd roll up his pant legs and go in, dry off on the sand. He'd have some oysters. Then, at night, he'd go back. Not to his room, but to that alley. And this time, he'd not take no for an answer. If she were booked, he'd get her to cancel. Tell her he'd make it worth her while. A big tip, breakfast even, a night at his hotel. He'd pay. Pay for the privilege, pay to pretend. He'd pay for Ida, all right, and whatever she was willing to do.

39

Sarah awoke with a splitting headache. She feared it was from the injury, that maybe something had burst inside, but the pain responded to aspirin and now she was just tormented. Mitchell. She had to do something about Mitchell, she just didn't yet know what. So instead, she stared at her watch, trapped in her room. Fifteen minutes. She checked again. Fourteen... thirteen... five... one. Finally, the hands read 10:00. She reached for the phone and dialed the station.

"Miss Kaufman! Sarah! Am I glad to hear from you!"

"Oh, Paige, you sound awful."

"I'm improving. You should've heard me the other day. My poor vocal chords. That's what I've been most worried about, my singing. But sweetie, I've been dying to know. Did you go to Tijuana, or what?" She coughed, deep and raspy. "I tried calling the Portsmouth and since you weren't there, I thought maybe you did."

"Yes, I went."

"Well, I'll be. Good for you! And?"

"Paige, I'm sorry to report that, uh, your source was wrong."

"What?" She coughed again, one hack leading to another until the spasm finally abated. "Pardon me. Boy, I hope you don't get this."

"That makes two of us."

"So what were you saying?"

"To make a long story short, it was the wrong Bradford."

"Huh?"

"A man named Bradford was holed up there, but he was British, and his first name wasn't Phillip."

"You kidding?"

"No."

"I can't believe it! Really. Wait till I get my hands on..."

"Don't worry. It seems to have been an honest mistake."

"I don't understand. I feel awful. Just awful. How could it be?"

"Part of the long story. But Paige...."

"Wait a minute. Let me grab the phone in the back."

Sarah heard the rustling of papers, clicking of shoes and the closing of a door. "Okay."

"I assume you know of the Sabrina Johnson murder," Sarah said.

"Of course, terrible."

"Well, has anyone in your office noted any similarities to Rita's death?"

"Huh? Not that I know of. Like I told you, they've put Rita to rest, in more ways than one. Why?"

"Well, there are some, if you think about it. Strangled women, found in the same neighborhood...."

"Gee, Sarah, I hate to burst your bubble, but that could describe a lot of people."

"I know, but just think about it, and maybe keep your ears open."

"Sure thing, but now, before you go any further, I've got something to tell *you* sweetie!"

"Oh? Something else about Rita?"

"No, unfortunately. You probably wouldn't trust me if I did! No, there was a fella here, came looking for you. Tall, grey, kinda good-looking, in an offbeat way."

"What?! At the station?"

"Yeah, Mitchell something."

Sarah was glad she wasn't standing. "What did he say?"

"That he was worried because he couldn't reach you. Asked Hodges to check around. Oh, and he said you might be with a man, a Mexican! He even had a first name. Carlos."

Sarah must be dreaming. How else? How in the hell else? "He told Hodges that? So are the cops...are they looking for me?!"

"I'm not sure. Hodges did put a man on it, but I don't know that there was any urgency about it. I didn't know what to do, but I sensed I shouldn't say anything to anyone. Before I spoke to you, that is."

"You did the right thing, Paige. Thank you. I'll straighten things out. With Hodges too."

Paige suppressed another spasm and then said: "So, uh, do you mind me asking? Were you with this Carlos fella?"

"All part of the story, Paige."

"Oh. Well, I'd sure like to hear it. This Mitchell, a boyfriend?"

"Was, is, sort of."

"One of those, uh? Seems nice."

"He is. I imagine he left a phone number."

"The Portsmouth."

Sarah nodded to herself. Naturally.

"Crap," Paige said. "I hear the boss rumbling out there. Better get back to work or he'll make me stay all day. So anything else?"

"Not right now. Maybe we could meet in person. It would take me some time to explain. It involves more about Sabrina, and then I could tell you about Tijuana, too. As soon as you can."

"Sure thing. How about dinner, tomorrow? My appetite's finally returning, and the doc told me that I'm not contagious. It'll be on me, for this fool's errand I sent you on."

"No, no. You were trying to help. But dinner sounds good."

"There's a place where they occasionally let me sing, and the food ain't bad. It's called The Lock, on Wilshire. Where are you staying now, by the way?"

"The Figueroa."

"That's pretty close. Seven o'clock?"

"Okay, if you're sure you'll be up to it."

"Sure, sure. I'll see you there…. Oh, uh, Sarah, I don't mean to be pushy, but you're gonna call this Mitchell chap, aren't you? If I had someone worrying about me like that, I sure would."

Sarah sighed. Paige was just that type, a bit too familiar but well meaning. A lousy judge of sources, but a good heart. "Yeah," she said. "I am."

40

Carlos paced in his concrete cell, three steps turn, three steps, turn. The cramped, cold space smelled of booze and piss, but he could have endured it indefinitely had he been certain of Andrés' safety. He tried to focus on his mother's reassurances. Only yesterday she was here, telling Carlos that Andrés had improved and was still home. According to Carlos' wishes, she had been vigilant, checking on the boy several times in the middle of the night. Ironically, Andrés was worried about Carlos, she said, and of course so was his mother, who stifled tears at seeing her son in jail. They were only allowed a fifteen-minute visit, with an officer breathing down their necks the whole time, so it was impossible to talk honestly. His mother kept asking Carlos if he had really done this thing he was accused of, and Carlos just kept saying that the only thing that mattered was Andrés. What timing. A little later and he might have made it to Mexico. That was the only good thing that had come out of this situation, his mother said. That her grandson was where he belonged. *Dios*, if she only knew.

Carlos had been in jail for four days and finally his attorney was on his way. He'd declined the public defender, even though there was a small chance that he might have already been out on bail had he gone that route. But the chance was too small. He needed certainty, someone with skill, and, most of all, someone he could trust. So he'd contacted George Miller, Jorge to Carlos and others of his ilk. George. Jorge. Part of the man's power was his ability to use both names, and all that they symbolized, to his advantage, sliding almost seamlessly between two cultures. It was also what made Miller, both *Señor* and Mr., highly in demand.

Footsteps! Carlos pressed his face to the bars eager to see Jorge's trademark white fedora. *Mierda*. False alarm. Only a guard. He stomped past Carlos, stopping two cells down, at the one in which a Negro man was being held for theft. Carlos learned that from the man himself, who, when Carlos was brought in, introduced himself as Tom, and said he wasn't no uncle. Carlos ignored him, but the guy was hell bent on talking anyway. He didn't steal anything he said, only borrowed a couple of apples and a sandwich from the grocery store. Would have replaced them when he earned a little money. He was just out of a job and hungry. Carlos had cringed. Borrowed my ass. As if stealing from a market wasn't a big deal. Petty crime maybe, but not for the grocer.

He sat back on the cot and thought of Jorge, his fine features, blue eyes and pale skin. No one would mistake him for a Mexican. But in fact, at twenty-one he learned that his grandmother's maiden name was Gomez, a chance discovery that he viewed as a sign. Indeed, even though he could have easily passed his entire life without anyone being the wiser, Jorge embraced this part of himself both personally and professionally, marrying a Chicana and devoting a good deal of his law practice to defending Mexican workers. He was an ardent supporter of the CUOM too, and his *gringo* credentials—raised in a white, middle class family, law degree from USC—made him a unique and formidable spokesman for the cause. There was only one problem. He believed wholly in the law, in the word as well as the spirit. For him, change would come not through circumventing it but through exploiting every possible legal avenue. He was enormously sympathetic to the Mexican plight, but not at the expense of his principles. Therefore, this initial meeting would be a delicate dance, because while Jorge undoubtedly suspected that Carlos was guilty, he might very well decline to represent him if he were certain.

Again, footsteps. Carlos sprang up.

"Mr. Miller is here," the guard said, unlocking the cell door.

"Thank you," Jorge said to the guard. "Come back in a half hour." He waited for the man to leave and then turned. "Carlos."

"Jorge," Carlos said, grasping the strong hand that was offered. The lawyer removed his hat and motioned for Carlos to join him on the cot, as if Carlos were the visitor. He then opened his briefcase and pulled out a pen, paper and what Carlos presumed was a police report. Jorge looked at Carlos intently, acquiring and conveying information without saying a word.

"Who?" Carlos said.

"Ernesto Basio."

"*Nito!* No! But *Nito* was…."

Again Jorge stared, his piercing gaze and nearly imperceptible headshake forcing Carlos into silence. Jorge didn't want to hear the end of that sentence. The less Carlos said, the better.

"Ernesto turned himself in," he continued, "gave Rochester Farms a heads up. They were able to ameliorate the damage."

Carlos pushed down bile in his throat. He wanted to howl. But all he did was grunt out: "What damage?"

Jorge gave a hint of a smile, a wisp of a nod.

"Salt. Ernesto admitted to salting their irrigation water. As soon as they heard, they flooded the area and were able to dilute it somewhat.

Carlos now just sat, trying not to twitch.

"He's in the Upland jail. Couldn't live with the guilt, he said. He gave a detailed account of the event, placing you in charge, the head of the operation. Rochester is going to cut him a deal."

Carlos still sat, stone-faced but boiling. Jorge must have felt the heat. *Nito*?! How could he? How could he? Jorge was probably proud of the fool, doing what he himself would do. "Are the others…?"

Jorge bore his steely eyes into Carlos once again. A warning. What others? How would Carlos know of any others?

"No need giving me your version of events," he said, when he was satisfied that Carlos understood. "We have only one option. We have to get you off on a technicality. I'm investigating that already and see some possibilities. There is no other way. This can't go to trial."

Carlos nodded. There was no other way if Carlos wanted Jorge as his attorney, that is. In his ethical universe, a man was entitled to a defense only if he told the truth, which ironically wasn't the way the system he followed so religiously was designed to work. But he was probably right anyway. Carlos couldn't lie, because there were in fact the others, who now would surely cave under pressure. No doubt they would be offered deals, too. It would be Carlos' story, which he hadn't even contemplated, over their collective truth.

"Short term, however," Jorge said, "we have to get you out on bail. We have a hearing tomorrow morning."

Carlos leapt up. "Tomorrow!"

"Easy, easy. You've got a road ahead of you. But I think I can convince the judge that you're not a flight risk."

Carlos swallowed. "No, of course not."

Jorge must have heard a hitch in Carlos' voice because he now said: "You're not a flight risk, right?"

Carlos gritted his teeth. "Absolutely not."

"The Rochester folks want blood, *hermano*. Mexican blood. They've given

Ernesto a break, but they'll be after you, no matter what happens here. You'll have to watch your back."

Carlos didn't need the lecture. And he didn't give a shit about Rochester. All that mattered now was Andrés. But he needed to say something. "Tell me, what do things look like, with the CUOM?"

"The union will go forward, despite, not because of this," he said.

Carlos averted his eyes.

Jorge returned the unused items to his briefcase, grabbed his hat, and stood. "Got a suit for court, *hermano*?"

"Of course."

"Good." He embraced Carlos and was off.

Self-righteous bastard, Carlos thought. Still, Jorge would find that technicality. And by that time, Andrés would be in Mexico. Then Carlos could handle the Rochester thugs. Then he could handle anything. His mother, Sarah, even *Nito*, who'd soon wish he were never born.

41

Sarah put the finishing touches on her make-up. Since talking to Paige, she had changed her clothes, and her mind, three times. But finally she'd settled on her black suit and on getting it over with. She would tell Mitchell everything. She thought of calling first, but it was Saturday. He liked to sleep in. Better to take him unaware, anyway, before he had a chance to put up defenses. She reapplied some lipstick, grabbed her gloves and started for the door. Just then, the phone rang. She nearly jumped out of her skin. Paige, she thought and picked up. But the voice was male.

"Sarah? Sarah Kaufman?"

"Yes?"

"This is Drake, you know, the Bradford's chauffeur."

"Oh? Yes, hello."

"I have some good news. Mr. Bradford has agreed to see you."

"What?"

"He wants to see you."

"Really?"

"Uh huh. And the reason I'm calling this early is that he actually would be able to meet with you today. I'm in town and could pick you up in a couple of hours."

"Today?" She thought of Drake, how hard he'd gripped her arm.

"I'm sorry it's such short notice," he said. "Mr. Bradford was in a receptive mood, given you knew his wife. And he thought he remembered you."

Remembered me? Hard to believe. But Sarah didn't think she told Drake that she'd met the man, so it must be true. Still, after Tijuana, could she risk it? That Bradford would see her, of all people. But then she'd asked. This wasn't out of the blue. Still…. "I don't know," she said, "I had plans…." But as soon as she spoke, an image of Jacob's mother flashed in her mind. Tears. Anguish. Her only son. If only Sarah had acted sooner, done something, anything.

"Oh," Drake said.

That poor woman. The terrible loss, the pain that would never end. Logically, Sarah knew that Jacob's death wasn't her fault. But she had stirred the pot, and then left it unwatched, left it to boil over. Rita. Sabrina. God forbid another. Maybe a coincidence, maybe nothing at all. But, if there were even the remotest possibility. "Wait," Sarah said. "Drake. I, I'll go. Yes."

"You sure?"

"Yes."

"All right. I'll be at your hotel at noon then. Oh, and you might want to bring a sweater. It's a little chilly where he is."

"Not far, I hope."

"No, near the beach. But you didn't hear that from me."

Near the beach. Huh. Okay, well, she wasn't leaving anything to chance. She immediately called back Paige, told her about Drake and Bradford. Paige was understandably shocked, and cautioned Sarah to be careful. But she also said that she was glad that Sarah still trusted her, enough to confide in her this way. She apologized again for Tijuana, wished Sarah luck and said she could hardly wait for tomorrow. If Sarah didn't show up, she added with a laugh, she'd let loose the hounds. Sarah laughed a little too and hung up. Paige. Limping through life, like Tillie. Sarah couldn't help but feel for her. She'd botched things, but perhaps it was for the best. Bradford would no doubt be more likely to open up to an invited guest than an intruder. It was a hard way to get here, but things worthwhile were never easy, or so someone said.

Sarah flagged a cab. She had two hours and felt a burst of courage, even a little excitement. Perhaps when all was said and done, Mitchell could help her. He enjoyed helping, feeling that he was needed. If he hadn't been there with her in Tennessee, she might have very well lost her mind. She exited the car, and took a few deep breaths. So much had happened. She might break down, but that would be all right. Mitchell was kind, sympathetic. He was a man who could understand mistakes, accept, even welcome, vulnerability.

Sarah smoothed her hair and glanced up at the hotel sign. The Portsmouth. Who would have thought? She pushed the revolving door. More than anything, she dreaded having to confront the clerk. Her only hope was that someone else was on duty, seeing that it was the weekend. But no, there he was. A few people were in line at the desk so Sarah waited out of view on a stool by the telephone booth. She fixed her hair again, imagining what the clerk would say when she inquired about Mitchell. "Oh so you're back after all. Have fun? Yeah, that fellow from Toledo is here, the one whose call you didn't return." But then…. Mitchell's voice! Deep, soft. Laughing. She turned so she could see a bit better. My God! It *was* Mitchell, loping down the stairs. Oh. But he wasn't alone. Not alone. A woman. Young. Beautiful. Mitchell, yes, tall and gangly, again in that jacket. Arm in arm! They stopped, faced each other. He cupped her chin, kissed her! Sarah eyed the exit, turned, tripped, pushed back through those damn doors and ran out of the hotel. Ran as fast as she could in her miserable heels. Tears welled up. She ran, dropped her purse, spilling the contents all over the sidewalk. She stuffed them back in, and ran. Ran and ran, then finally stopped and caught her breath.

So. He was not so worried about Sarah. Not that worried. Sarah hailed another cab, sniffed and wiped her eyes. She wanted a drink. Desperately. But Drake would be there soon. What's good for the goose, she thought, and started to sob. Back at the hotel, she cleaned up and opened her notebook. She started to write down what happened. *I went to the Portsmouth....* but couldn't finish a sentence. Instead, her pencil spurted out words, related, but singular, in no chronological order. *Ego. Unmoored. Fool. Pathetic. Paige. Carlos. Chump. Drake. Bradford. Murder. Rita. Beach. Sabrina. Carlos. Mitchell. Mitchell. Mitchell. Drink.* She checked her flask. *Empty.* She wrote that word, too.

She found her way downstairs. Drake was waiting. He came around and opened the door.

"Hello," he said.

"Hello." Sarah scooted in and sat numbly. Drake talked, but she had no idea what he was saying. She must have responded, though, because he nodded. Then, finally, silence. She tried to focus on Bradford, on what she would say, but her mind wandered back to the Portsmouth, to that unbelievable sight. Her eyes filled again. She gazed out the car window. Shrubs. Eucalyptus. Pine. A house. Dirt. Rocks. She didn't give a damn. About any of it. Nothing mattered. Nothing, she thought, until she realized that they weren't at the coast at all. No. They were climbing. Up and up. Yes, they were climbing, nearing the Hollywoodland sign. There it was, the letters huge and white. "Hey," she said. "Drake, what are you doing? Where are we going?!"

42

The hostess pointed to a chair at the counter but Mitchell wanted a booth, so he waited. He needed space this morning, space to indulge his memory. A blubbery family of four lingered over their empty plates. He tucked his newspaper under his arm, inched closer and hovered. They ignored him at first, but ultimately gave in and waddled out.

Mitchell wiped off some leftover crumbs and slid into the leather seat, still warm from the generous body heat. He browsed the menu and then let his mind drift. He'd asked Ida to join him this morning, but she declined, saying she had an appointment with sleep. "You're quite a fella," she said, kissing him before waving good-bye. He smiled. Quite a fella, and she was quite a gal. He'd enjoyed himself. Immensely. Too much. He knew what Ida was. Knew that she was only doing her job. Every look, every word, every touch. Each had a monetary value. She was good at it, so very good at making him feel special. Sarah never said those things. Never did those things, at least not to him. *Buttermilk Pancakes. $1.25.* Maybe he should have paid her.

"What'll you have?" The scrawny waitress stared at her tablet, suspending her pencil in the air.

"Ham and eggs, coffee."

"How you want the eggs?"

"Over easy."

"Over easy," she said, never raising her eyes.

Sarah. Mitchell felt a twinge of guilt. Why should he? Well, today he'd maybe, no not maybe, he *would* learn exactly where she was. He'd head over to Sparks' place after breakfast. Again, twenty-four hours, the dick had promised. If she were in L.A., he'd find out. But Mitchell was in no hurry. Not anymore. The waitress delivered the coffee. He shook his head. That was a lie. He couldn't wait to get there. Ida had helped his nerves, but he was still anxious as hell about Sarah. He gulped the coffee, too fast, and burned his tongue. Shit. He scraped his teeth over the burn and made it worse.

He lit a cigarette, opened the paper and read: *ENERGY GONE OUT OF JULIAN TRIAL.*

That an overissue of stocks occurred is indisputable. But teasing out all the facts will likely take months, maybe years. In the meantime, Rosen and his cohorts walk free. Rosen's testimony yesterday revealed nothing new. The defense team appears to have a kitchen sink strategy, throwing out so many numbers and obscurities that one forgets who's on trial and for what. The crowd has thinned, from boredom as much as illness, Judge Doran stifles more yawns than coughs, and even the attorneys look as if they wish they were somewhere else.

Ha. Telling it like it is, Mitchell thought. More like an op-ed, but damn right. He turned the page.

SUSPECT RELEASED IN THE SABRINA JOHNSON CASE. A Mexican man who had been detained for questioning in the murder of the aspiring actress was released yesterday. Although the lead was promising, the police stated that the man had a rock solid alibi. Officer Hodges of the Broadway station said that this was only a temporary setback, that he believed that they were closing in on the killer.

"Hodges. Christ," Mitchell said. He scanned and turned the page again.

A bail hearing is scheduled today for Mr. Carlos Martinez of Boyle Heights. Mr. Martinez was arrested for his alleged involvement in the sabotage of agricultural giant, Rochester Farms. Mr. Martinez, a local businessman and owner of several grocery stores, was arrested for the alleged spiking of one of the farm's irrigation channels with large quantities of salt. Mr. Martinez has pled not guilty. According to investigators, Martinez was centrally involved with the formation of The Mexican Worker's Union, and they believe the plot was retaliation for Rochester's resistance to the organization.

Hmm. Carlos. The name irked him, but Mitchell had a soft spot for unions and couldn't help but bow to the boldness of the plot.

"Here you go," the waitress said, delivering Mitchell's meal while performing a balancing act with several other plates. Her appearance belied her strength and skill.

"Ah, thank you." Mitchell folded the paper and dug in. He was starved.

He scooped the runny yolk with a biscuit and finished the ham in three bites. He sipped his coffee this time, smoked, checked his watch then motioned for the check. Soon he was on his way back to Poirot.

∎∎∎

"Ah. Mr. Dobrinski."

"Well?"

Sparks again prolonged the suspense, straightening a diploma that hung on the wall.

Mitchell cleared his throat.

"She's here, all right."

Mitchell sat up.

"She's staying at the Hotel Figueroa. For women, mainly. Built by the YWCA. She's alone. Here," he said, handing Mitchell a photograph.

Mitchell stared at the blurry image. "When was this taken?"

"Last night, near the hotel."

Mitchell was relieved, in a sickish way. "That's some quick work. You must have a dark room."

"Of course."

The shot wasn't a close up, but he could see that it was definitely Sarah. Determined stance, hair a little mussed.

"We found her pretty easily," Sparks said.

Mitchell reached for his wallet. "Good job." And it was. So much for Hodges and his incompetents.

"Glad you are satisfied," he said, taking the cash and counting it. "Professional, prompt and prudent."

Mitchell nodded. And proud of yourself. Proud Poirot.

They shook hands. Mitchell ran down the stairs and flagged a cab. The driver pulled over and Mitchell got in. "Where to?" the man said.

"The Fig…"

"What's that?"

"I'm sorry," Mitchell said. "Changed my mind." He handed the driver a dime. "For your trouble." He bolted out of the car, removed his jacket and slung it over his arm. Sarah was okay. He needn't rush, run over there like some desperate fool. He strolled back to Pershing Square and sought out an empty bench. He sat down in the middle, rested his arms on either side and watched the pigeons poop and peck. There were hundreds of them. The sun slanted on the sidewalk, rapidly drying some rogue initials in a patch of newly poured concrete. A furry mutt lifted his leg on a nearby palm tree and then approached Mitchell wagging his half-curled tail. Mitchell leaned over to pet the pup but a shrill voice ordered him to "come here," and he scurried off.

Why rush indeed. Bradford, Rita, all of that. But so much more. So much more to say. It wouldn't be easy, and he'd been up all night. Ida, Jesus Christ. Better to be rested. He needed an appointment with sleep himself. After that, he'd go to Sarah's hotel. Why was she staying at that place anyway? Alone, Sparks said. So many questions. He'd ask them all, demand the answers, and tell her everything. Mostly.

■■■

The next thing Mitchell knew it was 7:00 p.m. But the light was strange. He looked out the hotel window. The streets were empty, the sun in the east. Huh? It was 7:00 all right, a.m.! Sunday! Mitchell shook himself and even checked his pocket compass before finally accepting that he had slept nearly eighteen hours. Was he sick? He felt his head, swallowed. He was groggy, his mouth tasted sour, but he otherwise seemed all right. Perhaps it had been the relief. And Ida. He wasn't a kid, for Christ's sake.

His thick stubble confirmed the truth. It was as if he'd been dead, not even waking for his usual midnight pee. He shuffled to the bathroom and splashed water on his face. Maybe Sparks slipped him a Mickey. Maybe he hadn't really found Sarah at all. The photo was a fake. Mitchell laughed at himself, but still he quickly shaved and dressed. By 8:00 he was sitting in a diner across from the Figueroa. At 9:00 he crossed the street and went in.

A woman with a pinched face and broad, freckled chest was tending the desk. A large cross hung on a wall, as well as around the woman's neck.

"Could you tell me what room Sarah Kaufman is in?"

"No."

"No?"

"I can ring her room for you. There's a phone over there."

Mitchell smiled. The strategy had worked. Had he just asked whether Sarah was a guest, she probably wouldn't have told him.

"All right," he said, picking up the receiver.

"But I don't think she's in," the woman said.

"Excuse me?"

"I'll try though."

She was right. Mitchell hung up and returned to the desk. "Do you know when she'll be back?"

"We're not allowed to give out that kind of information, sir."

That wasn't a no, Mitchell thought. "I understand. But look, I am a very close friend of hers. I know you're doing your job, and I admire you for it. I work for a newspaper and am here covering the Julian Pete trial. Here," he said, showing her his *Blade* identification card.

"That really doesn't mean anything to me. Rules are rules."

"Of course. I just wanted to tell her something about her sister, Tillie. Poor woman. But it can wait."

"Her sister?"

"Oh yes. Sarah, I call her Sarah, of course, lives with her sister, and her brother, Harry. Tillie's been terribly worried about Sarah. Rather frail, you know. By the way, ma'am, that's a lovely crucifix, topaz isn't it?"

She blushed. "Yes, thank you."

"My mother used to have one like that. Reminds me that I wanted to attend church today. Never like to miss, even when I'm out of town."

"Oh? So you aren't Jewish, like your friend?"

"Oh no. Don't let this nose fool you."

The woman blushed again, tittering.

"Well, I'll be off then," Mitchell said, turning to leave.

"Uh, sir?"

"Yes?"

"Miss Kaufman left me a message. Just for me. Didn't want me to share it, but…"

"Oh?"

"It was kind of odd, and since you're a friend, and her sister, and…"

"Yes?"

"I'm actually relieved to tell someone. Miss Kaufman said, well, just a minute." The woman opened a drawer, removed a slip of paper and read: "Please ring my room at ten p.m. If I don't answer, call again in the morning, and again in the afternoon. If I still don't answer, please call The Lock Restaurant at 7 p.m. Ask for Paige Chastain, and tell her that I will be delayed. Signed, Sarah Kaufman, Room fifty-eight."

"May I see?"

She handed him the note. That was Sarah's scrawl all right.

He handed it back. "So you'll call her room tonight at ten then."

"Tonight? No, that's the problem. She wrote this yesterday. Gave it to me on her way out, in the afternoon, said it was very important."

"Yesterday? You mean she hasn't been back?"

"I don't think so. I wasn't here all night of course, but I tried calling again before you arrived. That's how I knew she wasn't in."

Carlos, Mitchell thought. She's with Carlos. But why? Why involve this clerk? And Paige. The gal with the limp. Must have something to do with Rita. "You were right to show me this. Can I use that pen?" Mitchell wrote down his name. "I'm at the Portsmouth. Will you do me a favor and have Miss Kaufman call me if she comes in? You can tell her that I was here." At this point, it didn't matter, he thought.

"All right. Do you think everything is okay with her?"

"I hope so."

"Me, too. She does seem like a very nice woman. Oh, Mr., Mr...." She sounded out Mitchell's name, "Do-bri-n-ksi, I assume you've told Miss Kaufman about the good news."

"Good news? Oh, oh, yeah. But you know, takes time with her people."

Mitchell exited the building. The sun was now blazing, white and harsh. He shielded his eyes and didn't notice a piece of glass on the ground. Stepped right on it, tearing the leather. Fuck, the shoes were only a year old. He lit a cigarette. More drama. More goddamn drama. He looked down one street and then another. Where the hell was she now? He loitered around for a while, checking the few cars that passed, scrutinizing the even fewer pedestrians. A cab pulled up in front of the Figueroa and let out a trim woman with dark swept up hair, but it wasn't Sarah. After another half hour, he decided to return to his room and write the Bishop article. Get something done. Maybe, just maybe, Sarah would call. If not, he knew where he would be having dinner.

43

Carlos yanked at his tie. Sweat poured down his back. The judge, a former Fresno prosecutor with a bullying reputation, had just granted bail, but set it at one million, guaranteeing that Carlos couldn't make it.

"It's all right," Jorge whispered. "You'll be out in a week anyway."

Carlos gnashed his teeth. "I can't wait a week!" Do something!"

Jorge turned toward Carlos and searched his eyes. He shook his head, then stood back up. "Your Honor, please. My client doesn't have that kind of money. He'd have to mortgage his markets, and his mother's house. His mother is in her seventies, your Honor."

Carlos lowered his head, but the attempt at humility didn't work.

"He can wait for the hearing, then," the judge said. "The border is too close for comfort. Mr. Martinez, I hear, is no stranger to Mexico."

"Your Honor, you can't really think this man sitting here is a flight risk. He's a responsible...."

"This is a serious crime, Counselor. I think your sympathy with the union is affecting your objectivity. Bail stands at one million dollars." He banged his gavel. "Next case."

"But Judge...."

"One more word and I'll hold you in contempt."

So that was it, Carlos thought. The judge was punishing Jorge for his views as much as Carlos for the crime. Prick! Talk about objectivity! Carlos scanned the room. If those cops hadn't had guns, he'd have made a run for it. As it was though, he just slumped over, feeling sick and impotent.

Jorge accompanied Carlos back to his cell, but his attitude had changed, and not in the way Carlos had hoped. Carlos thought that maybe this outrageous decision would prompt him to claim foul, to demand another hearing, a different judge. But Jorge said he would do nothing of the kind. He couldn't afford to alienate the man any more than he already had. This wasn't the last time he would argue before him. If it were a legal point, Jorge would push forever, but not when it involved judicial prerogative. Besides, Jorge said, he was extremely troubled by Carlos' outburst and what he had seen in his eyes. Something beyond the sabotage charge, something he wanted no part of.

"Meaning what?" Carlos said.

"Meaning I wonder if you should find yourself another lawyer."

"*Qué?!*"

"I've learned to read faces. And I see desperation, and danger, in yours."

Carlos wanted to strangle him, bash his head against the bars. But instead he said: "You're wrong. All you see is concern for my family. Andrés has been sick, and I'm worried about my mother. I need to be with them. That's all."

Jorge sighed and shook his head. "If you care about them so much, why did you....? Never mind. Don't answer that."

"Jorge." Carlos swallowed, pushing down bile and his pride. "*Por favor, hermano.*"

Jorge sighed again. "If you're lying...."

"I'm not," he said, lying.

Another sigh, deeper and longer. "All right."

"*Gracias. Muchas gracias.*"

"I'll see it through," Jorge said. "And there really is nothing to worry about. I've found the route."

"Route?"

"The technicality. One that's bullet proof."

"Oh?"

"A precedent. This very judge ruled on it before."

"Really? What is it?"

"Best I don't tell you. So you see, I am not afraid to take him on."

"But...all right."

"That's it. Let me do the work. Seven days. Until then, you're a model prisoner, understand?"

Carlos nodded.

Jorge called for the guard and left without shaking hands. Just as well because Carlos didn't want to touch him either. Groveling was not Carlos' style, and he would never forget that Jorge had made him do it. Still, the man was his best shot at freedom. This "route" he had found sounded a bit too convenient, but he had gotten people out of very tight spots before through such legal maneuvering. And on one point he'd been absolutely right. There had been danger in Carlos' eyes, and in every other part of him. What Jorge saw was a caged animal, one who would do anything to protect his young. And for now, that "anything" was talking to Andrés, telling him what he must do. It was the only way.

Carlos waited for the slop, also known as lunch, to arrive. The mess hall was small and stuffy. There were only about twenty prisoners, most of them *gringos*, but they were all pressed together, knocking elbows and legs. He felt like the slice of meat in the stale, white bread sandwiches that would soon be delivered.

He acted hungry like the rest, but he wasn't. He'd heard that one of the guards working the lunch shift, an ex-junkie named Johnny, took bribes, if the dough matched the deed. Johnny was nearby, and so, after everyone was served, Carlos got his attention. He asked to use the toilet, knowing that the guard would escort him there. When they were out of earshot, Carlos whispered his offer: he would pay him two hundred dollars to arrange a private visit with his son. Private, he emphasized. He had to be alone with him. Carlos would get the cash from his mother. The guard raised an eyebrow, but didn't blink. He was a father himself, he said, and understood. He would make it happen. Of course without the money, he would have told Carlos to go to hell and turn him in. But there was money, and for that Carlos was grateful. The urgency of the situation would finally force the conversation that Carlos had dreaded, and thanks to a little corruption and greed, it would happen in the most unlikely place he could have imagined.

44

o in the end, Ohioan, Ronald Bishop, like so many others, mistook Julian's siren song for a clarion call. Bishop was wealthier than some, luckier than others, but no less human and no more villainous. Indeed, his collapse on the stand seems to have been the result of delicate nerves rather than guilt, although, as with everyone involved in this scheme, the truth may never be known for sure. Did Bishop know Ted Rosen? Yes. Both the father, who he insists had no knowledge of the overissue, and the son, from whom, as he swore under oath, he expected no illegal favors. Mr. Bishop is back home now, probably still shaken, certainly not as rich, but hopefully a little wiser.

Mitchell read through the final paragraph again. The two-page article, with the photo, if Bishop sent it in time, would have to do. He wasn't going to invest a minute more in it. What with ruminating about Sarah, checking for messages that never came, and even calling The Figueroa a couple of times, the piece had taken five hours to complete, four more than it should have. Still, it was a wonder that he finished it at all, given his growing concern. Again. Nobody could sustain this kind of rollercoaster of emotion forever. At some point either his heart or mind would surely give out.

It was 5:30 p.m. Shadows flitted through the room haphazardly, as if uncertain of their object. Mitchell switched on a light, scattering them even further off course. He shaved and dressed. At 6, he called for a cab, and at 6:30 the car pulled up in front of a windowless, moody looking place on the nine hundred block of Wilshire. Mitchell's eyes were immediately drawn upward to a sculpture of an old padlock, a quaint reminder of a time before codes and combinations, when all that stood between a man, and treasures and secrets was a simple twist of a key. Underneath the object, in bold red letters, glittered the restaurant's name, positioned at a steep slant.

He pushed open the door and entered a softly lit room with low chairs and round tables. Romantic, if slightly sleazy. Like Ida, Mitchell thought. It was the kind of space where serious drinking must have at one time been done, or perhaps still was. Maybe down those stairs that Mitchell glimpsed on his way in. A worn, ebony baby grand was angled in the corner and butted up against a mirrored wall. Gold-framed oil paintings unevenly lined the red velvety walls. Mitchell squinted and saw that they continued the restaurant's theme, each a variation of a padlock: one latched to a small safe, another to a bicycle wheel, another a little girl's diary. He smiled, despite himself, appreciating the idea and the effort. The lock appeared again on the restaurant's matchbooks, several of which Mitchell snatched just as the maitre d' approached. "Do you have a reservation, sir?" he said, frowning at Mitchell's cache.

"No, no I don't."

"We're pretty crowded tonight."

Mitchell glanced at the empty tables.

"It's early," the man said. "You could take that spot over there, if you'd like."

Mitchell looked to where he was pointing. A slab of wood with a bench, squeezed in for more seating, it appeared, in view of the keyboard but slightly out of the way of the other tables. "Perfect."

The maitre d' handed Mitchell the menu. "Beef stew is good," he said.

It wasn't long before the place indeed started to fill up. Every time the door opened, Mitchell felt a rush of adrenaline but thus far it was wasted energy. He kept his eyes peeled, ordered a shrimp cocktail—for starters, he told the waiter—and checked his watch every second or so. By 6:45 he'd nearly gone through a pack of cigarettes. At 6:55 he started to get up to buy another but sat back down when he spotted Paige. Softer looking in this light, hair fiery and down about her shoulders, but definitely the woman he had met at the station. The limp was obvious, more exaggerated than he remembered. Perhaps it was the heels. What women wouldn't do for vanity.

Mitchell raised the menu and pretended to browse while watching Paige with one eye. The maitre d' took her coat, joking with her familiarly. She was shown to a table for two on the other side of the piano, giving Mitchell an unobstructed side view. She settled into the chair, her red waves flowing over a furry white sweater. She whispered something to the waiter, and he soon returned with a coffee mug. She pulled out a tiny bottle from her handbag and emptied the contents into it. Then she sat back and sipped, checking her own watch about as often as Mitchell did his.

7:00 p.m. 7:15. People were ordering and eating, mostly the stew from what Mitchell could tell. Smoke swirled in the air, lending an ashy tinge to the savory scent. 7:20. A phone on a pedestal near the door rang. "Shit," Mitchell said under his breath. "The Figueroa." The maitre d' answered and motioned to Paige, who had already begun to rise. She picked up the receiver, spoke briefly and then returned to her seat. She removed a cigarette holder and a pack of Lucky Strikes from her handbag, the red and white packaging recognizable even in this light. *Reach for a Lucky instead of a Sweet.* That ad had run in nearly every magazine imaginable, targeting women on a diet. Paige was svelte; perhaps that's how she stayed that way. She rifled through her handbag again, felt around her table and in the pockets of her sweater. Here was his opportunity. Mitchell hurried over, struck a match and leaned in.

"Thank you," she said, cupping his hand. Her nails were long and painted the color of her hair. Only after taking a few drags did she look up to see who come to her rescue. She smiled seductively, and then widened her still harshly made-up eyes. "Hey, it's you!" she said, exhaling a stream of smoke, after which she coughed a few times. "Mitchell, right? At the station. What in the world are you doing here, honey?"

"The same thing you are, I think."

"Sarah?"

"Uh huh."

"How did you know?" she said, motioning him to sit.

Mitchell gave her the Reader's Digest version of the events that led him to The Lock, and even then omitted some of the central facts, including that he had been to see Bradford, that he knew Sarah had been in Tijuana, probably with a man, and what he had learned about Rita. What he did say, however, was that he knew that the call Paige received was from The Figueroa, and that it meant that Sarah might be in some kind of danger.

"You're a sly one, Mitchell," she said, "although I wouldn't worry. We just had plans to meet for dinner, and she couldn't make it. That's all."

"Oh come on, there's more to it than that. I know you're probably trying to protect her, but right now telling me where she is the way to do that."

"Look, you've got it all wrong. I even told Sarah to call you."

"What?" Who was this woman, and how did she know so much? "Well, she didn't. You, or your boss, should have contacted me anyway. I filed a police report, remember?"

"That's kind of a long story."

"We don't have time for stories. If you know where Sarah is, tell me.

"I...I...."

"Goddammit. Where is Sarah?!"

"I'm right here."

Mitchell froze, except for his mouth, which involuntarily opened. He couldn't tell if the blood rose to or drained from his face.

"Sarah!" Paige said.

Mitchell looked up. It was indeed Sarah, or a ghostly doppelganger, hovering over them in a blue gossamer dress. "Mitchell," she said, her voice trembling.

So many questions, but none would form. He wanted to hold her, wrap his arms around her and sob. But he just sat and frowned. She looked thinner, drawn. Her full lips were pale and chapped. From kissing? He in fact wondered if she wasn't a wraith, especially in that filmy outfit. A lover's gift? Then Paige said: "I think you two need some time. I'm still a little sick anyway. I can wait to hear the news. Tomorrow?" she said to Sarah.

Sarah nodded. "Yes, yes. We *must* talk."

Paige rose, touched Sarah's arm and left.

Sarah took Paige's seat. For minutes neither of them moved. They said nothing, and yet Mitchell felt that they had talked to exhaustion. "Let's get out of here," he finally managed to grunt out.

"Wait," she said. "I need to get my coat." She returned from the checker with a wide-cuffed mink. Definitely a gift, Mitchell thought. He let her struggle with the sleeves. She could put on the monstrosity herself.

For a while they just walked. Mitchell smoked. Their heels sounded on the pavement, hers sharply, his muffled. Both were painful to the ear. Then Sarah slowed her pace. "Mitchell," she said, "what do you know?"

Mitchell took a deep drag and blew out a feeble smoke ring. "Enough. Carlos."

She reached for his hand. "Oh, Mitchell."

"Don't!" he said, pulling away.

She looked down. "All right. But so much has happened. More than you can imagine."

"I think I've pieced together a few things."

"Like what?"

"Skip it."

Sarah now stopped. "Don't you want me to fill in the gaps?" Her usual gentle tone had a brittle edge to it.

It was dark, but a street lamp lit up the contours of her face, the slope of her eyes, the bump on her nose that he always found so endearing. Now that she was here, inches away, her lips bearing the traces of god knows what, he wasn't sure he was ready. It depends on which gaps you're referring to. Why don't *I* fill *you* in about Rita first."

"Rita! What do you know about Rita?"

That question, of course, took a while to answer, but it gave him a focus, a relatively objective way to proceed. They bought some coffee and made their way to a bench in Pershing Square. It was nippy outside, but the bench gave them the space they needed.

Mitchell assumed that Sarah would be shocked to hear about his interview with Bradford. And she was, shocked and amazed that Mitchell had gotten the access that she thought no one else had. "No one else but me," she said.

"You? What do you mean?"

"That's where I've just been, Mitchell, with Phillip Bradford, for the last twenty-four hours."

Mitchell thought she was lying until she provided the details. The whole thing began, she said, with a surreptitious trip to the Bradford home. There she met Drake, their young, college student chauffeur. An image of Fred, the dolt who drove Mitchell to Bradford's, popped into his head at that description. Obviously, not the same, unless he was a master of disguise.

Sarah said that for a while she thought Drake might have had a hand in Rita's death, and for a few terrifying moments, she feared that he would have a hand in her own as well. Drake had arranged for the visit to his boss, and had driven Sarah to one of Bradford's several properties, a deserted, sprawling ranch house. He had initially said they were going to the beach, but instead headed for the hills, literally. Up around the Hollywoodland sign and beyond. That was the point Sarah became truly afraid, especially when Drake asked her to put on a blindfold for the last part of the drive. But in fact, he was simply doing his job, Sarah said. Bradford really did want to talk to Sarah, to this woman who claimed to be Rita's friend, who Bradford actually did remember because Sarah was the only person Rita said she liked that day at the Julian offices.

"Incredible," Mitchell said. "First me, then you."

Sarah nodded and shivered, even in the skin of that dead animal. "That's only the beginning," she said. "Bradford told me that he was dying, although that was evident. A nurse was in attendance. He was propped up in bed, all bones and in terrible pain."

Now Mitchell nodded.

"He then said that over the past few days he had done a lot of thinking. Rita, he knew, had cheated on him, and he despised her for it. It was her race, he had convinced himself. Marrying a Mexican. They all had loose morals. What did he expect?" he said.

"Same thing he told me," Mitchell said.

"But those thoughts had begun to gnaw at him, as much as his disease. He started to remember when he first met Rita, how lovely and innocent she was. How hard she'd tried to live up to his standards. How poorly she was treated by his friends. And so slowly he had come to accept that in some ways he had been responsible for her behavior. Not that she was blameless. Not that he didn't still, even in his physical agony, curse her for her infidelity. But he had come to forgive her."

"Ah, death bed mercy," Mitchell said.

"Yes, but more than that. Much more. He went on to say that he now allowed himself to believe, to acknowledge, that his wife was probably murdered."

Mitchell widened his eyes. "Really? Well that's something. I'd like to think I planted that seed. But go on."

"He confessed that he had lied to the police about her heart. Rita had been healthy, he said, and now, at the end of his life, he wanted to put things right. *Tikunn*," Sarah said.

"What?" Mitchell said.

"*Tikunn*. A Hebrew term for making the world right.

"Bradford's not Jewish."

Sarah frowned. "I know. But that's what he meant all the same. I couldn't believe what I was hearing, Mitchell. Finally, my own view validated, by the one person who would truly know. Drake had informed him about my encounter with Rita at the courthouse, and now he wanted to hear more. And so I told him, about how Rita had pleaded with me, about her terror, about how after reading about her death, I had been convinced that there was more to it. I told him that I had been pursuing the matter ever since, hitting one dead end after another. When Bradford asked why I had been so persistent, doing all this for a woman I barely knew, I said for the same reason he just gave. That I needed to put something right.

"Jacob," Mitchell said.

"I suppose, to start with anyway."

"Was Tijuana one of those dead ends?" Mitchell asked.

Sarah groaned. "You do know a lot."

"Well?"

"Can I have a cigarette?" Sarah said.

"A new vice?" he said, lighting one for her. She ignored the question and took a few puffs. "The deadest, I thought at first," she said. "But now, I'm not so sure."

Mitchell forced a blank look. Had she thought her feelings for Carlos had died and now come back to life. "Meaning what?" he asked as indifferently as he could.

She took a sip of coffee. "Yach! Cold. Have any hooch?

"Sarah…."

"So you're still clean?"

Mitchell considered the question. "Yes." Today, he said to himself.

"Hmm."

"So? Tijuana?"

"I'll get to that. First, as I said, I was with Bradford for quite a while. I stayed the night."

"What?!"

"I said I was with him for twenty-four hours. I meant it."

Keep cool, Mitchell told himself. Besides, he wasn't exactly worried that Bradford had taken advantage. "And?"

"He wanted to talk more," Sarah said. "But it was late, and he couldn't go on without sleep. He doubted if he had more than a week left. Wouldn't I please oblige an old, dying man, especially when he had more to say? He even had a change of clothes for me, a few of Rita's things that he had stored there. They might not fit exactly, he said, but they'd do. This dress, this coat," Sarah said, pointing to herself. "Rita's."

"Hmm," Mitchell said, masking his relief. "Speaking of clothes, did you ask him about the shoes?"

"Indeed I did," she said, opening her handbag and pointing to some squished heels. "I brought them with me. Rita had small feet." Sarah pursed her lips. "Hodges was telling the truth. Bradford didn't want them, not then. And now, well, what was the point? He asked me to keep them." She sighed and shook her head. "At any rate, I agreed to stay. I finally had the audience I'd been seeking. The nurse made me an omelet. We even played some cards, and then she showed me to a room with a four-poster bed and private bath. It was really quite comfortable."

"Daring of you."

"Out of necessity. But I did sleep. Wherever we were, and it couldn't have been too far from the city, it felt like the ends of the earth. Ghostly quiet and pitch dark. I awoke early, though, and tiptoed around until I found Drake leaning against the car outside. The terrain around the house was dry and rocky, but the sky was exquisitely blue. Drake now knew as much as I did because Bradford had ordered him to stay in the room with us, to serve as a kind of witness, I supposed. Drake said he'd been up for hours thinking about it all and wishing he had done more. He'd suspected that Rita was seeing someone on all those trips into town, but felt it was none of his business. For that matter he still felt that way. But she'd been afraid, he said, and he hadn't taken her seriously. Sarah said she told Drake not to be too hard on himself, that this was still all speculation anyway, and that whatever the cause of her death, there was probably nothing he could have done to prevent it."

"How did he take that?" Mitchell asked.

"Like the platitude that it was."

"Then what?"

"At noon Bradford woke up. The nurse bathed him and then called me and Drake in. He looked even worse, if that were possible, but in between the rattling and hacking, the grimacing and shaking, we resumed a semblance of a conversation. It was very focused, intimate, almost spiritual. We shared our guilt, our understanding that one kind of hatred could be used to justify another. I did most of the talking, telling him how I thought overcoming prejudice was one of life's hardest challenges, that it was never totally accomplished. Bradford said that he had not yet overcome it himself, that even now he thought Rita's race was a factor in her behavior. But he felt this forgiveness was an important step. He wanted me to agree, Mitchell. And of course I did. He wasn't a religious man, he said, but he sought a kind of absolution. Can you imagine? Me, a Father confessor?"

Mitchell smiled a little.

"But this wasn't the end, not by a long shot." Sarah closed her eyes. When she opened them back up, they were glistening. Her mouth quivered.

"Does it have to do with Tijuana?" Mitchell said.

"In a way."

"Bradford mentioned his advertising business."

"Uh huh."

"He said he was proud of most of his work, but that there were a few campaigns, one in particular that, as he had with Rita, he had just recently come to feel differently about, that he had come to somewhat regret."

"Oh?"

"Yes, but I never discovered which one. Because at that point, he screamed out and his breathing became ominously labored. Drake got panicky, and the nurse rushed in. She took his vital signs and upped his dose of medicine, morphine, I think. From then on, he slipped into and out of awareness. He moaned and rambled nonsensically. Except for the last thing, the last coherent thing he uttered...."

Sarah closed her eyes again.

"Yes?"

"Bradford had glanced at Drake to make sure he was listening, and then in an already dead-sounding voice said: "I know who killed my wife."

Drake and I both sat up. We waited, transfixed.

"Her old lover," he said. "Carlos Martinez."

Lover? Mitchell thought. He got that idea from me, too, actually took in what I said. But...wait a minute. "Carlos? Carlos? Not...."

"Yes, one and the same."

"Jesus. Why him? You must be, I mean...quite a coincidence. Horrible for you."

Sarah sighed. "To be honest, I was sickened, but not shocked. I had already come to think this was possible."

"Why?"

"Many reasons."

Mitchell felt a touch of glee. Whatever she would say now wouldn't hurt so much. "It's freezing out here. Let's go somewhere. I want to hear the rest without my teeth chattering."

"All right. Somewhere quiet, though."

Mitchell stood up. "My room?"

"Mitchell...."

"Just for privacy, Sarah."

"I didn't mean...."

"Come on."

The first few minutes in his room were excruciating. Suddenly they were really alone, with only a chair and a bed to sit on. Sarah, no doubt, was thinking of Carlos. Despite everything, she had been with him, here in this hotel. Mitchell thought of Ida. He could still smell her. But the tension soon eased. Mitchell plopped on the bed, Sarah took the chair and, after guzzling two glasses of water, recounted the bizarre events in Tijuana as well as those that led her there. Mitchell still winced when she spoke of her attraction to this man, but pitied her too, for she was almost certain that the whole thing was a set up, that Carlos never cared a whit for her.

"I have a theory," she said. "It must have been Carlos who was following Rita that day. And therefore, he must have seen me. Most likely he was in the courthouse himself. Drake confirmed that Rita was there. After Carlos...after he killed her, he then surely realized that I could be a problem, so he tracked me down at the trial and the dissembling began. It was a lucky break for him that my search led me to Tijuana. Almost too lucky. I even wondered if he might somehow know the person who supposedly spotted Bradford, the wrong Bradford, and planned that part of the deception, too. It's still possible I guess. I was going to talk that over with Paige. But in any case, had I stayed in Tijuana, I'm sure I'd be dead by now."

Mitchell lit a cigarette and offered one to Sarah. "You don't sound like this is speculation," he said.

"Huh?"

"You said you told Drake that Rita being murdered was speculation. Perhaps you, we, should keep that in mind."

"Oh, well that was before Bradford identified Carlos as the probable killer. But, well, yes, of course there's a chance that we're wrong. But at least now there is more to go on. For one thing, when I go to Hodges, I'll bring Drake with me." Sarah paused, turning something over in her mind. "I have another theory," she said. "Have you read about this Sabrina Johnson?"

"Sabrina?"

"The young woman, the actress found strangled."

"Oh, yes."

"I think Carlos might have been involved in her death, too."

"Oh brother. Why is that?"

"Their bodies were found in the same neighborhood, both with ligature marks. And I know that Sabrina was seeing an older Mexican man. Well, at least dark. I talked to her roommate, Jill."

"A Mexican suspect was released, you know. Solid alibi."

"No, I didn't know. I told Jill that she should tell the authorities."

"You *have* been busy," Mitchell said.

Sarah sat back in her chair. "You too, Mitchell. And not just with trying to find me."

"Yeah, I've been at the trial. Ronald Bishop and all."

"Uh huh, but I didn't mean that either."

"What do you mean, then?"

"I saw you."

"Saw me?"

"Here, in the lobby. With a woman."

Mitchell's face burned. "You saw me? How?"

"Actually, I first glimpsed you in court. Those coat patches are a giveaway."

"What? Why didn't you say anything?"

"I wasn't ready. But Paige urged me to seek you out, and I would have eventually anyway. So I came here, but…well, it doesn't matter. You're entitled."

"It didn't mean anything," Mitchell said.

"Sure it did. All of this means something."

Mitchell was silent.

Sarah got up and sat on the bed. She took his hand. "We've got a lot to figure out. For now, though, I could really use your help. If you can stay that is."

"I can stay. But what about you? What about Obee? You've been gone quite awhile."

"Yeah, he's already threatened to fire me."

"Pshaw. He wouldn't go that far. You saved his life, for Christ's sake."

"You didn't hear his voice, but, yeah, I think I'm safe for a little longer."

Mitchell quelled the knot in his throat. He squeezed Sarah's hand and released it. "So why in the world would Carlos kill these women?" he said.

She stood and paced around the room. "That's the million dollar question. Why? It was good to have Bradford's validation, but he didn't give a clue about how he'd come to that conclusion."

"I did suggest to him that it might be a lover," Mitchell said.

"Yeah, you told me, but Rita supposedly had more than one affair. Several, Bradford implied. So why Carlos? What did Bradford know about him? I mean, certainly Carlos is a liar. And he uses women as playthings. Girls too, at least one as young as eighteen. But that describes a lot of men. A killer is something else. A couple of times I felt uneasy with him, I guess, but it's still hard to fathom. And yet, I of all people know that monsters come in every shape and size."

Mitchell wasn't interested in the man's dimensions, or in exactly what setting Sarah had felt uneasy. "What about his work? Anything there?"

She shook her head. "He owns a few grocery stores, supposedly a successful business owner. Unless he lied about that. I've thought about scoping them out. He's also political, involved in some union business."

"Hold on! That's where.... Wait." Mitchell jumped up and got the newspaper out of the trashcan. "I knew I'd heard that name, he thought. Not just Carlos. Carlos Martinez. Read this."

Mitchell watched Sarah's eyes trail down the article. She sucked in breath. Her mouth dropped. "I can't believe it!"

"Same fellow?"

"Yes! It has to be. Sabotage! So that's what he was up to."

"Says he couldn't make the bail."

"Right," she said, looking at Mitchell with an expression he knew meant trouble.

45

arah literally felt lighter, although that could've been because she actually was. She had lost a few pounds, both from eating irregularly and nearly constant anxiety. Mitchell had even commented on it, and not in a flattering way. Mitchell. Finally, the secrets were out, the wounds, if not mended, exposed to the air. When she saw him at The Lock, sitting with Paige, she started to shake, half wondering if an earthquake had hit. The sight was jarring, so out of place. One of her lives converging with another. But it was in fact Mitchell, and he was there, looking for her.

Paige had been right to bow out, but her departure left a painful void. Sarah's chest had pounded, her hands had sweat. She had taken Paige's seat and felt as if she were being swallowed up by nothing. Neither she nor Mitchell had been able to breathe, let alone speak. But finally, they got past the shock, skimmed over the hurt and compared notes, realizing that in addition to butting heads with Officer Hodges, they had each been granted a face-to-face with Phillip Bradford. Out of all the people in L.A. clamoring for an interview, the dying man had turned to them for an audience. The one in a million probability of such an occurrence was something Sarah just accepted for the moment. Accepted, and as in the other near misses and coincidences she'd experienced on this trip, would try to make the most of.

She was still processing it all as she dressed for what would surely be the most challenging of those experiences yet. As she powdered her nose, she thought of the drive to the Bradford's, the relief of arriving there in one piece. Drake was a decent chap after all, indeed had been like a son to the couple. She dabbed a little perfume on her ears, chest and wrists. And Phillip Bradford himself. An oligarch who thought he could buy Rita's love and loyalty. Or at least that's how Sarah interpreted it. He was arrogant and prejudiced, but in his last hours he had tried to make amends. And if Sarah had anything to do with it, his legacy would include helping solve two murders and keeping a madman off the streets.

It was for that very madman, Carlos Martinez, she was now preparing herself, mentally and physically. In one hour, she would be visiting him in jail.

She would have eventually seen the article herself, but she was glad that Mitchell was the messenger. When she read about Carlos' incarceration, it was as if the light had poured into that crummy hotel room, almost blinding her with its beauty. Already behind bars! It was too much to hope for. Yes, she would go to Hodges, but first she wanted this chance. To ask, to accuse, to perhaps even catch a hint of an admission. Sarah had feared that in his current state, Carlos would deny her request for a visit, that she would have then had to ask Paige for help. But the opposite was true. According to the warden, he was not only amenable but impatient for it. That seemed strange, but then Carlos was always plotting. And, of course, he didn't know what Sarah knew.

She zipped her skirt, which was even looser than a few days ago. She buckled the belt on the last hole and tucked in her white silk shirt. That day, she carefully positioned her hat and pulled down the black netting. She wanted that barrier. The final touch was Rita's coat and the black, ostrich feather boa. This she had purchased at a gift shop when she first arrived, eons ago it seemed, a souvenir direct from the famous Cawston Ostrich Farm in Pasadena. Then, when all that lay before her was the trial and the conference, she thought she might take a side trip to the farm itself, see the ostriches up close and pick up a few more trinkets. But that was then. Today, she wrapped the soft plumes around her neck, imagining, with a chill, that once Carlos heard her out, he would want to strangle her with it.

She pushed the elevator button and waited. No stairs today. She needed to conserve her energy. After Mitchell put her in a cab last night, she had wanted nothing more than to sleep. Yet events compelled her to write, to record her experience with Bradford, Drake, and most of all with Mitchell. She skipped back to earlier pages in her notebook, again to the scratched out image of the two selves, and then ahead to when she imagined herself into pieces. She turned to a blank page and sketched another figure, a female whose limbs were in the right place, but barely attached to her body. At the points of intersection, where the leg communicated with the torso, for instance, she drew little sparks. Then she went to sleep. This morning she didn't feel so much electrically charged as less lopsided, a little more in balance. Not quite centered, but close.

The elevator opened, and Sarah headed for the exit.

"I'm so glad you're all right," Mrs. Parks called out. "You know, I called the restaurant, like you asked.

Sarah turned. "Oh, I didn't see you there. Yes, you weren't here when I came in. Thank you. I appreciate it so much."

The woman nodded. "I prayed for you, too!"

Sarah smiled. "That was very kind."

"And your sister."

"What?"

"Your friend told me about her."

"Ah. Well, thanks."

"Of course!"

Sarah hurried out and hailed a cab. "County jail," she said.

The driver turned and frowned. "Nasty place."

"I'm sure." She thought of Mitchell. He'd offered to come with her but she declined. This she needed to do alone. Still, she was glad he would be at the Portsmouth, only blocks away, waiting for her.

"Why's a nice lady like you going there?"

"Visiting a friend."

"Oh, well, you never can tell, I guess."

No, Sarah thought. You can't.

"Well, be careful."

"I will," she said, wondering if she should have played it safe and asked the dear Mrs. Parks for another prayer.

46

arlos lay on his cot staring at the ceiling. His body yearned for sleep but his mind couldn't rest. He was shocked that Sarah had asked to see him. She must have read about him in the paper, probably gloating over his arrest, coming to have her say. But he'd agreed immediately. Indeed, he was glad she was coming, would accept the condemnation, and then do everything in his power to make her understand. In other words, he would lie again. But not about everything. The thought of seeing her actually made him a little happy, took a bit of the sting out of all the rest. Now, more than ever, he needed a friend, even one who hated him. Most importantly, though, he had to discover if she was still on Rita's trail, if she'd picked up another scent, or, if, as he'd prayed, she'd given up.

He'd replayed his visit with Andrés so many times that he had begun to question his own sanity. He could hear their voices, the tone and pitch, rising, falling, the screaming, the thuds and scraping of his son's shoes as they took him away. How could he have let it go so wrong? He thought he was prepared. Ready for the worst. He turned on his side, scrunched up in a fetal position, and wound back the clock again, to yesterday, when Johnny followed through on his part of the bribe:

"Andrés, *mijo.*"

"Pop!"

They embraced as the guard locked the door behind them. The room was deathly grey, a concrete box with a table and two chairs, the walls like the sides of a tomb. But they were alone. Andrés pulled back and looked at Carlos with the innocent, frightened eyes of a *niño.* "Pop. Jesus, you look terrible."

"I'm fine. I'm just glad to see you're better."

They embraced again and then sat down. "Pop," Andrés said, "can I do anything? Beat up somebody for you?"

"Andrés, Andrés. No, no. This thing will work itself out. Believe me."

"Grandma's pretty mad at you."

"I know. But listen, son, we don't have much time. I have to talk to you about something else. How have you been, you know, otherwise? Calm?"

"Sure, Pop."

"Good. I want you to stay that way. Promise me."

Andrés nodded.

"Now, remember, before I was locked up. You remember, you started to tell me about some *chicas*, some women."

Andrés looked down. "Yeah, yeah. I remember."

"Well, I want you to tell me now about that. Right now."

"Oh, Pop, that can wait. It's nothing really."

Carlos grabbed his son's arm.

"Ouch! What are you doing?"

"Now. Tell me."

"All right, all right."

Carlos sat back, ran his fingers through his greasy hair and waited.

Andrés licked his lips. "Well, Pop. You know, you know how I've always admired you. You know, you're so much in my eyes."

"Yeah, son."

"Well…. I wanted to be like you. Live like you."

Carlos' stomach churned. He wanted to shake the words out of Andrés. "Go on."

"Remember, you used to see Rita Bradford?"

Carlos closed his eyes, clenched his fists under the table. "Yes."

"Well, you know what you told me. About her and that other one. Sabrina. Remember when you introduced me to her?"

"Yeah, I remember." His worst fears, his very worst fears.

"I…I was with them, you know. Like you."

"With them?"

"I wanted what you had. To feel what you felt. I wanted to get back at them, too."

Oh, *mijo. Mijo, mijo.*

"I'm so sorry, Pop."

"Tell me."

"Well, I, you know, I made love to them. Not love, not love. Had sex with them."

"Sex? You had sex with them?"

"Yeah, Pop. You were right. They were easy, easy to find and easy to lay. I told them they were pretty, flattered them, like you did. The older one really liked that."

"And then what?"

"I left them, just like you. After I told them I loved them."

"And then?"

"What do you mean, Pop?"

"Andrés. I know. I know that you…that you…" His throat seized up. He swallowed and reached for his son's hand. Softly, Carlos thought. Speak softly. "You hurt them, didn't you?"

"Hurt?" Andrés giggled. "I don't know, Pop, maybe a little. They didn't seem to mind."

Carlos yanked his hand away and slapped Andrés hard across the face. "This isn't a joke!"

"What?" Andrés put his hand up to his cheek, glaring at Carlos. Tears welled up in his eyes."

"You killed them."

"Kill?! Kill?! Are you serious? I fucked them, Pop. Fucked them! I didn't kill them. How can you even? How….?"

"Andrés. Andrés. Listen. Both women are dead. You know that."

"Dead? What are you talking about?"

"Andrés, think. Think! This is no time for evasion. I have a plan to help you, but you must tell me everything."

Andrés shook his head, contorted his features. "No, no. No! I didn't kill anyone!" Then he covered his ears, like he did during one of his attacks. He pounded on the wall. "Guard! Guard! Get me out of here! My father's crazy!"

Johnny stormed in, a gun in his hands.

"He's crazy! Crazy!"

"My son is sick," Carlos whispered.

Andrés started fighting Johnny, who called out for help. "I'm not sick! I'm not a murderer! I'm not a murderer! Let go!" Andrés kicked and scratched Johnny, struggling to free himself. Two other guards quickly appeared. Andrés tried to fight them, too, but they overtook him and dragged him out.

Carlos sat motionless, staring at the chair that had toppled over in the struggle.

In a few minutes, Johnny returned. "You didn't tell me your son was violent!" the guard said. "This might cost me my job, you idiot."

"I thought he'd be okay. He has a history of...of psychological problems, but he'd been fine lately. Probably seeing me here triggered it. He, uh, sometimes imagines things," Carlos said. "Please see that he gets to the hospital. Mental ward. He needs care. Whatever he says, pay him no mind. Oh, and please, please, no word to his grandmother. I'll tell her."

"You don't dictate the terms, buddy. I don't give a crap about some old Mexican bitch. And if you know what's good for you, you'll never say a word about the nature of our agreement."

Carlos would have knocked out his teeth, if he'd had any. But he just said: "I'm sorry."

Another guard led Carlos back to his cell. Later, he returned and told Carlos that Andrés was in fact in the hospital. Bad shape, the doctors said. They'd sedated him. He'd have to stay there awhile. He also said they didn't need to tell Carlos' mother for now. She'd find out soon enough. Carlos sighed in relief. The apology and restraint had been worth it.

Carlos turned on his other side and stretched out his legs. So Andrés was in the County again. Not pleasant, but at least he'd be safe, relatively speaking. It was true. A Chicano was better off in a mental ward than a jail, even if he had to undergo some of their barbaric treatments. Carlos remembered when they had wanted to try out the new shock therapy on Andrés after a particularly bad episode. At the time Carlos refused before the doctor could even make his case. But now? Now he'd choose a lobotomy for his son over a hanging, or, almost worse, being prey for all the jailed up perverts. Carlos could take care of himself in prison. No one would dare try that kind of shit on him. Andrés, on the other hand, was unaware, innocent, as absurd as that sounded given what he had done. Indeed, the depravity of some men, especially those who viewed their target as inherently inferior, was surely something his son knew nothing about. Besides, with Andrés in the County, there was hope, once Carlos got out.

Carlos smelled under his arms. He stank. He needed some soap and water, and soon. Where the hell was that *bruto*? Carlos peered out of the bars, looking for the guard who would usher him to the shower. He looked, but all he could see was Andrés, the panic on his face, the outrage over Carlos finally saying what they both knew. "I'm not a murderer! I'm not a murderer!" Carlos had underestimated the power of his son's defenses. The boy simply couldn't face the truth. If Carlos thought for a moment that someone else could have committed these crimes, he would chase that person to the ends of the earth. But who else? Who else knew these women, so vastly different and yet guilty by the same, unique association? Who else had the story pounded into him? Carlos had been stupid and selfish, telling his son, his tormented, impressionable son about this kind of revenge. Of how, if he could get away with it, he'd strangle them. Strangle! He'd used those very words. Who else? Sex, Andrés said. To be like his father. To feel what he felt. The idea tore at Carlos. But as God or the devil as his witness, he would give up his life to know that it had only been that.

"Ready?" the guard said, unlocking the cell.

"Oh, so you're finally here," Carlos said.

"Shut up and get going."

Carlos stood under the blast of cold water and lathered himself up. He let the spray trickle into his mouth. Salty, he thought, remembering why he was in this hellhole. Goddamn *Nito*! He rinsed and brushed his teeth. His nails were filthy, but he wasn't allowed a scissors, so he cleaned out the grime with his toothbrush. He dried off and in ten minutes total was back in his cell.

47

Now that she was here, about to be frisked, Sarah felt weighed down, heavy with anticipation. So much depended on how she acted. And in some respects, she really would be acting. After all, the man she was about to accuse of murder had been someone she thought she loved. Someone she'd given herself to, who in return deceived her to the core. This was a lot to demand of herself. She wasn't a cop, and she wasn't a robot. Her feelings ran the spectrum. She was horrified at the crimes and humiliated that she had let her emotions blind her to the truth. She had not seen Carlos since Tijuana, and she feared that in spite of everything, she might let something slip, let him see how much he'd hurt her, give him the satisfaction of knowing that no matter what he did, his power over women was undiminished. She pursed her lips, tightened her fists. No. She couldn't let that happen.

"This way," the guard said, leading her down a concrete hall to the visitor's room. Sarah had been to the prison in Toledo more times than she could count. Then there was Tennessee, that visit to Jacob, right before… She took in a deep breath and forced herself to concentrate.

"Handbag needs to stay with us," the guard said.

Sarah knew the routine and handed it over.

"You cold?" He was referring to Rita's coat.

"Yes," she said. "I had the virus, still recovering."

"Oh." He patted the pockets and quickly pulled back. "All right. Sit there. Mr. Martinez will be here in a minute."

Sarah took the chair. Between them would be that filmy, scratched partition with a tiny opening through which they would speak. She twisted her rings and listened for footsteps.

The door soon opened. "Okay," the guard said, "here you go. Fifteen minutes."

Carlos took his seat and scooted in. His hair was longer and silver stubble accompanied his overgrown mustache. "Sarah," he said.

For a moment Sarah couldn't speak. She gazed mutely through the glass, thinking this was a bad idea. He looked pathetic in that striped garb, vulnerable even though his muscles were bulging out of the sleeve. But then, suddenly, right there in front of her, like a divine text, like the Ten Commandments to Moses, appeared her well-rehearsed script. She could see it clearly, and her vocal chords responded. "Carlos, I'm not here for personal reasons."

"Oh?"

"No."

"Well, can I at least say how sorry I am about what happened."

"You can say it, but it doesn't mean anything."

Sarah saw him eyeing the coat, recognizing it.

"You look beautiful, Sarah."

"Maybe it's because of what I'm wearing."

"*Qué?*"

"I'll bet you tell a lot of women that they're beautiful."

"Sarah, please, I thought you said…"

"Rita, for instance."

Carlos sat up.

"And Sabrina? Sabrina Johnson."

Sarah did everything in her power to hold his gaze. "I've seen Phillip Bradford. He told me about your affair with Rita."

Carlos swallowed. He eyed the guard. Then he turned back. He leaned as close as he could to the opening, and whispered. "What if I did, Sarah?"

Sarah squelched a moan. "What if you did? That's quite a statement."

"Meaning what?"

"You're already here for one crime. I intend to make you stay. I'm going to the police, Carlos, this time with Phillip Bradford's blessing."

Carlos hung his head. "You don't know how wrong you are."

"We'll let them decide that."

"Sarah, do you know how many people have affairs?"

"With two women, who both happened to wind up dead?"

"The simplest solution isn't always right. Yes, I knew them. But why would I harm them? Why?"

"Only you know that."

Carlos shook his head again. A strange, ironic expression flitted over his face. "Well, then let's talk facts. If I recall correctly, Sabrina Johnson was killed while I was, well, doing what I'm locked up for. In fact, I read about it when I returned to Agua Caliente, looking for you. The dates, Sarah. They don't fit."

Sarah opened her mouth, but nothing came out.

"And Rita. Rita was killed while I was at Agua Caliente too, right before it opened. I know, because I also read about it there. There are dozens of witnesses. Even my enemies would attest to it. Even Raul. Did you think about any of that?"

Sarah felt her heart race. Timing, dates. How could she not…? "Well, I…"

"I couldn't be in two places at once. You can check all of this out. So, go. Go to the cops. Tell that guard over there, if you want."

Sarah's mouth was a desert, her insides a cactus. She started to stand.

"Wait, please."

"What?"

"Please don't go."

What? she thought. Did he want to revel in her humiliation? Surely it was written all over her face. But he wasn't smiling. He seemed desperate. Why shouldn't he be? He was in jail! Still, she felt a tug, a flicker of sympathy. So she sat.

"I didn't kill them, Sarah," he said.

"So you said."

"*Dios, Dios.*" He bent over and sobbed. His body was heaving spasmodically, so much so that Sarah had to fight an instinct to say something comforting.

He sniffed and looked up. "Forgive me," he said, choking back more tears. "Here's what I want to tell you. When it comes to women, I'm a louse. I admit it. I was a louse with Rita, and a louse with Sabrina, but that's all, a louse. And at first, with you, it was a game, like all the rest. The fact that you happened to meet Rita, that you'd concocted this murder mystery, were chasing down a ghost, well, that was a bit of luck. It raised the stakes, made it all the more of a challenge. But Sarah, my feelings for you. They changed. They were real. They still are."

What thing was he conniving now? Sarah thought. His watery eyes looked sincere, those same black eyes in which she had lost herself. She didn't know what the hell to believe. She had to get out, think. Go over the timing. The timing! But she heard herself say: "Were you ever really married to Rachel?"

He sniffed again, wiped his nose on his sleeve. He leaned back, appearing to consider. Then he motioned to the guard who came to his side. Carlos asked him something. The man nodded and then Carlos said to Sarah: "Before you leave, ask to see my ring. They've got it. Look inside, at the inscription. There's your answer."

"More games?"

"Just read it."

"Time's up," the guard said.

Carlos shook his head. "No, please, not yet."

He grunted. "Two minutes."

"Sarah, Sarah. I didn't do it. I didn't. I swear. But I, but I know…"

"But you know what?" Sarah said.

He cocked his head, then squinted, as if he were trying to read her mind. Sarah waited, breathless.

"Nothing. Nothing," he said.

"Okay," the guard said. "Let's go."

The door closed and he was gone, leaving her spent and reeling. "But, I know…" After all that, "But, I know….?" Those words were like bullets, piercing through the veneer of surrender. Sarah had been ready to give up, go home for real. Carlos had shamed her beyond measure. The timing, the dates: evidence so basic that hadn't even crossed her mind. In one fell swoop, her case fell apart. But now. "But I know…." Three little words that would force her back into the thick of it.

She shuffled out in a daze, picked up her handbag and started for the exit. The ring! She turned, asked the desk cop. He gave her a queer look, called for the guard who soon appeared with a small box labeled "Carlos Martinez." He rifled through it, and then laid the ring on the desk. Sarah put on her glasses and picked it up. She fingered the youth-giving stone and then the thick gold. She could now see the etchings on it clearly. They were flames. Flames licking the metal. Flames of love? She held the ring up to the light, where the pale gem gleamed, its facets revealing a hint of a rainbow. And then she looked inside, almost afraid, as if it would burn her. *Rachel.* She returned it to the guard and headed to the Portsmouth.

■■■

Sarah hung up the phone. "I'm such a fool," she said. She pushed open the booth and dragged herself back up to Mitchell's room.

"Well?" he said

"Carlos was telling the truth. I spoke to Esperanza, the maid who was such a help to me at Agua Caliente. She did some checking. He was there for several days before the place opened. I don't know how I could've been so stupid. And the phone call cost a bloody fortune."

"Well, don't feel too bad, I'm a goddamn reporter, and I overlooked one of the most basic questions. When? The when. But remember, Carlos admitted to the affairs. That's no small potatoes. Don't forget about Bradford. He thinks Rita was killed and that Carlos did it."

"After you planted the idea."

"Not Carlos specifically. Anyway, maybe in Sabrina's case, Carlos came to L.A., did the deed, and then caught up with his *banditos*."

Sarah groaned.

"Sorry, not very funny."

"And not plausible either."

"So what do you think he meant? By the 'but I know' business?"

Sarah shrugged. He wanted to tell me something, something significant I think, and then changed his mind. "But I know...who did?" Is that what he meant? But I can't be sure, and what am I to do about it?"

"Well, you know my theory. When stumped, do something mindless."

"Do you have a suggestion?"

"Actually, I do. I got a gash in my shoe. A piece of glass missed my foot by a millimeter. What do you say we find a shoe repair, walk around and let the air get into our brains?"

"What's with all the shoes on this goddamn trip?" Sarah said. "All right. And some food? I haven't eaten."

"Perfect."

"Mitchell, I don't have to tell you how grateful I am."

Mitchell glanced at her. "None of that now. Like you said, there's time."

"Right. Hey, I know! I know of a place, for your shoes. There's a deli around there, too."

"Boy, you get around."

"More than I'd like."

"How'd you find it?"

"Rita's shoes, they were from the store. I had hopes, but nothing came of it. The owner is very nice, though. Even had me over for dinner. One of my people."

"Ah. Should I watch my wallet?"

Sarah frowned.

■■■

It was past noon by the time they reached Brooklyn Avenue, and Sarah's stomach was growling. They stopped for lunch at the Plate Deli. The corned beef looked fatty, but Sarah ordered it anyway and had to stop herself from licking her plate. It was like old times, sitting with Mitchell across from her, demolishing his usual pastrami on rye. Once every couple of weeks they went to the deli in Toledo, vowing to try something new but always ordering the same thing. Just now, there was tremendous comfort in this simple act, even though Sarah knew that it was really only the habit that was familiar. Everything else had changed.

The shoe store was bustling. Sam was engaged with a customer and another was waiting. Sarah browsed the racks, with Mitchell awkwardly in tow. Sam did have a good selection, she thought, as she picked up a dark blue heel with a white leather trim.

"I've got more colors in the back," Sam said.

Sarah turned to his voice.

"Well, hello, there! You still in town? I'm surprised."

"Yeah, still here. How are you, Sam?"

"Busy, thankfully. And you?"

"All right. This is my friend, Mitchell. He's got a bit of a shoe problem."

"I hope not the kind you had."

"No, no."

"Good. Sit," Sam said. He untied Mitchell's wingtips and slipped them off. Hmm. Let me measure you. Twelve and a half. Those are some feet. I don't know if I've got anything."

"Actually, I was just hoping for a fix. See that tear there."

"Oh." Sam inspected the shoe. "Well, I'm not a cobbler, but since you're here with Sarah, give me a minute." He took the shoe in the back and soon returned with it patched. "Best I can do."

"That's jake," Mitchell said. "What do I owe you?"

"No charge."

"Oh, no, please."

Sam shooed Mitchell away. "I'd be pretty stingy if I tried to squeeze you for that."

There's a Jew for you, Sarah thought.

"Well, thank you," Mitchell said.

Sam eyed the customers and then turned back to Sarah. "Hey, uh, whatever happened with that Mexican lady, anyway? I've checked the paper but haven't seen anything."

"That's a tough question. I'm not sure."

"Did you end up going to that street, Marianna?"

"Yeah, nothing there."

"Shame. You know if you wait a minute, Marvy will be here. He's only got a half day. He's coming to help."

"Oh, I'd love to seem him." Sarah turned to Mitchell. "Marvy's Sam's son. Very smart boy."

"Smart ass, you mean."

Sarah managed a tired laugh. "How has he been, Sam?"

"Usual. But really, since you said he was okay, I've let up a bit."

"Not *too* much, I hope."

"No no. There he is now."

Marvy came running in, out of breath and flushed. "Hi, Dad."

"Look who's here, Marvy. Remember Miss Kaufman?"

"Oh, yeah, yeah. Hi."

"Hi, Marvy. How are you?"

"Okay. Gotta get going. Dad said I could work the cash register, today. Right, Dad?"

"Yeah, just make sure you don't put an extra quarter in your pocket. You're getting paid enough as it is."

"Yeah, yeah."

"I'm not jokin'."

Sarah smiled. "Well, I see that things are indeed okay, Sam. We're in a bit of a rush. It was good to see you, and thanks for helping my friend here."

"Yes," Mitchell echoed. "Thank you very much."

"Oh, Sarah. Before you go. He came closer and lowered his voice. "You know it's funny. Did you read about that girl, oh, uh, some actress that was murdered on Pomeroy?"

Sarah stopped. "You mean Sabrina Johnson?"

"Yeah, yeah. I think that was her name."

"What about her?"

"That was pretty close to where, to where…."

"Rita?"

"Yeah, to where Rita was found."

"Yes, it was. What about it, Sam?"

Sam rubbed his chin. "Well, Henrietta and I were talking. We remembered about Rita, you know since you told us about her and all, and then this girl, found so close."

"And?"

"I think that was the same area where all those folks got sick a few years back. Right before we moved here. Anyway, we just thought it was kind of odd. Not odd, but you know…"

"Sick?"

"Yeah, you know, Mexicans live there mostly. I guess it's not surprising, really. The real estate broker said it was just Mexicans who got it. But they had to burn down some of their houses. I've been trying to think of the name of that other street. The one where it started. What was that damn street?"

"Rachel," Marvy yelled out.

"What's that?"

"Rachel Street."

Sarah turned to Marvy, in what felt like slow motion.

"That's right," Sam said. "How'd you know that, kid?" Sam said.

Frankie Alcantar once talked about it. Nobody in school believed him, you know, because of his two names and stuff. But he said it was the plague. Remember? I told you that, Dad."

"Shush!" Sam grabbed Marvy's arm. "Don't say that word."

"No, Dad. Really, Frankie said they blamed it on the Mexicans. They said Mexicans weren't clean, that they couldn't wipe the dirt off themselves. But Frankie said that was a lie. I remember because the day Frankie told us about it he was going by Ben Washington, and the teacher stuck him in the corner. He said his grandmother's house was burned and that some men told Frankie's family to keep quiet. You remember that?"

Everyone in the store now slowed too, as if under some spell.

Sarah clutched Mitchell's hand and walked over to Marvy, who was pushing the register keys.

"Stop playing with that!" Sam said.

"Okay!"

"Sam," Sarah said softly, "houses were burned?"

"Yeah, a few. But Marvy's nuts. It wasn't that horrible disease."

"Sam, can I talk to Marvy, outside maybe?"

"*Oy*, I wish I hadn't mentioned it."

"There was a reason you did, Sam. Something struck you. Now, can I talk to Marvy? You know that I wouldn't say anything to upset him."

Sam sighed. "It's a good thing I like you, Sarah. Go ahead, but be quick."

Marvy followed Sarah and Mitchell to the sidewalk. "Marvy," Sarah said, putting her hands on his shoulders, "who did you mean by 'some men'? You said some men told his family to keep quiet."

"I don't know, that's just what Frankie said."

"Tell me more about Rachel. Rachel Street."

"Like Dad said, that's where Frankie, or Ben, said the first person got sick."

"And then what? Then what did he say?"

"He said they had to hide it. And then burn some of the houses. There were rats and things. Some of the people didn't have homes anymore, and I don't know what happened to them. Died, I guess. I don't know."

"I see. It must have been kind of scary, to hear that."

"Yeah, but the teacher said Frankie was making it up."

"What do you think, Marvy?"

"I think he was telling the truth. I like Frankie, and Ben, too."

"You know, I like you, Marvy. You've got a good heart and a quick mind. You keep being Frankie's friend. And Ben's."

"What about Dad?"

"Your dad needs time, that's all. And you can help him. Do you understand what I'm saying?"

"Sort of."

"I think you do. Now, you better get back to work or your dad might give the job to someone else!"

Marvy waved and dashed inside. Sam came back out. As Sarah started to say good-bye, he gave her a hug and whispered: "Please, Sarah, don't take this plague stuff seriously. You know how kids are, and, uh, it's bad for the customers." He pulled back and sighed. "If I'd thought that disease had been anywhere near here, you think I'd have risked it? Remember, it was because of my daughter's health that we moved to the Heights in the first place."

"Yes, I remember. Don't worry, Sam. I'm not interested in spreading rumors, or germs. Besides, no matter what it was, it happened a few years ago, right?"

"Yeah. But people have long memories."

"I understand."

"It was nice to meet you, Sarah. Truly."

"You, too. Oh, Sam, before I go, you asked my opinion about Marvy, and I told you I thought he would be fine, and I do. More than fine. You asked my opinion and now I'd like offer you a little advice, if you don't mind."

He furrowed his brow. "Go ahead."

"The fact that Marvy has compassion for Frankie should make you proud, whether or not everything the boy says is true. My professional opinion is that Marvy will be a great man, if you encourage this part of him, the part that feels or at least tries to understand what other people feel. Maybe he'll even be a doctor, Sam, someone who could help people like Frankie, like the people on Rachel Street, like your daughter."

Sam's worried, blue eyes filled up. "You know how to get to a fella, Sarah."

"I mean it."

Sam smiled. "Message received. Now, go, and give my regards to the snow!"

■■■

"Well, your strategy sure worked, Mitchell," Sarah said after they took their seats on the bus. Good thing for that nail."

"Yeah, I'd like to say I did it on purpose."

"I think it was Rita."

"Oh God. Don't get wacky on me."

Sarah gazed out the window at City Hall, its Egyptian lines towering Sphinx-like in the blue sky. "No, although it's tempting to believe in some guiding force. Everything coming together like that, Sam bringing up Rita, Marvy knowing the name, even the luck of him being off school. Had any of it been askew, I would have never learned that the poor, deceased Rachel was a street!

"Rachel still could have been one of Carlos' wives."

"No. Saying that he was married to a Jewish woman was part of his game. Those flames etched into the ring, the burned houses, the name. It all fits."

"Things have seemed to fit before and then split at the seam. Remember the timing?"

"I know, that's why I'm going to see Paige before anything else. She's lived in this city a long time, works for the cops. She'd know, first, if it were true, what really happened, and maybe even have an idea about how Rita and Sabrina might be connected. One thing I can tell you. Carlos is angry about how history treated his people, and Rachel Street must be part of that anger. Perhaps the very center of it."

The bus rumbled over a deep groove, almost pushing Sarah into Mitchell's lap. She ignored the pleasing sensation and straightened herself. "As I see it, Mitchell, there are three pressing questions. Who are the 'they' Marvy mentioned? How are 'they' connected to Rita and Sabrina? And how is all of that related to what Carlos stopped himself from telling me, the 'But I know....' Get the answers, my dear Watson, and I think we will be very close."

"Christ, Sarah. The last time you talked like Sherlock Holmes I wound up at a KKK induction."

"Don't worry. All you need to do for now is stay at the hotel. I'm calling Paige as soon as we get back."

"Aye, aye, Captain, but I think I'll first spend a few hours at the trial. To keep up appearances, you know."

"Good idea." She smiled at this slip into banter, as if all were normal. For a moment, they were their former selves.

"At least we know Ted Rosen isn't a murderer," Mitchell said.

"Never say never, but you're probably right. He's just a slimy crook."

"By the way, what ever happened to your conference?"

"Don't remind me. I saw Jean, so that was good. But, well, I lost the book there, the one you gave me. *Oi!*"

"Oh?"

"Yeah. Another long story. No pun intended. I'm really sorry though. It upset me."

"It's just a book."

"With Sinclair's signature."

The bus slowed and screeched to a halt. "Pershing Square," the bus driver said.

Sarah followed Mitchell to the exit and waited for the doors to open. "I never found out what happened to Bunny," she said.

"Bunny?"

"The protagonist."

"Oh yeah. That name. How could I have forgotten it? Want me to tell you?"

"Only if he turned out okay."

"Better wait then."

"Oh no."

The doors opened. They disembarked and gave each other a perfunctory hug.

"See you later," Mitchell said.

Sarah nodded as she flagged a cab.

48

Paige was already there, waving to Sarah with one hand, a cigarette in the other. She had been glad that Sarah had called her at work. Things were slow and she was very anxious to hear all. She was too excited to accomplish much anyway, she said, because The Lock had just hired her for the next five nights. Her own gig, not a fill-in. If she could bring in an audience, they would consider a more permanent arrangement. Her voice was still a little rough from being ill, but regular saltwater gargles were helping. Sarah congratulated her and said that one of these days, before Sarah went home, they would have that dinner they'd had to postpone and celebrate. For now, they had agreed to meet at the bench near the station.

"Well, finally," Paige said as Sarah approached.

"Finally, yes," Sarah said, facing an overdone but still somehow alluring vision in pink. Lips and cheeks; dress, shoes and hat. In the pink, Sarah thought. Paige was over the virus and had been given a chance to live out her dream. The color no doubt reflected her mood.

"I want to hear everything," she said. "Everything. Beginning with Tijuana. Jeepers, honey, I'm still so sorry about that whole mess. But I let *you know who* have it. Boy, was he embarrassed. He did really believe the man he saw was Bradford, but he also admitted to relying on rumors."

"Water under the bridge," Sarah said.

"Well, at least if you tell me about it, I can suffer vicariously."

So Sarah obliged, recounting the drive down the coast, the hotel, casino and, most importantly, the situation with Carlos.

Paige nodded as Sarah spoke, as if nothing could surprise her. As if she heard this kind of far-fetched plot every day, which, given her line of work, was possible. Then Sarah began to relay her experience with the real Bradford. But before she even got to her panic at seeing the Hollywoodland sign, Paige interrupted. "Sarah, could you first tell me a little more about Carlos."

"Oh, there will be more. Just wait."

Paige glanced shyly at Sarah as she flicked ashes on the grass. "No, I mean something different."

"Different?"

"Promise you won't laugh at me."

"Why would I?"

"Sarah, as I told you, I've had rotten luck with men. Not much romance. My leg, you know. They like my face but always seem to have somewhere to be when they see me walk."

Sarah shook her head. "I'm so sorry. But you're lovely, Paige. I'm sure there's a great guy out there who'd be thrilled to have you."

Paige sighed and bit her lip. "Do you mind indulging me a little? Woman to woman. I mean, do you mind telling me what this Carlos fella did? What he was like. What he said. You know."

"What do you mean?"

"Well, physically, and you know, that kind of thing."

Sarah stiffened. She had consciously skimmed over that part. It was none of Paige's business. Besides, the thought of it now made her sick. "I don't think that's necessary."

Paige lowered her eyes. "Of course. Forgive me," she said.

Sarah touched her sleeve. "It's all right." But she really didn't think it was. Such a strange request.

"You must think I'm demented."

"No, no. Of course not." And then Sarah again thought of Tillie, who had never been with a man. Only once did her sister talk to her about the effects of that kind of rejection, how it battered her self-image, shaped her outlook on life. It was so painful that Tillie forbade Sarah to ever mention it again. But she did like to hear about the niceties of Sarah's love life, the gifts Mitchell gave her, the restaurants they went to, the outward tokens of affection. Take that several steps further, Sarah thought, with a more worldly and tougher sort of woman, and well…. Sarah turned to Paige, who looked utterly dejected. "Actually, Paige, I don't mind a little girl talk. But before I start, you must know three things. First, Phillip Bradford said that Carlos was having an affair with Rita. Second, he now believes that Rita was killed. Third, he thinks Carlos is the killer. And there's a fourth. I think Carlos may have done it too, if I can just clear up a few details. Still want a play by play?"

Paige's mouth fell open. She just managed to catch her cigarette. "Bradford! Wait till the boss hears about this. He will hear about it, right?"

"In due time."

"How are things with Mitchell, by the way?"

"Okay. Well?"

"Well, to answer your question. Yes, I still want to hear, if only to confirm my suspicions that all men, except for your Mitchell, are beasts."

That didn't quite make sense to Sarah, but she went ahead, describing the night at the Biltmore, the dancing, the caressing, the passion that continued for days, reaching a crescendo in Tijuana before crashing to the ground. Carlos' sultry look, deep kiss, firm muscles. She indeed told all, and was shocked that in the telling, that in conjuring up the memories, her loins involuntarily tingled. Mind and body, inseparable. As for Paige, she listened with closed eyes, seemingly enraptured, no doubt experiencing a few tingles herself.

"Okay, that's enough," Sarah said.

"You loved him," Paige said, rousing herself out of her half stupor.

"I thought so."

"And he pretended to love you."

"Yes. Pretended. Although, even yesterday, he claimed that his feelings were real."

"Yesterday?!"

"Yes, that's what I was about to tell you."

"Well, please then, go on!"

So Sarah did just that. Paige now listened attentively, nodding and shaking her head at a narrative whose improbability had just grown exponentially. Mute expression seemed a fitting response. But when Sarah got to the part about Carlos being arrested, Paige broke her silence. "I knew about the Carlos in jail, of course," she said, "the union fellow. He's the talk of the town. But I had no idea he was one and the same. That's just too much, Sarah. Too much!"

"Yes," Sarah said, "and I hope that you might just hold the key to keeping him there."

"Me?"

"Do you know about an illness, a bad illness, in nineteen twenty-four, in the Mexican quarter?"

Paige's eyes nearly bugged out of her head. She looked around as if checking for spies. "You don't mean the…the…plague?" she whispered.

Sarah nodded. So she did know.

"How did you find out?" she said.

"Oh, I have sources."

"Well, they're certainly better than mine then. Jesus, honey, yeah. There really was a plague here. Pneumonic was the term they gave it. The Force worked with the city on that. Nobody much was aware of it because they kept it under wraps. A lot of hush, hush. Awful business. Homes burned. People displaced. Many died. They finally contained the thing, but there was a lot of bad blood."

"In what way?"

"Not what the city needed when they were trying to court investors and potential residents. I mean, people come here for their health! They sort of portrayed it as a Mexican disease. You know, not due to their living conditions, but to their race."

"Ah. You do know a lot about it."

"Well, like I say, the office was involved. I was kept out of a lot, but you know I'm always listening. But Sarah, what does this have to do with Carlos and Rita, and all that?"

"Motivation, Paige. Do you remember exactly where the disease hit? The exact neighborhood? The streets?"

"Hmm. Only one. Rachel. Rachel Street. The first patient, a young boy, I think. He died there."

Sarah's eyes burned, as if staring directly at a noon sun. "Where was Rita found? And Sabrina?"

"Not on Rachel," she said.

"No, but..."

"Oh, wait a minute. Wait a bloody minute! Pomeroy. Pomeroy and Marianna. That *is* the same area!"

Sarah grabbed Paige's hand, which was shaking as much as her own. "Who was behind the effort, you know, to keep it under wraps?"

"Oh, well that would be the Chamber of Commerce. Advertisers. Health Department."

"Advertisers. Advertisers like Phillip Bradford, for instance?"

Paige's eyes widened again. "Yes. Yes! He was on that campaign, I'm sure of it."

"Any documents on that?"

"Check the new library. The stuff won't be easy to find, probably scattered, but it's there I'd bet."

"Good idea. Oh, and Sabrina Johnson's father was a doctor," Sarah said. "A doctor who worked for the health board. Her landlady told me about that."

"Holy cow!"

"I know."

"But why would Carlos kill these women? They didn't do anything. And Sabrina was so young. It seems so...so...out of proportion."

"Not, perhaps, to someone who has been harboring the kind of resentment Carlos has. He is bitterly angry, Paige, over the treatment of Mexicans and Chicanos, and the feeling goes back a long way. It's been simmering since the Mexica-American War. Before that even. I imagine this cover-up, or whatever you want to call it, took him past the boiling point."

"He talked to you about all that?"

"Yes. In fact, he was quite eloquent. I learned a lot from him. And I sympathized. But as you well know, criminals can be smart, manipulative. They have their own logic. Carlos no doubt convinced himself that these vicious acts were just. Like the salting of the water. That's my theory anyway. However, there's a tiny problem."

"What's that?"

"Carlos can account for his whereabouts at the time of both deaths."

"Tiny? That's a huge problem, Sarah. At least where the cops are concerned."

"Yeah. I know. But first things first. I'm eager to see Carlos' response when I bring out the Rachel card. Oh, wait. Let me show you what I'm going to take with me," Sarah said, removing the embroidered handkerchief that Carlos gave her from her purse. The red and yellow zigzags, curling up to a point, licking the edges of the fine white linen, reminded her of that day in downtown Tijuana, when everything was aglow. Intricate in design yet simple in meaning, or so she had thought. "Carlos said he never thought he could fall in love again after Rachel. But he had. I was his flame, he said, his sweetheart, and this token, which he said Rachel once owned and his mother made, was a symbol of those feelings. But obviously that was another lie. This is a symbol of death, not love." Sarah handed it to Paige, who unfolded it and fingered the design. "Perhaps both," Paige said. "It's beautiful. The stitching. Took a lot of work."

"Yeah. I was moved when he gave it to me. What a fool."

Paige handed it back to Sarah and lit a cigarette. "Ha." She shook her head and sighed. "Goddamn men."

"Right." Sarah said.

Paige then stood. "Well," she said, "I better go."

"Back to work?"

"Uh huh. I'm so sorry this happened to you, honey. But I'm glad I could help a little after all. I'll tell ya, though, if Carlos has an alibi, the cops won't touch this."

"We'll see," Sarah said, watching Paige limp away toward the station. Everything fit. It all fit. Except, as Paige said, "huge problem, cops won't touch this." Or as Mitchell put it, "break at the seams." Except, except all of that. Maybe Carlos had someone else do it, Sarah thought. That was a possibility. "But I know...." who did, she mentally added. She sat for a while more. The air was fresh, the patch of grass near the bench young and green. A delicate eucalyptus blew lightly in the breeze, its fragrance hitting Sarah in sweet waves. Such a gentle tree. Those branches couldn't hold a neck, a body. Poor Jacob. He didn't have a chance with that old hickory.

49

itchell swung open the door at the first knock. "Christ, Sarah, I was getting worried about you again."

"Sorry. I walked back."

"Well?"

"I'll tell you on the way to the library."

"You want to read? Now?"

"Come on. It closes at nine p.m."

Mitchell looked at his watch. It was only four, but he grabbed his jacket, with the patches, and let her lead. Sarah said that Paige had confirmed that an outbreak of plague, the Black Death, had indeed occurred here in '24 and advised a search of library documents. Sarah wanted to return to the prison the next day armed with as many facts as possible. Throw them in Carlos' face and let him try to deny them. According to Paige, the Chamber of Commerce attempted to cover up the illness and cast it as an ethnic matter. Bradford's ad agency was a part of that effort, as was Sabrina's father, a health board official. To Sarah, their murders were Carlos' twisted form of retribution.

It was a compelling hypothesis, Mitchell thought. He remembered that Bradford had told him how one of his campaigns saved the city. Could this be the one he was referring to? And was it the same one that he told Sarah he had begun to regret? Compelling indeed, and yet. They were still working from the unproven premise that Rita was murdered. And then there was the issue of timing. But Sarah emphasized that she had now identified a motive. Any cop, any attorney would say that was a major accomplishment. "Yes, it is, Mitchell said. "And I'm impressed. "But…."

"I know, I know!" Sarah said, as they drove past the courthouse. "How was the trial today, by the way?"

"More of the same. I talked to one of the other reporters who said he doubted if we'd see the end of it in our lifetime."

"I'll see Ted go to jail if I have to rise from the dead."

"The library is here on Fifth," the cabbie said, "between Flower and Grand. Quite a place. Pretty new, finished just last year. An architectural hodgepodge.

You see, you've got your Egyptian parts and your Italian influences. See there?" he said, as he pulled over in front of the massive concrete structure. "On the top there's a pyramid in mosaics, and tiled suns on the sides. Then there's that hand holding the torch, the 'Light of Learning.' Course there's some statues of snakes and other Eastern type creatures. One of the biggest libraries in the country, they say."

"Thanks for the tour," Mitchell said, handing him a generous tip.

"Most people think cabbies are dumb. I like to prove them otherwise."

"Well, I've never thought that, but you certainly made your case."

They walked in and headed straight for the reference desk. It was a beautiful building, with statutes and chandeliers and grilles, but Sarah was too focused to notice. "We'd like to see anything you have from the fall of nineteen twenty-four," she said.

"Anything?" the attendant said.

"Anything and everything. Newspapers, magazines, health records."

The woman sighed. "Could you be a bit more specific?"

Sarah told Mitchell she didn't want to go into detail, lest she raise suspicion, or, based on the reaction of Sam and Paige, start a panic. "I'm afraid not," she said. We're just researching the period, a personal project." The woman shrugged. "Well, let me see," she said, and in a half hour returned with reams of material. Most of it was irrelevant, but there was enough, a paragraph here, a list there, comments, questions, statistics. Enough that by closing time they had the facts, more than Sarah wanted. The "light of learning" had indeed shone down, but the knowledge it imparted was of the darkest sort.

50

t was midnight by the time Sarah was back in her own hotel room. She fell asleep instantly but awoke with a start an hour later, drenched in sweat. Enormous black rats, images from a nightmare, were still swarming in the darkness. She sat up and switched on the light, trying not to hyperventilate. After a few minutes, her breathing leveled off. She got up, changed into another nightgown, and splashed some water on her face. Then she propped herself up on the pillow with her journal and composed a fragmented paragraph, the only form she could muster.

October. Rachel Street. Cough, fever, aches. Numbers growing. Screams, convulsions, deaths. Quarantine. Ropes, guards. Hospitals. Specimens. Mercurochrome. Intravenous drips. Mexican quarter. Spreading. Pomeroy. Marianna. Federal government. Secret codes. Black Death. Bodies mounting. Men, women, children. Raze the homes, kill the rats. Poisons. Petroleum, sulfur, cyanide. Slash and burn. Condemn. Destroy. No rebuilding. No compensation. Stealth. Burn the houses, burn the culture, burn out the race. More names. Lawsuits. Cover-ups. Ten thousand plague abatements. No provisions for the homeless. Pomeroy, Marianna. Rachel.

She concluded with a line that stuck with her from Southern California Business, a magazine the librarian had included in the stack of materials: *Anglo Saxon civilization must climax in the generations to come.... The Los Angeles of Tomorrow will be the center of this climax.*

She put down her writing but was afraid to go back to sleep. She and Mitchell had discovered beyond a shadow of a doubt the horror and injustice of 1924. City officials indeed appeared to have used this medical tragedy to further Mexican stereotypes, scatter residents, and attempt to remake this part of the city in their own image. *The Los Angeles of Tomorrow.* Understandably, people like Carlos would not accept that particular future without a fight. If only he had gone about it differently.

"We're a good team," Mitchell said before Sarah left.

"Yes," was all Sarah answered, but right now she thought how very right he was. If the situation wasn't so delicate, she would hop a cab, bang on his door and beg for comfort, the kind he was so good at providing. But instead she nodded off, battling more rats, trapped in a putrid blaze, waiting for morning.

■■■

"Who'd you say this is?"

"Sarah. Sarah Kaufman. I visited Mr. Martinez the other day."

"Just a minute."

Sarah could hear muffled sounds. A hand over the receiver.

"You're a friend of the prisoner?"

"Yes, a friend."

"Hold on." Again, the hand. Longer this time. "Ma'am, you better head to the County Hospital."

"What's that?"

"There's been an accident. Pretty serious. I'd hurry."

Sarah hung up the phone. Then she dressed and did exactly what she was told. She hailed a cab, stated her destination. But she felt oddly detached, as if this shattering news involved a total stranger, as if it might not spell the end of everything. Catatonic she thought, but she wasn't that lucky. She was too aware of herself for that. Now that she was being escorted to Carlos' room, the sights and smells, the agonies all about her came roaring into full relief.

She went over the cop's words again as she followed him down the hall. Carlos somehow got a knife and had tried to stab a guard. The guard fought back, grabbed the weapon. But Carlos was in a rage, came after the guard again, who then had no choice. In self-defense, he shoved the blade into Carlos' gut. Deep wound. Condition, grave.

Sarah was trembling, sweating, the lump in her throat about to give way when the officer seated outside his room said: "Okay, go ahead."

"Is he conscious?" Sarah said.

"Barely. His mother is on her way, so make it quick."

Sarah had been in enough hospitals, visiting the sick, volunteering in children's wards. She'd seen her fair share of broken limbs, burns, even gunshots. But the sight of Carlos, his blood-soaked bandage, the IV solution dripping down that tube and into his arm, was chilling. Still, she inched closer. His eyes were shut, his breathing shallow. She sat on a chair near the bed, watching the path of the fluid from the bottle to his hand to the bruised spot where the needle was inserted. "Carlos," she said. "Carlos."

He moaned and half-opened his swollen eyes.

"Carlos," she said, louder.

He turned. "Sarah," he whispered. "Come, come near." She moved in, her face almost touching his. "This wasn't an accident." His lips were cracked and white. "I was attacked, unprovoked."

Sarah shook her head. No! She'd had enough of these lies. She had her mission, and she would not be deterred. "I know about Rachel," she said. "Rachel Street, the plague, all of it. I know why you killed them."

He turned away, closed his eyes and moaned again. "*Andrés, Andrés.*"

"Carlos!"

"My son, my son."

"Your son? What?"

He turned back with wild eyes. "He's here, in this hospital, Sarah. The mental ward. *Andrés.* Sarah, my son! Didn't know what he was doing. *Por favor, Dios, Por favor. Por favor.* Don't let them arrest him. It was my fault, my fault…"

His eyes closed and his face went slack. Delirium, Sarah thought, just as she heard a woman screeching, wailing. The officer walked in. "Time's up. His mother is here."

The hunched woman flew past Sarah unseeingly. "*Mijo, mijo, mijo!*" She threw her small, fragile frame over Carlos' body, the blood staining her white blouse. Carlos let out a deep, grinding rattle. And then silence. Silence. "*Mijo! Mijo! Doctor! Doctor!*" White, more white. White coats, white shoes, white faces hovering over the dark, Pieta-like scene. Stethoscopes. Pulse. Injection. Pulse. And then, out of nowhere, a priest. "In the name of the father, the son, and the holy ghost." Another injection. No response. No response.

"I'm sorry," the doctor said.

His mother howled and fell to the floor. "*Padre, Padre!*"

The priest gently raised the woman up and pressed a rosary into her hand. "He is with God, now," he said.

Sarah stumbled out of the room, down one hall then another until she reached the door to the stairwell. She pushed it open, then leaned over, gagging. She wanted to vomit, rid herself of the torment she had just witnessed, but nothing came up. That poor woman, so broken. And Carlos. His strong body, lifeless, his twisted mind still, but surely not at peace.

Sarah eased herself down on the step. The past few weeks rushed past her; the naïve bliss, the psychic fractures, the grim realizations. Now, there would be no closure, no justice. Her throat grew tight, tighter, and then finally, tears. For herself, for Rita and Sabrina, for that pitiable mother. That mother. The love for her son, the sacrifices she must have made. What did Sarah know of it? She was barren, a shell of a woman. It was all happening again. All again. And again, as with Jacob, Sarah had failed.

A group of young nurses pushed open the door. Sarah turned to the wall. Don't talk to me, she thought.

"You okay, ma'am? "

"Yes."

They skipped down the stairs twittering about some intern one of them had a date with. They giggled, as if they were at a dance. This was a hospital for Christ's sake! Didn't they know someone had just died?

The door closed behind them. Died. Carlos had just died. God. But even at the end, he was playing her, wasn't he? An unprovoked attack? But. But. What about that other babble? His son, he said. Andrés. She closed her wet eyes. Could it be? He'd lied about everything else, why not this? She felt her brain trying to work, to calculate the possibility. A father's love. That could be powerful, too. Her own father's certainly was, risking all he had to protect his children. "My son. Andrés." Here, in this very hospital, mental ward. "My fault," Carlos said. "Didn't know what he was doing." Didn't know what he was doing when he did what? Sarah thought. When he did *what*?

Sarah sat up. Perhaps that wasn't a delusion. Perhaps, just perhaps, those were the most lucid, honest words Carlos ever spoke. His son. "But I know...." Yes, Sarah thought. That would explain...so much. She walked back down to the entrance, checked the directory and took the elevator to the fourth floor.

●●●

"Is there an Andrés Martinez in there?" Sarah said, motioning to the locked double doors.

"And who are you?"

"A friend of his father's."

The nurse stiffened. "Oh."

"I was just visiting Mr. Martinez."

"In prison?"

So it was true, Sarah thought. It was true! And the nurse obviously didn't know the rest yet. "What's wrong with the boy?"

"I'm not allowed to give out that information."

"Sorry. Of course."

"Can I help you with anything else?"

"May I talk to his doctor?"

"He's not in."

"Look," Sarah said, "I have reason to believe that your patient might have committed some very serious crimes. And there is something else. The father just died. He's downstairs, on the second floor. Or maybe in the morgue by now."

The woman looked at her as if she belonged behind those doors, too. "I'll check out your story," she said, as if talking about the weather, "and take appropriate measures. But I'd advise you go to the police. Remember, this is a hospital."

"But…" And then Sarah stopped. No. No more, she thought. No more buts. No more buts, ands or howevers. Only a period. "I'll do that," she said, and headed for the station.

▪▪▪

It was over, out of her hands. She told the authorities what she knew, what she suspected. She didn't even care that it was Hodges who took her statement. He listened this time. Why? Because it turned out they already had a lead on Andrés. He was, in fact, their prime suspect in the murder of Sabrina Johnson. The guard who Carlos attacked had put the pieces together from a prison informant, and that is why Carlos attacked him. Andrés had the time, the wherewithal and a motive. So now, with Sarah's statement about Phillip Bradford, and especially with the chauffeur to confirm it, they would reopen the case on Rita.

Like everyone else, Hodges advised Sarah not to "spread the plague," meaning keep the past in the past. That seemed wishful thinking at this point, since it was now obvious that the motive for murdering these women was directly related to the outbreak and its aftermath. Surely the whole city would be talking about the event once the press got a hold of it. Unless, of course, they didn't, unless the "powers that be" colluded again, changed the story, altered the motive to suit their vision. Or maybe that wouldn't even be necessary, since Andrés' attorney would no doubt mount an insanity defense. In which case the whole thing could be presented as a minor episode in the city's history that Andrés had greatly exaggerated or even fabricated. But she had no desire to argue. It wouldn't change anything. So when Hodges said that he just had her best interests at heart, she nodded, although if ever called upon, she wouldn't hesitate to give her unedited point of view.

"That's being smart," he said, his thin lips curving into a self-satisfied smile.

The officer's newfound concern for her was touching. Now that he had one Mexican in the ground and another probably locked up for life, he could afford to be magnanimous to a Jew. But Sarah had to admit the evidence against Andrés was convincing. He was a disturbed young man, had been in and out of hospitals all his life. Apparently had a few violent episodes. The informant had learned that Carlos had bred hate into him, brainwashed him to such a point that he probably believed he was saving the whole Mexican race by carrying out these heinous acts, not to mention making his father proud. When Carlos told Sarah that it was his fault, he no doubt had come to realize the damage he had done.

"You've performed a mighty fine service, Miss Kaufman," Hodges said. I apologize for not taking you seriously before."

"Tell that to the mother, the grandmother."

"Aw, now, those people are tough. She'll get through."

Sarah swallowed whatever traces of anger she had left and made for the exit. But Paige had been listening in the wings and once again came after her.

"Sarah, I heard. Terrible news."

"Yeah. Well, at least it sounds as if they have their killer. Insanity defense, I imagine.

"He'll never get out."

"No, and he probably shouldn't. But he'll be institutionalized rather than imprisoned."

"I wouldn't count on it. Insanity's hard to prove, especially in this town. Everyone's a little nuts."

Sarah shook her head. "Oh? I don't want to hear that." She didn't want to hear it, but knew from her own work that it was probably the case. In the area of criminality and mental health, Toledo, of all places, was more progressive than many cities, due in large part to Obee's work on the issue.

"Well, then let's talk about something else. I imagine you'll be leaving now."

"As soon as possible."

"Well, why don't you and Mitchell come by and take in my show before you go."

"I'd like that. I still owe you that dinner, too."

"Just come and hear me sing and we're even."

"Sounds as if I get the better end of the deal, but okay."

"Ducky," Paige said.

■■■

Cheat, liar, criminal. Carlos had been all of them. But not, apparently, a murderer. That made it a little easier for Sarah to imagine that what he had said about having feelings for her was true. Easier to pretend that they had both transcended their biases. Easier to believe that for a moment they had loved each other not as Mexican and Jew, but as man and woman.

She stepped into her grey chemise with the deep V-neck, the one that Mitchell bought her last year. It could have used a string of pearls, but that seemed inappropriate just now. Better to leave her neck bare, soft and unbruised, moving at will, pulse unimpeded. Better to appreciate it than ornament it. It wouldn't be long before the police would discover that Andrés had strangled Rita, just as he had Sabrina. With what? Her scarf? A rope? It didn't really matter. Hodges said that Andrés was known for his strong hands, that a friend claimed that he could squeeze juice from an orange without even peeling it.

Sarah brushed some powder on her chest and the small bit of cleavage only a dress of this cut could enhance. She knew she had done the right thing. But she was aching, tormented over the consequence. In telling the police about Andrés, it seems she had likely denied Carlos his dying wish that his son not go to prison. Carlos knew that an institution, however grim, was where Andrés belonged. But each city was different, and according to Paige, this one would be out for more blood. Aching. Tormented. What was wrong with her? She should be glad that she helped keep a psychotic off the streets. But she couldn't help it. The victory felt hollow, as if she exchanged one failure for another.

Again she thanked her lucky stars for Mitchell. He had supported her beyond any reasonable call of duty. If she'd had to go back to her hotel room alone after all this, she would have likely drunk herself blind. But there he had been, listening to the final, numbing installment, sharing the burden. If he'd taken even a sliver of delight in knowing Carlos was dead, he didn't show it. He responded with understandable shock, an abundance of sympathy and a long, healing embrace. It was an intimacy she needed, affection without the possible regret of sex. And then he purchased their return train tickets for Ohio, for 3 p.m., the day after tomorrow.

∎∎∎

They were not in a partying mood, but they needed to eat and Sarah really did want to see Paige perform.

"There she is," Mitchell said, pointing to a sexy photograph pinned to a scrap board behind a glass encasement. *The Lock is proud to announce a limited engagement of local crooner Paige Chastain! With Cuban wonder Piti Cabrera on the piano.*

Sarah smiled. "She must be ecstatic."

There was a table available up front, but they opted for one in the back. It was quieter, and this way they could surprise Paige. She was on in half an hour.

"Lamb chops?" Mitchell said.

Sarah nodded. If that dish was on the menu, Mitchell knew that was a sure bet.

"How can all these people look so happy?" Sarah said. "As if this were just another day."

"Life goes on."

"A cliché from the reporter who said he'd rather pass on a story than resort to using even one."

"I guess I'm getting soft."

"Oh, speaking of writing, I've been keeping a journal. Or notes or something."

"Really? That's great."

"Yeah."

"I don't suppose you'll let me see."

"I don't think you'd want to."

"Oh, right, probably not. You know what, though? For having gone through so much, you look nice."

"Is that supposed to be a compliment?"

Mitchell smiled. "Didn't I buy you that dress?"

"You know you did."

Mitchell lit a cigarette, adding more haze to the already smoky room. "Want one?"

"No. I think those days are over. They don't agree with me."

"Good," Mitchell said.

They both leaned back in their chairs, their eyes drifting from one depressingly cheerful table to the next.

"Looks can be deceiving," Mitchell said, reading her mind.

"That's two!"

"Two what?"

"Clichés."

"That one was intentional."

Sarah raised her eyebrow.

"Nice sound," Mitchell said, motioning to the pianist.

"Very," Sarah said, studying the striking young man playing a Latin tinged jazz. She tried not to think of Carlos, reminding herself that Cuba and Mexico were not one and the same. But that music. And the man, Piti Cabrera, could have been Carlos twenty years ago. Or perhaps Andrés now. Dark skin, full lips, thick black ringlets that fell around his neck. He swayed and closed his eyes as he played.

The chops arrived just as the overhead lights dimmed. From a side door, Paige emerged in a sequined black gown that glimmered under a spotlight. Her red hair had been straightened, giving her a more severe look, but she beamed at the clapping and whistles.

"Good evening, everyone," she said.

The crowd returned the welcome and clapped again. She extended her arm to Piti. "Isn't he something?" The clapping intensified. "Yes, amazing musician. But let me tell you a little secret. He is also quite the romantic." Piti grinned as he played a few whimsical notes. "If you were here an hour ago," Paige said, you might have seen him lower the piano's music stand with one hand while still playing with the other."

One person called out, "Yeah. I did see that."

"You know why?" Paige said.

"Why?" everyone said.

Because he wanted to see his sweetheart in the mirror, see her as he played. The spotlight shifted to a doe-eyed beauty, who melted under the glow. "Now that's something, isn't it?" Paige said.

Piti bowed his head and threw the girl a kiss. "My inspiration," he said in a charming accent.

Paige clapped along with the audience. "Boy, to have someone feel that way about you."

Sarah could feel Mitchell's eyes on her, but dared not look up.

"To belong to someone," Paige said. "To say I'm yours. He's mine. And to those waiting in line? Sorry, but I was here first. I mean, it's about fairness, don't you think? Whoever gets the...the...well, the *resource* first has the rights to it. Know what I mean?"

Everyone laughed. "Yeah!" they said in unison. I'd drink to that if I could!" someone said.

Sarah had started to take a bite of meat. She pulled back the fork and held it midair.

"Yes, indeed," Paige said, "I think that is a little rule we should follow, in life and in love." And then Piti added some chords and changed to a minor key. "Captured," Paige said, as the sultry melody began. "The song is called 'Captured.'"

> "*I tried to get away from your burning lips*
> *I didn't want to play with your burning lips...*
> *I tried to get away from the flame but the flame tossed my heart*
> *And I'm captured yes I'm captured..."*

Paige was a natural on stage. She held the microphone as if it were a baby, tenderly, lovingly. And her slight laryngitis actually lent itself to the song's steamy, obsessive quality.

> "*And I'm captured yes I'm captured*
> *There is nothing I can do*
> *I can't back track there's no track back*
> *I am yours heaven open its doors*
> *And as I wandered through*
> *Captured by you*
> *Captured by you*
> *I couldn't get away get away from you..."*

Whistles, cheers, and more applause. Paige belted out a few more tunes, and then took a break. She spotted Sarah and nearly floated to their table, her limp even seeming to benefit from the approval.

"Wonderful," Mitchell said. "You're a hit!"

"Thank you! I'm so glad you came. What did you think, Sarah? The truth?"

Sarah smiled, but only just. "Haunting."

"Ooo, I like that description."

"Who's the song by?" Sarah said.

"Anonymous," Paige said. "Hey, you two, how about a nightcap at my place after the show. A *real* night cap."

"No thanks," Sarah said. It's been a very long day."

"I know. That's why I thought you could use a drink. I make a mean sidecar. You'll forget everything."

"I don't mind, Sarah," Mitchell said.

"No, I'm tired."

Paige frowned. "I understand. Well, listen, I gotta get back. Will you write me, Sarah?"

"Sure."

"Good," Paige said. "Have a safe trip."

Sarah watched Paige maneuver through the tables, shaking hands, accepting tips as she headed toward a heavy-set man sitting alone. She took the chair beside him and leaned on his shoulder. He had red hair, too. Sarah peered around a customer who was partially blocking her view. Red hair, and, from here anyway, a slight resemblance to Paige.

"She really is great," Mitchell said.

"Mitchell."

"I'd never heard that song."

"Mitchell."

"I think she might really make it."

"Mitchell!"

"What?"

She sighed.

"What is it?"

"Something isn't right."

"You're not feeling well?"

"No. And I'm not hungry."

"You want to go?"

"Yes."

"Waiter," Mitchell said, "check please."

In a few minutes, they were in a cab, and Mitchell said: "Sarah, you're not really sick, are you?"

"No."

"What then?"

"Maybe nothing."

"But that means maybe something."

"Yes."

■■■

Sarah grabbed her glasses and her journal, and turned to the entry she'd made on the train. *Deauville of the Americas, Proust, Raul warns me, 'Don't trust Carlos.' Esperanza.* "No. No, it was before that," she said aloud. Before that. She turned back a page. Her eyes scanned the text, her own banal writing now more potentially important than anything she had ever read. "Where was it? No. Not there. Earlier." She flipped back further. *I didn't learn who Timothy Bradford was until after being examined in the infirmary. I had passed out for only a few seconds.* No. No! Sarah knew Carlos had mentioned the rule of capture with respect to oil, stocks and that damn C. C. Julian. First come, first served, he said. But he also drew a parallel, in reverse, in describing what was done to the Indians. Yes, now she remembered. It was that first day, the very first day! Yes, there was the page. There! And there, the translation. The missing link. The exact line. She knew she'd copied it down. *'Whoever gets to the resource first has the rights to it.'*

She sat back on the bed and removed her glasses. What were the odds that two strangers would use that rule, that law, as a symbol? How many people call a person a *resource*? And that song. "Captured." The burning, the flame. What were the odds? Sarah now thought back to when she had met Paige. Offering to help Sarah with Rita, with Bradford. Steering her to Tijuana. There was only one explanation. Only one. Paige had to have known Carlos. They had to have known each other.

Sarah felt as if she had turned that puzzle, the one she thought she'd solved, upside down, scattered the pieces every which way. But rather than being an unfathomable mess, they were realigning of their own accord, like the letters of a Ouija Board. She got up and picked up the phone. "Could you please connect me with the Portsmouth Hotel?"

itchell took two stairs at a time. He never dreamed he'd be back here, let alone for the reason that he was. But Sarah had made an incredible kind of sense when she called last night, and the significance of her observations had not diminished in the light of day. Indeed, it seemed that with the dawn came even greater certainty.

"She's hasn't disappeared again?" Sparks said, straightening his tie.

"No, no. But I do have another job for you, if you're interested. First, though, I've gotta ask you. Do you know Officer Hodges, at the Broadway station?"

"Of course. Everyone in this business does. Done some work for him."

Mitchell exhaled. "So he would trust you?"

He sniggered. "Look at this," he said, turning around a framed photograph on his desk so Mitchell could see it. It was a shot of some sort of banquet, with tables of uniformed cops, one of whom was Hodges. Next to him sat Sparks in a white tux. The two were smiling broadly.

"Does that answer your question? Now, what is this about?"

"Are you familiar with those new listening devices?" Mitchell said.

"A dictograph?"

"Yeah."

"I'm a dick, ain't I? The Feds use 'em at speakeasies quite a bit. Why?"

"Do you have one?"

"No. Too expensive. But I know how to use it. I could rent one for six bucks. Eavesdropping on her?"

"Well, actually, in a way." Mitchell explained the situation, and by the end the little man was intrigued. This was far more interesting than a runaway wife, and he might even make the papers. "Where would it happen?" he said.

"Train station. You know the waiting area has those benches that back up to each other."

"Ah, yes, I see. I could put the box underneath where they'll be seated. I'd only have to be a few feet away. The wire wouldn't be a problem."

"I'd hoped you'd say that. Sarah's already thought up a clever reason for meeting in one of the quieter spots there. She's scheduled a little farewell toast with the woman."

"Clever, but she'll have to be careful. Plainclothesmen crawling all over the place."

"She knows. Uh, Ray, this isn't illegal, is it?" Mitchell said.

"I wouldn't do it if it were."

Mitchell frowned.

"Okay, maybe I would. But no, it's not."

"Well, then?"

"When did you say?"

"Tomorrow."

"You're lucky. I just happen to be free."

That's what he said the last time, Mitchell thought, shaking his soft hand.

52

The loudspeaker sounded again. "Last call for Denver. Track nine." Paige was already five minutes late. Sarah checked her watch and glanced over her shoulder to make sure the detective was still there. His wide-brimmed hat hid the headset, and he looked relaxed, like a regular guy reading a book, which was the point. She turned back and fidgeted with her rings. Her stomach was in knots, and the knots were in knots. Paige had quickly accepted when Sarah asked her to meet her here, but maybe she'd had second thoughts. Sarah's unpacked suitcase sat at her feet. Maybe Paige didn't buy Sarah's story of wanting to share a few snorts before boarding the train home.

Sarah took out her compact and powdered her nose. Mr. Sparks had gotten permission to set up the dictograph earlier, so everything was in place. Mitchell had helped with the positioning, setting the amplifier and wire as far under the bench as possible. He assured her it was out of view, but to be safe, Sarah added a layer of security with the strategic placement of her suitcase. A few well-dressed passengers came and went, the highly polished floor echoing their footsteps. Another announcement: "Southern Pacific bound for Orange County. Track thirty-one."

"Prettying yourself up for me?"

Sarah jumped. "There you are. You snuck up on me."

"Where's Mitchell?"

"Oh, he'll be here. We have a few hours yet."

"You picked a good spot, Sarah," Paige said winking.

"Yeah, farthest from the tracks, so I assumed it would be the least crowded."

"You appear to be right," Paige said, sitting down.

First task accomplished, Sarah thought.

"I'm so glad to see you, Sarah," Paige said, opening her purse and pointing to a flask. I was disappointed the other night."

"I know. I was a wreck."

"Well, you're here now." She wrapped the flask in a chintzy scarf and handed it to Sarah. "And don't worry. I can smell a cop from miles around," she said, surveying the room.

Sarah prayed that wasn't true. "I do hope you're over your illness," she said, taking a sip.

"Completely. But how are you doing, Sarah? After all you've been through. They've arrested the Martinez boy, you know."

"No, I didn't know," Sarah said honestly.

"Yeah," Paige said. "But let's not talk about that." She swigged and passed it back. "Here."

Sarah sipped but pretended to gulp. She wanted Paige to do the majority of the drinking. "You really were great," she said. "Your singing."

"Thanks. They've held the show over, you know."

"Not surprising. Congratulations."

They passed the flask unobtrusively back and forth, keeping their eyes peeled. Sarah encouraged Paige to talk, asking her meaningless questions to keep her engaged and at ease. But at some point she had to up the ante. And so after twenty minutes, just as the arrival of the Northern Express was announced, she said: "Hey, after you left our table, you sat down with a man. You looked pretty chummy. Have you been keeping something from me?"

"I wish. That was my brother, David. I should have introduced you, but he's a little shy."

"Oh. You never mentioned him. What does he do?"

"Do? He's uh, a security guard."

"Where?"

Different places."

"He must be happy for you."

"Oh, you wouldn't believe how much. We're very close. He'd do anything for me." Paige said, slightly slurring her words.

It's now or never, Sarah thought, just as a little girl skipped by and looked at Sarah as if she knew her plan. "It's so funny. That comment you made, about being first to the resource."

"What's that?"

"You know, at The Lock. You introduced that eerie song, 'Captured,' by saying that the one who's first to the resource has the rights. It's funny."

"I know, that's why I said it."

"No, not that kind of funny. Strange funny. Because Carlos said that exact same thing."

Paige was silent.

"Yeah, he explained the rule of capture to me, you know, having to do with property, when someone discovers oil, for example. You know, like C. C. Julian. First come, first served. But Carlos had his own version of the rule, and he used it symbolically, just like you. Word for word."

Paige pulled in her chin and frowned. "So?"

"Coincidental, don't you think?" Sarah said.

Paige fanned herself and returned the flask to her purse.

"Remember this?" Sarah said, handing Paige the handkerchief that she had stashed in her pocket. You said it took a lot of work."

"So what?"

"You didn't say *takes* a lot of work, you said took."

"What the hell is your point? Takes, took. Who cares?"

Sarah pressed the handkerchief to her lips.

"You crocheted this, didn't you?"

Paige burst out laughing. A deep, guttural, boozy laugh. But Sarah didn't blink. She stared and held her gaze.

Paige started to stand, but Sarah dug her fingers into her arm. "You knew Carlos, didn't you, Paige. You knew him. You loved him."

She blanched, then smirked. "You're crazy."

"You loved him, and he left you, didn't he?"

She shook her head, contorted her face.

"I don't know how you did it," Sarah said, "but you killed those women. You're the one we've been looking for."

Paige yanked out of Sarah's grasp.

"Jealousy," Sarah continued with rapid fire. "I was focused on the complex. That's what prevented me from seeing the simple truth that was right in front of me."

"I do believe you've finally lost your mind," Paige said.

"He left you. He was disgusted by you. By your…your handicap, your defect."

"No! He wasn't! He…." She sucked in air, as if trying to breathe her words back.

Sarah closed her eyes and exhaled.

Paige stood and smoothed her still-straight hair. She was trembling, but her expression was smug. "You really believe that Hodges would take you seriously for one second? Haven't you learned anything?" She leaned over and in a raspy whisper said: "You think I could strangle anyone? Little me. A gimp? I'm going back to the station right now. Going to warn my boss about this insane encounter. I'll tell him the *kike* is at it again."

Sarah watched Paige until she disappeared from view. Her blouse was soaked, her ring finger raw, but she gathered her courage and turned around. The detective was fiddling with his hat. She stared at him, unable to bear another second of suspense. And then, finally, he looked up. Looked up and nodded.

53

The cabbie pulled over and parked, then came around and opened the door.

"I'll only be a minute," Sarah said.

"Take your time. We're very close."

Sarah clutched the bouquet and walked over to the ravine. She didn't know the exact spot, so she randomly chose a shady patch of moist dirt. She dug a hole with her fingers and planted the lilies. They drooped, but for now they added a brightness and touch of color to this place of death. Sarah climbed back up and surveyed the nothing of a hill, the run-down properties nearby. "Yes," she said. "*Me acuerdo de ti.* I remember you, Rita."

She got back in the car. They drove past Pomeroy and then down Rachel. Sarah asked the driver to go slow. There was no way to really tell, except for maybe that charred-looking fence, these empty lots. Mostly there were just houses, a child on a bike, a dog. She rolled down the window and breathed in. If that really was the faint smell of ash, it was probably someone burning leaves. Sarah checked her watch. Okay, she said.

He drove east and soon pulled over again.

"How long did you say?"

"Fifteen minutes."

"I'll be here."

Sarah swallowed, walked up the cracked steps, and knocked.

The door opened. "Come in," Carlos' mother said.

Sarah sat in the colorful room while the mother made tea. There were Mexican artifacts, a crucifix, photographs of Carlos and presumably of the young man she was here to see. An Aztec blanket covered a birdcage.

His mother returned. She was worn and weathered, dressed in black, her white hair in plaits. She arranged the turquoise cups and matching pot. "Andrés will be right here," she said.

"Mrs. Martinez. I know it's little comfort, but I wanted to offer my condolences."

"*Gracias.*" She pulled a tissue from the cuff of her sleeve and dabbed her eyes, wiped her nose.

"Miss Kaufman, right?"

"Yes."

"I wanted to say something before I leave you to Andrés." Her voice was thin and shaky.

"Of course," Sarah said.

"I am a religious woman. I believe my *Carlito* is in a better place. But I still miss him beyond words."

"Naturally."

"I understand you're Jewish."

"Yes."

"Well, what I wanted to say was that I have never liked your people, because of what they did to Jesus."

Sarah just nodded. This was one person with whom she had no desire to do battle. Not now, not ever.

"But, I am so very grateful for your, your help in this. For giving me back my Andrés." Then she broke down, her wafer-like body heaving in emotion. Sarah reached out and the woman fell into her arms. Sarah cried a little too, holding her until she quieted.

"Now," she said, pulling away. "I'll get Andrés."

Sarah wiped her eyes and sat up. She poured herself some tea and thought of how similar the house was to her own. Exchange that red plate for a white, that cross for a candle, and nothing was different. A family lived here, with all the pain and love that goes with it.

"Hello."

"Andrés," she said, standing. "I'm, I'm so very happy to meet you."

Andrés sat down and took a cup. The very image of his father, she thought. Taller, even more handsome.

"I heard that you tried to help my pop," he said.

"After a fashion."

He said nothing more. They sat sipping. It was up to Sarah. She had asked for the visit.

"It must have been frightening for you, being locked up and all."

"Sure. Mostly for the reason I was put there though. I've been in hospitals before."

"Well, that's what I wanted to talk to you about. All I wanted to say to you was that your father...I'm sure you know that your father loved you."

He clenched his jaw.

"I know it didn't feel that way," she said.

"No."

"He did though."

"Funny way to show it. I just can't believe he would think that of me."

"I know."

"You know? What do you know about it? You don't know me."

"No, but I knew your father. I know how people who love so much can make mistakes. Andrés, back in Ohio, I work with young people, counsel them sometimes. I know you've had problems, with controlling your thoughts, and with other things. I know how difficult life can be if you're not quite like everyone else. It can be tough to fit it. And if you're smart and sensitive, like you, like your father knew you were, well, things can seem pretty dark sometimes. Now, with your dad gone, I'm sure things seem overwhelming. But I just wanted to tell you, to beg you, to continue to get the help you need.

Andrés hung his head.

"And I don't know," Sarah said, "but I thought maybe, if you, well if you felt like it, we could, occasionally, write to each other. You could tell me about your problems, and the good things, too. I've never had any children," Sarah said, her throat tightening again. "Andrés, this would be as much for me as for you." Then she stopped. She was breathing fast, as if she were running a race. She'd said her piece.

Andrés was silent, his head still down.

"Well," she said, "I'll go."

Finally he raised his eyes and smiled just a little. He offered his hand, on which, Sarah just noticed, he wore Carlos' ring. "Maybe," he said.

■■■

It was their last day in L.A. and the weather had cooperated in spectacular fashion. Light breeze, seventy-five degrees, and a sky that almost redefined the meaning of blue. The City of Angels. *Ciudad de Lós Angeles.* Today living up to its better self.

Sarah linked Mitchell's arm as they headed down Spring Street. They were both pensive, still digesting the details of Paige's unexpected and startling confession. As Sparks told it, that is, for along with Hodges and the public defender, he had been present for it from beginning to end.

Upon returning to work, Sparks said that Paige blurted out her version of the conversation with Sarah. And Hodges was at first more than ready to believe her. But Sparks was quick on his heels, and once Paige was confronted with what he called his "unimpeachable" account, she fell to the floor and became hysterical. Hodges then was unmoved, and once Paige realized Sparks wasn't going anywhere, she agreed to talk, almost appearing relieved. She didn't even ask for a lawyer, but Hodges made sure one was there anyway.

Sarah was right. Paige and Carlos had been lovers. For ten years, Paige said, the relationship had been her reason for living. Carlos had been more accepting of her than anyone she'd ever known. That's why she'd lost control, incriminating herself when Sarah, hoping for that very reaction, suggested otherwise. Carlos had loved her, she insisted, body and soul, and in return, Paige was fiercely loyal. Carlos had confided in Paige about everything, and she kept his secrets. She befriended his mother and his son, who loved and trusted her. In fact, it was Paige who nudged Andrés to pursue Rita and Sabrina. She more than anyone else knew Carlos' mind, she said, the depth of his resentment over Rachel Street, how he longed for revenge. And she was also acutely aware of his fear about Andrés, that one day his son might snap. She knew because she listened, because she was always there, even when Carlos cheated, which he did from the very beginning. Those women meant nothing to him, she said. He used them to mete out justice. As long as she was the one he turned to, as long as he still made love to her, she didn't care.

Sparks said that while Paige spoke, she appeared to be in her own world, not talking to him or Hodges, but to a third person, her eyes fixed on the space between them. Her expression was soft, warm, as if it were Carlos himself in the room. But then, suddenly, she gazed directly at Hodges with one of the bitterest looks the detective had ever seen. Her whole being seemed to harden as she explained how a year ago Carlos started to grow distant. He made excuses, left without notice, and worst of all, no longer desired her. After all she'd done, satisfying his every whim, even sacrificing her career. Oh yes, she said. She took the job at the station for Carlos, to keep him informed. She was panicked, furious and profoundly hurt. But more than anything, she wanted him back. She had a right to him. And that's when things clicked. Yes, she said, she had a right. She knew the rule. Carlos had told her about it often enough. The rule of "fucking" capture, she said. She knew it backwards and forwards, in all of its mutations. And she decided that she would demonstrate just how well.

It was frightening, Sparks said, to hear her. So cold. She was like ice with a crown of fire, he said. She continued, saying that a fully formed plan had come to her in a dream. If she did away with these two women, the ones Carlos pretended to love, the ones he so regretted telling Andrés about, he would surely turn to her again. For then he would believe that Andrés was the killer, and he knew that Paige was the only one who would understand. He would need her. And indeed he did. As soon as he read about Rita and where the body was found, he called, begging for help. He was grateful beyond words, far beyond words, when Paige promised to do what she could to keep the cops off Andrés' scent. It wasn't that hard, she said, given their willingness to accept Bradford's account of Rita's health. And when Sarah came into the picture, he needed her even more. Yes, she told Hodges, she was responsible for everything. It was she who alerted Carlos to Sarah's inquires, suggested the "accidental" meeting at the trial. No woman could resist his charms, and Sarah took the bait. It was also she who encouraged Sarah to believe that the department intentionally attributed a heart attack to a woman they knew had been murdered.

Sparks said that on hearing that last statement, Hodges grimaced as if in pain, making the detective think that it was possibly true. Worse things had happened under the officer's watch. But Paige said that she'd confided in Sarah about it to stoke the fire, to compel her to go to Tijuana, a trip Paige had arranged, knowing full well, as every performer did, about the famous British singer hiding out there. Paige knew all along that he wasn't the Bradford Sarah was after. Of course, she said, the plan wasn't perfect. She wasn't thrilled that Carlos would need to be intimate with Sarah. But it was a small price to pay for having him so completely back in her life.

Sarah bristled, even now, recalling that remark. Sparks had narrated this part of the confession as matter-of-factly as the rest, but he couldn't conceal a slight gleam in his eye. He had tried to appear objective, but Sarah could only imagine what he'd really thought.

At this point, though, Sparks said Paige's expression changed, or rather grew blank, as if she were devoid of emotion. She had thought she could handle it, she said. But Carlos stayed in Tijuana too long. With no word, no postcard, no nothing. Her imagination and jealousy took over. She needed to get his attention again. Thus, Sabrina. A different street, but a name and a place he would recognize. And like clockwork, Carlos called, desperately worried about Andrés, pleading again for Paige to help. He had returned to L.A., but was arrested for that brainless act. Then she got sick, and Carlos couldn't make bail. Still she had hope. Until the final straw, the day Sarah showed her the handkerchief that Paige had spent weeks making for him. The one that he'd said he would never part with, that he'd sworn he would take to his death. Paige felt devalued and debased. And then she thought. If this, what else? Perhaps, he would take her down with him. Say something off hand, or under questioning. Reveal that they had been lovers, that she knew Andrés. And so.

Sparks told Sarah that by this time Hodges, in addition to being as dumbstruck as Sparks was by this account, was steaming mad. At the facts, of course, but also because it was beginning to sink in how dangerously he had been duped. All this time, thinking he was helping a cripple who no one else would hire. He stopped the interrogation, telling Sparks that he had to have a drink, otherwise he'd kill her, right then and there. In front of God and even the attorney. After he calmed down, the session resumed. Because of course a major question remained. How? How in the hell did she do it?"

The answer didn't surprise Sarah. She had half-guessed it herself. It was her brother, David, the one Paige said would do anything for her. She was, however, chilled by the plotting, by the twisted way Paige reeled him in, by how readily she sacrificed her own flesh and blood.

The upbringing Paige described to Sparks was eerily similar to her own. Sparks said that Paige and David had lost their parents when they were young too, and had lived together for many years. David had the build of a wrestler but, like Sarah's brother Harry, was sweet and generally mild mannered. The only thing that would stir his anger was when people teased Paige. That was true of Harry with Tillie. But unlike Harry, David had gotten into fights over it as a kid. And as time went on, he grew even more protective. If anyone looked at Paige sideways, he'd threaten them. This got to be a problem, Paige said, and ultimately had led them to living separately and seeing each other less frequently. No one even knew she had a brother at the station. Nor did Carlos.

Sarah drew Mitchell closer. The pavement sparkled under the sun. They passed a palm and then a eucalyptus. The now familiar scent filled her with profound sadness. Harry and Tillie. She longed to see them, tell them she loved them.

Paige said that David eventually found that his physical strength and mentality were a good fit for being a guard, and that he had worked as one in different facilities for years. He had gone by the name David Chase because he'd hated the French, even though that was his heritage, and that was just fine for Paige. The less in common the better. But suddenly she had seen his potential. He became a central part of that dream. So she'd rekindled the bond, made dinner for him, took him to movies. He was a loner, and she was his only family, something like a lover but without the sex. And then she'd begun planting the seed. She'd confided in him about Carlos and the woman who had stolen him from her. Rita. A woman who Paige said had sent her cruel messages, calling her at all hours shouting demeaning names. Paige said she had told the cops, but they couldn't do anything about it.

Sparks said that though the room was darkening, Paige brightened, that she seemed to be reliving the scheme, relishing in its ingenuity. She said that she had started out by having David follow Rita, had told him that she wanted only to scare her. David had never killed anyone, and this was a way of preparing and desensitizing him. But then, after a while, she told her brother that the vicious messages hadn't stopped, that she was becoming depressed, so much so that she'd thought of suicide. The next step, well, it han't been that hard, Paige said. And she'd used the same tactic with Sabrina. Carlos had even been easier. David had worked at the jail, knew the administrator and some of the boys. He'd offered to fill in a few nights, including, of course, the night that Carlos was attacked. Information about inmates flowed like water, and so David had quickly learned about Carlos' infamous visit from his son. A little arm-twisting here, a little payoff there, and David had had Carlos to himself. He'd just had to think of Carlos with his sister, Paige said, envision him using and discarding her, and the deed was as good as done.

"You think her brother is in custody yet?" Mitchell said, as they walked up the courthouse steps.

"Probably. I feel sorry for him in a way. Paige destroyed him by using his love."

"No good ever comes out of that."

"No."

They sat in the courtroom to take some photographs. The trial was in recess, wouldn't resume for a week. Whether Ted or any of them would be convicted was anyone's guess. Mitchell took a couple of shots and they left.

"You saved that boy, Sarah. Some redemption for Jacob."

"There's no redemption. The two aren't the same."

"But you saved the son, the grandson. And you helped to exonerate Carlos."

"Yes, that's true. Carlos was obviously no angel. But he did some good things. He took care of his family. And he helped me, Mitchell. He made me see things in myself, some that I didn't want to see, but needed to. And the union apparently is going forward. Perhaps he paved the way for the community, left a legacy. He did something for his people."

"Speaking of that," Mitchell said, you know, I really didn't tell the whole truth about Bunny."

"What?"

"You know that he gets involved with unions, too."

"Yeah, but does he die?"

"Eventually, I assume."

"What do you mean eventually?"

"Everyone does."

"I mean in the novel."

"I know. Hey, I've got an idea. Let's go into that bookstore and I'll buy you another copy."

"It won't be as good. No signature or anything."

"Maybe it'll be better. Besides, don't you really want to know what happens?"

Historical Notes and Acknowledgments

This book is a work of fiction but much of it is based on fact: the historical setting, the Julian trial, many of the characters and other crucial events are true. Most of the trial testimony is direct too, word for word, altered only when necessary for narrative flow. Countless historical texts informed my writing, but several splendid books had particular research value: *The Great Los Angeles Swindle: Oil, Stocks and Scandal During the Roaring Twenties* by Jules Tygiel; *My Friends Call Me C. C.: The Story of Courtney Chauncy Julian* by fellow Sunstone Press author, William Gardiner Hutson; *Whitewashed Adobe: The Rise of Los Angeles and the Remaking of its Mexican Past* by my brilliant, former dissertation committee member, William Deverell; *Becoming Mexican American: Ethnicity, Culture and Identity in Chicano Los Angeles, 1900-1945* by George J. Sánchez; *Satan's Playground: Mobsters and Movie Stars at America's Greatest Gaming Resort* by Paul J. Vanderwood; *A Bright and Guilty Place: Murder, Corruption and L.A.'s Scandalous Coming of Age* by Richard Rayner; and *The Los Angeles Plaza: Sacred and Contested Space* by William David Estrada.

First and foremost, I want to thank Jim Smith of Sunstone Press for his continuing belief in my work. Thanks to Esther Eastman, Ralph Stahlberg and all the reference librarians at The Los Angeles Law Library for their tremendous help with rounding up (several times) the trial transcripts. And the same to the folks at the San Diego Model Railroad Museum for helping me with historical train schedules and routes. Many thanks to my writing group—Sally Pla, Sarah Sleeper and Dare Delano—for their insightful critiques and friendship. A sincere word of thanks to editor extraordinaire Jackie Giordano for saving me from drowning in a sea of commas and from other deadly grammatical sins. As usual, thanks beyond words go out to my family—cousin and graphic artist, Lauren Kahn, for once again designing a stunning book cover, and husband Dean and children Benjamin and Brooke for their editorial assistance, encouragement, love and patience. Special thanks go out to my mother, Rhoda Kantor, for her careful proofreading and always (and I mean always) being there for me, and to my father, Dr. Marvin Kantor—"Marvy" in the book—for all of his reminiscences and keen sense of history.

Readers Guide

1. What do the title and the quotes that begin the book suggest about the story? Discuss your initial impressions and compare them to the way the narrative actually unfolds.

2. How does the Prologue influence your expectations of events yet to come?

3. Do you feel yourself empathizing with or judging Rita? Do her Mexican heritage and/or class influence your view of her? If so, how?

4. Sarah is self-critical. Why? How does that stance manifest itself? What decisions are related to it? Does it hinder or help her, or both?

5. Discuss the intersections of race, religion and class in the book.

6. Protagonists typically change and grow over the course of a novel. Discuss if and in what ways this happens to Sarah and to the other central characters.

7. There are three points of view in the novel. How does this affect your understanding of events and of the characters' motivations and feelings? What are the benefits and limitations of such a format?

8. A good deal of actual history is woven into this story. Identify things you believe are true but didn't know before reading the book. Are there sequences where the historical details remove you from the plot?

9. What are your expectations of an historical novel? What of the line between truth and fiction in such a work?

10. What are your expectations of a mystery? How does this book meet them? Disappoint them?

11. Discuss the role of Upton Sinclair's *Oil!* in the book.

12. How do the beliefs and assumptions of the characters influence their actions and interactions with other characters?

13. What is the thematic relationship between age and youth in the story?

14. Discuss the relationship between place (Southern California, Los Angeles, Tijuana) and behavior as it is portrayed in the book. Think of other regions in the country. Can any parallels be drawn?

15. Consider the coincidences that help to further the plot. Are they credible? Are there any supernatural type (*deux ex machina*) moments, and if so, how do they impact your response to the novel.

CPSIA information can be obtained at www.ICGtesting.com
Printed in the USA
BVOW08s1643260315

393400BV00001B/1/P